Suicide Note

By: *Matthew Daniels*
#TheRealBookWorm

"Create an enemy for the people to hate.
They will be so busy hating the created foe
that
you will be left to move with stealth and
further solidify your hold over them."
                        The Real Book Worm

Suicide Note
-Introduction-

You wanna know what I hate? I hate people that try to make it seem like the ghettos, projects, and poverty-stricken neighborhoods across America is all that. They want you to believe that if you weren't raised in the slums then you missed out on some hell of an experience. I hate when people brag about how hard they had it as if being born a victim of oppression is a badge of honor. As if going to the penitentiary was a rite of passage that welcomed youngsters into the wonderful world of adulthood. Now don't get me wrong, I think it's a beautiful thang whenever someone, boy or girl, finds the strength to overcome the madness and excel to new heights. I just think that a lot of the movies and books and songs coming out today tend to generally depict a "born with less but hustled my way to the top" type of story. Everybody can't be Scarface though. The odds of that happening are slim to none. The majority of ghetto babies end up just like me. But since my story doesn't have a fairytale ending, no one wants to tell my story. They figure it's too graphic, fucked up, and filled with a sense of hopelessness. Reality is reality though. For a lot of us, life's a bitch. No matter how hard we try, setbacks and failures are all God has planned for our existence. I would say that I hate God too, but what good would that do? I've never seen Him, heard Him, or spoke to Him, so really, He doesn't owe me shit. On the cool, I'm not sure God even exists. I guess I'll know in a lil bit. Oh, I ain't told you? I just took 32 Xanax pills straight to the head. And on top of that I just swallowed 3 grams of dope. HA! 32 Xanax pills and 3 grams of crack. That was all the drugs I had after busting my ass trying to come up in the street game. What an empire!! HA! What a fucking empire. Well, I guess I better fill ya'll in on how I got to this point before my heart bust. Like I said, don't nobody wanna to tell a story like mine, so fuck 'em. I'll tell my story myself. Just consider this lil narrative as my suicide note. Hey, I like how that sounds. Say, whoever finds this tape recorder after I'm gone, do me a favor. If they do make a movie or write a book about my life, make sure that they use that as the title. Suicide Note…

CHAPTER ONE

"Yo what's up nigga? Pass the mothafuckin' blunt. What you tryna to do? Hog all the weed?"

A.B. looked over at his homeboy Steel with a straight face and exhaled slowly. The secondhand marijuana smoke exited his lungs smoothly and united with the cool night air.

"So, what if I was?" A.B. answered. "I paid fa' this shit anyway."

"Nigga!" Steel exclaimed, reaching out and snatching the lit blunt out of A.B.'s grasp. "I paid fo' it the last time."

A.B smiled at his homeboy before turning his attention back to the task at hand. Even though A.B. and Steel had been best friends since the first grade, every now and then they would try each other just to check and see if one of them was getting soft. The two of them had been raised in the same apartment complex called Church Village in a small town called Dickinson, Tx. Population was a whopping 22,000. Don't be fooled by the name of the name of the apartments though. It was closer to the devil's playground then a village of church folk. Pretty much every type of crime imaginable got committed in Church Village. Drug sells, prostitution, assaults, murders, and one of the most common, statutory rape. There wasn't anybody running around forcing women to have sex, but the young girls around there grew up fast. It was nothing to see a 30 something year old man with a 13-year-old girl.

A.B. and Steel were 15-year-old hustlers. They didn't hustle in Church Village though.

Niggas around there were too cutthroat for them. They liked to dip off to the edge of town to get their money. The Highland Projects were their claim to fame.

A.B. and Steel sat crotched down behind a row of bushes that lined the back of the projects. They had only been selling dope for about 4 years and maybe 3 months of that was spent at Highland, but they had come up with what seemed like an airtight hustle plan. From the street no one could see them stashed away behind the foliage, but they could see them easily. All they had to do was post up and wait.

While Steel focused on the intoxicating effects of the THC, A. B. kept his eyes glued to the road. Why get so caught up in one measly ass blunt that you miss an opportunity to make enough bread to buy 100 blunts? That was the difference between A.B. and Steel. Steel was about his scratch, no doubt, but he got sidetracked easily by all of the traps the game had out there. Growing up on the bottom with barely enough to eat at times, Steel didn't know how to act once he started making a little money. It was like he was hustling for clothes, weed, liquor, and hoes.

Steel was in love with the lifestyle of a hustler/ gangster. A.B., on the other hand, had a plan. He could see the big picture. Yeah, a couple hundred dollars in the pockets of a ghetto child did make him feel good, but there were cats out there that came from the same neighborhood he did, and they had a couple thousand dollars to play with. Why couldn't that be him? And A.B. wasn't stupid. He knew that the same way he scored from the 4 figure niggas, the 4 figure niggas had to be scoring from the 6 figure or more niggas. A.B. wanted to be that 6 figures of more nigga. The way he saw it, he was 15 years old right now. If he played his cards right, he could easily have $100,000 to $1,000,000 saved up by the time he turned 20. That was his goal. To make a cool million by the time he turned 20 years old and then retire. If he invested that million the right way, he would never have to work a single day in his life.

A.B. peeked through the bushes. His hearing was keen, and he could swear that he had just heard a car approaching. He cut his eyes at Steel. Steel was puffing away at the blunt like he had to play catch up for all of the times A.B. had hit it. A.B. loved to grind with Steel. It really wasn't hard to beat him to the punch.

The Highland Projects were shaped like one huge square and they sat on their own block. There were four buildings that lined the four streets with a busted playground in the center. A.B. watched as cars' headlights cut through the darkness on his right side. If the driver hesitated at the corner of the projects, they were looking for drugs. Well, sometimes A.B. would run up on an unsuspecting motorist and scare the living shit out of them. But even then, when he didn't make any money, he got a damn good laugh out of the deal.

Just as A.B. had hoped, the small four door car made it to the corner and stopped.

"Who is th…." Steel had noticed the vehicle too late.

Before he could even finish his question, A.B. had sprang out of the bushes and was running full speed towards what he now could tell was a dark blue Chevy Cavalier.

His competition with Steel wasn't the only reason he had to rush to make the sell. To his knowledge there were at least 3 dope houses inside the Highland Projects and 2 weed houses. Some of the clientele that were frequenting the area were coming specifically for either him or Steel, but the majority of the money was for the dealers that already had the area on lock. Technically, what A.B. and Steel were doing was called Short-stoppin'. They were basically stopping the smoker short of his actual destination and trying to move their own product in place of someone else's. A.B. justified his actions by saying that if you wanted to be a true hustler you had to do just that... HUSTLE! If you sat up in the comfort of a trap all day long, you should expect someone with a go-getter attitude to stand outside and cut into your profits. Short-stoppin' was a dangerous, but so was being broke. The woman in the Cavalier saw A.B. running towards her car and waited. She was one of the few customers that actually came around looking for either A.B. or Steel. A.B. jogged around the front end of the car and hopped into the passenger seat.

"Make the block." He instructed her.

The woman did as she was told. Out the corner of her eye, she watched A.B. scan the area in all directions as she drove past the set of bushes, she knew concealed Steel. The woman couldn't help but to feel a tingling sensation ignite inside of her pants as she took A.B. in with her eyes. He was definitely fly in his black jeans, Roca wear tee, and black and yellow Roca wear jacket. His hair was freshly braided straight back, and his silver dollar sign shaped earring looked clean in his left earlobe. She knew that A.B. was only 15 years old, but how he carried himself was intoxicating.

"So, what you tryna do Layla?" A.B. asked, pulling a sandwich bag full of crack rocks out of his inside coat pocket.

Layla's eyes zeroed in on the sack and her focused instantly switched from pleasure back to business. Layla struggled to get her hand into the skintight blue jean shorts she was wearing. A.B. studied her curvaceous frame and licked his lips. He couldn't understand how Layla managed to stay so fine even in the midst of her addiction. Most of the addicts that he encountered looked like they had one foot already in the grave. Not Layla though. She somehow managed to hold onto her weight and carry herself in a pretty decent manner. At times her clothes were in desperate need of a trip to the Laundromat but at other times she looked like she had just stepped out of Neiman Marcus and spent a grip. Tonight, she was closer to the dirty Layla. Her clothes were clean, but she had on some short ass blue jean shorts and a pink fruit of the loom t-shirt. Her sandy blonde hair was pulled back into a basic ponytail and it was obvious she wasn't wearing any make-up. She didn't look pale without make-up like most white women but her 35-year-old face had small craters in it directly beneath her light blue eyes.

Layla exhumed a neatly folded one-hundred-dollar bill and held it between her index and middle finger.

"You wanna spend the whole hundred?" A.B. asked, working to untie the knot he had placed in the sandwich bag to keep his rocks from falling out.

"Yeah." Layla answered, "But I don't want that."

She motioned with her head towards the sack of rocks A.B. had on his lap.

A.B. looked at her confused. If she didn't want work, what did she want? Or did she think that he had some of that stepped on and whipped to the point of no return work that had flooded the streets of Dickinson in recent weeks?

"What's wrong with my dope?"

"Ain't nothin' wrong with it. At least I hope there's not. I just don't want to spend my money on a bunch of rocks."

Layla balled up her fist around the c-note.

"I want one solid piece that I can bust down myself." She told him.

A.B. wasn't sure what she was trippin' on, but he wasn't about to just let no hundred-dollar lick slip through his fingers because of a special request. He didn't have one big slab on him, but he did have some more work over at his apartment in Church Village.

He re-tied his sandwich bag and turned his attention to Layla.

"If you want it." He said, returning the sack to his coat pocket. "You have to take me to go get it."

Layla shrugged her shoulders to let him know that she didn't mind taxing him to where the dope was. As long as she got one nice sized hundred-dollar piece out of the trip, she was good.

Layla came to a stop at the only stop sign around the projects.
"Where we headed?" she asked, waiting for A.B. to tell her in which direction she should go.

"Just keep straight." He answered, adjusting the seat to make the ride more comfortable.

Steel peered out through the bushes as Layla's car pulled off again before A.B. got back out. He puffed on the weed and wondered where they could be going. The normal routine was to hop in the car, make the sell while circling the projects,

12

then get back out at the corner and return to the bushes. Neither one of them had ever rode off with a lick and left the other one there alone before. They were really out of bounds trying to get money in a hood that wasn't their own, so safety always was an issue.

Steel patted his pants pocket. Good. His pocketknife was still there. He hoped he wouldn't need it but there were no guarantees in the streets.

"Maybe Layla's just trying to get more dope then her money can buy and A.B. has to wrestle with her?" he thought.

Steel eased back against the building. Whatever was going on, A.B. shouldn't be gone for too long. And if he was, that just translated into more money for him. That thought made Steel smile. It had been a while since he knocked down the mall and he wasn't feeling that at all. It didn't make sense to him to be out on the frontline all night every night and not treat himself when the loot came. If selling dope didn't help you enjoy life, why the fuck would you risk your life trying to sell it?

Steel noticed a small truck pull up to the corner and stop. When the driver hesitated at the stop sign Steel sprang into action. By the time they had made the block and he had made it back into the bushes, Steel was $40 richer. He added the two worn twenty-dollar bills to his small but growing stack of feddy and patiently waited on the next stang to pull up.

Layla had driven about four blocks before she decided to ask A.B. what was bothering him.

"What's wrong?" she asked.

A.B. turned around in his seat and looked out the back window for the fourth time since they left the Highland Projects.

"Why you think something wrong?" he asked in response.

"Hmm. Let's see." Layla placed her hand on her chin and sarcastically acted as if she was in deep thought.

"For starters, you keep on turning around and looking out the window. If it's the laws you worried about just sit back and relax babe. I know how to drive plus I got a license and insurance on me. You good."

A.B. ran his hand along the top of his braids.

"Believe me lil mama." He began. "A.B. ain't ever been afraid of no pigs. I'm just thinkin' bout my boy Steel back there. I probably shouldn't have left him by himself."

"Ya boy Steel a man ain't he?" Layla asked, confused as to what A.B. was worried about. "He can take care of himself."

"Naw. It ain't like that Layla. Of course, my partner a stiff nigga, but we ain't from 'round there. You know how cats be hood plexin' and shit. If them niggas catch Steel slippin' and beef, he ain't gone back down."

Layla thought about what A.B. had just said. She didn't know a hell of a lot about what goes down in the streets, but she did know that the different gangs, sets, neighborhoods, and turfs were always fighting, stabbing, and shooting at each other.

"Do you wanna go back and get him?" Layla asked.

A.B. wiped his mouth and glanced out the window. Steel was his road dog for real. He wouldn't be able to live with himself if something happened to him over a hundred dollars. A.B. weighed his options.

"Yeah." He finally answered. "Let's go back and get him."

Layla flipped on her blinker and made a left at the very next corner she came to. She didn't mind doubling back to get Steel. If that's what A.B. wanted her to do then that's exactly what she was going to do. Layla had only been scoring her work from him and Steel for about 6 months, but in that seemingly short period of time she had fallen for A.B. It was something about how he carried himself that she was attracted to. And it didn't hurt that he was cute. A.B. didn't know it yet, but Layla was intent on making him her man. The only roadblock she could foresee in her plans was the fact that she smoked crack. But A.B. smoked weed, wet, and popped pills himself. A drug was a drug, right?

Steel couldn't believe his luck as he hopped out of another vehicle with twenty more dollars in his pocket.

"This bitch finna start rollin'." He said to himself excitedly heading back over to the bushes.

He was almost there when a dark blue Chevy Cavalier pulled up alongside of him.

"Damn." He thought. "I wish A.B. would've been gone a little bit longer."

Layla rolled down the window on the passenger side of the car so A.B. could talk to Steel.

"Ah say homie." A.B. began, looking around nervously. Sometimes the projects were hot as hell and he didn't want to get jammed up by the law in such a compromising position.

"Gone ride over to the Village with me while I pick somethin' up. You don't need to be chillin' out here by yourself."

Steel knew why A.B. wanted him to ride out with him. He was just thinking the exact same way a few minutes ago. Steel glanced down at the twenty-dollar bill in his hand. Things had changed a little bit since a few minutes ago. The licks were starting to pick up and he knew that if he scratched off just when things were getting good, he would be fucking himself out of some much-needed funds.

Steel slid the twenty in his pocket.

"Naw." He answered. "Ya'll go 'head. I'm gone sit back and make this money."

A.B. looked up and down the street one more time. He had kicked it with Steel long enough to know that it wasn't any arguing with him. Once he had his heart set on doing something, he was gone do it. No if, ands, or buts about it.

"You got ya blade?" A.B. asked.

Steel whipped out his trusty pocketknife and flicked it open.

"This bitch like American Express baby." He responded. "You never leave home without it."

A.B. couldn't do anything but laugh a little. He knew his homeboy was a soldier for real. In a lot of instances Steel would be ready to escalate that plex to full blown drama way before he would.

Layla was always amazed at how similar A.B. and Steel looked. Especially since they always dressed alike. The only main difference between the two was Steel stood about 2 inches taller and was slightly slimmer than A.B. Plus, Steel was a couple of shades lighter than A.B. too. Other than that, the two of them could easily pass for brothers.

A.B. turned his attention back to Layla. He still wasn't o.k. with the idea of leaving Steel there by himself, but at least his homeboy had protection. Reluctantly, A.B. lightly slapped Layla on her thigh with the back of his hand.

"He cool." he told her. "Let's ride out."

Steel watched the car pull away from the curb and heard A.B. call out that he would be right back. Once they hit the corner and disappeared down the street, Steel ducked back into his position behind the bushes. The blunt that he had been smoking on with A.B. was gone, so he patted down his pockets in search of another one.

"Damn." He cursed, when he remembered that A.B. had all of the other blunts on him.

Steel jumped out from behind the bushes and sprinted in the direction that Layla had driven. The corner of the block wasn't far away so he reached it in a matter of seconds. Unfortunately, though, a vehicle with four wheels could move a hell of a lot faster than an individual with two feet. He could barely make out the Cavalier's tail lights several blocks down the road. Trying to flag them down would be useless.

"Fuck." He mumbled under his breath. If it's one thing that Steel needed to stay focused while he was out hustling, it was weed. The sacred herb known formally as either cannabis or marijuana. It had the power to calm, soothe, and relax. Yes sir. There was nothing Steel enjoyed more out on the block then a pair of lungs filled up continually with THC.

"A.B. bet not bullshit and procrastinate." Half of the ride from the projects to the Village was made in total silence. Layla was observing A.B. out the corner of her eye but no matter how hard she tried she just couldn't read him. He stayed looking straight ahead and kept his expression blank. Realizing that if she waited on her passenger to spark up a conversation, she would be waiting a very long time, Layla took it upon herself to begin a dialogue between her and her secret crush.

"Why you stop hustling' in the Village?" she asked.

The question caught A.B. off guard. He had been fantasizing about the day that all of his hard work and late nights would pay off. The day when he could sit back and relax without a care in the world.
Cocking his head in Layla's direction, he allowed his mind to return from the pleasantness of his future back to the harshness of his present.

"What you mean?" A.B. asked her.

Layla shrugged. "I remember when I first met you, you were hustling' out in Church Village. Then, out of nowhere, you told me to start looking for you over in the projects. I was just curious as to why you switched up. Don't you still live in the Village?"

A.B. thought about the question. It seemed kind of strange to him that Layla would be asking him all sorts of personal questions. One of the first rules to the game that he had learned was to keep everybody out of your business. Especially your customers. The streets got so grimy at times that virtually no one could be trusted.

Attempting to dodge the question, A.B. looked away from her.

"Shit happens." He replied smoothly. "Sometimes you gotta do something different just to keep the competition guessin'. If you get too comfortable, you start makin' mistakes."

Layla caught the hint. He didn't want to let her get too close. Their relationship was business. Strictly business. She wasn't about to give up that easily though. She just needed to find a new way to approach him. One that wouldn't cause him to put his guard up. Layla made the rest of the trip in silence, but her brain was working overtime.

Back at the projects, Steel had waited as long as he could wait. There was no telling how much longer A.B. was going to be and he was ready to smoke now. Steel had been hanging around long enough to know which apartments sold weed, but he had never actually purchased any before. He would always cop his blunts from one of his people on the other end of town and just bring 'em over with him. He ain't like fucking with people he didn't know but desperate times called for desperate measures.

Steel stood stiff in front of number 110. He was nervous, but no one was paying any special attention to him. They were too busy doing they own thang to care about yet another customer of the local weed man.

Steel inhaled and exhaled his anxiety and knocked on the door. He made sure not to knock too loud. A heavy-handed knock was almost always interpreted as the police. Well, either the police or a woman scorned. Whenever a female was hurt badly enough by a man, she became capable of anything.

Only a few seconds passed between Steel's final knock and the sound of footsteps rustling in the direction of the front door. Steel played the encounter over in his head.

"Buy the weed and then burn off." He thought to himself.

Simple.

Steel listened as the person on the other side of the red door began unlocking the many deadbolts that kept their dwelling secure. Butterflies started to flutter around in his belly. He felt a little foolish because he had been purchasing and smoking weed since he was like 10 or 11. The apprehension he was now experiencing was reminiscent of the first time he had ever went to the weed house alone. The feeling might have taken him further down memory lane, but the door swung open before he could really get lost in his thoughts.

The light from inside the apartment stretched out a few feet into the darkness and illuminated Steel. Both he and the weed man examined each other quickly. The man at the door looked like he had just gotten out of the penitentiary. Standing around 6" even and probably weighing in at 250lbs., the jet black, and tattoo covered, muscle bound dud made Steel think about those silverback gorillas he had once saw on the Discovery Channel. The handle of a revolver was clearly visible rising up from the man's waistband because he wasn't wearing a shirt.

"Wassup?" the Silverback asked in an extremely throaty voice.

"Ummm." Steel responded nervously. "Ya'll got some bud?"

The Silverback frowned up and scanned Steel from head to toe. He was no doubt debating if he wanted to sell him any weed or not. Steel was a new face. A lot of times people didn't like to do business with a new face. There were always issues of trust. But one of the ironies of the weed game was that while even though the weed man didn't 'like' to sell to people he didn't know; he almost didn't have a choice. Any thriving weed house grew by word of mouth. And word of mouth guaranteed a steady flow of new clientele.

Apparently deciding that Steel was a legit customer, Silverback stepped to the side and told him to come in. As Steel entered the apartment, he looked down at Silverback's gun one more time.

His pocketknife didn't mean anything now.

Once inside, Steel noticed 3 more men sitting on a brown couch immediately to his left playing Madden on a 52-inch big screen T.V. When he crossed the threshold of the door, all 3 of them simultaneously looked up at him. Although they were all different sizes and shades of black, they were all tatted up, shirtless, and strapped, just like Silverback. So, just like Silverback, Steel assigned them all primate names in his head. The short, slim, braided up dude was chimp. The red nigga with the pretty boy features, gold fangs, and good hair was Orangutan. And the big lip, 6"6, butt ugly cat was dubbed Baboon. Even though Baboon was the tallest of the bunch, and the animal baboon was the smallest primate out of the 4, Steel felt like the dude's face was jacked up just like those pink asses God had cursed baboons to run around with.

Silverback shut the door behind Steel and locked it.

"How much money you got?" Silverback asked, stepping up behind Steel a little too close for comfort. His chest almost touched Steel's back. Trying to hide his growing uneasiness, Steel took a couple of steps away from him and turned around.

"Just let me get 3 of 'em." Steel told him, pulling a 20 dollar bill out of his pocket. Silverback kept his expression cold as he stepped back up to Steel and closed the gap he had tried to create.

"Naw lil daddy." Silverback said, placing his right hand over the handle of his revolver. "I ain't ask you how much weed you wanted to buy. I asked you how much money you got."

For the first time since deciding to score some weed from the projects Steel was 100% sure that he had made a mistake. He could hear Chimp,

Orangutan, and Baboon getting up off the couch behind him. His mind quickly did the math. 4 niggas with 4 guns vs. 1 nigga with 1 pocketknife. It didn't take a rocket scientist to figure out the outcome of that one. Steel's only hope was conversation.

"Come on my nigga." He pleaded, raising his hands in surrender.   "Why you boys wanna do me? All I want is some bud. I ain't lookin' fa no beef."

Out the corner of his eyes, Steel could see that the troop of primates had him surrounded. Orangutan and Chimp were smiling. It was hard to tell what Baboon was doing. His face constantly made it seem like he was in pain. Silverback remained masked up. True to his name he was obviously the most aggressive of the four.

"Why?" Silverback smirked for the first time. "You think we don't know who you is? Be real lil daddy." Silverback extended his arms out to his side. "This here our 'hood. Don't nothing go down that we don't know about. You and ya lil homeboy been comin' out here pretty regular lately. The streets talk. Ya'll ain't just doin' no major hustling, but ya'll doin' a lil eatin'.""

Silverback placed his left hand on Steel's shoulder. "We ain't gone rob you, nigga. Ya'll sell dope. That ain't got shit to do with us. But since ya'll doin' it in our hood, ya'll gotta break bread with the old heads on the block. You feel me?"

Steel looked around and made eye contact with each member of the group. There were no more smiles. Everyone meant business. Steel wasn't sure what kind of business they meant though. If they weren't gonna rob him, what did Silverback mean about breaking bread?

When Steel neglected to answer whether he felt him or not, Silverback continued anyway. "So how much money you got?"

Steel thought about it. There was no way he was going to get out of there with his cash, so he just decided to do things the easy way.

Digging in his pants pocket, Steel pulled out a wad of cash. He was now grateful that he had the foresight to put some of his money up in his shoe.

Silverback snatched the stack and flipped through the bills. "20… 30… 35… 55… "He counted out loud as he made his way through the 5's, 10's, and 20's.

"140… 160… 165." He stopped once he made it to the last bills. "You got $165." He informed Steel. Then, he folded the wad back how it was when he took it from him and shoved it in his pocket. Steel wanted to protest but that revolver had him on hush-mouth.

"Go get 'em." Silverback instructed Chimp.

Chimp obeyed. He walked over to a duffel bag that was resting in front of the brown couch. He dug around in it for a minute, retrieved two sandwich bags with weed n 'em, and brought 'em over to Silverback.

"Here." Silverback said, handing the bags over to Steel.

Steel accepted them and examined the contents carefully. Weed was his thing. He liked to refer to himself as a marijuana connoisseur. He had been buying and smoking weed so long that he could eyeball a sack of weed and make a damn good estimation about how much it weighed. After looking at the two bags, he came to the conclusion that they only contained an ounce apiece.

"What's this for?" Steel asked, even though

he had a pretty good suspicion about what was going on.

Silverback and the rest of the troop backed up off of him giving him a little room to breathe.

"That's what you just bought." Silverback answered.

Steel looked at the weed. "Two zones?!? He asked in disbelief. "At the most that's only $80. I just gave you $165. Where the rest of it at?"

Silverback laughed out loud. Even his laugh was deep and intimidating. As if cued by some unseen computer prompter, all the other primates began laughing too.

Steel thought, "A bunch of fuckin' followers!"

"What's so funny?" Steel asked, beginning to get agitated. If it was one thing he hated, it was being the butt of someone else's joke. He always told people that he was not there for their entertainment.

Silverback finished laughing and got back into his serious mode. The others, as expected, followed suit.

"That's all you getting lil daddy." Silverback told him, stepping back in close. "I said we weren't gonna rob you. I ain't say nothing about not taxing yo ass. That's all part of you breaking bread with the O.G.'s 'round here." Silverback pointed his index finger and poked Steel in the chest with it. "Just be glad I gave you two zones and not two blunts."

"Man… that's some hoe ass shit nigga!" Steel shot out before he had time to think about what he was saying. As soon as the word "nigga" had crossed his lips, he regretted the entire statements.

Rage instantly registered on Silverbacks face. "Hoe ass shit?!" he repeated. "You callin' me a hoe?"

Steel put his hands out in front of him and backed up. "Naw man." He said, backpedaling like a crawfish. "It was just a figure of speech."

Steel had only taken maybe 3 steps backwards when he felt the barrel of 3 pistols press up against him. He was literally terrified now. His big mouth was about to get him killed. And all over some weed. Steel was now wishing that A.B. was there.

Silverback moved with quickness and agility his huge frame made seem impossible, and in one second he punched Steel with a bad ass jab. Pain shot through his left eye as he collapsed backwards into the guns and tumbled to the floor. On his way down, the bags of weed flew out of his hands and up into the air.

The back of Steel's head hit the carpeted floor with a thud and Steel quickly slid into the realm of unconscious thought.

His last conscious thought was, "Where's A.B?

"Ooooo A.B.!!!" Layla howled as A.B. gripped her waist tighter and rammed his rock-hard dick deeper and harder into her sloppy wet pussy hole.

"Yeeeah bitch!" A.B. said smiling. "Take that dick! Take that dick!"

Both A.B. and Layla were butt naked inside of A.B.'s apartment in Church Village. Layla was on all fours with her nice sized ass cocked up and a dip in her back. A.B. was on his knees behind her trying his damnest to bruise up that sweet pleasure box Layla had been keeping marinated between those snow-white thick thighs. A.B. wasn't sure how they ended up fucking in his bedroom with his crack addict mother and 5 year old sister in the living room listening, but he wasn't trippin'. If he had known Layla's pussy was this good, he would have traded her some dope for it a long time ago. Layla, on the other hand, knew exactly how she ended up with A.B.'s dick stretching her walls. She had cleverly seduced him.

Euphoric sensations zigzagged throughout Layla's entire body. She bit down on the pillow like a crazed animal and closed her eyes tight.

"Uuuugghh…" she moaned through the fabric.

It had been at least 4 months since her pussy had received a good pounding. 4 long hard months. The conversation leading up to the actual sex had had her already wet, swollen, and tender. Her coochie was like a boa constrictors death lock. It was pulsating, throbbing, and squeezing the life out of the chocolate covered meat stick that had dared to intrude upon the sanctity of its chambers. As her well lubricated wall muscles continued to contract, her lover/abuser continued to drill deeper and deeper. He was no doubt in search of the creamy white substance that only the truly skilled was worthy enough to bring forth from within her.

A.B. clenched his jaws and watched as his tool repeatedly disappeared and reappeared. Layla's ass jiggled with the force of each thrust. He couldn't help but wonder how superb her sex must be without a condom if it was this intense with one.

A.B. was caught up in the moment. He raised his right hand high and slapped Layla's butt cheek just hard enough to make it sting.
She spit out the pillow and whimpered like a lost puppy. The sound she made turned A.B. on.

He raised his left hand and smacked her left butt cheek.

Layla was enthralled by his aggression. "Yes Daddy." She cooed, rocking back and forth as he rammed her. "Handle this pussy."

Then she started throwing it back.

"This my pussy?" A.B. asked, absolutely loving the dirty dialogue that was going on between them.

"Hell yeah this yo pussy." Layla answered. "I been waiting so long to put you in this pink. Mmmm. I don't want no dick but yours A.B." Layla threw her head back and moaned loudly.

"Oooooo SHIT Baby! If you want this pussy, it's yours!!! I swear daddy… ungh… oouu I swear daddy!"

A.B. reached out and grabbed Layla's ponytail. He tugged on it.

"Ahhh." She groaned.

"Shut-up bitch." He commanded. "Shut-up and take it."

He tugged at her ponytail again. This time, Layla simply moaned through sealed lips.

A.B. slowed down his strokes. He wanted to enjoy the time spent inside of her. He eased his dick out all the way leaving only the head in. Then he closed his eyes and slid back into her wetness until his pubic hairs pressed up against her asshole. The sensations were electrifying. He tugged at her hair and eased out to the tip of his dick again.

"That's right." He told her in a soft and sexy voice as he once again filled up her hole. "This my pussy. I'm gone do this pussy how I want to do this pussy."

Layla heard his words and smiled to herself. She knew she had some good sex. Now that she had broken the ice and started putting her pussy on him, it wouldn't be long before she got what she really wanted.

A relationship.

Layla fully submitted to A.B. for the remainder of the fuck session. Whatever daddy wanted… daddy got. Layla was an old school female. She knew how to leave a man sprung, and she had used every trick in the book on her young, money-minded stallion. She still had one more ace up her sleeve though. Something that was sure to seal the deal and ensure that he would be fending to fuck her again as soon as she dropped him back off.

A.B. laid on his back while Layla rode his dick like a professional cowgirl. He wanted her size 36c breast bounce around wildly. It wasn't long before he felt that familiar tingling down in his bowels. His eruption was near. He was ready to nut too. That would make all of his pumping and sweating worthwhile.

As the sensation grew, he felt himself getting to the point of no return.

"Shit." He groaned. "I'm finna cum. Keep goin' Layla. Keep goin'."

That was Layla's cue. She was waiting for him to get ready to nut so she could really blow his mind.

Layla bounced on his dick 3 more times then quickly hopped off. Moving quickly, she snatched the rubber off of his tool and replaced it with her mouth. A.B.'s toes curled up as Layla's lips wrapped around his shaft and she began sucking his dick like there was no tomorrow.

"Mmm! Mmm! Mmm!" she moaned. Layla was hungrily trying to slurp out his prize so it wouldn't be wasted.

The spit inside of her mouth made her oral

cavity feel just like her vagina. The sucking, slurping, and noises was too much for A.B. to take. He could hold back no longer. A.B. reached down and grabbed two handfuls of Layla's hair. Then he forced her to swallow every inch of meat he had. She gagged slightly but she didn't dare pull away.

"Fff… fff… Fuuck!!" A.B. cried out as his load erupted against the back of Layla's throat. His entire body tensed up as he force fed her all that he had to offer.

Layla eagerly swallowed every single drop that shot from A.B.'s dick. As she drank his cum, she was making a lasting impressed.

Once A.B.'s dick was completely drained, only two thoughts flashed through his brain.

"This bitch is the truth!"

"Wait 'till I tell Steel about this shit!"

CHAPTER TWO

"I'll be back." Was all A.B. said to his mother Samantha and his little sister Sandra as he led Layla from the only bedroom in the apartment, through the living room, and out the front door. It didn't matter to Samantha that her 15-year-old son was just having sex in her house with an older woman. It didn't even matter to her that she could remember going to high school with the woman. And what really should've bothered her, but didn't, was the fact that when she was a freshman at Dickinson High the woman her son was with was a senior. Nope, none of that fazed her at all. All she cared about was the $50 and the gram of dope her son had just given her. By the time A.B. and Layla had pulled away from Church Village, Samantha was zulooed out and little Sandra was once again forced to fend for herself. It's a good thing she was used to it.

Layla couldn't stop grinning as she drove A.B. back over to the projects. He was back to his ol' tight lip self, but she didn't need him to speak this time. She already knew what was on his mind. Layla had started smoking dope when she was just 21 years old. Her and her friends had graduated to it when the cocaine they had been snorting began to lose its edge. She could remember back in grade school when her teachers use to warn that marijuana was a gateway drug. She never did understand the term "gateway drug" until she moved on to the harder drugs herself. Once she had started using marijuana on a regular basis, she became hooked on the feeling of being intoxicated.

After a while her body built up a pretty strong tolerance for weed, so no matter how much she smoked she could never feel that same high she felt when she had first started using. The only thing that made sense at the time was to move on to a stronger drug.

Layla was actually one of the most popular girls in school. Dickinson was predominately black, but she was one of the few white girls who was so consistent in holding it down when her home girls needed her that she was accepted. It didn't hurt that she was built like a sister too. When she got strung out on crack though, it seemed like all of her friends turned their back on her. And not only that, none of the men wanted to have sex with her anymore. This was a major problem because Layla was a major freak. I mean, she was a straight up sexaholic. Ever since her 32-year-old math teacher, without remorse, popped her 12-year-old cherry, it seemed like she needed dick for her world to turn right. A lot of times it didn't even matter who the dick was attached to. As long as it was seven inches or better and slung right, she was good.

Layla never had a conscience about a man she was with. She would fuck his brother, best friend, father, or son. And if the timing was right, she would even romp around with his sister, home girl, mother, or daughter. She wasn't really into women though. She only went bi when she had some really, really, really good dope. That A-1, straight drop left her pussy so wet that anyone, man or woman, would do.

All of that changed when she met A.B. 6 months ago. His style and finesse was so unique. He was definitely going places. And she wanted to be right there by his side when he reached the top.

Her attraction went much deeper than materialism. Of course, she was attracted to his hustle, but she was feeling his entire swag. She didn't even know how deep her feelings for him ran until maybe 2 months after she had met him selling dope in Church Village. Things had gone from bad to worse for Layla and she somehow found herself with barely enough money to feed herself and pay her bills. Her addiction wasn't trying to hear it. It still demanded to be satisfied. So, Layla resorted to what most women in her predicament would resort to. She found herself hemmed up by 3 working class men who obviously weren't getting fully satisfied at home by their wives. They took her to one of the sleaziest motels in Dickson and took turns shoving their adulterous dicks in her pussy, ass, and mouth. Even though she had charged them $75 a piece, and that $225 was desperately needed, all she kept thinking about was A.B. She knew that if she were his woman he would not have approved of her behavior.

By the time she was finished turning her trick, she was covered with cum that rightfully belonged to 3 unsuspecting housewives and filled up with a sense of shame and guilt that she had never experienced before. After she cleaned herself up, she made a promise not to degrade herself like that again. A.B. deserved a respectable woman. That was the last time she had sex until just a little while ago. And now that she had worked her magic on the man she really wanted, she was confident that he would be more than willing to fill the sexual void she had whenever she wanted him to.

A.B.'s mind wasn't anywhere near on the things that Layla assumed his mind was on. Yeah, the sex was live, and yeah, he couldn't wait to do it again, but something else had begun to bother him as soon as he recovered from his nut.

His homeboy Steel.

He had gotten so caught up in satisfying his flesh that he had left his road dog out there alone for far too long. He was fucking up. One of the cardinal rules to the game was 'ALWAYS STAY FOCUSED'. Right now, his focus was supposed to be money, not hoes.

As if his brain had been programmed to relate such situations to Biblical stories, A.B. began thinking about some of the Proverbs his mother had read to him as a young boy.

Lust not after her beauty in thine heart;
Neither let her take thee with her eyelids.
For by means of a whorish woman a man
Is brought to a piece of bread...
Let not thine heart decline to her ways, go not astray in her paths. Her house is
the way to hell, going down to the Chambers of death...

As the story goes, King Solomon, the man responsible for penning most of the words found in the book of Proverbs, had at least one thousand women at his disposal at all times. A.B always found that fact mind blowing. If Solomon really did have one thousand women, he could have sex with a different woman every night for damn near 3 years straight. A.B. rationalized that any man capable of juggling that many different women could be unquestionably trusted on matters that pertained to women.

A.B. wasn't really religious. In fact, he wasn't religious at all. His mother Samantha was extremely religious though. She used to go to church every day of the week. The thing A.B. respected about his mother was that she never tried to force her beliefs off onto him. She did, however, share her beliefs with him. It was because of his mother that he had the knowledge about the Bible that he did. Ironically, it was also because of his mother that he never decided to really believe in God himself. He couldn't understand how God, if there even was a God, could allow one of his most loyal subjects to fall into the type of existence that his mother had fallen into. Samantha wasn't just a crack smoker; she was a full-blown crack head.

Anybody in the game could tell you that there was a major difference between smokers and crack heads. A smoker could hold down a job, find time for their families, and refrain from cleaning out the bank account. A smoker did the drug; they did not allow the drug to do them.

A crack head, on the other hand, was the complete opposite. A crack head couldn't maintain if their life depended on it. And quite often it did. A crack head didn't work. They stole, prostituted, and orchestrated petty scams. Their family always came second to their addiction. Crack heads never had to worry about cleaning out a bank account because they weren't about to put money in a bank to begin with. If given the chance they would clean out someone else's bank account, but they very rarely had one of their own. All of their cash went straight to the local drug dealers. A crack head did not do the drug, they allowed the drug to do them.

Unfortunately, A.B.'s mother was a crack head. He knew from their frequent long talks that at one point she was a smoker. Samantha was weak-minded though, and she started smoking at the tender age of 14. She was in a relationship with a 25-year-old that had turned her on to crack in an attempt to pimp her out. His tactic worked. After only 2 months of hardcore drug use, Toad, the 25-year-old, had 14 year old Samantha turning tricks day in and day out. He eventually slipped up and rented her out to an undercover police officer. Toad ending up serving time in the Texas Prison System, and Samantha ended up with a habit and a detrimental lifestyle that she just couldn't shake.

A.B.'s father was one of Samantha's customers. She had no idea which one it was so A.B. had to accept the fact that he would never know his real father.

In a sick way, A.B. was lucky that his mothers' addiction was as strong as it was. If it wasn't, he wouldn't be alive today. Samantha had told him that she had gone to a local clinic to see about getting an abortion. Her doctor, a 42-year-old Iranian man named Masul Abu-Kahr, had asked her 101 questions about how she got pregnant and why she wanted to abort the child. Believing that her story would ensure a government funded abortion, she told him the whole truth and nothing but the truth.

After hearing her story, Dr. Abu-Kahr made an appointment to perform the abortion. He also made a strange request. He told her that he would pay her $300 if she had sex with him before she aborted the baby. As expected, she agreed. At the time she was about 2 months pregnant, so she didn't feel any guilt. After all, the baby wasn't even developed yet.

Samantha never understood why her doctor wanted to get her in his bed before she aborted the child until the night she was actually in his bed. While he was plunging deeper and deeper into her 16-year-old pussy, he kept going on and on about how good pregnant pussy was. He said that it was tighter, wetter, and extremely warm. That gave Samantha an idea. Instead of going through with the abortion, she used her pregnancy as an excuse to raise the price of her sex. While the other girls were offering just plain pussy, Samantha was offering pregnant pussy. The bigger her belly got, the more she made men pay.

By the time she realized how much time had passed she had given birth to a surprisingly healthy baby boy. Anthony Tyrone Boon. Also known as A.B. After her baby dropped so did the demand for her sex. Samantha scrambled trying to get pregnant again but not too many men were willing to risk having unprotected sex with a prostitute. And even when they did neglect to use a condom, they rarely ever came inside of her. They would either bust all over her porno-style or force her to swallow every drop porno-style.

A.B. thought about how Layla had just drunk his load. That was exactly how his own mother had done countless men.

"Life's a bitch." A.B. mumbled.

Layla took her eyes off the road momentarily when she heard A.B. speak.

"What was that?" she asked, only hearing the word 'life'.

A.B. shook his head and dug around in his

coat for a blunt.

"Just thinkin' out loud." He told her.

A.B. found what he was searching for and wasted no time putting some fire to the tip of it. He suddenly felt the need to escape reality. He allowed the marijuana to relax his mind while his eyes observed the Cavalier's headlights slicing through the darkness maybe 15 feet ahead of them. He was ready to get back to the Highland Projects where the money was at. Stacking his chips always made him feel better. When the hard white was transforming into soft green things didn't seem so hopeless. He could see tomorrow when he was hustling. Tomorrow was a million dollars later, but if he stayed consistent it was possible. Everybody had a dream. Elevating above the rest was his. As long as he headed in the direction of success, all seemed right in the world.

Layla drove down the last block before coming to the projects.

"You want me to drop you off at the corner or over in front of the bushes?" she asked.

A.B. thought about it. "Drop me off at the bushes." He answered finally. He might as well get valet all the way. After all, the bushes were only a few feet away from the corner.

As soon as Layla turned onto the street that lined the projects, A.B. began scanning the area for his homeboy. When he didn't see him anywhere, he figured that Steel was either hidden in their post-up spot or making a sell. Either way he was no doubt close by.

Layla thought her eyes were playing tricks on her. The light from her headlights spread out far enough to just barely illuminate the bushes off to her left. She squinted as she pulled the car to a stop.

"A.B." she said in an unsure voice, keeping her eyes glued to the scene. "What is that?"

A.B. was about to climb out the car when her question caused him to hesitate. Trying to follow her gaze, he asked, "What's what?"

Layla's eyes got wide when it started to register what she was looking at. She cut her eyes at the practically brand-new pair of black and yellow Air Force Ones on A.B.'s feet. The shoes that were attached to the legs sprawled out underneath the bushes were an exact match. Layla knew from experience that Steel and A.B. often dressed alike.

From the looks of it, it didn't seem like Steel had just laid down to rest.

"Is that…" Layla said, pointing a somewhat trembling finger. "Is that… Steel???"

She already knew the answer to her question, but she hoped like hell that she was wrong.

At the mention of his road dog Steel, A.B. scanned the area more thoroughly. His heart skipped a beat when he came across what had Layla so shaken.

"STEEL!!" he cried out jumping out the passenger side of the car and flying across the grass in the direction of his homeboys' limp body. When he reached the spot where Steel was laying, he felt himself get lightheaded. Even in the darkness he had no difficulty deducing what had happened. Someone had fucked Steel up bad.

His left eye was purple, black, and swollen shut. His mouth was slightly open and A.B. could see that is lips were busted and his teeth were stained with blood. He had a 3-inch-long gash going across his forehead but it was no longer leaking. The blood was dried up and smeared across his face. The way that his clothes were ruffled, and the position his body was in, made A.B. think that he was attacked somewhere else and his body was dumped behind the bushes.

A.B. felt himself flipping out. "Fuck man!" he called out placing his hands on his head not knowing what else to do. He looked up and down the street, but the culprits were no doubt long gone by now.

A.B. dropped down to his knees and bent over with his ear next to Steel's nose and mouth. He looked dead, but there was a slight possibility that he was still holding on.

"Is he…" Layla couldn't finish the question. She had left her car running in the middle of the street to come and offer her assistance.

A.B.'s heart was beating fast. He couldn't lose his best friend like this.

Not like this!

He held his breath and listened intensely for any signs of life.

"Fuck!" he cried out, not hearing or feeling any breathing. A.B. clutched Steel's shirt with both hands and shook him. "Come on Steel." He begged. The emotions of grief, loss, frustration, anger, and pain began bombarding his senses. Even though Layla was standing there watching him he couldn't stop the tears from building up in his eyes.

Steel's limp body rocked side to side as A.B. thrashed him about.

"Hell Naw!" he yelled at his childhood friend through the sobs and tears.   "You can't die on me!"

A.B. shook him harder as memories of their past together rose to the forefront of his mind like a bittersweet fog that had the ability to both terrify and calm by cloaking the obvious and, masking reality.

"Wake up!" A.B. screamed.

Layla stood with her left arm holding her body and her right hand covering her mouth. She had seen a lot of 'hard to swallow' images in her lifetime, but this was by far one of the most disturbing. She felt so powerless to help. All she could do was stand idly by while the man that she was growing to love pleaded with his closes companion to wake up. There was only one problem. People that were asleep would wake up if you wanted them too, but people that were dead would not.

A.B. buried his face into Steel's chest and cried like a newborn baby.
"It's my fault." He wailed. "It's all my fault."

A.B. knew better than to leave Steel out there by himself for so long. But nooo. He not only had to go make that hundred-dollar stang, but he also wasted time getting his rocks off.

As the tears flowed freely from his eyes, he felt Layla's hand begin rubbing his back in a reassuring way. He somewhat blamed her too for his road dog's fate, but the comfort she was providing made him feel good.

"It's gone be alright." He heard Layla's voice say.
Although he knew that she was right there beside him her voice still sounded a thousand miles away.

"Ssnniff… steel." A.B.'s voice was soft and weak. He hadn't done any kind of strenuous work, yet he still felt worn out and exhausted.

A.B. released his hold of his fallen comrades' shirt and gently laid his head across his chest. Out of all the obstacles he was forced to overcome in his short 15 years of life, this episode had to be the hardest by far.

Closing his eyes in a moment of silence, Anthony Boon reflected on some of the good times he had shared with Steven Woolard. As Layla gently moved her soft hands across his back and shoulders, A.B. drifted calmly into the past.

His mind went all the way back to the time when… Do-Do!

A.B.'s eyes shot open. Do-Do… Do-Do… Do-Do!

"It can't be?! He thought in disbelief.

A.B. listened harder. Do-Do… Do-Do… Do-Do!

The sound was faint, but it was unmistakable. A.B. was hearing the rhythmic sound of Steel's heartbeat. He knew his boy was a fighter. Energized by the prospect of saving his friend, A.B. shot up to his feet, startling Layla.

"He's alive!" A.B. told her as he bent over to pick Steel up off the ground.

"What???" Layla couldn't believe it. It had to be a miracle.

A.B. grunted as he slung the dead weight over his shoulder and then made a beeline for Layla's car.

"We gotta get him to the hospital." A.B. called back to her.

She was still shocked that Steel might actually make it, but A.B.'s words caused her to act. She sprinted over to her car, helped place Steel in the backseat, and the next thing she knew she was flying down FM 517 heading in the direction of the Utopian Center Hospital.

The next hour went by like a blur. It was all so surreal that A.B. had a difficult time processing it all. The lights of the stores they sped past in their race against time. The other vehicles on the road that blew their horns and extended their 'fuck you' fingers at the white broad driving like a bat out of hell. He was demanding that she drive faster. She was swearing that was as fast as the Cavalier would go. There was a constant string of encouraging words for Steel coming from both of them. Hold on! You're gonna make it! Everything will be alright! You're too strong to die! Steven Woolard is a survivor!

Then came the pandemonium at the hospital. Them busting into the Emergency entrance and demanding assistance. Doctors tried to calm A.B. down. Their efforts were in vain. He raised hell until something was done about his friend. Much to the dismay of the people who were there long before him, his unruly attitude was awarded with V.I.P. service. When Steel was wheeled away to the operating room on a stretcher, the waiting room erupted with protest. The people had learned a valuable lesson that they were now trying to use to their advantage. 'The Squeaky Wheel Gets The Oil'. Plain and simple.

Waiting on a word from one of the doctors about Steel's condition was excruciating but waiting on a word was all he could do at this point. So, wait on a word is exactly what he did.

"Here. You need to drink something." Layla extended the can of Sprite that she had just purchased from the vending machine out in front of A.B.

A.B. had been sitting in one of the 3 chairs that sat out in the hallway next to the O.R. that Steel was in. He was bent over with his face inside of his hands. Long ago his eyes had gone dry, but he was still feeling the pain of his homeboy's situation.

He rose his head up slowly and encountered a smiling Layla. She was still there. The only relationship she had with him and Steel was a seller/buyer one but for some reason she didn't just bounce after taxiing him to the hospital. She had stayed right by his side every step of the way. She hadn't even dipped off to smoke the work he had sold her.

"You know you don't have to be here." A.B. told her for maybe the sixth time.

Layla rolled her eyes and sat down next to him.

"Why do you keep telling me that?" she asked frustrated. "I know I don't HAVE to be there. I already told you, I WANT to be here."

For some reason her concern him. He peered at her deeply and tried his damnest to read her. What was her angle? Did she even have an angle?
Layla offered the Sprite once again like a stranger presenting a peace offering to an unsure neighbor to show that they meant no harm or ill-will.

A.B. eyed the beverage suspiciously and hesitated. Then he asked, "Why?" His expression was now serious. She had indeed told him several times that she was hanging around simply because she wanted to, but he had never just flat out asked her why she wanted to. Was there something she hoped to acquire by staying?

"Why do you WANT to stay?"

Layla pulled the soda back close to her head feeling a bit foolish. It seemed like the harder she tried to get close to him; the harder he tried to push her away.

Silence lingered in the air as Layla struggled to find the right words, she should use to answer his question. Her dilemma was a unique one. How do you tell your dealer that you want to become his woman?

She took a deep breath and continued to stare into the metal top of the soda can. "You wouldn't understand." She told him.

A.B. wasn't a psychic or anything like that but he could tell from Layla's body language and tone of voice that she wasn't there for any selfish reasons. His first assumption that she wanted to weasel more dope out of him seemed to be wrong. There was obviously something going on with her that he had somehow missed.

A.B. reached over and placed his head on Layla's chin.

"Hey." He said softly, making her lift her head up so he could look her in her eyes. "You can't judge a book by its cover lil mama. Just tell me what's on ya mind and we'll go from there."

Layla was melting under his touch and smooth words. He had a way of making her want to just open up completely and leave herself totally exposed to the scrutiny of his thoughts. Yet and still, she held back and chose her words carefully.

"It's like this..." Layla proceeded to tell A.B. that she really cut for him. She told him that the only reason she had never stepped to him was because she wasn't sure how he would react. To her, her drug of choice was frowned upon, but everybody that used drugs used a drug that someone else frowned upon.

A.B. sat quietly while he tried to take it all in. He had no way of knowing that she felt that way about him. He thought that the sex talk only meant that he could fuck her whenever he wanted to. It surprised him to find out that she really meant she wanted to be his girl. Really, the fact that she smoked crack didn't turn him off like she thought it did. His mother smoked it too, so he couldn't see dope smokers as the scum of the earth. It just wasn't in him. He had never considered Layla as girl material though. And even now he wasn't ready to just make her his woman. Relationships like that took time to create. You needed a bond first. Layla showed that she understood that concept of building a bond when she said that the main reason she wanted to stay was because she wanted to spend some time with him. She said that the only way they would get to know each other as more than just buyer/seller was by spending time together and talking.

Once she had finished explaining herself to the best of her ability, she pulled her face away and turned her gaze back to the top of the soda can. She didn't know how A.B. was taking all that she had admitted to. Her heart rate had increased slightly, and the palms of her hands began to sweat. She was nervous. She had laid it all out on the table. Either he would reject her or accept her. She wasn't sure how she would react if he rejected her.

The few seconds that passed after she finished speaking felt like a lifetime to her. She closed her eyes. He wouldn't respond. She had struck out. Or maybe not. Layla felt A.B.'s hand brush up against hers. She opened her eyes to investigate. In an attempt to accept the peace offering that she had presented to him, and to grant her access into his world, A.B. gently took the Sprite from her hands. She watched in amazement as he tapped on the top to kill any fizz and popped it open. Then he took a swig. She had gotten through to him. Layla's heart fluttered with glee.

A.B. swallowed the swig of sprite and leaned back in his chair. Layla had initiated the bonding process so now the ball was in his court.

Staring straight ahead at the all-white wall, he talked about the most important thing that was on his mind at that present moment.

"I remember when I first started kicking' it with Steel." He began. He was using a somber tone as he referred to his homeboy fighting for his life behind him on the operating table. "We wasn't nothin' but 6 or 7 years old. We had the same first grade teacher. A white lady named Mrs. Wilson…"

All of the first graders had been released for recess. Anthony, he wasn't known as A.B. yet, loved recess. It was his favorite time of the day. Not because it provided him with the opportunity to play, but because of use it offered him an opportunity to come up. Anthony had found a hustle at a young age. Growing up with a mother that could very rarely be depended on had a way of making a kid super-independent. Anthony was no different. He caught on early on that if he wanted to eat on a regular basis, he had to find a way to feed himself. So that's exactly what he did.

Anthony spent his time outside of school walking from store to store stealing candy. The first couple of times he did it he was nervous and scared. Luckily though, his hunger was stronger than his fear. Otherwise, he never would've perfected his craft.

His time at school, specifically recess, was spent selling his stolen candy to the kids at school who had normal parents that gave them allowances. Anthony was on his money way back then. The haters were on their bullshit way back then too.

One day Anthony was on his hustle and a couple of kids from around 23rd St. came around knocking' what he had going on. Even back then the kids were beginning to break off into the different groups they saw the older kids in the neighborhoods break off into.

"Let me get one of those snickers." Robert and Jonathan said, approaching Anthony over by the monkey bars. Robert was a chubby brown skin kid from 23rd and Jonathan was a chubby high yellow kid from the same part of town. Neither one of them had ever bought any candy from him before so Anthony was instantly suspicious. He zipped up his backpack to keep them from inspecting his merchandise.

"Give me fifty cents. Anthony told them in response o their request for a snickers bar.

Robert smiled a toothy grin. "We got yo money." He said. "We'll give it to you after you give us the candy."

Anthony clutched his backpack tightly. "Naw homie. I'll give you the candy after you give me the money."

Robert and Jonathan exchanged glances. Anthony knew what was coming next. The kids from 23rd were just as broke as him. A lot of their parents were strung out just like his mother. But instead of them finding a way to capitalize off of the rich kids like he did, they resorted to preying on people like him. He was far from weak, but two on one put the odds heavily in their favor.

"How about we just take the candy and don't give you nothing?"
The two kids took a step closer to Anthony and he backed up. A quick scan of the playground let hi m know that the teacher wasn't paying any attention, and neither were any of the other kids. Not that he expected any of the other kids to help him. Anthony was a loner. He didn't even run with the group of kids that were from Church Village like he was.

Robert and Jonathan continued to advance on him. Running was not an option. To be labeled as scary was the worst thing you could be labeled as. Realizing that his only real choice was to fight, even though he couldn't win, Anthony dropped his backpack behind him and prepared himself for the confrontation. The kids from 23rd laughed.

"Oh. You gone fight us for it?" Jonathan asked grinning.

Before Anthony could even respond or swing, a tall skinny kid named Steven Woolard came out of nowhere running full speed up behind Robert and Jonathan. Anthony wasn't sure whose side he was on but Steven didn't leave him wondering for long.

He ran up straight behind Robert and used his right foot to kick a field goal with the kids' crotch.

"Ahhh…" Robert hollered in agony as the intense sensation of pain not only brought him to his knees, but also blurred his vision. Robert fell over onto his side. For the first time in his life he found himself teetering on the edge of a mental blackout.

Jonathan spun around and watched in horror as his friend collapsed. "What the hell are you doing?" he shouted.

Anthony didn't give Steven a chance to respond. He took a page from his newfound friends' playbook and used Jonathans sack to kick a field goal of his own.

A.B. couldn't help but to laugh out loud at the distant memory. His laughter brought both Layla and him back to the present.

"After that..." A.B. said smiling. "Me and Steel became best friends. We rode for each other right or wrong."

He took another drink of his sprite. He was surprised at how better he felt after sharing his story with Layla. She was a good listener. She didn't interrupt or make stupid comments. She just sat back and let him narrate.

The two of them locked eyes for a minute. Layla was silently praying that he felt the connection that she felt. A.B. was wondering why he felt so comfortable around a lady he barely even knew. Their moment was cut short, however. One of the doctors who had been operating on Steel exited the room.

A.B. leaped out of the chair and stepped in front of him anxiously rubbing his hands together.

"So…" he asked, trying to read the doctors expression. "Is he gonna be alright?"

The doctor adjusted the face mask that hung loosely around his neck and rubbed his mouth. A.B. couldn't see any hope in the doctors' eyes. They were filled with sorrow.

"Your friend…" The doctor began, knowing it was best to just say it and get it over with.

"He didn't make it."

A.B. felt like he had just been hit by an 18-wheeler. He couldn't even scream, cry, or protest. All he could manage to say was a weak, "nnnoooo…"

His head dropped and the waterworks started all over again. As Layla embraced him from behind, his legs got weak. He couldn't believe that he had lost his homie, got him back, and then lost him again all in less than two hours.

"I'm sorry." The doctor told them. "But whoever beat him up really did a number on him. There was so much damage to his cerebral cortex and frontal lobe that he was practically brain dead long before he reached or operating table. All we could was fight to keep his body alive, but... but he just shut down and we were not able to revive him."

A.B. felt the room start to spin so he sat down and buried his face in between his knees.

"It's o.k." Layla whispered to him. "Steel was like a brother to you. It's o.k. to grieve."

The doctors watched the pair for a few more moments before he just couldn't take it anymore. Everyone thought that once you delivered the bad news that you lost a patient so many times you somehow got numb to the family's reaction. That just wasn't true. For Dr. Abu-Kahr it felt like it got harder and harder each time. Even though he use to perform abortions some years back, he never got use to the idea of lost life. And looking at the blonde woman comforting the friend of the deceased, he figured he never would.

"I'm really, really, really sorry." Dr. Abu-Kahr said, apologizing one more time before walking off and shaking his head.

Through his sobs, A.B. wondered what he should do next. For as long as he could remember Steel had been right by his side. That was his partner in crime. His road dog. His Ridah! A.B. looked up at the white tiled ceiling through water-logged eyes.

For the first time in his life he felt completely lost. For the first time in his life he could no longer see tomorrow.

CHAPTER THREE

Samantha paced back and forth across the living room floor. She looked a hot mess. Her white with thin black stripes skintight spandex shorts were dirty and dinghy. Her purple halter top was filthy too. Samantha had sacrificed her weight, ass, and breasts a long time ago so her attempt at rocking form fitting clothing was pathetic. They were clinging to her bones and accentuating her physically debilitating lifestyle. She hadn't washed her hair or took a bath in 3 days. The little twigs she called hair was wild in some places and matted down in others. Her foot odor floated freely through the air because she was barefoot. But none of that was the really fucked up part. The really fucked up part was that 5-year-old Sandra was wallowing in the same 3-day old filth as her unfit mother. Sandra was sitting on A.B.'s bed in the back, watching cartoons. The only clothes Samantha had put on her was one of A.B.'s white t-shirts and a pair of panties she had on her way too long.

"Where you at?" Samantha asked impatiently, peeking out of the living room window. She was twitching, fidgeting, and scratching places on her body that didn't even itch.

She adjusted her weight from foot to foot. "Come ooonnnn." She urged. "I need you man. I'm fiendin' bad right now."

It had been a full 3 days since Samantha had seen her son A.B. The last thing he said to her was that he would be back before he walked out the front door with that white lady. She didn't know if he was in trouble or what.

The streets had told her that A.B.'s best friend Steel was found beaten to death that very same night.

Since then, A.B. had gone missing. No one had seen him, and no one knew where he was at. The situation had left Samantha with a whole host of problems.

Not only did people speculate that her son was somewhere dead in a ditch, but also her dope supplier and financial support was gone. A.B. was the man of the house. He was the sole wage earner and provider. The money and dope he had left her ran out that first night. Samantha still needed to get high though.

Assuming that A.B. would show up sooner or later and take care of things as always, Samantha started getting work on credit from a local drug dealer named Menace. Menace lived in the Village, but he was rarely ever there. Like A.B. his days and nights were spent chasing' that bread. Menace was a 28-year-old stocky cat that had never worked a legit job a day in his life. His hustle game was on point though. He accepted no shorts and no losses.

Menace had earned the tag 'Menace' too. He was one of the cutthroat individuals that A.B. and Steel were trying to avoid by hustling in the projects instead of the Village. Menace was the type of dude who would plex with you if you refused to buy his shit, tax you when you did buy his shit, and plex with you again if you complained about the price. That nigga attitude was like Debo from Friday. Everybody knew and respected Menace, but nobody liked him. He didn't give a fuck about anybody but himself though. Menace did what Menace wanted to do whenever Menace wanted to do it.
Samantha heard the bass from the two 15's in the trunk of Menace's blue Delta 88 before she saw the actual car pull into the parking space in front of her apartment.

Menace swung his car into the parking space rapping along with Z-Ro as the song blasted from his speakers.

"Finally I found me...man FUCK THESE HOES!"

Menace killed the engine and examined himself in the rearview mirror. He had just left the barber shop so his haircut and edge up was fresh. All he rocked was a bald fade. No tapers, no afros, and no braids. He smiled at himself and admired the six platinum teeth that covered his top row. Diamonds spelled out his name. The two teardrops under his left eye was a testament to what could happen to a person that was fool enough to cross him. Some people had tattooed teardrops just for show, but his were earned by putting in work, and almost everybody knew it. He was in T.Y.C. from age 12 to age 18 for those teardrops. To him they were like his bars and stripes.

Satisfied with his face, Menace climbed out the Delta and checked out his clothes. Black Dickies, white wife-beater, and a pair of black and white Chucks.

It was about 2:30 in the afternoon and the Village was crunk then a bitch. The place was crawling with lil bobblehead ass hoes, lil new to the game hustler's old school cats, and dope fiends. Everybody either spoke, waved, or gave the universal head nod when Menace made eye contact with 'em. He knew the smiles plastered across their faces were more artificial then the flavoring in a package of Kool-Aid, but he loved it none the less. The streets were a warzone. And anyone involved in a war knew that fear was stronger than love. The fact that they never portrayed their true feelings of hate while in his presence made sure that he continued to hold the most powerful hand. His hand was the iron fist of a dictator. Disobedience equaled discipline and discipline might just constitute death.

Menace left the cowards to their meaningless existence and strolled up to Samantha's front door. She knew that he didn't like having to knock so she pulled the door open for him as soon as he got close.

"Hey Menace." She said all polite and sweet. "You got here fast. I thought it would take you longer than that."

Menace ignored her comment and walked to the middle of the living room. There was nothing in it but a couch to his left and a radio to his right. How someone could let themselves live like that he did not know.

Samantha closed the door and Menace turned around to face her with his arms folded across his chest.

"120." He told her. "You got somethin' on it or what?"

Samantha walked up to Menace rubbing on her left elbow.

"You know I'm gone pay you yo money baby. It's just been a while since I heard from my son. But as soon as…"

"Hold up." He said cutting her off. "You mean to tell me you called me way the fuck back out here and you ain't got 'NONE' of my money?" He looked around and shrugged his shoulders. "I know you ain't call me for some mo' credit."

Samantha was expecting him to react like this. She was already $120 in the hole. And here she was trying to get more.

"I know, I know, I know, baby." She pleaded. "I need to get you yo money. You ain't doin' this shit fa yo health. You tryna get paid. You a businessman."

She placed her hands on his chiseled pecs.

"That's why I got you baby. I understand where you comin' from. It's just my sorry ass son. That lazy mothafucka owe me some money right now. I swear baby, as soon as he takes care of me, I'm gone take care of you. You got my word Menace. Just pleeese baby. Please look out for me one more time."

Menace smiled on the inside as Samantha attempted to fast talk him. It amused him how the drug he sold had the power to make a person turn on their own family. He knew her son. He was one of the few youngsters that were really about they scratch. Word was that that boy was stankin' somewhere though. But if he was alive, Samantha was willing to rack up an enormous bill with him that A.B. would have to pay. He didn't mind. He knew that A.B. had some loot. There was just the matter of his reputation. He couldn't keep letting her off the hook when she failed to come up with what she owed.

"Come on Samantha." He said grinning. "I know you good for it. I just don't like it when you lie to me over the phone and say that you have my money when you really don't."

He reached out and grabbed her chin with his thumb and index finger.
Rubbing her chin with his thumb, he said in a soft voice, "That shit really pisses me off."

"I'm sorry Menace." Samantha closed her eyes and apologized. She could sense the handout coming. All she had to do was pout and play that sympathetic role a little while longer.

"I wasn't trying to play you or anything

baby. I just needed a hit. That's all."

Samantha felt Menace's hand leave her chin and she mentally pictured how big a rock he was about to give her. She decided to keep her eyes closed until he presented her with what she wanted.

Menace was about to break her off, but he had to discipline her first. He could tell her a million times not to do something, but he knew that her addiction was strong. It was strong enough to cloud her judgment. The only way to make his point sink in was to provide her with a preview of what would happen if she continued to disobey him.

While she waited patiently with her head slightly bowed and her eyes closed, Menace balled up his fist as tight as he could. Then, without any kind of a warning, he cocked his upper body to the left and swung up and back with all of his might.

His knuckles connected with the right side of Samantha's face hard. Her head snapped to the left and her small frame rocked backwards with the force of the blow.

The sound of the fist to face collision, and the following THUD of Samantha's body hitting the floor, echoed throughout the tiny apartment and entered into the ears of a suddenly frightened Sandra.

She turned her head in the direction of the bedroom door and listened to the yells and screams coming from the living room. Her heart was beating fast and her eyes were wide as she heard her mother's voice.

"I'M SORRY MENACE! I'M SORRY MENACE!" her mother cried, as a man's voice responded with a string of curse words that included, "Stupid Bitch! Fucking Whore! Lying Slut!"

Sandra had been around enough violence to know that her mother was being beaten. Even though fear had her little body trembling, she climbed off the bed and slowly inched towards the door. She made sure to tiptoe and be extra quiet. There was no telling what the mean man would do to her if he found her.

Sandra made it to the door and listened. She was doing her best to breathe as shallow as possible.

The man's voice said over her mother's cries, "I'm gone give you what you want. But yo ass gone have to earn it this time, and you still gone owe me two bills tomorrow."

Sandra placed a shaky hand on the cold doorknob. Before she turned it she said a silent prayer to Jesus asking that the mean man don't see her.

Finishing her prayer, she said 'Amen", took a deep breath, and cracked open the bedroom door. What she saw was something that no 5-year-old girl should ever have to see.

The mean man was tossing her mother's clothes to the side and he had her mother down on all fours like a cat or a dog. She was all the way naked and her bottom was facing the mean man. Sandra instantly became paralyzed with a mixture of fear, embarrassment, and overwhelming confusion.

"What's the mean man doing to mommy?" she thought.

To her horror, her mother stayed like that while the mean man unzipped his pants, pulled them down around his ankles, and got down on his knees behind her. Sandra shivered at the sight of the mean man's hairy booty.

Samantha hollered loudly as Menace rammed his

tool into her asshole raw. He didn't wear a condom, use any type of lubrication, or ease his way in. He just jammed her up with his meat and pounded away without any consideration for the extreme pain he was inflicting on her.

Samantha had experienced anal before, but it was never like this. Menace was long and thick, and he gave her all that he had.

"OOOHHHH..." Samantha wailed as she felt the lining inside of her ass tear from the rough, dry thrust.

Sandra wasn't sure what was going on, but she knew that the mean man was hurting her mother. Knowing that made her hurt also. It all became too much and Sandra started to cry.

"Mommy!" she called out.

Samantha was in too much pain to hear her daughter calling out to her. Menace heard her though. He continued to pump but turned his head in the direction of the bedroom door.

Sandra made eye contact with the mean man. The evil looking expression he gave her made her think he was the devil. Sandra slammed the door shut and ran as fast as she could into the closet. He had seen her. Why didn't she just stay quiet? He might come hurt her next. Sandra could still hear her mother through the closed door. The sound shook her to the core.

Not wanting to be next, Sandra buried herself beneath a pile of dirty, musty, smelly clothes and pressed her little hands to her ears as hard as she could. She wanted desperately to block out her mother's voice. Unfortunately, it didn't work.

After seeing Sandra, Menace drilled Samantha even harder. Not only did she willingly put her son in debt with him, but she also allowed herself to be taken by him in front of her daughter. He felt as if he owned her.

Samantha endured the abuse for maybe 5 more minutes before Menace was stimulated enough to deposit his load inside of her wounded rectum. When he withdrew, she collapsed onto the floor and reached down to hold her anus. She could feel the blood. Menace was satisfied. He stood over Samantha and pulled his pants up. After adjusting his clothing, he fished a sandwich bag out of his pocket. He opened it, inspected its contents, and then dug out a slab of dope worth $50 on the streets.

As he stepped over Samantha's body, he dropped the work in front of her face and headed towards the front door.

"Don't forget." He told her as he walked out without looking back at her. "The bill is $200 now."

Everybody was watching him exit the apartment. The look on their faces told him that they had heard everything. He liked that.

Samantha saw the $50 piece and scooped it up quick. Her asshole as burning but she dealt with the pain. She grimaced and winched as she scrambled over to the radio where her pipe and lighter were at. Menace had ensured that she wouldn't be able to sit down for a week, so she positioned herself on her knees as she crammed a piece of the work she had just got onto her pipe. A few seconds later, the dope was crackling on one end of her pipe and her lips were wrapped tightly around the other.

She inhaled as deeply as she could. Trying to get as high as possible, she held the smoke in her lungs until she thought she was going to pass out. Sweet, blissful, euphoric intoxication. At that moment her swollen jaw, busted lip, and ruined asshole no longer mattered. She thought about what she had just been subjected to for a gram of dope. Was it worth it? She put some more flame to the work and sucked in paradise. Holding in the smoke, she glanced down at her still nude body.

"Yep." She told herself, trying to make the letter "O" with the exhaled smoke. "It was worth it."

Outside, a Dickinson High school bus was dropping off the teenagers that lived in and around Church Village. In another part of town, a 13-year-old bi-racial girl named Alize was getting off a Dickinson High school bus in her neighborhood.

Almost all of the boys that went to a school at Dickinson High wanted to be with Alize and almost all of the girls wanted to just be her. She was easily in the top 5 as far as pretty girls went. Being a mixed breed, her mother was white and her father was black, genetics had blessed her with a skin tone so caramel smooth that she attracted men just on the strength of her look. She had jet black hair that hung down all the way to the small of her back. Her eyebrows were bushy, her eyes were slightly slanted like an Asian, and she had dimples. Her body wasn't developed all the way like a grown woman's yet, but she had enough curves and beautiful facial features to be classified as sexy.

Alize wasn't the type to thrive off of attention though. She would've enjoyed life more if she had been born ugly. At least then she would've been able to fade into the background and go about her business unnoticed. Alize was probably the only anti-social popular kid on the face of the planet. Even though she wanted people hanging around her like she wanted a hole in her head, Alize hung with a clique of girls known around the way as the Valley Park Girls.

Valley Park was a small sub-division in east Dickinson that contained homes worth between $45,000 and $75,000. The families there weren't poor but they weren't rich either. They were somewhere in between. The area was known as Valley Park because of the neighborhood park found at the center of the sub-division. The park was called Valley Park. All of the Valley Park Girls used it as a hangout.

Alize's clique wasn't too deep. There were only 5 of them altogether. Whenever she was around her friends Alize played the role, but all she wanted was to be left alone.

It seemed like their little gang contained all the necessary races and the stereotypes that coincided with them.

First there was LaQuisha Williams. If they had decided to label each other, LaQuisha would no doubt be identified as the leader. She was a 15-year-old dark skinned sister with a ghettofied attitude, short hair, and a boxing game that even the niggas weren't sure they wanted to test.
The title of Second-in-Command would have to go to Melissa Gomez. Melissa was a 14-year-old Hispanic chick with 3 big sisters and 2 little brothers. Her big sisters had already married and moved out the house. Melissa wouldn't be far behind. At the age of 14 she was already pregnant and engaged to an 18-year-old Hispanic boy who worked for her father's lawn care business. Melissa didn't let her pregnancy slow her down though. She still drank, smoked, and got into fights. She wasn't as good with her hands as LaQuisha was, but she was still pretty nice in the paint.

Then there was Krystal Starr. She was the same age as Alize, and in the same grade, but both of her parents were white. She had blonde hair, blue eyes, no butt, and even less brains. Krystal was known as a slut, but she liked to consider herself as kind-hearted. If she had sex with one dude and didn't have sex with his friends too then the friends might feel bad. What others seen as group sex she saw as sympathy sex. Last but not least there was Ming Vu. As you could probably guess, Ming was the Asian of the group. And true to the stereotype she was something like a genius and built like 6 o'clock. Straight up and down. No bumps, no curves, no nothin'. Ming was only 14 years old but she had been skipped up so much that she was already a senior. Ming was a bookworm. She was still a virgin, she never fought alongside the other girls, and she would only smoke weed when LaQuisha or Melissa forced her too. Ming was basically the odd one. LaQuisha liked her though. It was something about her innocence that she respected. Ming Vu's ghetto pass was like platinum on the strength of LaQuisha.

Behind closed doors Alize was more like Ming then any of the other girls, but when in public she walked, talked, and acted like LaQuisha. Alize was somewhat a stereotype herself. She didn't know if her black father was dead, in prison, or making power moves on Wall Street. She always told people that her father abandoned her and her mother. The truth was a little rawer than that. Alize's mother was on drugs. She wasn't as bad on them as some people were though. Her mother still managed to go to work every day and provide a pretty decent life for the two of them. Alize's mother told her that when she was younger, she use to get high and have a lot of wild and unprotected sex. When she found out that she was pregnant the list of possible fathers was so long that she never even tried to find the right one. She said that she couldn't see herself going through DNA test after DNA test like those women who appeared as guests on the Maury show. Alize pictured her mother being a white girl like Krystal back in the day. She would never admit that though. In her mind it was better to have a deadbeat dad then a slutty mother. It seemed like everybody had a deadbeat dad. Her lie helped her fit right in.

The school bus dropped the Valley Park Girls off at the edge of their little subdivision. All 5 girls lived on the streets that surrounded the park, so every day when they got off the bus, they would walk each other to the park and then split up to go to their individual houses. The walk home was always spent the same way... gossiping. The Valley Park Girls talked about any and everybody. To be up to date on all of the latest news was mandatory.

"Say Melissa?" LaQuisha said getting her pregnant friends' attention as they walked. "Did you see that nigga A.B. at school today?"

Melissa walked with a waddle, resting her hands on top of her ever-growing belly.

"Ummm." She answered, chewing on her Winter fresh gum like her life depended on it. "Now that you mention it, naw, he ain't come to school today neither."

LaQuisha shook her head. "Damn. That's fucked up. Maybe them same fools that killed Steel got his ass buried somewhere."
Krystal twirled her hair around her finger.
"Awww." She cooed in her innocent little girl voice. "That's so sad. He was fine too. Why couldn't they have killed someone ugly? Like... Albert Lundy."

Ming held her books close to her chest and pushed her sliding glasses back up her slender nose. "You shouldn't say things like that Krystal." She admonished. "Just because Albert isn't attractive like A.B. or Steel doesn't mean he deserves to die."

LaQuisha's face lit up. "Whaaat??" she asked smiling. "You think A.B. is attractive?"

Ming started to blush.

LaQuisha poked her in her arm playfully and said, "Let me find out you secretly wanted A.B. to pop that cherry."

Ming's mouth dropped open. "I did 'NOT' say that!"

LaQuisha's language was something that Ming figured she would never get used to. She was always so vulgar.

All of the girls got a good laugh at Ming's expense. Ming didn't mind though. She was always joked with because she was the only virgin in the clique. When her home girls were high and drunk though, and their tongues were loose, each one had expressed their desire to be like her if they could. LaQuisha always told her that she could be like the rest of them in 5 minutes if she wanted to, but none of them could ever be like her. She had held onto her prize and she was proud of herself. Ming wanted her future husband to be the first and only man to make her feel how her friends said sex made them feel.

"Well," LaQuisha said, placing her arm around Ming's neck. "Maybe we can help you find another crush since A.B.'s dead."

Ming was about to protest LaQuisha calling A.B. her crush but Alize spoke up before she could say anything.

"A.B. isn't dead." Alize told them.

All of the girls looked at her.

"How do you know that?" Melissa asked skeptically.

Alize thought about how she knew that A.B. was still alive. There was no way that she could tell them the truth. The truth would no doubt bring on a flurry of questions that she really didn't want to have to answer.

Staring into the enquiring eyes of her home girls made her regret even speaking up on the subject of A.B.

Alize shrugged and tried to play it off.

"Weeell, I don't know for sure, but I don't think he is. I mean, if they would've killed him when they killed Steel, why weren't their bodies found together? It wouldn't make sense to kill one and kidnap the other. A.B. people don't have no money to pay off no ransom. If they did, he wouldn't be selling' dope."

The rest of the group allowed Alize's words to sink in. What she was saying made a lot of sense. LaQuisha eventually brushed it off and changed the subject.

"Guess who got caught suckin' Craig dick at the movies?" she challenged.

As the girls proceeded to beg to know who Craig's latest conquest was, Alize let out the breath she had been holding. She was thankful that no one had asked her any more questions about A.B. In the future she had to be a little more careful and think before she spoke. The rest of their walk together she just listened.

By the time LaQuisha got through filling them all in on the situation she had dubbed the movies 12 scandal it was time for them to split up and go their separate ways. Since it was a Friday night and they didn't have school tomorrow, LaQuisha told them that she would call them to discuss what they would be getting into. As usual, the girls hugged and headed towards their lives outside of the clique.

Out of all 5 girls, Alize and Ming had to enjoy splitting up more than the rest of them.

Alize brushed her hair out of her face with her hand and put a little more pep in her step. The two-bedroom, red brick home that her mother was renting to own never looked better. She paused momentarily at the curb to check the mailbox.

Empty.

Her mother was a receptionist for the Willis, Winn, and Stone Law Firm and her workday wouldn't be over with until 6:00 that night. Alize was looking forward to the 3 hours of solitude.

"Well," she thought, taking out her house keys and walking up the driveway. "Semi-solitude."

For the past few days, her and her mother had entertained a most unusual houseguest. But perhaps the word 'entertained' didn't quite fit the scenario. All their guest did was lay in bed. Whenever they felt themselves building up a little energy, they would do drugs until their body shut back down. It was more like her and her mother periodically checked on their houseguest to make sure that they were still breathing.

The locks clicked and the keys jiggled as Alize entered her home through the front door. From the looks of her house, you wouldn't be able to guess that her mother had an addiction. For the most part their crib was laid. Black leather sofas, matching love seat and end tables, 52-inch flat screen television, and an 8ft. x 6ft. aquarium that contained the same orange and white fish that had starred in Finding Nemo. And all of that was just in the living room.

Both bedrooms were furnished with the Rooms To Go Cindy Crawford home collection. Alize had queen sized bed and decorated everything with the colors purple and black. Purple and black were the Valley Park Girls official colors. All of their rooms looked similar to one another.

Alize's mother had a king-sized bed and she decorated her room with white and gold. She said that men loved to relax under a set of satin white and gold sheets.

Each room also had its own T.V., radio, D.V.D. player, and huge walk-in closet. It was obvious that the people over at Willis, Winn, and Stone paid her mother well. And to think, all she had to do was answer the phones. At least Alize hoped that was all her mother had to do.

Alize crossed the plush living room and headed towards her mother's room to make her routine check on their house guest. The closer she got the more audible a strange noise was becoming. She stepped into the hallway and faced her mother's door.

"Sssssss…"

Alize gave a confused look. She recognized what the noise was, but she wasn't expecting to hear it. She opened the bedroom door and the hissing noise got louder.

"SSSSSSS…"

It was coming from her mother's personal bathroom. They had two full bathrooms in their house. Each one could only be accessed by going through one of the bedrooms.

Alize looked at her mother's bed. For the very first time in 3 days their house guest wasn't wrapped up under the covers. He had finally decided to get up and take a shower.

Alize crept into the room silently and eased over to the bathroom door. It was wide open. She could see a man's naked outline through the shower curtain.

Alize smiled, folded her arms across her chest, and leaned up against the door jam. Dude was apparently her mother's new boyfriend, but Alize thought he was fine as hell too. She didn't want to step on her mother's toes or nothing like that, but she did want a sneak peek.

For the longest she had wondered what he was packing, and she wasn't about to pass up this golden opportunity to find out.

Lucky for her he was rinsing off and she didn't have to wait very long. She heard the water cut off, seen a hand emerge from the inside of the shower and grab the curtain, and then she stared as the hand pulled the curtain back.

A.B. made eye contact with a grinning Alize and froze. He didn't know if he should apologize, shut the curtain, or what, so he just stood there. Alize looked his nude frame up and down and licked her lips. She now knew why her mother didn't mind shacking up with a dude that her daughter went to school with. A.B. was nicely hung. She looked at his tool one more time and locked the image away in her memory bank.

"Hmph." She said, cocking one of her eyebrows and nodding her head in a downward motion as if to point at his piece.

A.B. followed her gaze and was happy to see that she had caught him at a good time. He looked back up and opened his mouth to speak but Alize rolled off the door jam and disappeared out of her mother's room.

She had left him speechless. Was she letting him know that she wanted to get loose? A.B. knew all about Alize and her little clique. They all had some wild reputations. All of 'em except lil Lucy Lu. Lucy Lu is what he liked to call Ming. Knowing how those Valley Park Girls got down, it was definitely a possibility that she wanted to let him cut.

A.B. grabbed his drying off towel and stepped out of the tub.

"Then again," he thought, wiping off his face. "Layla might've shot her at me to see if I would bang up her daughter."

As enticing as the lil half-breed was, A.B. knew that his best bet was to let her make it. It sure would be playa to knock down a mother/daughter combo though.

CHAPTER FOUR

A.B. sat on the edge of Layla's King size bed wearing nothing but a pair of black boxer briefs. Since he had been laid up with Layla over in Valley Park, she had bought him a couple pairs of brand-new boxers, socks, and t-shirts. All of his clothes were still over in the Village, but he hadn't felt like going to get any of them. Today was his first time taking off the outfit he had on when Steel died. Losing someone so close to him and really taken its toll. His whole world had suddenly gone haywire and he was just now making an attempt to get back on track. A.B. knew that no matter how many times a real nigga might fall a real nigga would always get back up.

Sitting on the nightstand next to the bed was a half-ounce of weed and four wet sticks rolled up in a piece of aluminum foil. Three hundred dollars, all the cash he had on him, was stacked neatly next to the bud. Layla had smoked up the rest of the work he had, but to her credit, she didn't take not one-dollar bill away from him. A.B. broke down the weed and thought about Layla. She had been keeping it so 100 with him that it scared him at times. She only left his side to go to work the entire time he had been out of it.

When she was around, she was catering to his every need and encouraging him to bounce back. Layla understood that he was a hustler. If he didn't get up and go hustle, then he was nothing. She also understood that he was no good to himself or anyone else in his present condition. Layla told him that she would hold him down however long it took him to mourn Steel. A.B. had to admit that she had been true to her word.

Once he had broken down enough weed to roll a nice sized blunt, A.B. laced the blunt with two of the wet sticks and put some fire to it. He had to hit the streets tonight. Business called. And A.B. wanted to be in a state of mind to handle anything. He knew that the P.C.P would do the trick.

True enough, A.B. hadn't been his money-minded, fully focused self lately, but he wasn't as out of it as he pretended to be. He had just simply switched modes. He went from hustle mode to plex mode. Someone had brutally beaten his best friend to death, and he had no intentions of just letting that shit ride. In the streets it was an eye for an eye, a tooth for a tooth, and a life for a life.

The past 3 days had been spent analyzing, plotting, strategizing, and hiding out. A.B. saw the situation like this: he and Steel knew the risk they were taking by short-stoppin' those niggas in the projects. If they had ever just flat out caught them cutting into their profits, they would no doubt want beef. A.B. figured that Steel had gotten caught by them fools while he was gone. They probably initiated plex, and Steel, being the type of dude, he was, didn't back down.

The fact that they tossed his beaten, bloody, half-dead body behind the bushes where him Steel use to post up meant that the killers wanted to send him a message. "We know what ya'll been doin'!"

A.B. couldn't know for sure but his instincts told him that he was next. There was no way he could allow himself to be seen on the streets until he knew who it was that was looking for him.

Cough! Cough! Cough!
A.B. hit his chest with his fist. That 'Boss Playa'

blunt he was smoking was hitting' hard.

Common sense had helped him to narrow it down to 3 people. There were 3 crack houses located inside the Highland Projects and it had to be one of them that were responsible. A.B. had no way of figuring out which one it was unless they fucked up and went around bragging, so he had no choice but to target them all.

Layla had told him that she would help him handle those fools and when the smoke cleared, they could start selling all of the dope in the projects themselves. She called herself a Queen Pen and A.B. a King Pen. A.B. wasn't looking that far into the future. It sounded good but he really just wanted to avenge his road dog's death. Setting up shop in the projects wasn't really his goal. He knew he'd need all the help he could get though, so he allowed Layla to hold onto her dream.

Layla and Alize seemed like the only tools he had so he had to be careful and play his cards right. One false move and he would be re-united with his home boy sooner than expected.

Layla was a smoker, and as a smoker she knew other smokers. A.B. figured that he could keep his hustle going through her. If she wanted to be down so bad, fuck it, he'd let the bitch be down.

Her daughter, Alize, was a freak. A freak that hung with other freaks. A freak that hung with other freaks and knew everything about everybody. A.B. hadn't given her a specific job in his mind yet but he could tell that she would come in handy sooner or later. All he had to do to come out on top was keep the females out front and call the shots from the background. He had learned long ago how to survive plex. Shadow Walk! A man can't kill what a man can't see. And likewise, a man can't dodge what a man doesn't expect.

A.B. inhaled, exhaled, and smirked.

"It's finna go down." He thought, holding the blunt in his mouth with his lips while getting dressed.

He slid on the same pair of black jeans but grabbed a fresh black t-shirt that Layla had bought him to put on. He needed to get Alize on his team. She was already feelin' him. Maybe if he put his pound game down on her she would happily be a puppet on his strings.

A.B. laughed out loud at the thought.

BossPlaya blunt still burning, A.B. went and knocked on Alize's bedroom door. All he could hear was Tyrese singing loudly on the other side. He was saying something about a zodiac freak and 'the signs of love making'.

Knowing that he would have to practically kick the door down for her to hear him over the radio, he just turned the knob and pushed it open. Inside, he saw Alize how he had never seen her before. She was sitting at her study desk with her back to him. All she had on was a purple bra and panty set. She was hunched over writing something down in her notepad. A.B. decided to use the fact that she hadn't heard him come into his advantage. It wasn't every day he got to see one of the badest females he knew wearing nothing but her undergarments.

A.B. stood in the doorway and studied her. Alize Scott had the most intoxicating complexion he had ever seen. Her long pretty hair swayed gently as she worked diligently at putting her thoughts down on paper. A.B. noticed how her shoulder blades protruded just a little behind her bra straps. Just being real, Alize could stand about 10-

20 more pounds, but she was sexy then a motherfucker as is. If her mother's body was any type of peek into the future for Alize, whichever man ended up with her had him a square business dime piece. No one could deny that.

A.B. strolled into the room and hit his blunt. When he got up close behind her, he bent over and blew out the smoke along her spine.

Alize shivered and felt a few goose bumps pop up as the unexpected breeze caressed her back. At first, she wasn't going to pay it any mind and just write it off as the A.C. but the distinct smell that accompanied the breeze made her look up.

Alize snapped her head around and gave A.B. an evil look.

"What the fuck are you doing in my room?" she asked, quickly snatching a white t-shirt up off the floor and putting it on to cover herself up.

"Did you come in here to get some kind of a peep show?"

A.B. took a step back and chuckled.

"Whoa lil mama." He told her, raising his hands up as if to surrender. "Pump ya brakes. I just came in here to ask you if you wanted to smoke this blunt with me. I wasn't trying' ta do you how you did me. I don't steal peeks. I wait until they're offered."

Alize smacked her teeth. What could she say? Even if he was there to look at her half naked body, she had opened up that door by spying on him in the shower.

It had been a while since Alize had smoked some wet. She liked how the high felt but it wasn't the kind of drug she did too often. That embalming fluid was some strong shit.

"I guess." Alize said, rolling her eyes and

getting up to turn down the volume of the radio. "But just for the record, if I had asked to see it you would've showed me, so technically I ain't steal shit."

A.B. watched her twist across the room. The t-shirt she was wearing wasn't a long one so he could see the bottom of her butt cheeks poking out from beneath it.

"Stay focused." A.B. willed himself silently. His stay in Valley Park had to remain business. If he allowed himself to be sidetracked by a woman again there's no telling what might happen. Losing sight of his goal when her mother spread her legs played a huge part in him losing his homeboy. He wasn't about to make the same mistake twice.

Alize bent over without bending her knees when she made it to the radio. A.B. hurried up and looked off. He redirected his attention towards the notepad Alize had been writing in.

"What's this?" he asked, scanning the page. "Some kind of diary?"

Alize walked up behind him, took the blunt, and hit it.

"Naw." She said exhaling. "It's a book. I'm not too far into it though. That's only like chapter three."

A.B. looked at her quizzically. He thought he had heard wrong.

"A book?!?" he repeated surprised. "You never struck me as the book writing type."

Alize put one hand on her hip. "And just what do you mean by that? You think I'm not intelligent enough to write a book?"

"Damn girl." A.B. responded. "Why you so confrontational? I ain't even say all of that. All I was saying was that I never would've guessed you were an aspiring author. I thought you and yo home girls were just party girls."

"Well," Alize said, closing the tablet to conceal her work, "you should never judge a book by its cover. There's waaay more to me then the Alize Scott you think you know."

A.B. made his was over to the bed and sat down.

"Is that right?" he asked.

"That's right." She answered.

"Mind telling me what it's about?"

That question shocked her. Not even her own mother had asked her what her book was about. Could he really be interested in what she was doing, or was he just making small talk while they smoked together?
Alize sat down in her swivel chair and passed the blunt. She was already beginning to feel the effects of the drugs. Her defenses were initially on high alert but the buzz that was kicking in mellowed her out a little.

"You don't have to pretend like you all concerned with what I have going on just because you are sleeping with my mama. Ya'll little relationship... arrangement ... or whatever it is don't make you my step daddy or nothing like that."

There she was shooting at him again. This time he decided to ignore the attitude. If he ceased to feed into the negativity, what would she do then?

"Pretend?" A.B. swung his legs onto the bed and propped his back up against the headboard. "Why you think I'm pretending to be concerned? For all you know, I could be writing a book too and just want to compare notes. Maybe you could help me with my plot and character development?"

Alize rolled her eyes. "You aren't writing a

book. You sell crack all day."

"Damn lil mama. You just told me that I should never judge a book by its cover, yet you are judging me right now. Yeah, I do what I do to eat but trust me, there's waaay more to me then the Anthony Boon you think you know."

He was good. Alize noticed how he kept on using her actions and words to justify his own. Whenever he brought to the light that he was only doing what she had done, it left her no good was to respond. It was like a communication checkmate. Her only option was to call his bluff and let him do the talking. That way she could gather ammunition off of his words instead of him doing it to her.

"Alright then," Alize said, smiling like she knew a secret that no one else in the world knew. "If you tell me what your book is about, I'll tell you what my book is about."

A.B. threw one hand behind his head and got comfortable. He wasn't writing any book, and judging by the smile on Alize's face, she knew that he wasn't writing any book. She just said that to make him admit it and to give herself a legit reason not to tell him about her book. A.B. wasn't about to admit to anything. He was going to continue to play along.

"Bet." He told her.

A.B. hit the BossPlaya blunt hard. He needed time to think. A book? What kind of book could he be writing? A mystery? A horror? A romance? Damn! What if she asks questions? How am I going to come up with an entire story that quick and keep all the facts straight in my head?

Think nigga think!

Shit, I can't hold this smoke in forever. She lookin' at me, still grinning. I bet she knows that

I'm stalling. Look at her. All smug. I cannot give her the satisfaction. Come on A.B.!

A.B. slowly exhaled the smoke. That's when it hit him. He remembered one of his big homies coming home from the penitentiary and telling him that he had spent his whole two years reading books. Tut, his big homie, said that there were hundreds of books floating around the Texas Department of Criminal Justice system that talked about nothin' but 'hood shit. The characters sold dope, got high, fucked hoes, killed people, went to prison, and stole cars, the whole 9. Tut said that some of them sounded like the autobiography of his life. The only thing different were the names.

"My book is an Urban book." A.B. told her proudly. "It's like the kind of book Eric Jerome Dickey, The Real Bookworm, and Zane be writing."

Those were the only 3 authors he could remember. When Alize's expression changed, he knew he had her going. He had just told her a type of book and named 3 well-known authors. All he had to do now was talk about his life but make up some different names and scenarios.

"I'm sort of like you." He told her. "I haven't gotten too far into my book yet neither. I'm only on... like... chapter five."

He remembered that she said she was only on chapter 3 so he made sure to outdo her.

It's basically going to be about hood shit." He told her, feeling more confident in his lie with each word.

"Jordan , the main character , is the only child of his drug addict mother. His father was one of her Johns, so he never met the dude. To Jordan, poverty is a bitch, so he..."

A.B. proceeded to tell her a realistic tale that

somewhat mirrored his own life. The more he talked, however, the more he ventured from reality to fantasy. In his make-believe book, the main character was so traumatized by all of the shit he encountered growing up in the ghetto that he vowed to get rich or die trying like the rapper 50 cent. He tried his hand at hustling, but mass distribution of illegal narcotics just wasn't in his blood. Jordan was more comfortable draped in black making mothafucka's drop out. He graduated from burglary to robbery and from robbery to kidnapping. The lick that was supposed to be his claim to fame was a job that consisted of kidnapping the biggest dope dealers' 18-month-old son and holding him for a one-million-dollar ransom.

A.B abruptly stopped talking and left Alize in suspense. The plot that he had just described to her sounded live then a bitch. She couldn't help but want to read the book.

"So, what happened to Jordan?" she asked fiending to know how the book was going to end. "Did he get paid? Did he get killed? Did he get locked up?"

A.B. could tell from her reaction that she liked the book. Hell, he liked it too. Too bad none of that was wrote down anywhere. He could probably sell a million copies of a book like that.

"Ah Ah Ah." He said, waving his index finger from side to side. "I can't just give you everything on G.P. How about you tell me what your book is about first, and then I'll 'THINK' about telling you how my book is going to end?"

Alize had to admit, she thought he was bullshitting her about having a book he was working on. Maybe there 'was' more to A.B. then she first thought.

"Alright." She agreed.

Fair was fair. She had said that she would tell him about her book if he told her about his, and he did. It was now her turn to share. She felt a little intimidated by his book though. He already had the entire story mapped out. All she had was a general idea and about 32 pages wrote. Hers wasn't near as action packed as his was.

"I don't have the whole thing in my head like you do, but I got the basic concept down."

She looked over at her tablet. "It's called, 'My Mask, My Costume, My Fraudulent Life '."

Alize rubbed her hands nervously in her lap. It felt awkward talking with someone she barely even knew about something her own home girls didn't even know about. She didn't want to tell them about her book because of how closely it mirrored her own life. If they ever would've read her book, they would've known that the face she put on for them and everybody else was just a mask. Deep down she wasn't the person that she pretended to be. On the cool, she wasn't even sure why she was about to open up to A.B.

Maybe it was because she felt obligated to keep her word? Or maybe it was because he might not even recognize the similarities between her and Zania, the main character? Or did she just feel safe because the drugs had made her lower her guard?

She gazed up and locked eyes with A.B.

Nope!

It was really none of the above. The real deal was that she sensed genuine interest in the dark brown windows of his soul. She had longed to share her true self with someone other than her diary. In this forum, she could reveal herself to a person who seemed eager to know her. If he liked the concept of the book, her self-esteem would rise, and she would have more strength to be herself. If he didn't like it, she could soften the blow by saying it was Zania that he didn't like and not necessarily her.

"The book I'm writing is an Urban book too." She began. "My main character is a teenage girl named Zania. Zania's mother is on drugs and her father is doing life in the pen. Seeing all the stuff that she seen growing up forced her to create an image just to survive and cope. Really though, Zania was a good girl…"

Alize went on to tell him that Zania witnessed her mother get beaten by drug dealers on numerous occasions. She also couldn't get to sleep on some nights because her mother use to trick to support them. The sounds of moans. groans, and headboards knocking would filter through the paper-thin walls they had in their small, cramped, efficiency apartment. She was always in fear of being raped by some perverted old man because even though she was young, her mother's so-called boyfriends would always stare at her with lust in their eyes.

Zania was a good girl with a titanium shell. Being aggressive was the only remedy for being afraid. So, she wore the mask of a gangster girl. All along, she hated the image she was forced to hide behind.

"The book is basically about Zania trying to overcome the madness she was born into." Alize grinned sheepishly. "She wants to be a writer."

A.B. sat up on the bed and looked deep into Alize's eyes. She turned away. Her book was deep. He had just hastily thrown together some criminal activity and passed it off as a plot, but her story actually had some depth to it. It made him feel sorry for Zania and she wasn't even real. It also made him think. To a certain extent, he was wearing a mask and a costume too. He played the role of a dope dealer loving the grind, but late at night, he tossed and turned over the hand he had been dealt. He ain't like the 'hood. He ain't like the streets. He ain't like the game. It had already cost him a mother, a father, a childhood, and a best friend. Come to think of it, if he didn't stay on his toes, it just might cost him his life.

A.B. rested his elbows on his knees and hung his head. Alize watched the blunt burn between his fingers. She didn't know if he was feeling her book or not. He was obviously contemplating hard about something. She didn't know it, but he was thinking about her.

After remaining in that position for about a minute, A.B. passed her the blunt and finally spoke.

"That girl... Zania... she's you ain't she?"

Alize quickly shook her head 'no'. She wasn't ready to admit that to him. That would be opening up too much.

"Oh nooo." She said. "She's just a representation of real teenage girls in her shoes. Zania is hundreds of girls. She ain't me."

A.B. knew that she was lying but he decided not to press the issue. He now knew what she meant when she said that there was more to her than he thought he knew. On the inside, she wasn't that Valley Park gangster girl that he knew from around the way. She was more like the female version of him. A child forced into adult shoes way too early. It's just that the streets version of adult men and adult women had him playing the role of a gangster/hustler and her playing the role of a down ass bitch.

"You know what?" A.B. asked. "We got a lot in common."

Alize leaned back in her chair. "How so?"

"Think about it." A.B. told her. "We pretty much come from the same place. The bottom. Our mothers are on drugs, we don't know our fathers, we both were placed into situations that made us deny who we really are, neither one of us actually like poverty and projects, and get this… we both write books. Come on girl. What are the odds?"

Alize couldn't help but chuckle at the last thing on his list of stuff they had in common. Hearing him rattle off his list made her think that he was right though.

"To be honest," A.B. continued. "There's only one major difference that I can see between you and me."

Alize cocked her eyebrows. "And what, pray tell, is that?"

"I've figured out a realistic way to do just what Zania is trying to do. I know how to overcome the madness, hard times, self-hate, and poverty. I got a 5-year master plan that's guaranteed to get me so far away from the ghetto that I can live the rest of my life without ever looking back."

A.B. stayed silent for a few seconds allowing his words time to really sink in. From their brief conversation he had acquired exactly what he needed to get Alize on his team. Everybody had a dream. If you can figure out what an individual's dreams are, you can more easily coerce them into helping you fulfill yours. You just had to let them see how helping you would ultimately help them. That was the 13th Law in one of A.B.'s favorite books, 48 Laws of Power.

'When asking for help, appeal to people's

self-interest, never to their mercy of gratitude. The shortest and best way to make your fortune is to let people see clearly that it is in their interest to promote yours.'

A.B. had indeed piqued Alize's curiosity. From the way that he lived, she figured his master plan had something to do with the dope game, but she wasn't sure if that's all he was about.

"So, she said, allowing her curiosity to get the best of her. "Are you going to tell me what this 5-year master plan is or do you plan on leaving me hanging like you did with your book?"

She bit. Now, all A.B. had to do was reel her in.

"I can show you better than I can tell you." He responded.

"Well, show me then."

"I can't right now, but tonight when Layla gets back, I'm going to go handle a little business. When I get back, if you still woke, I'll lace you up. I think I can trust you."

"'Think' you can trust me?" Alize shot at him swiveling her neck. "I ain't even told nobody that you been at my house. Not even my girls, and me and them are like family. With all of the stuff that's going around about you right now, I'm probably one of the only people that you 'CAN' trust."

Her implications that the streets were talking about him got him on point.

"What you talkin' 'bout?" he asked. "What stuff has been going around about me?"

"Well, for starters, everybody thinks you're dead. Either that or... "

A.B. paid close attention while one of the Queens of gossip filled him in on what was being said about him. All of this was need-to-know information. If he wanted to be able to make the right moves, he needed intelligence from someone that had their ear to the streets. He knew that Alize would come in handy. She was already making herself extremely useful and he hadn't even talked her into joining his team yet.

The only time he interrupted her was when he went to get the rest of his weed and wet. He wanted to keep her smoking. Smoking and talking.

CHAPTER FIVE

A.B. sat inside the driver's seat of Layla's dark blue Cavalier and stared out at the full moon through the windshield.

"The moon." He thought. "An assassin's best friend."

Enough time had passed since his road dog's death. Retribution was due. Half a bar off of Tupac's song Hail Mary was repeating over and over in his head.

"I ain't a killer but don't push me…"

He would be the first one to admit that premeditated murder wasn't exactly his thing. Selling dope and making money got his dick hard. But every O.G. he had ever talked to all told him the same thing. You can't pick and choose what route you gone take all the time. For the most part, you have to stay ready to keep from getting ready. There were plenty of rules, codes, and laws that supposedly governed the streets, but anybody in the streets knew that the rule that superseded all others was 'THERE ARE NO RULES'. Anything and everything goes. It didn't matter that he didn't go out looking for drama. Drama found him when his friend found out firsthand if heaven and hell was real. Now he had to embrace the drama, tuck tail and run from the drama, or fall victim to the drama.

A.B. picked the fully loaded, all black, .38 snub nose up off of his lap. For him, the choice had already been made. He was going to embrace the drama.

From his position parked about a block up the street from the Highland Projects he had a line of sight that grazed passed the back window of his first target. All of the doors to the apartments in the projects faced towards the inside so he only had to worry about nosey neighbors.

This was his first time going back to the projects since the night Steel got killed. He was grateful that the side he chose to conduct his stakeout on wasn't the same side where he use to post-up. Thoughts of his friend was helping to fuel his rage so that he could see the mission through, but if he dwelled on it too much his mind would become his greatest adversary.

A.B. checked the hot pink pager that was resting in the passenger seat. He knew it hadn't gone off because he didn't hear the beep, but he checked it anyway.

"Come on Layla," he whispered, watching the window. "Here's your chance to show daddy you down for whatever. Do ya thang girl. Do... yo... motha... fuckin'... thang."

A.B. closed one eye, aimed the revolver with both hands like the cops he saw on T.V., and mentally pictured Steel's killer.

This first hit was no doubt going to be the easiest out of the three. Alize had told him that the three top theories about his whereabouts were dead, held hostage somewhere, or in another town hiding out in fear of his life. Since he knew that the killers knew the first two were false, he was placing all bets on number three. The killers assumed that he had skipped town. He couldn't blame them. Him and Steel had been involved in plex before, but nothing so serious that it was kill or be killed. Steel was the only one of them that had a reputation for being aggressive but even he hadn't killed before. A.B. was the more passive of the two. He would be more likely to squash the beef then to escalate it.

His slow to anger attitude was once his downfall. Now, it was more of an asset. Because of it, no one expected him to attack. That's why the first hit was going to be so easy. Well, as easy as a hit could be. He had the element of surprise. After tonight, that would be taken away. The streets would know that he was still in town and seeking revenge. That would no doubt put the other two dope houses on high alert. Getting to them would take some serious planning. He was up to the challenge though. He had come up with a scheme so live to pull off this first hit, he surprised himself. Who would've thought that the hustler could transform so gracefully into the gangster? A.B. sure didn't.

At first Layla didn't want to go along with the plan. At least she said that she didn't. But A.B. got the impression that she was only refusing because she thought that's what he wanted to hear. After a few kind words, a promise not to hold it against her, and a reference to her as the Queen Pen of Highland Projects, Layla was more eager to play her part then he was. The Bible wasn't bullshitting when it said that the tongue was a bad son of a bitch.

Sticky, a 5'7 130 lbs. tar black brother, sat on the couch inside of his trap massaging his growing member through his G-Unit jeans. He had already taken off his red G-Unit t-shirt and tossed it to the floor. As he stared lustfully at Layla's nude body, he had only one thing on his mind. Getting a piece of that thick ass snow bunny.

It was Layla's idea to go after Sticky first. She didn't have an inside tip that named him as the killer but she had bought work from him before, so she had some inside knowledge on how his operation was run. The main thing that put his head on the chopping block early on was the fact that he hustled alone. She knew that A.B. didn't have any real experience at that black mask shit so she told him to start off small. After he got a taste for blood, and a little hands on training, he'd be more mentally equipped to tackle the bigger fish.

Layla was only charging him a 20-dollar piece of crack for a blowjob and some pussy. Sticky thought that he had won the lottery. A bitch like Layla was worth way more than that. If he had been thinking with the big head, that alone would've raised a red flag. Unfortunately for him, he wasn't. Layla bit her bottom lip seductively and ran her fingers across the top of her trimmed pussy hairs.

Talking like a baby, she said, "You want me to suck your dick baby?"
Sticky nodded his head yes and licked his lips. Layla breathed out sexily as she slid two of her fingers into her hole.

She was wet.

Real wet.

Sticky's dick became rigid and stiff as he watched Layla pull her fingers from her pussy, slide them up her stomach, between her breast, and then placed them inside of her mouth.

She slowly sucked her juices off of them giving him a preview of the treatment he was about to receive.

Then she asked, "Do you want me to suck on your big... black... dick until you shoot your cum all the way down my throat? Huh baby?"

"Hell yeah." Sticky responded. She was driving him wild with how nasty she was talking. Most of the times he tricked with dope fiends they wanted him to hurry up and nut so they could move around. Layla was taking her time. Sticky made a mental note to become one of the white girls' regular customers.

"Good." Layla told him, "cause I just looove how dick and cum taste."

She strolled over to where Sticky was sitting and dropped down to her knees in front of him. More than ready to get his joint done right, he started to unbuckle his pants.

Layla grabbed his hands and looked up at him.

"Let me do that Baby." She told him. "All you gotta do when you with me is sit back, relax, and enjoy the best head of your life."
Sticky liked the sound of that. He just smiled as Layla gently pushed him back into the cushions on the couch.

Layla undid his pants, unzipped them, and pulled them, along with his boxers, down around his ankles. His dick twitched as the blood rushed into it.

"Daaamn baby." She cooed, wrapping her hand around his swollen meat. "I hope I can make all of this fit."

"Just do your best." Sticky said, with his head laid back and eyes closed.

Layla rolled her eyes. She was just being sarcastic, and he thought that she was for real. He had lived with his dick for twenty-something years so she thought that she should know by now that he wasn't working with anything.

She shrugged. Maybe he had only fucked females that didn't have the heart to tell him the truth. 3 ½ inches fully erect is closer to a clitoris then a dick. She wasn't going to get any enjoyment out of this. Well, making him drop out would be nice. Sticky hustled hard then a bitch. She just knew he was sitting on something fat in that apartment.

Layla bent her neck and hung her head just above the tip of his penis. Then she stuck her tongue out and licked around it teasingly. She ran her tongue across the head of his tool until it shined from her saliva.

Sticky moaned when he felt her wrap her lips around his head and start to French kiss it. He could feel her tongue squirming around in her mouth as she sucked and kissed on the tip.

Then she dropped her head and swallowed his entire dick. He could feel her nose pressing up against his pubic hairs. Layla began massaging his nuts as she went up and down along the length of his shaft.

"Hell yeah girl." Sticky moaned, reaching down to run his fingers through his hair. "Suck on that dick like I'm paying' you to do it. Mmmm. Swallow that mothafucka."

Layla bobbed her head faster and faster. She was creating so much spit that it was sliding down his balls and making a small puddle on the couch. She knew that that's what men liked. A lot of spit made the mouth feel like a sloppy wet pussy.

Sticky's meat disappeared and reappeared like magic. He opened his eyes and gazed down at his purchase. Every time she would take him into her mouth, he could see the top of her ass. He couldn't wait to bang that pussy up from the back. The deal was two nuts for a 20-dollar piece. One nut in the mouth and one nut in the pussy. Layla was sucking his dick so good that the first nut was going to come quick.

When she started making noises as she ate that dick, Sticky really got into it. He leaned back, grabbed her hair with both hands and started rocking his body thrusting his dick into her mouth. His balls slapped against Layla's chin as he mouth fucked her harder and harder.

Layla saw her chance. While Sticky was caught up in forcing his little midget dick down her throat, she felt around for his pants and dug around in the pockets.

"Ooohhh shit." He groaned, pounding away at her lips. "You a lil freaky ass bitch ain't you? You like it when a nigga long stroke them tonsils!"

Layla rolled her eyes as she pulled out his cell phone and carefully punched in 7 digits. He wasn't even big enough to make her gag and he was bumping about stoking her tonsils. Niggas with little dicks had some nerve.

Sticky was pumping so hard he had broken a sweat. The springs in the couch were squeaking and everything.

"Here it come." He announced when he felt himself about to blow. "This what you been waitin' on girl."

Layla pressed talk on the keypad and the cell phone dialed the number.

"Here it... here it... here it come." Sticky clenched his jaws, arched his back, and closed his eyes tight. "Uuuggghhh!!!" he groaned as his cum sprayed across Layla's tongue.

Layla placed the phone to her ear and listened.

"Come on." She thought, willing the phone to hurry up and connect the call. Sticky would open his eyes in a second.

As Sticky jerked and felt his final few drops being sucked from his tool, Layla was sending a 3-digit code to a hot pink pager stationed about a block away.

"Damn." Sticky said out of breath." I need a break fo' I can get up in that pussy."

He released Layla's hair and opened his eyes. She was rising to her feet pointing at her mouth and pointing towards the bathroom.

It took Sticky a couple of seconds to catch on to what she was trying to say.

"Oh yeah." He told her, waving a hand. "You can go rinse your mouth out."

Layla did need to rinse out her mouth, but her top priority was unlocking the bathroom window. Sticky rubbed on his stomach and chest as his eyes followed the side to side motion of Layla's nice plump ass. He couldn't wait to penetrate her.

A few seconds later, through the hard to explain magic of technology, the hot pink pager that Layla had left with A.B. began to beep.

BEEP! BEEP! BEEP!

His gaze shifted from the windshield to the passenger seat. Even though he had been anticipating the page since Layla gave him a kiss and climbed out of the vehicle, a horde of butterflies appeared out of nowhere and swarmed the inside of his belly.

A.B. swallowed hard. Holding the weapon in his left hand, he retrieved the pager with his right. Holding it up to his face, he could feel his heart begin to beat faster. A single drop of fear fell into his lake of emotions and rippled out disturbing his calm composure.

"I hope this isn't her." He thought, hesitating with his finger over the button that would confirm if it was time to act.

"Maybe something went wrong? Maybe Layla decided that tonight wasn't the right night?

Maybe the page was from Alize and she was wondering where the two of them had gone? Maybe... maybe..."

A.B. thought about Steel.

"Maybe my home boy watching' me right now?"

The idea made him frown up in disgust at himself. They had always sworn that they would ride for each other no matter what consequences the trip might bring. Be it harm, be it imprisonment, or be it death. And here he was wishing he wouldn't have to follow through with his oath.

A.B. apologized to the all-seeing spirit of his fallen comrade for his moment of sickening weakness and applied pressure to the button. The 3-digit code that Layla had dialed into Sticky's phone stared up at him from the display screen.

"321"

The code was simple. It was meant to represent a countdown. Three... two... one... time to get down to business.

Tossing the pager to the side, A.B. inhaled deeply. "This fa' you Steel." He said to the ominous glow of the full moon. "If this one of them cats that caught you slippin, I'm finna send him to the other side with you so you can pay that hoe back."

He stuffed the gun into the waistband of his black jeans and stepped out into the cool October night.

"If this ain't one of them niggas," he continued, pulling the hood of his ash gray Sean John sweater over his head, "just be patient."

A.B. scanned the scenery.

Nothing.

Nobody.

It was beautifully desolate, deserted, and

quiet. To his knowledge, there were no potential witnesses. But even if there was, all they could say that they saw was a figure wearing a gray sweater and black jeans walking around in the area.

A.B. started down the street in the direction of the projects. Tonight, he was a ghost. A shadowy vision. An angel of revenge, judgment, and death. With each step he felt a surge of adrenaline rush through his veins and cause his heart to pulsate with the power of the pistol he was carrying. He had no idea that the sensation of planning another human's death could be so invigorating. With another man's life dangling so precariously over the abyss of extinction, he was somehow being supercharged with feelings of being more alive and alert than ever before. Layla was on to something when she said that once they had taken care of Sticky the rest would come easy. He hadn't even killed Sticky yet and he was already getting hooked on the high of predator vs. prey.

By the time A.B. had reached the window that led into Sticky's bathroom he was ready. He didn't even hesitate. He just eased the windowpane up as quietly as he could, grabbed the windowsill, and hoisted his body up and over the ledge.

Once inside, he found a crude message from Layla and smirked.

Using what he could only assume was her pussy juice; Layla had drawn a barely visible smiley face on the bathroom mirror. She had told him that she was going to write the words 'Hey Boo" but he assumed she decided not to because it would have taken too long.

The sounds of Sticky grudge fucking his bitch made their way to A.B.'s ears inside the bathroom. He wasn't sure why but hearing Layla squeal with another man inside of her was rubbing him the wrong way. She said that she was going to have to pretend she was liking it but A.B. didn't know if she was pretending or not. All he knew was that Sticky was digging her out for real. There was nothing pretend on his part.

A.B. crossed the bathroom and stood next to the cracked door. He could tell from the noise that Layla had him in the living room to the left. A.B. felt confident that he would catch Sticky off guard. He was so busy getting laid that even if he had a pistol, he wouldn't be able to make it to it in time.

A.B. gripped the handle of the .38 and retrieved it from his waistband. Then he slowly pulled the bathroom door open.

"Alright baby." He whispered to himself, leaning up against the wall. "Bring it to this fool."

He sucked in air through his nose, blew it out of his mouth, and adjusted his hold on the gun.

"Let's get it."

With that, A.B. swung around into the hallway and extended the weapon out in front of him. It was a straight shot to the living room. He could see the back of Sticky's butt naked body bouncing up and down on the couch. Layla's snow-white legs were spread eagle and sticking straight up in the air.

A.B. stopped.

"Who this pussy belongs to? Who this mothafuckin' pussy belong too?" Sticky was demanding to hear that Layla's sweet love box belonged to him.

"It's yours baby! It's yours baby!" Layla howled.

Sticky was stroking with so much force that A.B. thought he was trying to reach her throat from her vagina.

"Whose?" Sticky asked again, loving every second of this cheap fuck.

"Yours baby." Layla reiterated.

This time when she said it A.B. thought back to the first time he had sex with Layla. She had told him that her pussy belonged to him. Now she was saying it was Sticky's. The thought infuriated him.

The entire plan that they had mapped out got chunked out the window. At that moment, it wasn't about Steel, revenge, or becoming a set for life King Pen. A.B. wanted Sticky dead for one reason and one reason only.

The hoe ass nigga was using A.B.'s pussy like it was his own personal trampoline!

Keeping the gun aimed at Sticky's back with his left hand, A.B. dug around in his pants pocket with his right looking for his pocketknife. Once he found it, he extended the 3-inch blade and strode with purpose in the direction of his target.

Sticky was in mid-stroke when A.B. came from behind him and drove the sharp metal deep into the right side of his neck.

Blood squirted from the wound as the blade pierced his jugular vein.

"Uuuugghh... hh...h..." was the only sound Sticky could gurgle out as the life swiftly drained from his flesh.

Layla stared gleefully as A.B. left the knife lodged in his prey's neck and shoved his dying body from on top of her.

"That's my pussy." A.B. declared.

Layla watched Sticky twitch and grasp uselessly at the murder weapon. The scene caused a flood to engulf her lower region.

"Oh daddy." She said with lust in her voice, turning her attention to A.B. "You so... you so... you so gangsta!"

Layla rose to her knees and pulled A.B.'s face to hers from over the back of the couch. The last image Sticky saw in this life was Layla's white ass. He had no idea what had just happened or why.

Layla shoved her tongue down A.B.'s throat. The two of them kissed passionately until Layla pulled away.

"Fuck me daddy." She begged, unzipping his pants aggressively. "Fuck me now! Right here. I want you to dick me down in front of that stupid motherfucker and show him who this pussy really belongs too."

Sticky was already dead. Both of them knew this. But he had died with his eyes opened and facing them.

A.B. dropped his pants, drug Layla over the couch, and bent her over doggy-style. As he plunged in and out of what he felt like was rightfully his, the two of them moaned loud enough to wake the dead.

Apparently Sticky was super dead because regardless how intense the session got, he never moved.

The sex inside the apartment of a dead man was strangely exhilarating. There was so much raw energy that A.B. could only contain himself for about three minutes. His rational brain told him that there was something very wrong with what he was doing, but his irrational brain had overridden his sense of decency and reason.

There he was, probing the inner walls of one of his customers, inside the living room of a deceased man, who was just minutes ago tricking with the exact same bitch.

Splatters of Sticky's blood stained his right hand and Layla's breasts. Why this had him turned on, he had no idea. Layla just had some strange effect on him.

A.B. contemplated on what he had just done after he coated Layla's insides with his eruption. He looked around the room in a daze. As Layla was rushing to put her clothes back on, she noticed the spaced out look on A.B.'s face.

"Baby." she called out, getting his attention. "Now's not the time to zone out on me baby. We gotta hurry up and find his stash and get the fuck out of here."

Her words brought him somewhat back to the present.

"I'm good." He lied, wiping his hand off on the couch.

It didn't come clean. It only smeared.

"You good?" Layla asked, pulling her halter top over her head.

"Yeah. I'm good."

A.B. headed to the back to search for the money and drugs. He initially wanted to just avenge his friend, but Layla told him that if he planned on murking the dope men he might as well rob them too. Why let the detectives collect it when he could benefit from it himself? The plan was to make Sticky drop out before killing him, but A.B had lost it. Once again, the Bible was right. In so many words it said that the pussy was just as bad as the tongue. It's kind of ironic how the slang term for a woman's clitoris is pearl tongue and the slang term for the labia is lips. A.B. guessed someone else had made the same connection a long time ago. A man could make a woman do some strange thangs if his mouthpiece was live enough, but a woman could make a man lose his damn mind if her sex was on point.

Once Layla was certain that A.B. was occupied in the bedroom, she scooped up her Baby Phat purse and pulled a pair of latex gloves out of it. The entire time she had been inside the apartment she was making a mental note of everything that she touched. She wasn't sure if the surfaces her hands came in contact with could be fingerprinted or not, but she didn't want to take any chances. Layla like to watch C.S.I. If the Dickinson Police Department had at least half of the gadgets and gizmos that the Miami Police Department had, her clean-up job had better be thorough.

Layla slid the gloves over her hands and went to work. First order of business was the murder weapon. You never... ever leave the murder weapon at the scene of the crime.

Speed walking to the kitchen that sat next to the living room, Layla rummaged through the cabinets that hung over the stove.
Sandwich bags. Every drug dealer had them. It didn't matter if they sold heroine, weed, cocaine, pills, or crack.

Withdrawing four of the bags from the yellow cardboard box, she made her way back over to Sticky. Kneeling down, she carefully grabbed the handle of the pocketknife with two fingers. She didn't want to get blood all over her gloves.

"Mhp." She grunted, not being able to extract the blade with only two fingers. A.B. had lodged it in his neck pretty good.

Layla glanced around the room. She needed something to wrap around it so that she could grip it tight and yank it out without getting blood on her glove. The last thing she wanted to do was spread Sticky's blood around the room. The idea was to give the homicide detectives as little to go on as possible.

Layla saw what she could use when her eyes passed over Sticky's shirt. She picked it up and used it like a glove to her glove.

"Mmmph." She grunted again as she tugged. This time the pocketknife came sliding out of Sticky's neck with a slicing sound. The noise made Layla shiver. She remained focus though.

Closing the knife with the t-shirt, Layla doubled bagged two of the sandwich bags and placed the knife inside. She then placed the murder weapon inside of her purse.

"Alright." She said, pulling a small hair comb out her purse. "Phase two."

She had made sure she trimmed her pubic hairs down low before leaving the house, but there was only one way to be sure that she didn't leave any pubic hairs or head hair tangled up in Sticky's body hair. Layla hunched down over his dick and slowly ran the comb through the hairs on his penis, testicles, legs, and ass.

A.B. was just about ready to give up. He had tossed around everything in the small bedroom. Sticky was just so damn filthy. He had clothes and shoes everywhere. The search wouldn't have been so bad if he didn't have to dig through pile after pile of miscellaneous bullshit.

For the life of him he couldn't understand how some of the cats he knew from the hood chose to make a criminal career out of home invasions. If the owners were at home to point you in the right direction it made sense but going blind like he was doing didn't. All Sticky had in the room was a bed, a dresser, and a radio. Scattered around the floor there were loose clothing and black trash bags full of clothes.

The closet go figure was completely empty. Sticky had to be the most eccentric dude on the block.

There were at least six trash bags that A.B. was tearing open and searching through one by one. He had chosen to tackle them last. With four down and two to go, A.B. was beginning to think that either the money and drugs were stashed in another part of the house or all of the drugs were sold, and the money was spent on clothes and shoes.

A.B. gripped the second to last trash bag and tore it open. As expected, it contained more clothes. A.B. picked the bag up off the floor and dumped the contents out. Becoming irritated and frustrated, A.B. kicked around the newest pile of Roca Wear, Akademiks, Sean John, 8732 and a whole host of other Urban clothing.

He scanned the mess.

Nothing.

"Fuck!" he growled. "What the hell does this dude need with all of this shit?"

Reaching out to check the last bag, his instincts told him that it would be another waste of time, but he had to do it anyway. He could leave no stone unturned.

Layla was in the living room finishing up her cleaning process. She had decided to leave Sticky shirtless, but she did put his boxers and pants back on. That way it wouldn't be obvious that he died while having sex. For all she knew she had left just enough of her fluids behind for DNA to place her at the scene of the crime. She hoped not but it was 2008. Medical science was so advanced that you couldn't put anything pass them.

Layla jerked her head in the direction of the bedroom when she heard A.B. begin to curse. She couldn't help but to giggle.

"He must've realized that there was nothing back there." She thought to herself. "Nothing but a shit load of clothes."

Observing the area, Layla stood to her feet. Everything seemed to be in order. The murder weapon was put up, her fingerprints were wiped away, and she had gathered as much of her D.N.A. as she could.

It was time for the two of them to get out of there.

Layla stepped over Sticky's body and tossed the cushions off of the couch.

"Baby! Baby!" she called. "I think I found something."

Layla bent down over the three cushions and unzipped one of them. A.B. came rushing into the living room just as she was pulling pout a handful of cotton and cash from inside of it. His eyes got huge. Once again Layla had come through. He never would've thought to check inside the cushions on the couch.

Layla looked up at him and used her innocent voice.

"I just wanted to do my part and help you search, and… look what I found baby. It was in the couch the entire time."

A.B. was so happy to see some actual loot that he didn't even pay attention to the altered scene. He had forgotten about the knife he left lodged in Sticky's throat immediately after he had done it. A.B. was a novice at committing a serious crime and at cleaning one up too.

"Let's get it and go." A.B. said, kneeling down beside her to pick up the cushions. They had already been inside the apartment for an extremely long time. The initial plan was to be in and out.

"Wait a minute." Layla told him. "We can't just climb out the window with these couch cushions and run a block down the street to the car. That would be crazy. Somebody's bound to think something strange is going on and call the cops."

A.B. wasn't thinking about it like that. A black dude and a white girl running down the street in the middle of the night would definitely raise some suspicions.

"So how are we going to get up out this bitch with the money and shit?" A.B. asked.

You gotta go get the car by yourself." she told him. "Pull it up to just outside the bathroom window, I'll come out with the money, hop in, and then we'll be home free."

A.B. liked the sound of that. Home free. He was more than ready to get back to Valley Park. The high was gone and the realization that he was now a murderer had begun to set in. He had just officially taken his life in a direction that was like a strong ocean current. All of his future actions must now be made with consideration to what he had just done. There was no going back.

As A.B. exited the apartment the same way that he had entered it, all he kept telling himself was that this was just the beginning. He still had two more hits to pull off, and neither one of them would be as simple as Sticky. A.B. made it to the car without being seen. At least he hoped he did. He was walking so fast that he really didn't keep his head on the swivel like he should've. Fuck it. He was still just a ghost.

He climbed in the Cavalier. The interior was cold. It matched his heart. A.B. shook his head. The image of Sticky wouldn't leave his mind. Those glossed over eyes. That slightly opened mouth. Those G-Unit pants.

Wait a second. G-Unit pants? Sticky was naked when I killed him.

"I'm trippin' for real." A.B. told himself. "I need some sleep."

He crunk up the car and pulled off.

"Naw. Fuck that. I need some weed."

A.B. made it to the back of Sticky's apartment and waited. It wasn't long before Layla tossed two trash bags out the window and then climbed out herself.

He felt a little better. Even though it seemed like he was slowly losing himself, at least he had somebody that was willing to ride it out with him. It was like he lost Steel but gained Layla. She was helping to fill that void and he appreciated her for it.

Layla tossed the trash bags into the backseat and climbed in next to A.B.

"I told you I had yo back baby." She reminded him smiling.

"Yeah." A.B. responded, applying pressure to the gas pedal. "You like the Bonnie to my Clyde."

"No, I'm not." Layla corrected him. "I'm the Queen Pen to yo King Pen."

A.B. cut his eyes at her and put distance between them and their victim. He had him one down ass bitch. "You right." He agreed. "You the Queen Pen and I'm the King Pen."

CHAPER SIX

Two days after killing Sticky, A.B. was cruising around the West end of Dickinson, Tx in a plain white 2004 Buick LeSabre with Alize Scott tucked away in the passenger seat. The windows were tinted dark, so he didn't have to worry about being seen. No one knew the car he was in neither. Layla had insisted on trading in her Cavalier for something new the day before. She said that they had spent too much time inside of Sticky's apartment and someone might've noticed it parked up the block.

A.B. had to give Layla her card. She was one sharp female. Layla was thinking so fast in tight situations that it seemed like she had done this type of stuff before. A.B. wasn't trippin though. Every move she made was a good move. He had no complaints.

"I still can't believe how much money ya'll got." Alize said, sipping on some Gold Passion Alize straight out of the bottle.

A.B. came to a complete stop at the stop sign, looked up and down the road, then continued driving forward.

"Sixteen thousand five hundred twenty-five dollars." Alize quoted for the umpteenth time.

She had been mesmerized by the amount ever since her mother and A.B. came home and dumped the cash all over her sleeping body. Normally she wouldn't have been home like that on a Friday night but LaQuisha had never called to make plans. Alize had found out on Saturday that her boyfriend had swung by and scooped her up. She couldn't knock her home girl for wanting to spend time with her man. That nigga was on the go so much that LaQuisha barely ever got to see him. None of the other Valley Park Girls had seen him at all. All they knew was his name. Tank.

Alize often accused LaQuisha of intentionally trying to keep him out the low but LaQuisha swore up and down that that wasn't the case. She said that she wanted nothing more than to flaunt her latest catch, but he always dipped in and out unexpected and refused to be introduced to anyone. In the two months that they had been fucking around she could tell that Tank was in the game somehow, but he never gave her too much information about his business. He said that the less she knew the better. He didn't want to have her in any way connected to his personal affairs.

LaQuisha and all of her home girls respected him for that. Most of the dudes they met acted like they were only coming around for some pussy and a scapegoat. They not only wanted to bring the drugs around them, but they also wanted the girls to hold the drugs. And out of all the places in the world they wanted them to put the work inside of their vaginas. As if the Valley Park Girls were walking and talking stash spots. All of them swore that they would never degrade themselves like that but at one point each of them (other than Ming) had transported drugs via their gap goodies. It's just some things they didn't want to share with the group. The funny part was that if one of them went ahead and admitted to it, they would all find out that they had all come across a dude they wanted to impress so bad that they were willing to do almost anything.

"I told you I got a 5-year master plan." A.B. said, making a left on Ester St. "You thought I was just talkin or what?"

Alize took another swig of her Alize.

"Naw. I ain't think you was just talkin." She answered. "I had just figured your master plan had something to do with hustling. I ain't know you was a jacka."

A.B. cut his eyes at Alize. They hadn't told her were they had gotten the money and the 8 ½ zones from. For all she knew he could have had that loot in a safe somewhere.

"Who said I was a jacka?" he asked, trying to feel her out. Maybe Layla told her what happened.

Even though it was Layla's idea not to say anything to anybody, she probably felt obligated to tell her daughter. After all, during their talk the night of the murder, both of them had agreed that it was necessary to get Alize in on the ultimate goal. She needed to know what was going on so she would know what to talk about and what to keep quiet.

Officially making Alize a part of the team was the main reason for their little Sunday drive. Layla had been called in to work and she told A.B. to use the time alone with Alize to help her see the vision. A.B. wasn't showing her the 'King Pen/ Queen Pen' vision though, he was trying to show her the 'Make it out the hood' vision.

"Nobody had to 'SAY' you were a jacka." Alize told him. "Regardless of what you might believe, I'm far from lame."

She swung her head to get her hair out of her face.

"All I had to do was put two and two together."

Alize placed her Alize bottle between her

thighs and used her hands to illustrate her point. The liquor was cold, but her body was warm.

Using her right index finger to count off on her left hand, she said, "For one, all you had was about three hundred dollars when you left Friday night. For two, I know for a fact that my mama doesn't have access to that kind of cash. Three, the two of you were so excited about the money that common sense told me ya'll were surprised to have it. And last but not least, that fool from the projects been all over the news."

A.B. thought about her reasoning. He guessed it made sense. When she laid it out all plain it did seem kind of obvious. They leave and come back with $16,000 cash and some dude turns up dead. He was somewhat impressed with her ability to see the big picture. The only thing that really concerned him was whether or not she could be trusted to keep her mouth shut about the whole thing. Alize was not known for her ability to keep secrets.

She had held down the information about his whereabouts pretty good. He had to give her credit for that. A.B. knew that she hadn't told anyone because no one had come looking for him. If she would've spread the word amongst her clique, those other chicks would've screamed the news from the tallest building in Dickinson. With that, she had earned a little trust. Besides, if she was to tell anybody about it, she would be fucking over her own mother in the process. A.B. had committed the actual murder, but by law, Layla was just a responsible as he was.

A.B. pulled over in front of an all-white one-story wood home on Ester street. The house wasn't that old, but it looked run down from years of neglect. There were patches of dead grass scattered across the yard, the screen door was barely hanging on by its last hinge, and what use to be flower bed at one point was nothing more than a rectangle of mud sectioned off by filthy stones and trash. Broken and discarded toys also littered the yard.

"The only thing I don't understand." Alize added as A.B. killed the ignition, "is why you had to kill him."

She faced him with genuine confusion etched across her face.

"I mean, did he try to fight back or something? Did he say he wasn't going to drop out?"

·The expression on Alize's face caused a strange feeling to start simmering in his stomach. She was obviously shaken by the idea that her mother and him could take a man's life. Truthfully, he wasn't all the way o.k. with what had happened neither. He had never killed before. The only thing that he could tell himself was that it was justified because of Steel. Only problem with that was this little voice that kept whispering in his head saying, "What if Sticky didn't have anything to do with Steel's death?" That would make it a senseless killing.

A.B. ran his palm across his mouth and chin searching for the right words to explain why what he did had to be done. After he thought, the only thing he could come up with was something that the old schools use to tell him.

"I'm just gone give it to you like it was given to me." He said, speaking slowly and seriously.

"The only exit strategy us ghetto kids have at overcoming the misery and hard times is something like a paradox. On the surface o it doesn't seem to make sense but it's one of the best methods that tried and true. In order for us to make it out the streets, we must first embrace the streets. We have to give ourselves over to the very thing that we hate and loath and mash the gas with no remorse, regret, or thought to the competition's feelings. Becoming a predator in the jungle is the only way you survive long enough and get enough respect to actually see some real cash. Then once you get the cash, you invest it, wash it, move out the hood, go legit, and most importantly you never look back."

He looked at her to see if any of what he was saying was sinking in. She was staring off into space.

"Have you ever wondered why God designed time to only move in one direction?" he asked.

The mention of God brought her back from the endless expanse of her mind.

"God?!" She repeatedly softly. "You believe in God?"

A.B. thought about his mother.

"God, Allah, Lord Krishna, Jehovah, the big bang… whoever or whatever is responsible for all of this."

He waved his hand in front of himself as if to indicate all of creation.

"Names aren't really important." He continued, dodging the question about his belief in God. "I'm just speaking on the laws that govern the universe. Have you ever wondered why time only moves in one direction? Forward?"

Alize considered what he was saying. She noticed how he didn't answer whether or not he believed in God and she decided not to push it. To a lot of people, religion was a sensitive issue. Even to her. She wasn't even sure if God existed herself and she guessed that A.B. was undecided like she was. Just being real with herself, she had never given much thought to the reason behind the direction in which time moved. It was one of those things that so effectively took care of itself that it never really crossed her mind.

Alize shrugged. "No. Not really." She answered.

"To me, "A.B. began, "it's because the present and the future are the only two aspects of time that really matter. Life is about goals, dreams and ambitions for the future. Once you get a clear understanding of what you want out of life, you do whatever you gotta do to make that dream a reality. In the end, what you've done or where you've been, isn't as important as whether or not you reached your goal."

A.B. opened the door to the LeSabre and placed one foot on the asphalt road.

"I'm no judge," he continued, pausing before exiting the vehicle, "so I can't say if doin' Sticky was right or wrong. All I know is it was necessary if we ever plan on making it out the hood. And to me…"

A.B. stepped out into the afternoon air.

"… That's all that really matters."

Alize allowed his explanation to marinate on her mind. It was the classic philosophy that the ends justify the means. She wasn't sure that she fully agreed with that, but she did want to reach a point in her life where all of her worries would magically disappear.

A.B. shut the door and Alize climbed out on

the other side. The sun was high in the sky and the weather was warm. The two of them could've very well been dressed for a hot summer day.

Alize was looking fly, as usual, in her black with purple stitching Capri pants and black t-shirt tied in the front showing off her toned, flat stomach. She knew that she would be extra sexy and cute with her belly button pierced but Layla was making her wait two years until she turned 15. Alize chalked it up to jealousy. Her mother never really gave a damn about anything she did except when it came down to enhancing her appearance. She had to give her mother credit though. Layla was still a bad bitch, but she was getting older. Her age was the enemy of her good looks. Alize was getting older too, but her age was only filling her out more. It seemed like her mother viewed her as competition sometimes.

Alize and A.B. strolled across the front yard and headed towards the front door.

A.B. was decked out in a light blue Sean John shirt and shorts set. On his head he wore a matching light blue du-rag that matted down the loose strains of hair around his braids.

"Who lives here?" Alize asked as they reached the front door.

A.B. knocked.

"One of Layla's friends." He answered. "I'm finna show you how this hustle game go."

Layla had already started the process of turning A.B. on to all of her friends that smoked. She had given him a cell phone with a number that everybody had already knew to call. He never talked specifics over the phone, he only needed an address. Since Layla knew all of the callers personally, A.B. didn't have to worry about selling to an undercover.

It had been a total of 5 days since he had last sold some work and he was fending to get back on his hustle. A part of him wanted to go and post up in either the Village or the Projects like he use to but he knew that that wasn't even an option. He already had people looking for him, and now that he had murked Sticky, they would know that he was looking for them too. That alone made every move crucial. He was now deeply involved in some life or death beef. All he was trying to do now was stay under the radar long enough to get revenge for Steel and make enough money to leave Dickinson and the streets alone.

A cool and very welcomed breeze blew in from the east and momentarily eased the effects of the afternoon sun.

Alize's hair shifted gently as she thought about how crazy the weather had been lately. One day it would be so cold that you could see your breath as if you were smoking, and on the very next day it would be so hot that a lot of the men wouldn't even wear shirts outside.

"I wonder if the hot, cold, hot, cold weather has anything to do with that Global Warming everybody keeps talking about?" she thought to herself.

Her thoughts were soon interrupted by the sound of the door being unlocked. She had never ridden around selling dope before, so Alize was a little anxious. Layla had smoked in front of her countless times before but ever since she turned about 10 years old she did her best to avoid and ignore that part of her mother's life. It was hard having a mother on drugs and Alize found that she could cope best by pretending everything was normal. If A.B. was right though, the only way for her to get out of her hard knock life was to jump headfirst into it for a set period of time. She wasn't exactly sure why his theory made sense. After all, money makes the world go around and the streets are easy access to money.

A.B. glanced up and down the block as they waited for the owner of the house to open the door. He noticed that almost all of the houses on Ester St. were in bad shape like the one he had pulled over in front of. His instincts told him that Felicia (the woman whose house he was at) wasn't the only smoker on the block. He made a mental note to use her as a plug to her neighbors.

After listening to a series of about 3 or 4 locks being undone, the person inside opened the door up wide. Alize almost laughed out loud at the appearance of the woman. Felicia was standing there in a wrinkled, brown and black sundress with one strap broken and tied together over her left shoulder. Her hair was cut into a bald fade hairstyle like only men and dikes wore. Felicia was also lacking shoes, make-up, lotion, and a good portion of her teeth. Alize could tell because the 30 something brown skinned black woman greeted them with a huge smile. The black, white, black combination of her grill made her mouth look like a piano.

"Heeey A.B.! Heeey Alize!" the woman said in a singsong voice as if the three of them were the best of friends.

"Ya'll come on in."

Alize looked at A.B. as Felicia politely stepped to the side and waved them inside.

A.B. simply nodded to let her know it was o.k.

As they stepped into the poorly lit living room, A.B. noticed two more people sitting down on the sofa. A man and a woman.

The man looked like he had just gotten off from work in his dingy pair of blue jeans and paint stained t-shirt. The woman looked like she had just turned a hundred tricks. She was wearing a pair of pi8nk shorts and a matching pink halter top. Her knees were scabbed up bad like she had been sucking dick in the middle of the street. The make-up she was wearing was caked on so thick that she looked like a black, Barbie doll, drug addict.

A.B. spoke to everybody as he went and stood in the middle of the living room. The lady was staring at him in a weird way, but he guessed she was just geeking and ready for a fix.

"So, what's up?" A.B. asked, turning to face Felicia. "What you trying to do?"

Felicia scratched her head hard.

"Ahhh." She signed with relief.

Alize wondered if the woman had fleas.

"My boy right there," Felicia said, pointing to the man on the couch with one hand and wiping the other off on her sundress, "is the one lookin' for some work. He got all the money."

A.B. turned his attention to the man. He noticed that Alize was staying close by his side that was common to him. A room full of smokers wasn't anything. He had grown up in an environment like that.

"What it do pops?" A.B. said.

Pops just stared at him for a few seconds.

"I don't know you." He declared finally. "You sho' you got some good work?"

"What?!?" A.B. shot at him looking around. "Am I sho' I got some good work? Come on pops.

Be real. You think Layla would send me over here if I had some bullshit dope?"

Felicia nodded her head. "Yeah Carl." She said. "This who Layla be fuckin' wit. She said she done tried his shit out and he got some of the ooowweee."

Carl frowned up at Felicia as if he didn't like her getting involved in his business.

"I'm just saying'." Felicia added, noticing his look. Obviously, Carl was about to fire the two sisters' up so Felicia didn't want to offend him. If she made him mad it would show in the amount of dope he gave her.

"I don't need you saying' nothing." Carl spat out. Can't nobody tell me what to spend my money on. Not you, not Layla, and not even Yolanda here."

He nodded his head in the direction of the woman sitting next to him. Carl wanted to put her in her place too before she could even consider bucking him.

A.B. had run across a million smokers like Carl. He was going to buy the dope. There was no question about that. It was just obvious to A.B. that he was about to spend a nice amount of change. Whenever dope fiends were about to spend big, they got big headed. They felt like the money allowed them a little leeway to call some shots.

"Aiight pops." A.B. said smiling. "You right. I feel where you comin' from."

A.B. dug around in his pocket for his sandwich bag full of work. Finding it, he pulled out a baggy with an ounce of hard white crack in it. All six eyes of the smokers zoomed in.

"If it was my money," A.B. continued, untying the baggy, "I would be cautious of how I spent it too. So, this what I'm gone do for you. I'm gone give you a sample... on the house."

A.B. shrugged.

"If you like it, we'll do business. If you don't, I'll ride out and you won't owe me shit."

Carl licked his lips and folded his arms triumphantly. He was in charge. A.B. broke off a nice sized dime piece and dropped it in Carl's hand. As he rushed to get his pipe, A.B said, "That's how A.B. do business my nigga. I don't try to fuck over nobody."

Yolanda snapped her fingers and leaned back smiling.

"That's where I know you from!" she exclaimed excitedly pointing at A.B.

"You Samantha's boy, ain't you?"

A.B. looked at the woman startled. It didn't surprise him that a smoker knew his mother or him, a lot of them did. He just wasn't sure if he wanted this particular smoker to recognize him. The streets were no doubt talking about how he had left Sticky leaking and he wasn't ready to resurface yet. He didn't need anyone knowing how to find him. Especially not someone who would quickly divulge the information for some crumbs... literally.

"I thought you looked familiar." Yolanda continued. "Boy, I remember when you weren't but this big."

She used her hand to measure about one foot off the floor.

"Dang you done grew up. You don't even remember me, do you?"

A.B. studied the woman's features. She did look vaguely familiar, but he wasn't sure if he knew her personally or if she was just some face from the streets. The expression on his face told her that he couldn't really place her.

Yolanda crossed her fingers and held them up.

"Me and yo mama use to be like this." She said. "Hell, we still kick it. I was over there at ya'll apartment in the Village yesterday. Samantha was telling me she ain't seen you in damn near a week."

A.B. rubbed his head.

"You say yo name Yolanda?" he asked, trying to remember if his mother had a friend named Yolanda.

Yolanda rolled her eyes and playfully slapped Carl on his arm. Carl frowned up and mugged her, but he remained silent. The quality of A.B.'s dope had his jaws locked. He was too high to talk shit.

Smacking her teeth, Yolanda said, "Carl old tired ass the only person that call me Yolanda. Everybody else just call me by my middle name, Yasmine."

A wave of recognition washed over A.B. when the woman identified herself as Yasmine. All at once the memories of her came rushing back.

"Aunt Yasmine!" A.B. said, slapping his forehead for not recognizing her sooner.

Yasmine wasn't his real Aunt but that's what his mother use to make him call her. When he was little, Yasmine would babysit him for days at a time when his mother would "forget" him at her house. She always smoked but she used to maintain on the drug better than she was obviously doing now. That's why he didn't know who she was. Yasmine never use to look that busted.

"I ain't seen you in a minute." A.B. told her. "What you been up to?"

Yasmine shrugged.

"Same ol' same ol'." She replied.

While the two of them played catch up, Alize listened to the conversation in awe. She couldn't believe that A.B. didn't recognize his own Aunt. Once they established who they were though, the two of them talked like they were the best of friends. She could tell that they cutted for each other.

"It's a small world." She thought.

Felicia had listened to the first half of their conversation, but her mind was really someplace else. She had abandoned their dialogue and was talking Carl out of a piece of the free rock that A.B. had given him.

"Why ain't you been over there to check on your mama and baby sister?" she asked accusingly. "You know Samantha worried sick about you."

A.B. looked away. The mention of his mother and Sandra quickly changed the mood. It forced him to remember Steel, Sticky, and his current predicament.

"I just been handlin' a lil business." He told her, not wanting to go into details. "I'm probably gone swang through there in a few days and check up on 'em. They'll be aiight until then."

Yasmine cut her eyes and tilted her head.

"I... don't know A.B." she said. "You might wanna go over there a little sooner than that. Shit done got crazy in the few days since you been gone."

A.B.'s heart rate threatened to speed up.

"What do you mean 'shit done got crazy'?" he asked, thinking about his little sister. "What happened?"

Yasmine raised her hands in the air.

"Now..." she said, not liking to be the

bearer of bad news. "It really ain't none of my business, and Samantha said she had it all under control, but I don't know."

A.B. took a step closer to her. He wasn't in the mood for any beating around the bush.

"Just tell me what's going down." He urged. "What does my mother think she has under control?"

Yasmine took a low deep breath. Everyone in the room was glued to the conversation now. Drama had a way of captivating any audience.

"You know Samantha." Yasmine began. "One way or another she's gone find a way to get high. Sometimes she'll even go to extreme lengths to feed her habit."

A.B. thought about the $50 and the gram of dope he had given her. That had probably run out that night. He silently cursed himself for the oversight. He had neglected his family and now there was no telling what Samantha had done in his absence. A.B. braced himself for the rest of Yasmine's revelation.

"When you took a long time coming back home," she continued, "Samantha started getting credit from Menace."

"WHAT?!?" A.B. cut her off yelling. "MENACE?! She been fucking with Menace? That nigga can't be trusted! He too fuckin' grimy!"

Alize looked on as A.B. started pacing the room with a mixture of anger, frustration, and fear plastered across his face. She had no idea who Menace was, but it was clear that whoever he was, A.B. DID NOT like the fact that his mother was doing business with him.

A.B. walked back and forth across the carpeted floor and tried to calm himself. Everybody in the room could sense his discomfort and chose to remain quiet.

Thinking to himself, A.B. thought, "I haven't been gone that long. What's it been? Four days? No... more than that. Today makes five days. She couldn't possibly be too deep in the hole. Then again... Menace always taxes people. Especially when they want credit."

A.B. did a few quick calculations in his head. Samantha could smoke whatever she got her hands on, but how deep would Menace let her get? That was the real question. He had to find out what she owed so that he could pay off her bill before Menace got tired of waiting. There was no telling what a dude as crazy as Menace would do when he got fed up with waiting.

Turning back to Yasmine, he asked, "Did Samantha happen to mention how much she owed him?"

Yasmine looked off for a moment and then locked eyes with A.B. once again.

"That's just it." She said slowly, as if it hurt her to continue to speak. "She doesn't owe him anything anymore."

A.B. was confused. There was no way Menace would just forgive a debt. Kind-hearted shit like that just wasn't in his nature.

Trying to make some sense of it all, A.B. asked, "How did she get the money to pay him off? Is she back working the streets?"

A.B. knew that his mother had no problem turning a few tricks to make ends meet. That's one of the reasons he so readily gave her dope. He didn't like the fact that she smoked but he absolutely abhorred the idea of her body to get high. If he had to supply her with crack to keep her legs and mouth closed, so be it.

"Well," Yasmine began, choosing her words carefully to answer his question. "It would probably be the best if you went and spoke with her yourself, but I will say this. Menace done set up shop in yo mama apartment and now he got all kinds of shit going on up in there."

She shook her head.

"Like I said... It done got crazy since you been gone."

A.B. couldn't believe his ears. Samantha had allowed Menace to turn their apartment into a crack house. What the fuck was she thinking? She probably just got so far in the hole that Menace just forced himself on her. He did shit like that.

A.B. quickly served Carl $300 worth of dope that he wanted and hopped back in the LeSabre. He didn't have his gun on him, and Alize was with him in the car, but he had to go confront the situation over in the Village. If not for Samantha, then for Sandra. His baby sister was probably scared to death. He knew that he was when he was her age and their mother had done the exact same thing.

As he sped across town, he had absolutely no problem visualizing the scene over at his house. Turning her home into the makeshift crack house for various drug dealers had become Samantha's M.O. over the years. To her it made perfect sense. The bills would get paid, the rent was always taken care of, and she had practically unlimited access to her drug of choice. In a way, the arrangement she had with her own son was reminiscent of that particular set-up. The only difference was that A.B. chose not to sell any drugs directly out of the house and he actually cared about the welfare and well-being of his family. The others only cared about one thing. Money!

A.B. gripped the steering wheel tightly with both hands as he rushed across town in the direction of the Village. He had no idea what he would do when got there but he knew he needed to get there.

Alize buckled up her seatbelt out of fear. Houses on the streets were going by in a blur and A.B. didn't seem like he was going to slow down any time soon. The news about his mother had him all shook up.

"Ummm A.B." she said, trying to calm him down. "Don't you think you should slow the car down just a little bit?"

A.B. flew passed a stop sign without so much as taking his foot off the gas. He couldn't hear Alize pleading with him to slow down and he damn sure couldn't hear the many honks of the irate drivers who were defiantly not feeling his complete disregard for the rules of the road. All he could hear were the various ghosts from his past, and all he could see were the graphic, disturbing, and all around fucked up images of scenes that played as the back drop for the horrifying situations and circumstances that made up his childhood.

In his mind eye he could see his yesterday. Not yesterday as in the day before today, but yesterday as in all of the years that made up his painful past. He could see the yesterday that pushed him into the drastic measures of his today. It was the yesterday that made reaching his tomorrow worth all of the underhanded and unlawful things he had done.

A.B. could see and hear his many 'Uncles'. They would come into his life for a couple of months, make his existence almost unbearable, and then break camp, never to be seen again. He never understood the strange noises his mother and uncles would make at all hours of the night. And not just his mother and uncles, but all of his uncle's friends too. It seemed like they all made weird noises with his mother.

They were all aggressive as hell too. If A.B. had a dollar for every time his mother ended up with a black eye… let's just say he would have enough dollars to last a lifetime.

He used to try to defend her. It was always to no avail. The only thing he could do was end up with a black eye too. At first, he felt good about that. To his young mind, one black eye on him was one less black eye on his mother. He was helping. But for some reason his mother started getting upset with him for helping. Something about running her money off. This he never understood because he thought that the goal was to run the uncles off. His mother wanted them to stay. Maybe she liked black eyes and fat lips?

It wasn't until A.B. started getting older that he was able to comprehend what was really going on. The 'Uncles'… they were about as much his family as the man on the moon. They were drug dealers. The odd noises emanating from his mother's bedroom were the sounds of sex. His mother was having sex with all of the drug dealers and all of the drug dealers' friends. But the friends weren't friends. The friends were customers. They were coming for drugs, sex, or a little bit of both. His house was a crack house/ whore house. And his mother was the hoe.

The white powder that looked like flour. The white stones his mother smoked. The nauseating smells coming from his kitchen. The stacks of money the drug dealers always had in abundance. It all began to make sense to A.B. at around age nine. By age eleven, he was trying to do it himself. The way he saw it, if his mother only allowed all of the bullshit to go on at their house because the drug dealers had money, if he became a drug dealer and had a lot of money, his newborn baby sister wouldn't have to grow up like he did.

"SSCCRREECCCHHH!!!"

The tires on the LeSabre squealed loudly as A.B. yoked the car into the Church Village parking lot. Alize clutched the sides of the seat holding on for dear life. A.B. didn't even attempt to look for a parking spot. He just pulled up behind the blue Delta 88 that was parked in front of his apartment. A.B. knew who the car belonged to. It was Menaces' ride. Seeing it caused him to come back to reality. He had enough on his plate right now. How was he going to manage to evict Menace after Samantha had already let him in?

Common sense told him that Menace wasn't going to leave until he was good and ready. And plex with one of the most ruthless cats in Dickinson was not something he was looking forward too. But still, that was his home, his family, his territory. He had to defend what was his. Plus, he had promised Sandra when she was only four days old that she wouldn't have to grow up like he did.

"Wait here." A.B. told Alize before climbing out of the driver's seat and speed walking up to his front door.

"As if." Alize mumbled, unbuckling her seatbelt and hopping out behind him.

She knew drama when she smelt it. The situation A.B. seemed caught up in was like a made for T.V. movie. Their day had started out so simple.

Ride around, get drunk, move some product, stack some chips. Now, in the blink of an eye, things were getting heated. Layla had given Alize specific instructions to stay close by A.B.'s side all day. She didn't want him trying to run off with the money and drugs. Trust was something her mother had told her should be issued out very sparingly.

A.B. pulled out his house keys as he walked with determination in his stride. There was no way he was going to break his promise to Sandra. All of his ripping and running in the streets wouldn't amount to anything if he couldn't provide a better life for his baby sister.

The Village was packed, and all eyes were on A.B.

"Nosey mothafucka's!" he thought.

They were no doubt getting the entertainment of a lifetime. A.B., who was rumored to be dead, had shown up at his mother's house where Menace had set-up shop. He hated to be coming out of hiding so prematurely but drastic times called for drastic measures.

A.B. wasted no time shoving his key in the lock and bursting through the front door like the Dickinson police. The scene he encountered was all too familiar. And yet it still had the power to turn his stomach inside out.

Samantha was on her knees in a white pair of capri and white wife beater vigorously treating Menace to a helping of oral sex. Whip 'em, a so black he looked purple dope fiend, was hard at work in the kitchen cooking up what could only be Menace's latest batch. Sandra was nowhere to be found. Good. At least she wasn't forced to witness the madness firsthand.

All eyes instantly pointed towards A.B. and

Alize. Whip 'em stopped whippin'. Menace stopped guiding Samantha's head. And Samantha momentarily stopped degrading herself.

She looked up from her meal and scowled.

"Who you think you is busting up in my life like that?" she questioned with an exaggerated twist in her neck. "You lost yo damn mind or something?"

"Me...lost 'my' mind?!?" A.B. stepped further into the living room. "Look at yourself mama. You the one trippin. What the hell you got goin on in here?"

Samantha released Menace's tool and stood to confront him. Alize, Menace, and Whip 'em stared on as the mother and son got lost in a heated argument. Even though they were all witnessing the exact same thing, all of them reacted to it in a different way. Whip 'em watched and listened nonchalantly. It didn't really move him one way or the other. Alize, on the other hand, felt sorry for A.B. It sickened her how his mother could really be upset with him and she was the one fucking up. She was even defending Menace. How could she take his side over her own flesh and blood? How could she go against someone she carried around for nine months? That just didn't make sense.

It was a beautiful thing to Menace though. He just sat on the couch with his arms spread out across the back smiling like a chess cat. The dude didn't even have the decency to put his clothes back on. He stayed with his pants and boxers around his ankles and his fully erect penis sticking straight up in the air. He even allowed thoughts of fucking the shit out of the caramel dip that had come in with Samantha's son to float around in his head.

Menace had anticipated the day when A.B.

131

would pop back up and he was proud to see that his brainwashing technique had worked. All Samantha could see was the piles of crack he kept in front of her. She was his.

A.B. indulged in the screaming match with his mother for as long as he could before the feelings of abandonment started to rise to the surface.

"YOU AIN'T NEVER LOVED YO KIDS!" he shouted, fighting hard to hold back the tears. "ALL YOU LOVE IS THAT SHIT!"

Samantha pointed a finger at him and warned, "You better watch how you talk to me boy. I'm still the mothafuckin' parent around here and yo ass is still the child."

A.B. threw up his hands.

"HA!" he hollered. "I stopped being yo child a long time ago. This..."

He dug around in his pocket for the baggy of dope.

"This right here is your child!" he waved it in her face. "It's all you ever cared about."

A.B. had been holding in his true feelings for so long that as the tide of pain crashed against his heart, his inner self was instantly transforming the pain into rage.

Going with the momentum of the moment he forgot all about the room full of spectators, and the fact that Samantha was his mother quickly faded away.

"You been choosin' this... this... this 'HIGH' over me my whole life!" A.B. accused, stepping up and getting in Samantha's face. "And now," he continued, "when I finally start to make some moves to provide a better life for Sandra, you fall back into the same fucked up style of parenting that you used on me."

He waved his empty hand around the room.

"I refuse to let my baby sister grow up like this. I'll be damned if I allow Sandra to be raised by a… by a… by a mothafuckin' dope head ass hoe like you!"

It seemed like everybody in the room gasped. Samantha couldn't believe her ears. A.B. couldn't believe his mouth. He had never talked to his mother like that before. For years he held his true thoughts inside. The pressure had just finally gotten to be too much.

Her sons' words cut through Samantha's false bravado and seared her soul like a red-hot branding iron. The entire room fell silent. 'Dope head ass hoe'! The truth of the slanderous term knocked the wind out of her. It was the real. She was addicted to crack and she often prostituted to support her habit. The drug dealer on her couch with his pants down testified to that. But still, he had no right to say that to her face. Especially not in front of everybody.

There were no more words she could use. Her son had just verbally crushed her. So, trying desperately to save face, Samantha reached back and brought the palm of her hand across the side of A.B.'s cheek as hard as she could.

"WHAP!"

The sound of the slap echoed throughout the house.

A.B.'s head jerked to the right, but his body didn't move. The blow stung like hell, but his mothers' feeble frame didn't wield enough power to make him stumble.

He stayed with his head cocked to the side and rubbed the inside of his throbbing jaw with his tongue. The slap was unexpected.

"Yeah," Samantha said, nodding her head in approval of the effectiveness of her reaction to his hurtful words. "With yo lil smart mouth ass. Next time you'll think twice before you form yo lips to tal... lgh... ggg..."

With absolutely no warning whatsoever, A.B. grabbed Samantha by the wild and unkept twigs she called hair and proceeded to force feed her the work he had in his hands. He was trying to make her swallow the plastic and all.

Years of neglect, abuse, and frustration took control of him.

"UUUGGGHHH!!!" Samantha's eyes widened as she struggled in vain to get A.B. off of her.

Alize watched in horror and Menace watched happily as A.B. transformed right before their eyes.

"IS... THIS... WHAT... YOU... WANT?" he asked through clenched teeth as he bulldozed her to the ground.

Memories of all the times his mother was too fucked up to protect him from the sick and twisted females she hung with began to resurface. He never wanted to do the things they made him do, and his mother never believed that it was being done.

"If you lick it long enough some ice cream will come out."

That's what they use to tell him. The white stuff hardly tasted like ice cream though. It was salty and nasty.

Samantha scratched at A.B.'s hands as the plastic baggy full of dope cut off her windpipe.

Alize screamed. "A.B. STOP IT! YOU'RE

GOING TO KILL HER!

A.B. shoved harder. Alize's voice was distant and inaudible. All he could hear was her gags. The sound made him think about Sticky. Yeeeah! He had taken a life before and he could do it again. Who cares if Samantha was his mother? His real mother had died long before he was even born. All that was left was this pathetic shell of a woman that would put her own five-year-old daughter in harm's way over a funky ass hit., He was actually doing her a favor by putting her out of her misery. She ought to be thanking him.

Samantha felt the blood filling up in her head. Fear had swept over her so totally that she didn't even have room left to be mad. All she could think about was self-preservation.

Samantha kicked weakly as her vision began to blur. The room started rotating slowly. Soon, darkness inched from the edge of her vision and ominously threatened to swallow everything around her. She couldn't believe she was dying at the hands of her own son.

Alize struggled with a course of action. She could both stand idly by and watch A.B. ruin his life, or she could somehow try to intervene. It wasn't technically her business but still… Her and her mother needed A.B. on the streets. He was no good to them behind bars. She knew what Layla would want her to do.

"A.B. NO!" she screamed as she leapt onto his back and loosened his grip on Samantha.

Samantha squirmed from beneath him while he wrestled with Alize. She sucked in the much-needed air in deep breaths. Samantha backed away from A.B., eyes still wide with terror, and rubbed on her neck.

"You... you tried to kill me!" she said, still out of breath. "Get the hell out of my house, Anthony, before I call the law."

Her threat was really a bluff tactic. She knew damn well if the police came to her house more than just A.B. would be going to jail. All she really wanted was for him to just leave. She had never been afraid of her son before, but at that moment he terrified her.

"Let me go." A.B. demanded as he tossed Alize off of his back.

She fell to the floor with an "Ooofff."

A.B. was still in attack mode and he wanted his prey. Looking up, he locked eyes with his mother as she backpedaled across the floor half on her elbows and half on her ass.

Letting the bag of dope go, he was about to rush Samantha again, but a familiar voice stopped him.

"Mommy." A frightened Sandra called out from the open bedroom door. She looked at A.B. and seen the same demonized face that she had seen on the mean man. Why was her brother hurting her mommy too?

The sight of his baby sister quickly calmed A.B. down. He wondered how long she had been there.

"It's o.k. Sandra." He said in his loving big brother voice. "Come here. Come to A.B."

When he extended his arms out towards her, she thought that he was going to hurt her too, so she bolted across the room and dove into Samantha's arms.

"Mommmyyy!" she cried, as the tears flowed like waterworks.

"Shhh." Samantha comforted her, rubbing

her daughters head. "It's gone be alright. Mommy not gone let nothin' happen to you."

Samantha could see her salvation in Sandra. There was no way in hell A.B. would hurt her.

"Shhh." She said one more time before turning her attention to A.B. "So, what you gone do?" she asked, clutching Sandra tightly. "You gone hurt yo sister too? Huh?"

Sandra's cries made A.B. realize what he was doing.

"What's happening to me?" he thought, scanning the room. Alize on the floor.

Menace with his dick still out. Whip 'em waiting for a moment of calm so he can finish cooking. Sandra crying her eyes out. And Samantha afraid for her life. How did it come to this? It seemed like for every step forward he seemed to take, fate stepped in and knocked him back two. He needed some air. Suddenly his apartment, his city, his entire world felt extremely small.

A.B. rose to his feet and staggered out the front door in a daze. Alize followed. He left behind his clothes, his dope, his mother, his sister, and a huge chunk of his sanity.

CHAPTER SEVEN

Layla smiled from ear to ear and ran her freshly manicured fingers through her hair. Today was probably the best Sunday she had experienced in a very long time. Here she was, relaxing in a nice warm Jacuzzi inside of one of the most luxurious hotels inside of Dickinson, Tx. The Marriott. She was completely naked, and the streams of incoming water were beautifully massaging her body. It was like she could just feel the tension of the past few months leaving her flesh and dissolving as if it never existed.

She had money, dope, a brand-new car, one hellafied plan to be set for life, and a boyfriend and daughter who were out and about moving the work she had stolen from Sticky. They thought she had been called in to work, but that story was made up. If chillin' in a hot tub at the Marriott was work, then Layla was the Queen of England.

The little white lie had helped her to find some much-needed alone time. Plotting was hard work. She had more than enough alone time before A.B. moved in. While Alize was at school Layla had the house to herself. The only stress had come from having to pretend like she still had a job. Truth was, she had been fired from her job at Willis, Winn, and Stone about four months ago. In fact, her sudden unemployment was the hard times that led her back to the activities of a prostitute. Her feelings for A.B. had kept her from getting back in too deep, but she still needed to make ends meet. She had bills to pay and a daughter to raise.

Petty scams and hustles had gotten her thru

so far but Layla knew she needed to see some real money. Finally, things were starting to go her way. All she had to do now was continue to play her cards right. A.B. was willing to help her eliminate the cats in the projects. She knew that if they could hit those other two licks on the right day, they would come out of it with more loot then they knew what to do with. They might not even need to set-up shop in the projects. They might get enough money to retire.

Layla dried her hand off on the towel she had resting on the ledge of the Jacuzzi.

"This is getting boring." She said, referring to the nature program she was watching on the T.V.

"Ain't nobody tryna hear about no endangered flowers deep in the jungles of Africa somewhere."

She scooped up the remote and aimed it at the T.V.

"That ain't got nothing to do with a bitch way over here in Dickinson, Tx. America."

Layla laid her head back as she surfed the channels. All of the rooms came with cable, so she had a good amount of stations to choose form. She was confident that she would find one with something interesting on it.

"Hmmm." She hummed. "Let's see now. Bullshit... bullshit... boring... bullshit... bullsh... wait a minute."

Layla raised her head up and slid around the Jacuzzi over to the side that was closes to the T.V.

"That look like the projects."

The news had been airing the story about the murder of Sticky ever since it happened, but the big as day title 'Breaking News' caught Layla's eye.

What new information had come up?

Was there a witness?

Did she forget something critical in her clean-up of the crime scene?

Layla turned up the volume. She had to know what they Knew.

"…unusual turn of events." The reporter was saying. She wasn't actually at the Highland Projects, but they had made a picture of the projects the background for her broadcast.

"Once again." She continued. "For those of you just tuning in, and those of you who need a re-cap, this is Antoinette Hall reporting to you live from the Channel 9 News station. This station has just received a call from a very reliable source, who wishes to remain anonymous, informing us that the stabbing death of Orlando Green is somehow connected to the beating death of Steven Woolard."

Layla gasped.

"What the fuck?" she asked confused.

"Yes." Antoinette said, as if she could hear Layla. "If you have been following the broadcasts of this station, which I'm sure you have, you will remember that a few nights ago a 15 year old boy named Steven Woolard was found beaten to death just outside of the Highland Projects shown here behind me."

She motioned toward the picture background.

"And more recently, a man by the name of Orlando Green, a.k.a. Sticky, was found stabbed to death inside of his home inside these same projects."

Layla felt her stomach twist-up in knots.

"According to our calling," Antoinette continued. "The murder of green was done in retaliation for the murder of Woolard. Now, we have to say that there is no evidence pointing to Green as the killer of Woolard, but our caller was the positive that the two crimes are related."

Antoinette raised one finger for emphasis.

"In fact," she added. "Our tipster even provided this station with the name of a man who they say sought the revenge for Woolards death. Woolards longtime friend and alleged partner in crime, Anthony Tyrone Boon. Better known on the streets as A.B."

Layla dropped the remote and her bottom jaw simultaneously. She couldn't believe it. This bitch, Antoinette Hall, had just plastered her man's full name and alias all over the news. And she even had the nerve to implement him in the death of Sticky.

Layla scrambled out of the tub.

"Anonymous caller!" she thought.

Who knew about what they had done except for her, A.B. and Alize? And even if someone else suspected it, why would they just dry snitch to the Channel 9 News? Why not call the police?

Layla rushed through the sliding glass doors that separated the Jacuzzi from the rest of the room.

Maybe they did call the cops?

"Shit!" Layla cursed out loud as she snatched up her all red robe off of the Queen-sized bed and wrapped it around her dripping wet and sudsy nude frame.

She had to think. The police weren't supposed to be involved. At least not yet.

She turned the other T.V., in the part of the room with the bed, to channel 9. She wanted to be tuned in if they said anything else.

Antoinette was only repeating herself.

Layla analyzed it. The reporter said that the

caller had called them directly. Why would they do that? If you wanted to snitch, wouldn't you just call the police?

She scratched her head.

"Maybe they ain't wanna snitch?" she guessed.

Layla shook her head and frowned.

"No." she responded to her own suggestion. "That doesn't make sense. They obviously wanted to snitch because that's exactly what the fuck they did. Snitch!"

Pacing the room, Layla was able to come up with only two possible scenarios that made sense to her. What if the caller had first called the police with their allegations, were turned away, and so they decided to go to the next best thing, the news? Layla knew that a lot of times in a semi-high-profile case that got news coverage, the cops received calls from damn near half the city with theories and hypothesizes about who did it and what for. If that was the case, the D.P.D might've written the snitch off as yet another conspiracy buff. Little did they know, the snitch was on point.

The other scenario Layla came up with was slightly different. She figured that the caller, for whatever reason, didn't call the cops at all. They went straight to the news. The only explanation that would explain a course of action like that was if the caller was involved in something themselves that would make talking to the laws directly a stupid move.

Layla knew that if the second scenario was what actually happened, the snitch was somebody from the streets. That made more sense because somebody from the streets would easily know A.B.'s alias and easily be able to connect him to

Sticky.

"They gotta be dealt with." Layla said, referring to the snitch. "But first I gotta let A.B. know that it's no longer safe out there."

Layla made her way over to the hotel phone. She didn't want to have to call A.B. from the room, but she could talk her way out of that one later. Her man's safety and freedom were way more important than here protecting the lie about her lack of a job.

Layla picked up the receiver and placed it to her ear.

Weird. No dial tone.

She was about to hang up the phone and try again when she heard someone breathing on the other end.

She paused. Apparently, she had answered an incoming call before the phone could even ring on her end.

"Ummm... hello." She said, wondering who the breath belonged to.

"We got a problem." The man on the other end told her.

Layla recognized the voice and stiffened up.

"How did you know I was here?" she asked, suddenly feeling the urge to peek out the window.

"I always know where you're at." The man answered. "But that's not important right now. What's important is this breaking news report I just watched on the Channel 9 news."

She knew he would be upset when he heard about the broadcast.

"This changes things." He added. "If you can't hold up your end of the bargain, then..."

"Who said I can't hold up my end?" Layla jumped in. "Look, I just watched the same news report and I'm already on it. I can handle it. Just give me some time."

The man was silent.

"We got a lot of money tied into this Layla.' He said finally. "I'm not trying to lose out because your little boy toy works sloppy."

"Don't worry about A.B." she said defending her man. "It's like I told you. He doesn't even know about you. He's in this for me and his boy Steel. I know for a fact that he's gonna play his part all the way to the end. His motivation goes deeper than just money. Revenge will make a man complete any mission regardless. This... snitch, whoever they are, won't stop me and my team. You have my word on that."

"Good." The man replied. "Because if A.B. goes down, he's going down by himself."

Layla heard the phone hang up. She prayed her plan wasn't unraveling.

The man who Layla had just been talking to, closed his flip-phone style Sprint cellular and dropped it into his pocket. He was already extremely aggravated because of the breaking news story, and the white man staring oddly at him through the bathroom mirror didn't make it any better.

"What the fuck you lookin' at?" he growled, silently wishing the white man would jump fly so he could have a reason to break his face.

The white guy jumped alright, but his ass didn't jump fly.

"Oh. I'm sorry sir." He apologized, quickly backing up in the direction of the exit.

"I didn't mean to intrude."

The white guy wasn't the least bit familiar personally with the streets, but he had watched enough gangster movies to know a mob boss call when he heard one. He also knew the possible consequences of becoming the enemy of said boss. The red and white 3-piece Versace suit the man had on didn't fool him. He could tell that the tall, muscular black guy behind the suit and tie was dangerous. The white man didn't want any trouble.

The man in the 'Sace suit glared at the white dude until he had backed all the way out the door. The cowards retreat was a bitter/sweet encounter. A part of him laughed at the fear he induced. Another part of him wanted to bang dude up like he used to do the Aryan Brotherhood and the Woods when he was doing his bid in the Texas Penitentiary on the Beto unit.

"Oh well." He thought.

The man's attire was flawless, but out of habit he adjusted his collar, his cufflinks, and smoothed out wrinkles in his jacket that only he could see.

"You one fine ass brotha." He said smiling to his reflection in the over-sized mirror.

Just that quick he was back in gentleman mode and ready to return to his date. If he stayed in the bathroom too much longer his lady friend would no doubt get suspicious. Females were the species that took all day in the restroom, not males.

Giving himself one more overall visual inspection, he decided that he was still fly and exited the bathroom.

The dining area of the Chez Jacques French cuisine 5-star restaurant was packed. It seemed like everybody in town had the exact same idea as him that Sunday evening. Chez Jacques had a strict suit and tie type of dress code so everywhere you looked you saw nothing but well-dressed men and women. It wasn't the type of environment you'd expect to see a man of his background and lifestyle in. But that's what separated him from the rest of the bunch. He wasn't confined to the back alleys and juke joints. He was able to fit in with the so-called 'high society' while at the same time locking down the ghettos.

He surveyed his surroundings. There were gorgeous, vivacious, beautiful women in every square inch that his eye came across. He wasn't lusting after them though. True, he greatly appreciated the perfection of all that is called and classified as woman, but his money was long as I-45. Any man with deep pockets so easily acquired female companionship no longer warranted top priority importance. It could be done at a moment's notice.

So, searching for eye candy was not his motivation. Making sure that his lady friend was one of the top 5 best dressed in the joint was. He had spent a nice lil chunk of change on her dress, so it was understandable that he wanted her to stand out. They had only been kicking it for maybe two months, but he really was digging his lil mama's swagger. She was gangsta when she needed to be gangsta and girly when she needed to be girly. Plus, her personality was so laid back and playa. She knew that he had loot, but she never pressed up on him about buying her things. Shorty carried herself like she had had nice things before. Of course, he knew that it was all an act, but she got credit for having the decency to contain herself around a made man.

Spotting his prize across the room, still waiting patiently at their table for two, he headed towards her.

She was looking absolutely stunning in the

matching red and white dress that he had bought her. The 7 karat diamond earrings sparkled in her sexy chocolate ear lobes. Her neck was void of any jewels per his request. To him, when anybody, man, or woman, accessorized every possible part of their body with jewelry, it screamed to the world of onlookers that they have never had shit. And now that they do have something, they want the whole world to know it. So, he chose to deck his beauty out in diamond earrings, a $3,500 tennis bracelet, and a toe ring to accentuate her expertly pedicured feet. Nothing more.

Never taking his eyes off of his dark-skinned dinner date, he strolled right up to their table and sat down.

"My bad LaQuisha." He apologized, startling her. "I had to go handle some business."

LaQuisha was still watching the channel 9 news broadcast when her boyfriend Tank walked up surprising her.

"Boy." She said, placing a hand over her chest. "You scared me."

Tank chuckled.

"You?! Scared?!" he asked sarcastically. "Not Ms. Billy Bad Ass."

LaQuisha playfully rolled her eyes and faced back in the direction of one of the TV's Chez Jacques had suspended from the ceiling.

"Whatever." She replied.

LaQuisha was still caught up in the news about A.B. Apparently, he wasn't dead. Alize was right. Dude was still alive and well. Well, if that anonymous caller could be trusted, A.B. won't be well for long. People that kill people get locked away in prison for a long ass time. And quite often they never touch down again.

"Is something wrong?" Tank asked, noticing for the first time how consumed LaQuisha had become with the broadcast. He was so caught up in his own reaction to it that he didn't pay her any mind.

Without looking away from the screen, she said, "I know those dudes. Well, not all of them. I know A.B. and Steel though. We all went to school together."

"Oh yeah?" Tank responded, sipping his wine.

He knew that they were all in the same age, but he never considered the possibility that they knew each other personally.

"Yeeeah." LaQuisha said, still zoning. "Me and my girls were just talking about them fools the other day."

She shook her head slowly.

"We all thought that nigga A.B. was dead."

Reaching for her glass of wine, she added, "Alize tried to tell us that A.B. wasn't dead though. I guess she was right."

LaQuisha shrugged and sipped on her wine.

"Alize?!" Tank repeated, suddenly looking very suspicious. "Who is Alize?"

LaQuisha looked at him as if he was joking.

"You know Alize." She told him. "She's one of my girls that I been trying to get you to meet, but you said you don't like meeting new people."

Tank leaned forward and placed his forearms on the table.

"What do you mean by 'one of your girls'? Is she a friend from school or something?"

LaQuisha smacked her lips.

"She's part of my clique. The Valley Park Girls. There's me, Krystal, Ming, Melissa, and

Alize. We all like this."

She crossed her fingers.

Tank could vaguely remember her telling him something about her little clique of gangster girls. He didn't pay it much mind though. Not until now. If one of them had prior knowledge about A.B. still being alive, that instantly made them a suspect in the snitching that just went on.

Tank suddenly found himself very interested in his girlfriend's clique.

"So." He said, trying to ease more information out of her without raising suspicion. "If ya'll called the Valley Park girls, does that mean all of ya'll stay in Valley Park?"

"Of course." She answered. "We all stay in houses that line the park inside of Valley Park."

"For real? I know this white chick named Layla that live out there around that park."

"Now I know you just joking." She said smiling.

"What?" Tank asked, genuinely confused. "Why I gotta be joking?"

LaQuisha studied his expression. He really didn't know.

"You serious, huh? She commented. "you know Layla, but you don't know Alize?"

Tank raised an eyebrow.

"Why are you so shocked that I know one and not the other? Just because they live in the same area don't mean I gotta know 'em both."

LaQuisha giggled.

"Naw Sweetie. They don't just live in the same area. They live in the same house. That white chick named Layla that you know is Alize's mother."

Tank's eyes grew wide. A million thoughts

erupted from that single revelation and caused an avalanche of questions to bubble up in his mind.

Layla has a daughter. Her daughter and LaQuisha are close friends? Her daughter was going around telling people that A.B. was still alive?

Tank stared off into space.

Is Alize the anonymous tipster that called Ms. Antoinette Hall at the channel 9 news?

"Uh sweetie." LaQuisha called. "Are you alright?"

Tank could only ignore her. His thought process was trapped inside a sphere of possibilities and deceptions that seemed to have a life of their own. One concept merged with one idea and the two of them conceived a theory. And that theory was now giving birth to feelings. Feelings such as anger and confusion. Simple-mindedness and wounded pride. Feelings that bred a desire for revenge.

'IS' Alize the snitch? What would reality bring along with it? If Alize is the snitch, then Layla can't be trusted. If Layla can't be trusted, I'm being played. If I'm being played...

LaQuisha looked on as Tanks' face contorted more and more into an expression of rage. She didn't understand why, but she knew it had something to do with what she just said about Layla and Alize being mother and daughter.

CHAPTER EIGHT

Layla had dialed the number of the cell phone she had given A.B. six times before she finally gave up. She was trying to tell herself the problem was something simple like a dead battery but a nagging voice inside of her head kept saying that both A.B. and Alize were in police custody somewhere.

She wasn't sure what she would do if that was the case. Neither one of them were legal adults and the juvenile system in their area didn't allow bonds to be posted. If they were in juvenile, the best she could do is get them a lawyer.

Not willing to give up that easily, Layla gathered her things, called a taxicab, and headed back towards her home in Valley Park.

The cab ride cost a good $11.50, but that was nothing compared to the peace of mind she got when the cab driver pulled over in front of her home and she saw her new, all white. 2004 Buick LeSabre parked in the driveway.

"Oh, thank God." She thought. "They're alright."

Layla paid the cabby and rushed into her home. The scene she encountered was unexpected.

A.B. was sitting down in the living room hunched over with his head in his lap. Alize was sitting next to him consoling him. At first glance the scenario made her think about the night she stood by A.B.'s side when Steel got killed.

Was Alize trying to push up on her man by being there for him in his time of need?

The spark of jealousy flickered but luckily it

didn't ignite. There were bigger things going on. Bigger than a possible man-theft.

"I guess ya'll already seen the news broadcast too." Layla said, crossing the carpeted floor and taking a seat on the other side of A.B.

Alize and A.B. looked at each other and then at Layla.

"News broadcast?! They both asked at the same time. "What news broadcast?"

"The one about A.B. and Sticky." Layla answered in a tone of voice that said they should already know what broadcast.

A.B. sat up and Alize's hand slid off his back. His face told the tale of tears shed. Something was really bothering him if he broke down in front of Alize.

"Me and Sticky?" he said, drying off his eyes. "We didn't see no news broadcast about me and Sticky."

He was suddenly very nervous. There had been several broadcasts about Sticky, but none about him 'and' Sticky. A.B. wasn't even sure what Layla was talking about and he didn't like the sounds of it.

How in the hell did they tie him in to Sticky?

Him and Layla played it smart. Didn't they?

Their execution of the robbery/murder was flawless. Wasn't it?

Layla analyzed what she had seen when she walked in.

"Hold up." She said, with an "I know ya'll didn't" look on her face. "If ya'll ain't been watching the news, what are you doing crying and what are you doing all up in my man's face?"

"Tttsss." Alize smacked her teeth, rolled her

eyes, and threw a small twist into her neck. "All up in yo man face? Mama please. You do not have to worry about me taking your man. Don't nobody want A.B. but you boo. Trust."

Layla gasped and placed her hands on her hips.

"No you didn't just get all sassy with me. Girl, who you think you talkin' to like that?"

A.B. could tell that the conversation was about to escalate into an all-out spit boxing championship match, so he intervened. He couldn't take another mother-child episode like the one he had been involved in earlier.

"Layla!" he said firmly, looking her directly in her eyes. "You really need to calm yo ass down and chill out. All that ol' charging you r daughter up behind me... you can miss me with that shit. For real."

"But A.B...."

"But A.B. nothing!" he told her. "You know how I feel about you girl. Don't ever come up in here and insinuate that either me or yo daughter would fuck over you like that."

Layla folded her arms and pouted. A.B. knew how to handle her. He knew that she had been through so much drama in her life that a weak man couldn't contain her. Her man had to be strong, firm, and assertive. At times, A.B. had to be downright aggressive. It was all good though. His mother's lifestyle forced him to grow up fast and to adapt a take charge type of attitude.

A.B. motioned towards Alize with his thumb.

"She was just holdin' me down while I digested the situation my lil sister in."

Layla felt a little embarrassed. She had all

but accused her 13-year-old daughter of sleeping with her man. If she had been right, the accusation would've been warranted. But since she wasn't, it only made her look bad. Jealousy was tacky no matter who was wearing it.

Layla lowered her voice.

"What situation is Sandra in?" she asked, trying to change the subject.

Alize was cheesing on the inside, but she refused to let it show. She remained calm, cool, and straight faced. A.B. had just checked the shit out of her mother on her behalf. She was shocked. He had actually stood up for her. And he took her side instead of her mothers. Even thought he was sleeping with her mother. Once again A.B. had shown her a side of himself that she didn't previously know was there. More and more she was beginning to feel like he actually cared about what she was going through.

Caring about what she was going through meant the world to a girl like Alize. Especially when it was a man who was doing the caring. In the society that Alize's generation was growing up in, a lot of the females were being raised without a loving male role model in their lives. So, it could easily be labeled as nature taking its normal course when a young woman got attached quickly to any man who showed her even a small portion of the attention she so desperately craved.

Who cares if he's a thug? He notices me and it makes me feel good.

Who cares if it's all bullshit game and lies? He compliments me and it makes me feel pretty and desired.

Who gives a damn if her only wants my body? He pursues me and it makes me feel like a woman.

So the fuck what if he's currently fucking my mother? He's attractive, intelligent, goal-orientated, protective of me, half my mother's age, and guess what...? He makes me feel like I deserve to have him fucking 'ME'.

Maybe this is what the early stages of love feels like?

A stinging sensation pierced A.B.'s heart when he prepared to fill Layla in on the drama surrounding his mother and little sister.

He let his chin fall to his chest and slowly shook his head. It was all still hard to accept.

"Baaaby." Layla whined sympathetically, gently caressing the nape of A.B.'s neck. "What happened? What got you acting like this? Is she sick or something? Did she have an accident?

A.B. was about to respond but Alize beat him to the punch. She could tell that he was still in emotional pain and she wanted to carry some of the load for him. He had been through a lot this past week. And now, to top it all off, he had flipped out , almost murdered his own mother, and left his little sister terrified of him and trapped in one hopelessly negative environment.

"Remember how you sent us over to Felicia house to make that money?" Alize asked.

Layla gave her daughter her attention and nodded.

"When we got there," Alize continued. "We ran into one of A.B.'s Aunts. I think her name was Jas... Tas... Yas... Yasmine. Yeah, that's it. Yasmine. A.B.'s Aunt Yasmine told us that..."

Alize went on to give Layla a play by play account of everything that went down. From the conversation with Yasmine, to the Nascar-esque race across town in the LeSabre, to the harsh reality of A.B.'s mother allowing Menace to set up shop in her apartment, to the attempted murder, to the frightened to set up shop in her apartment, to the attempted murder, to the frightened and helpless Sandra. Alize didn't leave anything out.

As she spoke, Layla's expressions seemed locked in a continuing cycle of confusion, disbelief, surprise, shock, anger, and empathy. It seemed to her like A.B. couldn't get a break. If it wasn't one thing, it was another.

Layla bit her bottom lip. She rattled off a few words of encouragement but deep down she knew that her touch couldn't soothe his soul. Especially seeing as how she had more bad news for him. There was no telling how he would react when she laid it on him that a Ms. Antoinette Hall had just recently been on live T.V. saying that she received an anonymous call naming him as the killer of Sticky. At the young age of 15 he might just have a mental breakdown.

"I'm so sorry boo." Layla said, giving him a kiss on the cheek.

"I'm aiight." A.B. told her. "I already pretty much know what I gotta do about that."

He shook the depressed feelings off and put his game face on. Really, he had absolutely no idea what his next move should be. His plate was already full with the mission of revenge he was on. There was no way he was going to let Sandra grow up like he did, and at the same time there was no way he was going to let them cats over in the projects get away with murdering Steel. He just had to figure out which issue should be addressed first. His baby sister or his deceased homeboy?

A.B. had been racking his brain with that

one. The best he could come up with was getting revenge first and rescuing Sandra second. After all, not only did the situation with Steel come up first, but only after dealing with those dudes in the projects would he have enough loot to provide for Sandra like he wanted too. So reluctantly, he decided to put today's developments on the back burner. He had to focus on the task at hand.

Revenge! Retribution! And Robbery!

"We'll confront the situation with my people later." A.B. decided. "Right now, we need to keep our minds on the mission that we been on. Payin' them sucka's back fa what they did to my road dog and getting paid in the process. So gone lace us up on that news shit you came in here talkin bout."

A.B. paused.

"Everything is still going as planned, ain't it?"

Layla slowly brushed her hair back attempting to stall. She had been hoping like hell that he would somehow forget she even mentioned a news broadcast. Of course, she realized that all of her wishful thinking was in vain but still she wished anyway.

Layla nervously chewed at her brand-new nails and turned her gaze away from the questioning stares of Alize and A.B.

How was she going to tell him?

How would he react?

She couldn't possibly keep it from him. Could she?

No! That would only make matters worse. He deserved to know what he was up against. It was the only way they could put their heads together and come up with an intelligent plan of attack.

Layla faced them once again and took a

deep breath.

"Just say it and get it over with." She thought.

"So?!" A.B. asked, shrugged his shoulders. "What did they say about me and Sticky?"

Layla laid her hands in her lap and swallowed the lump that was in her throat.

"Now don't be mad baby." She told him. "We still got things under control like we always did. But some hating motherfuckers done apparently made an anonymous snitch call to the channel 9 news with you name in their mouth..."

Layla proceeded to tell A.B. and Alize about the drama she had stumbled up on. She didn't approach it like Alize did. Her story was far from a 'tell all' account of her day. She intentionally left out the part about chilling at the Marriott and the part about her little phone conversation with Tank. Those two details would bring along with them questions that she didn't want to have to answer.

Instead, she ran with the story about being at work. She told them that she had seen the broadcast on the break room T.V. inside the Willis, Winn, and Stone Law Firm building. She even went on to describe what was said in great detail.

A.B. listened closely to what the news reporter said. He paid even closer attention to Layla's two possible explanations of why someone would go to the media. He had been around her in enough situations to know that she was sharp as hell when it came to street shit. Her theory about what was going on was no doubt close to the truth. The only brick wall was figuring out who this anonymous caller was.

There were roughly 22,000 people that referred to Dickinson, Tx. As home sweet home and any one of them could be the snitch. Layla narrowed the search as much as she could by guessing it was a person from the streets.

But who? Did the real killers see how A.B. had done Sticky behind Steel and catch that pussy? Were they trying to get him off of the streets before he could get his hands on them too? Could they actually be so afraid that they would dry snitch?

A.B. wasn't used to causing that type of fear so he wasn't sure if his ego was making him miss something. Who said that the call came from the killers? Nobody. That's who.

One thing was for sure though. Whoever the snitch was, and whatever the snitches reasons, their actions had A.B. sweating bullets. He was now the suspect in a murder. And not just any murder. A murder that he was actually guilty of committing.

A.B. rubbed his damp palms off on his shorts. His mind was racing.

"Is there any evidence linking me to the crime?" he wondered.

He replayed the event over in his mind.

The stakeout. The coded page from Layla. The entry into the victim's residence. The sounds of sex. His anger. His rage. His fury.

The kill shot. Pocket knife to the throat. The slightly insane, extremely exotic sex in front of the body. The piles of clothes in the back. Layla finding the stash. Him going to get the car. Fleeting thoughts of G-Unit jeans on a body that should've been nude.

Hmmm. G-Unit jeans? A.B. strained to re-live that night.

"Baby." Layla called, threatening to interrupt his thoughts.

He simply held up a finger. He was deep in

the recollection of the event. And he did not want his concentration broken.

Layla got the hint. Her and Alize silently watched him think.

A.B. had never thoroughly picked apart the events of that night. Now that he was, he was seeing things he never saw before and considering things that never once crossed his mind.

Sticky 'was' naked when he killed him. But somewhere between him searching the room and Layla finding the stash, she had put Sticky's pants back on him.

What for?

A.B. dug deeper. Was... was she wearing gloves when he came out the bedroom?

A.B.'s pulse quickened.

She was! She was wearing gloves.

He cut his eyes at Layla suspiciously. Maybe there was a perfectly good explanation for all of that? She looked innocent enough. Pretty blonde hair. Light blue eyes. Cute face, sexy lips, smooth neck...

A.B. gasped on the inside.

He had left his knife lodged inside of Sticky's neck. Why when he exited the bedroom it was gone? The knife was the murder weapon. It could get him a life sentence. What had she done with it? Where was it at right now?

He remembered her telling him that she had cleaned up the crime scene. Maybe she got rid of it and the wrong person found it?

"What did you do with the pocketknife I used to kill Sticky?" he asked Layla.

She was caught somewhat off guard.

"I told you." She answered. "I disposed of it."

A.B. rubbed his chin.

"You don't think the anonymous caller somehow got their hands on it, do you?"

Layla considered the possibility. It was highly unlikely.

"I seriously doubt it." She told him. "For someone to have that knife, they would've had to have me around from the moment I yanked it out of Sticky's neck. And to be following me around they would've had to already know I was involved with the crime. Didn't nobody but the two of us know that we were going after Sticky that night."

A.B. nodded his head in agreement.

"You right." He said. "Besides, if the snitch had the knife then the cops would have the knife. And if the cops had the knife it would've been them on the T.V. and not that reporter lady."

Alize jumped up off the couch and covered her mouth with both of her hands. She gasped.

A.B. and Layla snapped their heads in her direction and looked at her strangely.

"It makes perfect sense!" she declared, eyes wide and covered with the glare of understanding.

Pointing at Layla, she said, "You said that whoever made that anonymous phone call is from the streets, right?"

"Well," Layla answered, wondering where her daughter was going with this. "I'm not 100% sure, but that would be my guess."

"Yeah. And that's a good guess." Alize assured her. "See, whoever made that call fits a pretty specific profile. They're in the streets. They can't afford to go to the police. They know A.B. personally and they have their ear to the goings on around Dickinson. Plus, they have some type of motive for wanting to mess over A.B. They gotta feel like he wronged them in some way."

Alize sat back down next to A.B. and started using a softer, calmer tone.

"Now I know you feel like that could be anybody." She said to A.B. "but if you really think about it, it's obvious who called the channel 9 news and why."

A.B. rushed through his list of information once again. He didn't know what Alize was talking about. It wasn't obvious to her.

Alize could tell that he was still drawing a blank. She closed her eyes and took a deep breath.

"A.B." she said after exhaling. "I'm willing to bet money that it was your mother that made that anonymous phone call."

For A.B., that statement made time stand still.

CHAPTER NINE

A.B. stretched out on Layla's bed and puffed on one of his special Boss Playa blunts. He glanced at the wall clock hanging on a nail directly in front of the bed.

9:30 am. Monday afternoon. Alize was at school learning about Christopher Columbus, pronouns adjectives and verbs, fractions, and a plant uses to transform sunlight into energy and food called photosynthesis. Layla was at work answering the phone calls from men and women (mostly men) who had made one too many wrong moves in the streets, and now the justice system was threatening to swallow them whole. A.B. wondered if he got arrested and charged with murder before he could leave town for good, would Willis, Winn, and Stone take his case as a personal favor for their hardworking receptionist? He sure hoped so. If he was a praying man he would sure be praying about it.

A.B. had no idea that Layla wasn't at work. She had taken the car and everything. Leaving him stranded in Valley Park. All he had to occupy his time was weed, wet, and porno flicks.

After two nuts, one inside of Layla before she left for work and one inside of a wad of toilet paper after she was gone, A.B. wasn't really feeling the flicks anymore. Maybe later after he re-cooperated some.

He hit the blunt and held the smoke.

As much as he didn't want to believe it, his own mother was trying to get him put away for life. She's the only person that made sense. She had access to all of the information that the anonymous caller gave to Antoinette Hall. She knew A.B.'s real name, the fact that him and Steel were best friends, and without a doubt she had been receiving daily updates on the latest rumor about her son. Plus, she had just a square business motive he couldn't really blame her for what she did. He had tried to kill her.

Last night, when him, Alize, and Layla were going over the possibilities, he remembered that Samantha had threatened to call the cops if A.B. didn't leave. Seeing as how Menace was using her apartment for his latest dope house, realistically she couldn't go to the cops. So either own her own, or co-conspiring with Menace, Samantha mad that fateful call to the channel 9 news shortly after him and Alize scratched off.

Putting that phone call into perspective with everything else that had been going on with his mother, he opted to believe that Menace had his grimy ass hands all over the situation too. It was probably his idea. The smirk that stayed on his face from the minute A.B. arrived, to the moment he left to A.B. that he was getting way too much enjoyment out of being the reason behind his families' downfall.

Menace didn't know it yet, or maybe he did, but he was now at the top of A.B.'s list. At first Layla tried to talk him out of going after Menace. She was saying that they already had two more people that had to get it too. That would be risky enough. Especially with A.B.'s name all over the news. They couldn't just ride around killing people like murder was legal. It was the most serious criminal offense. It deserved a certain amount of respect.

A.B. was able to rationalize it by pointing

out that Menace had a lot of money too. He even had more than Sticky. Plus, how could they let the snitching slide? That would compromise his whole reputation. Nobody respected a coward or a hoe.

Slowly but surely Layla was able to see things his way. She understood that the snitching had to be addressed. The only thing she didn't like was the fact that going after Menace was an unexpected turn of events. Everything else had been mapped out to the "T". In Layla's mind, spur of the moment crimes had a tendency of getting even a mastermind locked up.

A.B. stared up at the ceiling and followed all of the exhaled smoke as it danced and drifted smoothly across the room. Layla had made a point that A.B. had thought about but tried to ignore.

If they had to go after Menace because he had something to do with the anonymous call, then they had to go after Samantha too. After all, she's the one who actually made the call.

This posed a problem. True, A.B. would've ended Samantha's life yesterday had it not been for Alize's and Sandra's interference, but he was caught up in the heat of the moment then. He couldn't see himself going through the motions of plotting his own mother's death. All of the things she had put him through had him at a point in his life where he wished things were different, but he didn't necessarily want his mother dead. He wanted to change her ways, not end her days.

Layla noticed his reservations and made a mental note about it. If it came down to it, he wouldn't pull the trigger on Samantha. She would have to do that one herself.

A.B. glanced at the clock again.

9:45 am.

Alize would be getting dismissed from school in about another five hours or so. At least... that's what A.B. thought.

Earlier that day, Alize got up, took care of her hygiene, got dressed, and headed towards the park to meet her home girls and catch the bus. When she got to the park, however, she suddenly changed her plans.

Posted up at the park, reclining back in a 2008 candy red Cadillac Escalade was LaQuisha, Ming, Krystal, and Melissa.

"Heeey Biiitch." LaQuisha sung, hanging happily out of the driver's side window. "Hurry up and get in so we can roll out."

Alize stood there frozen.

What in the world was LaQuisha doing in a ride like that? A candy Escalade sitting on 24 inch chromed out rims? And... and are those screens falling from the sky?

Alize rubbed her eyes and pinched herself. She had to be dreaming. There was no way any of this was real.

HOOONK!

The sound of LaQuisha blowing the horn of the head turning S.U.V. made her jump.

"Do I gotta drag yo ass up in here kicking and screamin' ?" LaQuisha shouted. "because I really don't feel like wrinkling my clothes up."

She opened the door.

"I don't feel like it, but you know I will."

Alize snapped out of the initial shock and jogged over to the S.U.V. Krystal opened the back door and let her in.

LaQuisha slammed her door shut.

"Now that we all here, let's ride out." She said, cranking up the R&B station and allowing

Jagged Edge to tell them how they felt like they had walked right out of Heaven.

"Funny." Alize thought, examining the matching red and white interior of the vehicle. "I feel like I just walked right into Heaven."

As LaQuisha pulled off, all 5 Valley Park Girls sang along with the song, bobbing their heads and snapping their fingers.

In between songs LaQuisha filled them in on what she was doing in a ride like that. Apparently, her new boyfriend Tank had let her use it. Plus, he had given her $5,000 to take her and her home girls out with. Ming was the only one who objected to skipping school, but LaQuisha and Melissa talked her into staying. It wasn't every day you could skip in so much style.

The first stop Alize suggested they make was over at one of the many weed houses scattered around town. She was trying to get high. High and drunk. Her home girls didn't know about all of the drama she had been involved in in the past few days, but the madness was taking its toll on her. Keeping secrets was never a really big problem for her but the nature of the secrets she was forced to keep were huge in comparison to the ones she held in the past.

Murder, money, and drugs!

Live News Broadcasts, snitches, and retaliation plots!

Those things weren't her. Hell, she didn't even know that those things were her mother. Over the past couple of months her mother had been acting stranger and stranger. To Alize, it seemed like something that sounded so perfect, flawless, and easy in the beginning, was nothing more than an 'enticing to the eye' pit of quicksand. Once you were foolish enough to jump in with both feet, your fate became instantly sealed. If you struggled, fought, and thrashed about, you would meet a swift panicky end. If you sat back, chilled, and rolled with the punches, your death would be excruciatingly slow.

A statement A.B. had once made kept on echoing in her consciousness. He had told her that in order to get out of the streets they had to first embrace the streets. She hadn't thought about it at the moment when he said it, but she definitely was pondering it now.

"What if you got swallowed in you attempt to get rich?"

Alize turned up a bottle of Bud Light and rushed 3 gulps of it. They didn't even have to make any stops to score some weed or buy some drank. LaQuisha's man had thought of everything. Along with the vehicle, and the money, he had also given LaQuisha two ounces of weed and a 24 pack of Bud Light. This nigga Tank was really trying to show them a good time. And he wasn't even around to enjoy any of it. Alize guessed that things between her girl and Tank were getting serious. Any man with any kind of common sense knew that the Valley Park Girls were so close, you pretty much had to befriend them all just to hold onto one.

Taking another drink, Alize called out over the stereo system in the front of the Escalade where LaQuisha and Ming were sitting.

"Damn bitch." She said to LaQuisha smiling. "Nandy red 'lac... 5 mothafuckin' G's... two zones of that sticky-icky...AND a 24 pack! Shooot. You must've put that pussy on Tank something serious last night to get all of this shit."

Melissa, who was sitting next to Alize in the

middle seat, gave Alize a high-five and laughed out loud.

LaQuisha grinned from ear to ear. She was feeling like a Queen right then and there. Her man had loot. And he didn't mind sharing some of it with her. All females enjoyed being the envy of friends and foes alike. LaQuisha felt like she was one of the realest women around, and now she was able to flaunt it. She had won her the type of dude 95% of the women on the planet wanted. A gangsta/gentleman that was handsome, nicely built, paid in full, and hung like a porno star. The 5% that didn't want what she had were probably either dykes or nuns.

LaQuisha quickly glanced back and then faced back towards the road.

"You forgot something." She said, basking in the glow of her newfound status. "I also got my man to fill the tank up before I rode out."

She pointed at the gas hand.

"You know a bitch had to pull out on 'F'. Okaaay?!"

LaQuisha gave Ming a high-five and the whole truck erupted into laughter. Even Krystal, who was in the backseat by herself and barely able to hear over the speakers, laughed hard and clutches her sides.

After the laughter died down, LaQuisha handed the blunt over to Ming. She always looked funny when she smoked. Ming would hold the blunt with her index finger and thumb like she was using her hand to express how small something was. Then she would slowly put it to her lips and inhale.

Ming couldn't deny that she liked being fucked up. She often wondered who wouldn't be able to find enjoyment out of an unusually large number of endorphins being released directly into the pleasure center of the brain. On a chemical level, doing drugs was fast, easy, and cheap (but sometimes expensive), happiness. Unlike her home girls though, Ming was extremely well read and knowledgeable about a lot of different topics. She knew all too well all of the negatives that came along with heavy and prolonged drug use. Ming had a future. A future so bright that her mother often called her 'sun', even though she was clearly her daughter. She couldn't see herself ruining it over a high.

The weed was already taking full effect even though this was only Ming's second time hitting the blunt in the rotation. That was another perk of not smoking on a daily basis. Whenever she did decide to blow it was just like her first time.

"Hey LaQuisha." Ming said, feeling less reserved with every puff. "Did you and Tank really have sex last night?"

LaQuisha cut her eyes at Ming.

"Naw girl." She responded. "We ain't have sex. I done had sex before and that wasn't it. Me and my boo made looove."

"Awww shit! Melissa exclaimed. "You know we want the details. Where at? How long? Good, great, or indescribable?"

"Yeah." Ming chipped in. "Was he gentle, rough, or a little bit of both?"

"Four-play? Lights on?" Alize inquired.

"Girl!" Krystal jumped in from the back. "Fuck all of that less than interesting ass shit. I'm gone ask what I know we all wanna know. How big was dude dick? Was he able to keep it standing at attention like soldier? How many times did he make you cum? And last but definitely not least. Does dude got any big dick, stay in the paint all night, make a bitch cum so much you'd swear his thang was caught in an avalanche, candy red Escalade driving, money so long he can give his woman 5 G's to spend on her home girls, type of friends you can turn the rest of us on too? Okaaay?"

High-fives and chuckles spread throughout the inside of the vehicle once more. Krystal had really put it out there.

"O.K. O.K." LaQuisha said, reaching forward to turn down the volume of the radio. "I know the rules. If ya'll wanna know then I gotta share."

She turned down the music and cleared her throat.

"Gather 'round little children," she said playfully. "Let me lace ya'll up on who mama was do… I mean, 'what', mama was doing last night."

"You had it right the first time." Ming joked. "'Who', you were doing."

LaQuisha smacked her lips.

"Anyway." She said. "Things had taken a turn for the worse at the restaurant, but by the time we made it to the room it was on and popping."

LaQuisha proceeded to paint a picture that was as vivid in all of the girls' minds as if they had witnessed it firsthand with their own eyes. On many occasions Melissa and Krystal had told her that she should try her hand at writing those freaky sex stories that got published in the XXX magazines. It was like you could actually get off to LaQuisha's rendition of a sexual escapade. She was live in that department. That's why even Ming loved to hear her stories. It gave her insight into how to not only blow her future husbands mind, but also how to get hers blown in the process. Expectations were always high when LaQuisha got ready to tell a fuck tale. And thankfully, she never once disappointed.

LaQuisha didn't want to be forced to mention that her man knew Alize's mother, or that he became upset when he found out Layla even had a daughter named Alize, so she decided to leave all of that out and just start from when they left the restaurant.

"It's a good thing we had already eaten." LaQuisha told them. "Because whatever it was that had my baby bothered made him want to leave Chez Jacques immediately…"

After hearing the news about Layla and Alize being mother and daughter Tank was furious. He felt betrayed! Lied too! Manipulated! And played for weak! There was no hard evidence to support his growing suspicions, but his instincts were screaming out DOUBLE-CROSS. In the streets, the stakes were always high. The penitentiary was packed with dreamers like him and the graveyard was filled to the brim with visionaries. Tank understood his vulnerability. He meditated daily on ways to strength his weaknesses but he by no means fooled himself into believing that they weren't there. In the game of money & dope, power & respect, jealousy & envy, and prison & death, an individual that lacks wisdom as to who they really are is destined to collapse like the home which is built with no foundation.

That's why so many young men and young women fall victim to the beast at an early age. They are destitute of wisdom, knowledge, and understanding. A child's teenage years are meant to be used as a period of searching. They are supposed to be trying to find themselves. Yet so many times they pretend as if they already know everything about themselves. To them, they know who they are and why they are here. This misconception is what leads to babies having babies, babies catching felony cases, and babies getting hit with 6 of the 17 shots fired in their direction by another baby.

Tank had been in the streets for a long time though. He knew that in order to stay on top he had to accept the fact that he could be p[played. If he felt like nobody could get over on him, it would be impossible for him to spot the back-stab. To Tank, anybody could be juiced. Even a dope fiend could juice a hustler. He wasn't happy about it, but he accepted it. And until he got some solid answers, Layla could no longer be trusted.

"Let's go." Tank instructed LaQuisha while rising to his feet. He needed those answers as soon as possible.

LaQuisha knew that now wasn't the time to argue so she just quietly obeyed. Tank reached into his pocket, pulled out a stack of hundred-dollar bills, peeled off 7 of them, and dropped the cash on the table.

Each one of their plates cost $120, the wine that Tank had ordered cost $300 per bottle, and the rest of the money was left as a tip. Their waitress earned that with her skin color and good looks. Tank was a sucker for a dark-skinned Black Queen and the Gabrielle Union look alike that smiled at him and his date all night was a nice piece of eye candy to compliment his meal. Plus, he might want to fuck her some day in the future and a $100-plus tip was a sure-fire method of staining lil mama's brain. She worked in an environment where all of her customers were caked up, but Tank was willing to bet that the rich white men that frequented the restaurant were more inclined to cater to the big breasted, bird brained, blonds. A man of his caliber was rare around there. How could she possibly forget him?

Tank strode through the eatery with LaQuisha right on his heels. He was a man on a mission. Making another phone call to Layla's hotel room wouldn't do his concerns proper justice. The two of them needed to have a face to face conversation. She was withholding too much information. He didn't like that.

Of course he understood that the fact that she had a child wasn't need to know info at first, but if this Alize girl was privy to information that could result in a news broadcast that could aid a criminal investigation, he needed to know about her because his personal interests were now compromised.

Tank made his way towards the exit with only one thing on his mind. 'Getting to the bottom of Ms. Antoinette Halls anonymous phone call and live news update.'

He was so caught up in getting out of Chez Jacques that he almost walked right passed and associate of his. Really, if the man wouldn't have spoken up, he would've passed him by.

"Tony." The 58-year-old Iranian man called out as Tank approached his table. "Tony Quentin. I didn't know that you were in here."

Tank stopped when he heard his real name recited and looked down. Upon recognizing the face, he instantly changed his own expression.

Forcing a smile that he really wasn't feeling at that particular moment, he extended his right hand.

"Doctor." He said. "How have you been?"

"Oh. Same thing different day I suppose."

Tank scanned over the pretty young thing

sitting across from the Doctor. He had to give him credit. The Doc always kept a bad bitch on his arm. His latest conquest seemed to be Puerto Rican. She was a high yellow female with exotic features and full Angelina Jolie lips. Tank couldn't really tell because she was sitting down but he guessed she was thick. Doc liked them thick.

The Doctor noticed Tank admiring his beauty and smiled even bigger. What good was money if you couldn't afford a woman that a poor man couldn't have? Gorgeous women were like the accessory for successful men.

"Where are my manners?" Doc asked. "Tony, this is Ashanti. Ashanti, this is my good friend Tony Quinten."

"How do you do, Tony?" Ashanti greeted politely.

"Please." Tank said, bowing his head. "Tony is just so formal. Everybody calls me Tank."

Ashanti shivered on the inside. A big black guy named Tank. He must can roll a girl over in the bedroom.

Grinning shyly, Ashanti responded, "O.K… Tank."

"Ummm." LaQuisha interjected with a whole lot of attitude. "And you can just call me his giiirlfriend."

She was not feeling this overseas ass broad flirting with her man right in her face.

Ashanti noticed the neck twisting black girl about to go off and she retreated. She wiped the smile right off of her own face.

"Feisty." Doc said still grinning.

Tank looked at LaQuisha and put his arm around her neck. Just that quick he was reminded of why he loved his Sistah's. They were gangsta. Just like him. He kissed LaQuisha's temple. Tank knew that in order to keep this from coming up later, he had to show LaQuisha some type of affection in front of Ashanti.

"She cool." Tank told them. "Baby just love her some tank."

"Well." Doc said. "Aren't you going to properly introduce us? I can't very well call her girlfriend the next time I see you two together."

"Oh yeah. My bad. Doc, this is LaQuisha. LaQuisha, this is one of my people from the other side, Dr. Masul Abu-Kahr."

Tank pointed at him.

"This man right here is a good dude, baby. If I call him, and I'm in a bind, he gone take care of me. Real talk. I just gotta take care of him in return. It may cost me a little, it may cost me a lot, but it's definitely gone cost me."

"Now Tony." Dr. Abu-Kahr said. "Paying for services rendered is all a part of doing business. You know that."

"Indeed, I do."

Layla and Alize flashed across Tank's brain. He was wasting time. He needed to get to that room before Layla dipped off.

"And on that note," Tank said, preparing to end the conversation. "We have to run. Me and LaQuisha have another engagement we need to attend to. How about I come by your house tomorrow some time and we can discuss what we need to discuss in private?"

Dr. Abu-Kahr sipped his wine.

"I'll see you then, Tony." He said.

With that, Tank and LaQuisha left their table, exited the restaurant, and climbed into Tanks' all black Chrysler 300. His 300 was all factory. He had left it exactly how he bought it off the lot. Within minutes of pulling out of the Chez Jacques parking lot, Tank and LaQuisha were cruising down the highway headed towards the Marriott hotel.

"You know I liked that huh?" Tank asked out of nowhere.

LaQuisha was staring out the window. They hadn't spoken since they got in the car. She assumed that whatever was bothering him was still on his mind. With the type of business Tank was in, LaQuisha knew that it was pointless to try and keep up with his mood swings and whatnot. The streets were stressful as hell.

"Liked what?" she asked.

"How you checked that hoe back there." He answered. "Watching a stiff bitch be a stiff bitch while still remaining a lady gets my dick hard."

LaQuisha felt her pussy quiver when he mentioned his dick. She absolutely loved his dick.

She playfully smacked her lips.

"Yo dick ain't get hard nigga. Quit lyin'."

"Lyin'?! Ain't nobody lyin'. As a matter of fact, my shit still rocked up right now."

LaQuisha glanced down at the dick print in his slacks. He wasn't bullshitting. She could clearly see a bulge. And it was twitching.

"What you gone do with that?" she asked seductively. Her mind was already in the gutter and there was no coming back.

"The question ain't what I'm gone do with it. The question is what are 'YOU' gone do with it."

LaQuisha knew what he meant. Tank loved to get his dick sucked while he was driving. That was a good thing though because she loved sucking his dick while he was driving.

She hesitated for a moment to tease him.

179

"You bet not wreck this mothafucka." She said. "Cause if I die, I'm gone come back and haunt yo lil nasty ass."

Tank eased the back of his seat down a little while LaQuisha went to work on his belt, button, zipper, and boxers.

"Mmmm." He moaned as she took him into her mouth and slowly started bobbing her head. "Yeeeah baby."

LaQuisha took her time and enjoyed her dessert. Tank's soft moans and gentle hands rubbing her head, neck, and shoulders was like encouragement to do a real good job. Her mother had always told her that the things she wouldn't do for her man another woman would. So LaQuisha didn't have any limits when it came to sex. Probably one of the only things she could say she hadn't tried was anal sex. The horror stories she had heard about how painful the first time was is what kept her from experimenting with that one. Everything that she did try though, she worked hard at perfecting. Her mother had also told her that if she couldn't perform a particular sex act very well, another woman could... and would. Those words of wisdom from the only woman LaQuisha respected 'AND' feared had her like an army recruit. She was trying to be all that she could be.

LaQuisha rose up until just the head of Tank's tool was in her mouth. Then she held that position while her tongue swirled around his flesh stimulating all of the various nerves that lived just beneath the skin.

Miniature lightning bolts of pleasure struck Tank from head to toe. He tilted his head back and embraced the warmth of LaQuisha's lips. She was one of the best he had ever had.

Giving her man head like a pro, LaQuisha tickled his tip a little while longer and then suddenly swallowed his every inch.

Tank flinched.

"Oh shit." He cursed. He could actually feel his dick brush past her tonsils before she pulled back up.

LaQuisha increased speeds. Working her neck oh so wonderfully, she slurped up and town Tank's thick black dick faster and faster.

Tank's mouth hung open slightly. He struggled to maintain his composure but LaQuisha wouldn't let him.

She released his pipe from the grip of her mouth and quickly wrapped her hand around his shaft.

Jacking him off, she looked up and asked in an extremely sultry voice, "You like that shit baby? You like how mama work that tongue for you?"

Tank could barely respond.

"Hell yeah." He moaned, fighting the urge to pull over at the next exit and take her right there in the car. "Hell fuck yeah."

LaQuisha smirked with satisfaction.

"I know you like it nigga." She told him cockily. "I got skiiills."

And with that, LaQuisha inhaled his dick once more and went back to work.

"HA! HA! HA!" Melissa burst out laughing, dragging all 5 of the Valley Park Girls from the hot and heated moment in LaQuisha's story and bringing them back to the inside of the candy red Cadillac Escalade.

"You crazy then a mothafucka, 'Quisha." Melissa said through her giggles. "You actually told dude that you know you got skills?"

LaQuisha came to a stop at the red light and turned around to face her home girl.

"Why not?" she asked smiling. "I got one of the meanness mouthpieces around this bitch., I ain't ashamed of it. I'm proud of it. 'Cause when it's all said and done, that's gone be one of those things that keep my man from creeping."

"Oouu! Oouu! Oouu!" Krystal said, pointing at LaQuisha from the back. "She ain't lyin' neither. I can't count the number of times a boy done came to me asking me to suck his dick because his girlfriend either won't do it or don't know how to do it."

Ming was shocked.

"You mean to tell me that random men, who are already committed to what their women think is a monogamous relationship, approach you with request for oral sex just because you are more experienced than their woman?"

Krystal looked at her like she was joking.

"Are you serious?" she asked. "Girl, I can't even count the number of times a nigga done came at me like that."

Ming thought about that for a few seconds. She was one of those women who didn't know the first thing about satisfying a man orally. Her future husband might sneak around too.

"So, what did you do?" Ming asked. "I mean, when they asked you for oral. What did you tell them?"

LaQuisha pulled off when the light turned green and jumped in the conversation.

"What did she tell 'em?!" LaQuisha asked. "She couldn't tell 'em shit. Her lil freaky ass was too busy sucking they dick like they asked her too."

Everybody but Ming almost died laughing.

Even Krystal couldn't hold it in.

Krystal shrugged. "I ain't do the ugly ones." She said, as if that somehow made it better. "Only the cute ones."

Ming's jaw dropped. She was appalled. Not at the fact that Krystal gave them head. Krystal was her homegirl, but Krystal was a slut. She was somewhat mortified by the idea of her future husband disrespecting the sanctity of their marriage vows for a girl like Krystal. The good girls always got brushed aside for the loose ones.

LaQuisha." Ming said, with a serious expression on her face. "I need you to teach me how to give a man oral sex, so he won't cheat on me with a girl like Krystal."

The entire S.U.V. fell silent.

"WHAT?!" they all asked.

"Awww hell." Melissa said, rolling her eyes. "Ming done got too high ya'll. She trippin'."

Ming turned around and frowned. She was indeed high then a bitch, but she felt like she was thinking rationally.

"I am not tripping." She said. "I listen to ya'll tell these types of stories all of the time. And on a lot of occasions ya'll tell stories of being with men who are already taken. Even married men. I don't want to be that blind housewife who doesn't know how to keep her husband happy. I want to have skiiills too."

Melissa started to debate but LaQuisha cut her off.

"Ya'll let her make it." She instructed them. "To be honest, I feel where my lil home girl is coming from. Can't nah bitch in this truck tell me they don't wanna be all they man want and need. I know I do. My mama raised me up like that."

She turned to Ming. "Don't worry 'bout it girl." She reassured her. "We gone chop it up about that. You know I got you."

"O.K." Alize said, speaking up. "Now that we got all of that taken care of, can we PLEEEASE get back to the story?"

"Oh yeah." LaQuisha said. "The story. My bad. Where was I?'

"You just told Tank that you a microphone wrecka." Melissa told her grinning at the memory.

"Yeah, yeah, yeah." LaQuisha remembered. "I got Skiiills. Okaaay?"

LaQuisha once again used her words to transport them all from the Escalade to the Chrysler 300...

LaQuisha smirked with satisfaction.

"I know you like it nigga." She told him cockily. "I got skiiills." And with that, LaQuisha inhaled his dick once more and went back to work.

In a very breathy voice, Tank moaned, "Ahhh."

Suddenly becoming caught up in the ecstasy produced and delivered by LaQuisha's mouth, Tank grabbed a handful of her hair and guided her slowly and gently at her task of servicing him.

The sensations had gotten to be too much. Tanks eyes closed in reaction to the waves of euphoria that were overtaking him.

While LaQuisha swerved and swallowed, Tank allowed the Chrysler to slowly swerve towards the vehicle in the next lane over. The driver of the other vehicle glanced to his right and saw a black man with his head cocked all the way back and his mouth wide open easing into his lane.

Tank had just begun to feel the pre-tremors of his bowel eruption when he heard a horn blast.

"HOOONK!!!"

His eyes shot open and LaQuisha's head shot up.

"Fuck!" Tank cursed, jerking the wheel hard to the right trying to avoid a collision on the highway.

LaQuisha's heart skipped a beat. The tires squealed and the car rocked as Tank struggled to get it under control.

On the other side of the highway, moving in the opposite direction, an A-1 taxi driver and his blonde-haired passenger looked on as the Chrysler 300 just barely dodged a possible six-car pileup.

"Look at that!" the cab driver said, as he drove passed the near wreck on the opposite side of the medium.

Layla spun around in the back seat of the cab and squinted out the back windshield.

"Was that Tank's car?" she wondered.

She had been so engrossed in her own thoughts and problems that she hadn't been paying any attention to any of the other motorist on the road. She had a crisis that demanded her immediate attention.

Straining to see the Chrysler that was now nothing more than a dot in the background, she decided that it wasn't Tank.

"You trippin'." She told herself. "Just because Tank somehow knew you was at the Marriott doesn't mean that he's everywhere. After all, dude not God."

"What was that?" the cab driver asked.

Layla looked startled. She hadn't realized she had been thinking out loud.

"Oh… nothing." She replied. "Just talking to myself."

"Well," the cabby said, "as long as you're

185

just talking to yourself, you're good. But if you ever find yourself answering yourself, 'THEN' you have a problem."

The cab driver laughed hard at what he thought constituted as a joke. His voice sounded like he had been smoking ten packs of cigarettes a day since the day he was born.

Layla forced a smile.

"Just drive." She thought.

Once LaQuisha was sure that Tank had the vehicle under control, she slapped him on his shoulder.

"Boy!" she snapped. "What the hell was all of that?"

Tank was shook up. He couldn't allow his girl to see him shook up though. He had to play it cool. He had to remain in charge of the situation.

"Come on boo." He said in his most laid-back tone of voice. "You know daddy not gone let nothing happen to you. I got you.'

He reached out his hand to caress her cheek, but she pulled away. Tank knew what was wrong. It wasn't so much that she was angry or mad, she was just scared. The majority of people that grew up in the struggle often supplemented artificial anger for fear. Fear could get you preyed upon in the streets. Anger could get you respect.

"That's my fault, Baby." Tank apologized sincerely. "It just got good to me."

LaQuisha still didn't respond. Her life had just flashed before her eyes and she was not feeling that at all. Tank decided not to press it. He knew that she would get over it. She just needed some time to be "mad" at him. He put his flaccid penis back into his pants and focused on the road.

By the time Tank pulled into the parking lot

of the Marriott, his intentions for going there had somewhat shifted. He still had plans on confronting Layla face to face but his gut instincts were telling him that she was no longer there. During the silence of the 'post-crash LaQuisha', Tank had time to really think. More than likely, Layla was on her way to find A.B. The young hustler was her problem. If she wanted to hold up her end of the plan, she had to keep him from falling victim to the police. Unless she wanted to fall victim. In which case she was probably setting the stage to cross out everyone. Including him.

After analyzing the situation, tank came to the conclusion that it was probably best he didn't get to confront Layla. A confrontation would expose too much of his hand before he had a handle on what was going on. He almost allowed his anger to cause to act on impulse. Animals acted on impulse. Humans thought things through. Tank had too much at stake to regress to the state of a beast. He would leave that type of attitude to the killers and jackers. He was a Don in the streets. Don's called shots. He could come up with a better way to get to the bottom of things. In fact, he felt like he had the perfect weapon riding shotgun in his Chrysler with him. He already had LaQuisha. LaQuisha had access to Alize. The only hurdle was figuring out the best way to capitalize off of what he had to work with. That shouldn't be hard. Tank was a military minded by nature. Planning was his thang.

Tank looked up at the huge blue and white hotel building as her pulled into a parking space in front of the office.

"In the meantime," he thought. "Why let a perfectly good trip to the most luxurious hotel in town go to waste?"

Tank left the car running and climbed out.

"I'll be right back baby." He said, shutting the door and disappearing through the office doors. LaQuisha stared mesmerized at the facility. The Marriott was the size of an apartment complex. It boasted well over 1,000 rooms. Naturally some of the rooms were better than others but all of them were top notch. LaQuisha had fucked with niggas with money before but none of them had ever took her to the Marriott. She had never been to Chez Jacques neither. Tank was introducing her to a way of life that she wasn't used to. She liked it though. She had been trying to be mad at him after he almost got them both killed but her attitude melted away as soon as she realized where they were headed. Either that or he had this Marriott visit planned from th jump. It didn't really matter to her. All she could think about was bragging about the experience to her home girls later.

LaQuisha daydreamed about what the room would look like. The image made her fidget in her seat.

"I'm gone fuck the shit out of Tank." She told herself.

Tank finished making small talk with the young white girl working the front desk, slid her $450 for the room, and casually strolled back out into the parking lot. In the short period of time it took him to walk into the office, rent the room, and walk back out, he had come up with a way to handle the situation he was in. With that little dilemma worked out in his mind he could really kick back, relax, and enjoy the rest of his evening with his girl.

The room that Tank had got was pretty close to the office, so he decided to just leave his car parked where it was at.

LaQuisha watched with anticipation as Tank walked his fine ass over to the driver's side door. He opened it, leaned in, killed the ignition, ands shut the door. Before LaQuisha knew what was happening, a silent Tank was leading her by the hand up to room number 307. She was fighting hard to contain her excitement. It wasn't easy though. The way Tank was just taking charge even though she was pretending to be mad at him was turning her on. There was nothing in the world like a strong black man.

Reaching the room they were headed to, Tank swiped the card key and pushed the door open. Then he spun LaQuisha's around, wrapped his arms around her waist and pressed his chest firmly against her back.

LaQuisha moaned softly as Tank's mouth sealed around the right side of her neck. The Unforgivable perfume that she was wearing found its way into her man's nostrils. The scent was like an aphrodisiac.

The two of them slowly entered the hotel room connected at the waist like Siamese twins. Tank wanted the cushions of LaQuisha's ass to feel the stiffness of his arousal.

Once inside, he kicked the door closed with the back of his shoe and it automatically locked. LaQuisha could barely inventory the room because of the pleasure that Tank was producing. Her eyes wouldn't stay opened and her mind couldn't focus on anything other than the tsunami in her thong. All she noticed was a huge bed with red and black blankets and pillows. A huge big screen T.V. A set of sliding glass doors, a desk, table, and a couple of chairs. Tank kept his lips wrapped around her neck

While he used his hands to pull up her dress. He only stopped kissing, sucking, and licking long enough to pull the dress up and over her head. He kissed her a few more times then stood back to look over his beauty.

Chocolate smooth skin.

Video girl fat ass.

Red bra and thong set.

Tank licked his lips and started to undress. LaQuisha turned around to watch. She never got tired of seeing Tanks body. He had done a few years in the pen a while ago, but he never lost the physique he had acquired while he was there.

Tank took off his jacket and dress shirt. LaQuisha stared hungrily at his jet black, 6 ft. frame. His tattoo covered torso made him look so dangerous it was erotic. A man like that could hurt her. He could hurt her in so many different ways.

Her pussy juice trickled down her leg leaving a streak of her sweet tasting liquid shining on her inner thigh. She rubbed her legs together and stimulated her clit.

Tank tossed his shirt to the side and started on his pants. LaQuisha played with her breast. She knew what to expect. Her man was packing a nice amount of meat. And he knew exactly how to work what God had blessed him with.,

Not wasting any time, Tank pulled down his boxers along with his pants. His thick tool was fully erect. It pointed ominously at LaQuisha's dripping wet vagina as if it was threatening to expand her walls passed the point of pleasure and reduce her experience to pure pain. She tore off her under garments and welcomed the challenge.

The two of them stood naked for a moment embracing each other with lustful eyes. Tank was quite possibly the epitome of male perfection and LaQuisha was so curvy, thick, pretty, and oozing with sexuality that she was Tanks perfect female counterpart.

Like statues of chocolate flesh. They both stood glossed over with flawless King and Queen appearances. Etched out from an enormous priceless black diamond and black pearl.

Tank's chiseled pecs and LaQuisha's ample breast somehow rose and fell in unison. The two of them were indeed on the same wavelength.

His expression said, "I want you!"

Her body said, "Come get me!"

His brain obeyed and sent the signal to his limbs. "Move!"

Tank eliminated the gap between them and embraced his equal. LaQuisha more than welcomed his body heat.

Their lips connected. Their tongues danced the forbidden dance. Strong hands explored a slender back and came to rest on the hills that sat just below the waist. The hills were soft. Soft as Charmin. Tanks fingers sunk into the hills. He gripped them tightly, and then released. He gripped them tightly, and then released.

LaQuisha stood on her tip toes every time the fingers grabbed. It felt so good to be stimulated in several places at once.

Lips were kissed. Tongues were licked. Ass cheeks were squeezed. And pussy lips were pressed up against by an anaconda.

Tank lifted LaQuisha up in the air. She wrapped her legs around him. They continued to kiss aggressively as Tank carried her over to the bed.

He laid her down gently. She crawled into a

comfortable position in the middle of the king-sized bed and prepared to be mounted.

Tank waved his index finger from side to side. It wasn't time yet for penetration. He wanted to take his beautiful companion to a level he had never taken her before. He wanted to express how he felt with action.

The strong hands wrapped around LaQuisha's ankles and tugged her back to the edge of the bed. When her butt made it to the edge, he lifted her legs straight up in the air and dropped to his knees.

LaQuisha couldn't believe it. She had sucked his dick a lot of times, but he had never ate her out. Her legs twitched before she even felt the wetness of his tongue.

Tank was at eye level with LaQuisha's delicacy. The aroma that emitted from her hot, wet, tight love box was sweet and inviting. He had never been the type of man to just lick on every woman he came across, but LaQuisha was sort of special to him. She deserved the all-out treatment.

Goosebumps skated across LaQuisha's body as Tank's warm breath blew across her garden. She could feel his fingers easing her lower lips apart.

Tank gazed at the pink flesh and licked his lips. He wanted them nice and wet. Then he leaned in and began to French kiss LaQuisha's goodies. He could hear her moan as his tongue probed her depths. The ridges of his tongue felt good to her.

"Mmmm." She cooed.

Tank had been holding out on her. He knew more about eating pussy than he let on. LaQuisha was loving his technique.

Tank's tongue slid in and out of her hole rapidly until LaQuisha instinctively reached down and tugged at his ears. Holding her lips open, Tank started licking up and down the length of LaQuisha's wetness. He went from the hole to the pearl tongue and from the pearl tongue to the hole. He made sure to lay his tongue down flat so he could hit a wider range of flesh.

Tank licked and kissed, LaQuisha moaned and cooed. The oral satisfaction went on for almost an hour. He was like an animal. He refused to quit.

LaQuisha tried to run from the pleasure. Tank pursued her.

She quivered, trembled and backpedaled. Tank crawled into the bed and continued with his mission. He was like an expert. LaQuisha found herself moaning louder and louder.

"Oh Tank!" she hollered. "Shit baby!"

Her pussy was like a blank canvas that Tank was using to paint his masterpiece of ecstasy upon. The brush strokes of his tongue were priceless. A rainbow of emotions arched across LaQuisha's body. The flood between her legs was reminiscent of the ancient flood that theologians say covered the entire earth back in Noah's day.

LaQuisha could feel herself reaching the point of no return. Deep within her and eruption was brewing. An eruption she could sense would be more powerful than all the others.

She began grinding her hips into his face. He didn't care. His mouth, nose, chin, and neck were all coated with LaQuisha's juices. Tank wanted more than her juices though. Tank wanted her orgasm.

LaQuisha's body rocked.

He was about to get his wish.

Her eyes rolled to the back of her head. Her back arched and she started to convulse.

"Ooohhh... ooohhh...OOOHHH!!!" she screamed in passion as her release gushed forth and covered her lovers face.

Surprisingly he didn't move. He continued to do his job until she was finished. Tank liked the way her satisfaction tasted.

LaQuisha was out of breath. She laid there, stretched out, slowly wiggling her body on the bed. The aftershocks of orgasm forbidding her from being still.

Tank sat up and looked down at his work. He was proud of himself.

Gripping his still rock-hard manhood, Tank licked her cum from off of his lips.

"My turn." He whispered, climbing on top of a writhing in euphoria LaQuisha.

Her lips parted as his girth penetrated her. SSSRRREECCHHH!!!

"Fuck!" LaQuisha yelled, as she abandoned her memory and slammed on the brakes of the Cadillac Escalade.

All of the girls screamed as they just barely avoided ramming into the back of the red Ford Explorer that swerved in front of them and then just stopped.

None of them were wearing a seatbelt so the near collision thrashed them all about. Once the truck was at a complete stop, Melissa grunted as she adjusted in her seat.

"Is everybody alright?" LaQuisha asked, not believing that she almost had a wreck while telling a story in which she also almost had a wreck.

Melissa clutched her pregnant belly and gritted her teeth.

"My... my baby." She groaned. "I need to go to the hospital."

Alize and Krystal started rubbing on Melissa's back.

"Oh my God." Ming called out looking at her friend. She could tell from Melissa's expression that something was wrong.

"Uuuugghh!" Melissa moaned. "It hurts. It... it hurts so bad."

"Don't worry." LaQuisha instructed her. "We ain't that far from the Utopian Center Hospital. Ya'll hold her down."

Alize hugged Melissa as she curled up clutching her stomach. Everything had switched up on them so fast. One minute they were riding around getting fucked up and trading fuck tales, then, out of nowhere, they were caught up in a medical emergency.

"We got her." Alize told LaQuisha. "Just hurry up and get to the hospital!"

LaQuisha nodded her head as she turned back around in her seat. What she saw when she looked out the windshield scared her more than the emergency concerning her pregnant friend.

Three black men had climbed out of the red Ford Explorer that she had almost hit. One of three men was short and slim. He was wearing a pair of black jeans with an ice white tee. One of the other men was a little taller. He was wearing a pair of Gucci shades, a golden silk shirt, and a matching pair of golden slacks. The third man looked like an ugly basketball player with his 6'6 frame, throwback Houston Rockets jersey, and red Dickies shorts on.

All of the three men had their own unique style but there was one thing they all had in common.

Guns!

Well, they had two things in common.

Guns, and a look on their faces that said they meant business.

"LaQuisha!" Ming called out. She had no idea what was going on. All she knew was that she wished LaQuisha would handle it.

Krystal and Alize looked up from comforting Melissa to see what had Ming so spooked.

"What the…" Alize muttered.

The short man with the white tee stood in front of the Escalade with the barrel of a shotgun pointed straight in LaQuisha's direction. It was obvious that if she attempted to drive off, the attempt would be the last thing she would ever do on this side of the grave.

LaQuisha and Ming raised their hands in the air and glanced at each other. Despair was etched across both of their faces.

The basketball player went to the side of the truck and opened up the door next to Alize. The one with the Gucci shades opened LaQuisha's door.

"Look." LaQuisha pleaded. "I'm sorry O.K. It was an accident. I didn't mean to…"

"SHUT-UP!" Gucci shades ordered her. "Just tell me where the bud at!"

"Bud? What Bud?" LaQuisha asked confused. "All we got is like two ounces." Her mind raced. They were robbing them. She didn't have any weed. She did have money though. Yeah. The five grand.

"I got some money." She offered. "You want the money?"

LaQuisha leaned over to grab her purse from off the floorboard in between her and Ming.

"BITCH!" Gucci shades shouted. "What the

fuck you doin'?"

He reached inside of the vehicle and grabbed LaQuisha with his left hand. Then he swung his pistol with his right hand and struck her on the side of her head.

"Ooowww!" LaQuisha cried out as the blow registered on her pain receptors.

"Hey!" Alize shouted. "You didn't have to do that!"

"What?" the basketball player asked. "Yo lil tough ass gone get it next if you speak up on my homeboy business again."

He aimed his weapon at Alize's head. She quickly came to her senses. They were at the mercy of the armed men.

"Like I said hoe." Gucci shades growled. "Don't play no mothafuckin' games with me. I know who this truck fa'. This that faggot ass nigga Tank shit. That hoe keeps weed everywhere."

He pressed the pistol up against LaQuisha's temple. She cringed as the cold steel chilled her skin. Her level of fear was so high that all she could do was close her eyes and start to cry. When they found out that she didn't have any of Tank's weed, they would probably kill all of therm.

"I... I don't know where Tank keeps his shit at." She whimpered. "He just let me drive the truck for the day so I could take my girls out. I swear!"

Gucci shades and basketball player exchanged glances. There was no way they were about to leave empty handed.

"Uuunngghh!" Melissa moaned. She was in so much pain that she wasn't even paying attention to the gun toting thugs demanding weed that they didn't have. "I re... I re... I really... need... to get... to the hospital." She mumbled through the burst of excruciating and intense pain.

Alize leaned in close to Melissa's ear and used her words to comfort her.

"It's o.k. girl." She assured her. "We gone get you to the hospital. I'm not going to let anything happen to you or your baby. Do you hear me?"

Alize rubbed her back a few times then turned back towards the man with the gun.

"You gotta let us get to a hospital." Alize pleaded. "She's pregnant and something is wrong with the baby."

Basketball player looked Melissa over. Then, in an extremely cold tone of voice, he said, "Shiiit. That bitch baby ain't mine, so why should I give a fuck about her or it?"

Alize felt anger surge through her body at the man's evil remark.

"You... you... you heartless son of a bitch!" she spat out.

That did it. The man had had enough. He curled his lips up into a snarl and reached in to grab Alize like the other man had grabbed LaQuisha.

She struggled against his grip, but he was too strong for her to break free.

BAM! BAM! BAM! BAM!

Alize screamed bloody murder as the man proceeded to severely pistol whip her.

"Leave her alone!" Ming yelled. "Please! Just leave her alone!"

Alize's friends were forced to watch helplessly as her beautiful complexion became stained with her own blood.

They were also forced to sit idly by as the three gunmen kidnapped all five of them and hijacked Tank's Cadillac Escalade.

The man with the Gucci shades said that

they better pray Tank was willing to drop out in order to ensure the safe return of his girlfriend and vehicle. If not, they were going to just murder them all on G.P. and cut their losses.

Tank seemed like the perfect boyfriend to LaQuisha. He didn't have any noticeable flaws. But now that one flaw did come up, it was a gigantic one. His actions in the streets had fallen back on her. And not just her, her and her friends.

LaQuisha hated to admit it, but she wasn't 100% sure that Tank was willing to give up whatever to get her back in one piece. There was a real good chance that if they didn't do something quick, this little situation was going to result in bullet holes and a 30-minute slot on the popular T.V. show, Unsolved Mysteries.

CHAPTER TEN

At approximately 8:00am, on a mildly chilly Monday morning, Tank was pulling up to a lavishly designed $550,000 red brick home on the North side of Houston, Tx. He was completely oblivious to the fact that just an hour and a half away in his hometown of Dickinson, Tx., three armed gunmen were following his woman and her home girls around waiting for the perfect opportunity to ambush them.

Tank eased the Chrysler 300 into the driveway and parked it behind a fully loaded Maybach Benz.

Killing the ignition, he nodded his head slightly at the Doctors test in vehicles. He had to give Dr. Abu-Kahr his credit. The man really knew how to enjoy his money. He carried himself with style.

When it came down to business, Dr. Abu-Kahr's record was impeccable. Never once did he try to fuck over Tank, and never once did he fail to do what he was called upon to do. The Doctor was one of the best assets that Tank possessed. His cost was through the roof though. He knew that he was Tank's only connection to the specialized services that he was willing to provide. It was all about supply and demand.

Really, the thing he loved about the Doctor was also the thing he couldn't trust. Dr. Abu-Kahr would do anything if the price was right. Tank needed a man like that at his disposal. The only problem was that the Doctor wasn't an official member of Tank's team. He held no exclusive rights to the Doctors services. That meant that at any given time, the Doctor could be called upon to aid one of Tank's enemies. And Tank knew that if the price was right, Dr. Abu-Kahr would swiftly switch sides. The man was loyal only to himself. Men like that were dangerous.

Tank stepped out of the car with a black briefcase in his hand. The winter air blew across the freshly manicured lawn and caused Tanks long leather coat to waft in the breeze. Tank closed his coat with his free hand and looked from the Benz to the briefcase he was carrying.

"I probably paid for that pretty mothafucka." He mumbled.

Tank stood there for a moment looking like a freelance detective in his leather coat that hung to his ankles, black slacks, and black snakeskin shoes. He quietly reflected on how he started doing business with Dr. Abu-Kahr when he was still just a teenager. Back before he was making any real noise in the streets. Back when his survival depended on how hard he could hustle. He understood no rules and embraced absolutely no morals. All he wanted to do was eat. By any and all means. It didn't matter if he had to hustle, steal, or kill.

Tank had first met Dr. Abu-Kahr when he was just 13 years old. The reason he met him was somewhat because of his older brother, Tyler. Tyler had been stabbed to death during a prison riot when Tank was just 16. But if it was one thing Tyler was remembered for, it was his way with the ladies.

Tyler was a certified, bonafied, stamped and sealed P.I.M.P. He use to always try and teach Tank how to follow in his footsteps, but Tank didn't have the patience to break a bitch. At the time , he would much rather rob a prostitute than manage one.

Tyler was about 14 years older than Tank, so he understood his mind state. After all, he was a young nigga with nothing to lose before. He knew that Tank would come around eventually. Unfortunately, Tyler got caught up and sentenced to 10 years in prison before he could successfully mold his younger brother. And even though he only had a dime, Tank's big brother never made it home.

For a while Tank tried to coach his brother's stable after he went to the pen. But you could imagine how a young cat would act with 8 different sluts at his disposal. He was 12 years old when Tyler got popped. And at 12 years old he lost his virginity. Not to a girlfriend from school, but to one of his brother's workers.

Tyler tried to keep Tank from fucking. He always said that once Tank fell up in some pussy, his personality would make him crazy behind it.

And guess what.

Tyler was right.

After Tank got his first taste of some pink, it was over. He forgot all about the hustle. He might as well have been one of the Johns. Instead of collecting money from the hoes, Tank just wanted pussy and head. He allowed his brothers workers to keep 100% of their earnings in exchange for sexual favors. Tank was a street nigga at a young age but there wasn't a pimp bone in his body. Within months of his brother's arrest, Tank had broken every single rule, code, and ordinance found in the Pimp's handbook. Not only did he take his foot off of the hoe's necks, he started trying to gal one of them.

Tank fell weak for one of his brother's younger hoes. Mesmerized by the tight pussy and deep throat, tank found himself having unprotected sex with her, cumming inside of her daily, and doing everything in his power to become the only man she was sleeping with.

The girl was just a few years older than Tank though. Prostitution was paying good, so she had no plans on leaving the business alone.

Eventually the girl got pregnant. So, Tank, believing that the baby was his, wrote a letter to his Big Bro bragging that he was soon going to be a father.

Tank thought that Tyler was going to be happy for him but that wasn't the case. Tyler wrote him back talking mad shit. He opened tanks eyes up to the reality that the baby wasn't his. And even if it was, a whore was not the type of female he should have a baby with.

Very reluctantly, Tank decided to follow his brother's advice. He had grown up without a father, so his big brother was the only strong male role model in his life. Even though Tank really wanted to be a father, he respected Tyler's advice. Big Bro had never led him wrong so far.

Following Tyler's instructions, Tank convinced the girl to go see an abortion doctor with him. It wasn't hard though. She didn't want a baby. She was too busy running the streets to raise a child.

As fate would have it, Tyler sent the young Tank to none other than Dr. Masul Abu-Kahr. Tyler knew firsthand how crooked Abu-Kahr was. See, technically, when a female under the age of 18 tries to get an abortion, a signature from a legal guardian is required. For the right price though, Dr. Abu-Kahr would overlook that.

Tyler had taken plenty of females to see the Doctor while he was on the streets. He didn't need pregnant women on his team. Having a child sometimes opened a woman's eyes to the negative lifestyle Tyler had them caught up in. He did not want any of his hoes trying to get their lives right for the sake of their baby.

Tyler even took some females to see the Doctor whether they wanted to have the baby or not. If they actually wanted to carry the child to term, he would lace the Doctor up ahead of time. Then he would pretend to be taking them to see a specialist for a routine check-up.

By the third visit to Dr. Abu-Kahr, the woman would all mysteriously have an unexplainable miscarriage.

"Too much stress." Is all the Doctor would say.

In those rare instances where the Doctor was called upon to abort a child that the mother actually wanted, his price tag went through the roof.

When Tank approached the Doctor, he used Tyler's name and he was good. Dr. Abu-Kahr even gave him a discount price. $300. Tank took the girl up to his office, paid the money, and that was that. He was through with the idea of being a father, through with the girl, and through with the pimping business as a whole.

Tank ran all 8 workers off and bought him a sack of rocks. He quickly traded in crack for marijuana, but he remained a hustler. He remained a loyal client of Dr. Abu-Kahr's over the years too. If he wasn't taking a female to him to get an abortion, he was tricking the female into going to see him. When the Doctor stopped performing abortions, Tank used him for prescriptions. He had access to every kind of pill on the market. Tank could've changed his name to Walgreens or CVS Pharmacy if he wanted to.

Once Tank started seeing some real money, the Doctor transformed into a real lethal connection. He once provided Tank with some shit that he used to murk one of his enemies and leave no evidence of foul play behind.

The lady he killed was a heroine junky named Bunny. That made the murder method of injection the perfect way to do her. The official autopsy labeled the cause of death as an overdose.

Tank returned from his stroll down memory lane and turned away from the luxury vehicle and faced the luxury domicile.

Tank knew that he had a nice home, but the Doc's shit was like whoa! It was Lifestyles of the Rich and Famous nice. Three car garage with stalls for his money green 2008 Lincoln Navigator, his yellow supercharged Lamborghini, and his Benz. The same Benz that was parked in the driveway.

Doc's home was 3 stories high with a built-in handicap elevator on the inside of it. The bushes that lined the two acres his home sat on had a theme. They were all trimmed and manicured to resemble Chinese Samurai Warriors. Doc often said that they were meant to ward off evil and protect him from wicked men's devilish intentions. But just in case the Samurai didn't do the trick, Doc had a state-of-the-art security system that was so live he gets alerted to visitors' presence before they even reach the house.

Strategically placed in several of the Samurai Warrior bushes are video cameras that send a live feed to monitors inside of the Doctors house 24 hours a day. The electronics and wires run from the bushes to the house via underground pipelines that were put in place for that specific reason. No one knew about the fact that a few of the

Samurai had functioning eyes unless Dr. Abu-Kahr told them. And as you can imagine Dr. Abu-Kahr told no one. In his mind, telling his secret would defeat the purpose of having them in pace.

Tank checked his Cardiae wristwatch. He already knew that it was around 8:00am in the morning, he just wanted to gaze upon the diamonds that accentuated his watches face. It was an expensive watch, but it could've been better.

He made his way up to the front door thinking of ways to expand his empire. Every time he made a trip out to Dr. Abu-Kahr's home it had the exact same effect on him. Seeing how large the Doctor was living made him want to step his game up. If he only hung out in the hood all day, he would never be motivated to go and get it. He would get comfortable around people he had more money than. If he went around people with more money than him, his hustler's instincts would kick in. The concept was basic human nature. It was mankind's insatiable desire for dominance, and his/her mastery over his motor skills, that catapulted him to the top of the food chain. Now, that same internal longing to be 'better than' is what drives mankind to obtain that which is unobtainable to another human.

Tank stood in front of the huge mahogany doors and waited. The one camera that the Doctor did tell him about was situated in one of the two stone lions that sat, mouths wide open, on either side of the 12x8 ft. cherry wood porch.

He wasn't sure which one was Abu-Kahr's third eye, but he did know that the Doctor always knew when he was there. Tank never had to knock, call, or ring the doorbell. All he had to do was show up at the predetermined time.

Just as Tank had suspected, Abu-Kahr was reclining back in the area of his home that he liked to call the command center, watching every single move his guest was making. He had done so much business with Tank in the past that his eyes lit up when he saw him step out of the car with his briefcase.

Black briefcase equaled stacks of green cash.

Stacks of green cash equaled a smile on the Doctors face.

A smile on the Doctors face equaled entrance to his sanctuary.

As the huge doors slowly opened inward, Tanks jaw almost hit the floor. Standing on the other side was a grinning seductively Ashanti. Tank immediately recognized the beautiful Puerto Rican from the night before.

The only thing different about her was her clothes. Last night she was decked out elegantly. Today, she was totally nude.

"Tony Quentin." She greeted him with her sexy little accent. "Or should I say, Tank?"

Ashanti looked him up and down as she said his name.

"Masul has been expecting you. Come on in."

Tank found himself at a complete loss for words. He was so stunned by how Ashanti answered the door that all he could do was stare lustfully at her ass as he followed her in.

The Doctors living room was exotic. But before you reached it you had to pass through the lobby. He called the area between the door and the living room the lobby because he often invited some of his patients to his house. The under the table jobs all came there.

The lobby was huge itself. Immediately after crossing the threshold of the front door, any visitors to the Doctor's humble abode found themselves feeling like Jesus Christ. The light blue marble tiles that covered the floor reminded Tank of the story about Jesus walking on water. Especially how there were winding white streaks scattered throughout the pattern. The white looked like the reflection of shape shifting clouds floating freely across a majestic sky.

Tank couldn't help but to take light and easy steps. He felt as if, if he took his eyes off of Ashanti's curves like Peter took his eyes off of Jesus, he just might begin to sink. It's a damn good thing Ashanti was easy on the old eyes.

Ashanti led him through the lobby quickly, but he still noticed his surroundings. Off to his right, about four feet away from the wall, the Doctor had a spiral staircase that led only up to the second floor. Tank always assumed that the only way to reach the third floor was to take the elevator up. He wanted to ask but he didn't want to pry.

Over to his left was the actual waiting area. The Doctor had 3 small ash gray couches situated in the shape of a 'U'. In the center of the furniture there was a brown coffee table with a pile of magazines on it. Dr. Abu-Kahr really went out of his way to make his home feel like an office.

At least, he tried to make the lobby feel like an office. After you exited the lobby and entered the living room, the Doctors eccentric nature once again reared its head.

"You can have a seat next to the Ivory's." Ashanti said, leading Tank into and artificial rain forest.

The Doctor had plants, bushes, flowers, and butterflies everywhere. Tank probably hated this part of the house most. The temperature was set-up to keep the room humid. The green paint on the walls was special ordered to last in the vegetation friendly environment.

Tank took a seat in the chair that was made out of artificial logs. Looking around, he sat his briefcase down next to what he guessed were the Ivory's.

"I'll go get Masul." Ashanti told him. Then she sashayed out of the room.

It wasn't long before Tanks leather coat had him on the verge of sweating like a slave.

"Shit." He mumbled, sliding out of the coat. "Why couldn't I just wait in the lobby?"

Tank pulled off the leather and glanced around trying to find a place to hang it up. It didn't surprise him not to see a coat rack anywhere.

"Fuck it." He said, deciding to just lay it on the floor next to his briefcase. "A lil dirt won't hurt."

Tank sat his leather coat down and then examined the four potted plants he had been instructed to sit next too.

"Ivory's?" he thought. "This shit bet not be poison ivory's"

He looked the plants over.

"Wait a second. There's no such thing as poison ivory. It's poison Ivy. Ain't it?"

He rubbed his chin and shrugged his shoulders.

"It doesn't matter. Long as I don't touch those hoes, I'm good."

Tank didn't know much about plant life. His level of education was limited. He was raised by the streets. One thing he did possess was good observation skills. And it didn't take long for him to realize that one of the four plants were different from the other three.

While they all were pretty much the same size, color, and shape, one of them had very unique leaves. The leaves of the odd plant were green with purple tips. The purple was small but distinct. Tank stared at the odd plant and wondered why the tips of its leaves were purple. Was it dying or something? Did the plant not know that autumn was over, and it was no longer under any obligation to change color? Or maybe, just maybe, it was supposed to look like that.

"That," Dr. Abu-Kahr said, creeping up behind Tank and making him jump, "my dear friend, is Photo-habi-vegatanis. Or as I like to call it, Purple Angel of Life and Death."

Abu-Kahr moved to stand in front of Tank. He was wearing a metallic silver robe with matching slippers. Tank thought dude looked like a foreign Hugh Hefner.

"You don't know it yet," he continued, "but you'll be using that plant one day."

Grinning slyly, the Doctor took a seat in the log chair across from Tank.

"Photo-ha... hobo... vegetable?" Tank repeated, trying to pronounce the name of the plant like Abu-Kahr did.

"No, no, no." Abu-Kahr corrected. "Photo-habi-vegatanis."

"Photo-habi-vegatanis." Tank said. "What's that? Like the scientific name of it?"

Abu-Kahr chuckled.

"Oh heavens no. I made that name up myself. Between me and you, Tony, I have no idea what the scientific name of any of my little green babies is. All I know is the potential of each one."

The potential? What potential?"

Abu-Kahr reclined in his seat while a still nude Ashanti delivered two lit cigars to him and his guest.

Abu-Kahr puffed on his cigar while he waited on his Puerto Rican honey to walk back out of eyesight. Her shaven vagina had Tanks undivided attention. Abu-Kahr was no fool. He knew that his conversation could not compete with Ashanti's beauty.

Tanks eyes stayed glued to Ashanti's sexy shape until she exited the room. A completely naked goddess had a way of making a man lose focus.

"Ah-hem." Abu-Kahr cleared his throat. "As I was saying."

Tank turned back to face the Doctor feeling slightly embarrassed. Well, it wasn't his fault. Ashanti was the one walking around all free. What man… or what straight man could possibly ignore all of that nudeness?

"I am a doctor." Abu-Kahr said. "And as a doctor it is my business to understand the potential of various species of plant life."

Tank was confused.

"What does being a doctor have to do with plants? I don't really see the connection."

Abu-Kahr wasn't surprised by Tanks ignorance. They had been knowing each other for years and Abu-Kahr knew that it wasn't really his fault. After all, the man had never even been to high school. The bulk of Tanks knowledge was acquired on the streets. And the streets only taught one subject.

SURVIVAL!

"The connection, Tony, is simple. Every single pill, liquid, elixir, powder, gel, or any other substance that is used for medicinal purposes started out just like this."

He motioned at the many plants.

"Without plants," the Doctor continued. "There would be no medicine."

Tank allowed this new information to sink in. He wasn't particularly interested in plants, medicine, or the correlation between the two, but what he had just learned caused him to view the Doctors living room in a whole new light.

All these years he thought that Abu-Kahr was just a few cards shy of a full deck but now the mini rainforest made perfect sense. The Doctor was harvesting his own medicine.

Tank glanced down at the Photo-habi-vegatanis plant. The one Abu-Kahr called Purple Angel of Life and Death. He had told Tank that one day he would be using it. Tank couldn't help but wonder what its name meant and why he would someday want it.

Tank puffed his cigar. It tasted funny but he just chalked that up to the fact that it was exotic.

"And what potential does the Purple Angel have?" he asked.

Abu-Kahr smiled. He knew that Tank wouldn't be able to resist asking about his most special plant. Its name alone was intriguing enough to spark a man's curiosity.

"Ahhh." Abu-Kahr sighed. "The Purple Angel of Life and Death. Quite possibly my most exotic... and also expensive plant."

The Doctor leaned in close to Tank and changed his expression to one that fit the level of seriousness his next statement deserved.

"Just a few small drops of the sap from those leaves injected into the bloodstream can slow someone's bodily functions, heartbeat, and brain activity so significantly that the person injected will be pronounced clinically dead. And as long as there is no autopsy done, depending on the amount of sap injected, that same individual will return to normal in a matter of hours or a matter of days."

Abu-Kahr leaned back in his seat.

Tank looked from the Doctor, to the plant, and back again.

Was he serious?

He couldn't be.

A plant that could make someone clinically dead and then bring them back to life? That's that science fiction type shit. The Doctor had to be just bullshitting him to see how gullible he was.

Tank glanced down at the purple tipped leaves.

Magic sap! Yeah right.

"Hmmm." Was all Tank said in response to the Doctors story. He wasn't about to feed into that.

"That's... interesting." Tank scooped up his briefcase and dropped it on his lap. "But I think it's time we came back to planet earth and go ahead and tend to the business at hand."

Tank unlocked the case.

"I called on you with a spur of the moment request, and like always, you came through for me. I must admit though, I sort of feel like you are taxing me heavy because you did the job before we had a chance to agree on the price, but business is business."

Tank popped the briefcase open and spun it around.

"As you requested," Tank told him, "Twenty-five thousand dollars cash money."

Abu-Kahr gazed greedily at the stacks of one hundred-dollar bills. No matter how much money his eyes had seen, and his hands touched, the sight of more of it that was destined for his bank account still had the power to reduce his state of mind to that of a kid on Christmas.

"Excellent." He said to Tank while still staring at Benjamin Franklin.

Abu-Kahr reached out to accept the briefcase but the sudden sound of 50 Cents voice caused him to pause.

"Many Men. Many many many many men. Wish death on me Lord I don't cry no mo'. I don't look to the sky no mo'."

Tank recognized his 50 Cent ringtone and patted down his pants pocket looking for his cell phone. Abu-Kahr looked at him silently.

"Have mercy on me. Have mercy on my soul. Somewhere my heart turned cold..."

Tank remembered that he had his phone inside of his coat pocket and snapped his fingers.

"Oh yeah." He mumbled as he reached down and fished it out. "Who could possibly be calling me this early in the morning?"

Tank retrieved his all red sprint cellular and examined the number on the display screen.

"LaQuisha?!" Tank said in a low voice. "I thought you'd be too busy ballin' wit ya lil home girls to be getting at me this early."

He pressed the clear 'TALK' button on his phone and greeted his girlfriend.

"What it do Boo? Ya'll havin' fun?"

"Baby!" LaQuisha cried into the phone that the kidnapper had held up to the side of her face.

"Baby they got me!"

Tank frowned up with confusion.

"What did you say?" he asked. "They got you?!"

"Some niggas!" she whimpered through the tears. "They talking 'bout money, weed, and all kinds of crazy shit."

Tanks eyes got wide. He listened as the sound of a slap echoed across the phone line.

"HEEELLLPPP!" LaQuisha screamed.

"LAQUISHA!" Tank hollered.

She didn't respond. All he heard was her cries being muffled like someone was shoving something into her mouth.

"LAQUISHA!!" he screamed again. "LAQUISHA! ANSWER ME!"

Panic submersed his emotions. It didn't take a rocket scientist to figure out what was happening. Someone had kidnapped his girl.

"What's up homie?" A male voice said calmly into the phone. "Look. This how this shit is gone go. I got yo bitch and four of yo bitches potnas. Hell, I even got yo bitch ass Escalade."

The kidnapper chuckled.

"And you got money." He continued. "Money and weed. So how 'bout we make a little trade? I'll give you what I got… if you give me what you got."

"Anything." Tank said without hesitation. "Anything you want. Just don't hurt 'em."

"Awww." The kidnapper mocked. "You don't want me to hurt 'em?"

He drew his foot back and kicked LaQuisha directly in the stomach. Tank could hear her muffled groan.

"Weeelll." The kidnapper continued. "It's a

little too late for me not to hurt 'em, but I will promise you this. If you just cooperate and do exactly as I tell you too, none of these pretty… little… bitches will get killed."

Tank hit his cigar hard. His level of stress had just gone through the roof.

"O.K." he told the kidnapper, exhaling the smoke. "O.K. Just tell me what to do and it's done."

The kidnapper smiled. This was going to be a piece of cake.

"Objective one." The kidnapper said in a more square business tone. "Go to wherever your stash is at and wait on my call."

"But when will you c…"

The line went dead.

Abu-Kahr looked concerned.

"That didn't sound good my friend."

Tank's head jerked from side to side as if he could find the answer to his problems somewhere among the vegetation. Obviously, he could not.

"I gotta go." Tank said, his mind in a distant place. "Something has come up."

He quickly sat the briefcase full of cash and the cigar down, picked up his leather coat, and dashed towards the front door. Abu-Kahr was saying something to him as he ran off, but Tank wasn't listening. He was too busy thinking about LaQuisha. She was suffering because of his lifestyle. She was in danger because of him.

As Tank was blazing out of the Doctors mansion Ashanti was walking back into the living room with a huge ass smile on her face.

"Did it work?" she asked eagerly. "Did he smoke enough of it before he left?"

Abu-Kahr looked down at the still smoking cigar Tank had left in one of his flowerpots. He was supposed to smoke the whole thing right there in that chair, but a strange phone call made him run off.

The Doctor eyed the cigar to see how much of it was gone.

Rubbing his chin, he said, "The drug I laced it with would have worked much better if he had smoked it all, but it will still get the job done. It will just take a little while longer to kick in."

Ashanti made her way over to the open briefcase.

"About how much longer should it take?" she asked, closing the case and rising to her feet.

The Doctor thought about it.

"My guess would be about 10-15 minutes." He answered.

"O.K." Ashanti said, heading out of the living room. "I'll make that phone call and let them know that Mr. Quinten will be unconscious in 10 minutes."

Dr. Abu-Kahr rose to his feet and walked swiftly behind the still nude Ashanti. Even though he had just sold out someone he had known for years, no feelings of guilt bubbled up inside of him.

All he cared about was how good his dick was going to feel penetrating the beautiful Ashanti on top of a pile of $25,000.

Indeed, the Puerto Rican was worth every penny that the Doctor was spending on her.

CHAPTER ELEVEN

"Come ooonnnn." Tank urged his Chrysler as he mashed the accelerator into the floorboard.

He was speeding down I-45 with a million thoughts racing through his brain. He couldn't believe that someone had kidnapped LaQuisha and her friends in an attempt to extort him. They must have a death wish.

Not too many people knew it, but Tank was way more powerful than he seemed to be. The prestige of being one the largest suppliers of marijuana was one thing, but it was defiantly not the only thing Tank had his hands into. He also had his hands slightly in the dope game. Tank wasn't the major man on the crack scene, but he was a genius hustler. He was strategically gaining ground in that area.

But what had to be his most intelligent and calculated maneuver was when he invested a huge chunk of his money into the founding of what was now an extremely lucrative business.

Tank, A.K.A. Tony Quinten, was a silent business partner in the operation of a criminal defense law firm known as Willis, Winn, and Stone.

His involvement in the company was completely behind the scenes. He never even went to the office building during normal business hours. The only time he stepped foot through those doors was in the middle of the night when no one would be able to see him.

Years ago, Tank came in contact with a lawyer by the name of Henry Willis. At the time, Henry was a peon working for another law firm in a small town called Hitchcock. Tank had a bullshit possession of marijuana charge that he hired Henry to take care of for him.

During their first meeting Tank found out that Henry had handled a few cases for his older brother Tyler back in the day. The two spent a while reminiscing about Tyler and a friendship bond formed. Even after the possession charge was dismissed the two of them stayed in touch.

Henry often expressed his desire to make senior partner at his job, but he kept getting overlooked. That's when tank had an idea. Any mob movie would show you that any boss needed two types of legit people on his squad.

Police and lawyers.

The police helped you avoid catching a case.

The lawyer helped you beat the cases you couldn't avoid.

Tank didn't have any cops on his payroll, but he saw an opportunity to get himself a lawyer. After months of working out the details and carefully planning things out, Tank provided Henry with the seed money he needed to start his own Law Firm. All they needed was one more lawyer. It was Henry's idea to bring in his best friend from law school, Marshall Winn.

Tank didn't want to be officially associated with the company, so he used the name Stone to represent himself. The reason being, he felt as if he were the cornerstone of the operation. He was the foundation, the base, the stability.

Hence the name Willis, Winn, and Stone Law Firm.

Tank pretty much allowed Henry and Marshall to run shit. After all, they knew the business. Tank used it to not only wash some of his dirty money but also to stash some of his dirty money. Some of his drugs were stashed there too. It was the perfect hiding spot. Nobody knew that a street Kingpin had ties to Willis, Winn, and Stone, so nobody would think to look there for a street Kingpin's loot. Well, as far as Tank knew his secret was safe.

Layla swerved around a purple minivan trying to keep Tank in her line of sight. It was hard going on a high-speed chase with one hand preoccupied with holding up a cell phone.

"7 minutes?" Layla asked, getting discouraged. "But he's flying down the highway doing at least 85mph. If he passes out behind the wheel, he gone crash."

"I'm sorry girl." Ashanti apologized. "But that's the best we could do."

"Best you could do?! I thought the plan was for him to go to sleep over there and I just come pick him up before he comes to."

"How was we supposed to know that something bad was going to happen to his girlfriend?"

"What happened to his girlfriend?" Layla asked. "What does she have to do with any of this?"

The Doctor stood on top of his bed and peeled off his robe.

"Ooohhh Ashanti." He called, gripping his manhood and slowly stroking it as it filled with blood. "I'm not paying you to talk to your little friend. I'm paying you to talk to 'my' little friend."

He smiled goofily.

Ashanti faked a grin and thought to herself, "What a pervert?"

"Look Layla," Ashanti said, "I know he was supposed to fall out over here, but he didn't. His girlfriend, LaQuisha I think, got into a fight or something and he rushed to go help her. Sometimes we just have to improvise."

She looked at the nude and masturbating old Iranian man and cringed.

"Both of us gotta do some shit we'd rather not do." She continued. "Just make something happen. He'll be out in about… six minutes now and he'll be unconscious for a good two hours. Think about the money Layla. We done came too far to let it slip through our fingers again."

Tank weaved around an 18-wheeler and shot passed it.

"Get the FUCK off the road!" He shouted.

Layla hung up the phone and tossed it in the passenger seat.

"His girlfriend LaQuisha?" she thought to herself. "I know not talking about my daughter's friend LaQuisha."

She quickly glanced at the cell phone then focused her attention back on the road. Something inside of her was telling her to pick that phone back up and call Alize. Chances are, the LaQuisha Tank knew wasn't the same LaQuisha that hung out with her daughter but there was only one way to find out for sure.

Layla licked her lips. Tank was still bobbing and weaving through traffic. There was no way he would drive like that over something as simple as a fist fight. Whatever he was racing towards was important. It was important as hell.

Layla jerked on the steering wheel to avoid colliding into the back of a Mrs. Bairds bread truck. The tires squealed and the delivery truck driver blew his horn. Layla's cell phone slid right out of the seat and landed on the passenger side floorboard.

"Well," Layla said, shrugging her shoulders. "Guess I gotta just call her after this madman loses control of his vehicle."

She wondered how she was going to pull off kidnapping a wounded man right after he's involved in an ugly highway wreck.

Layla gripped the wheel and pushed the Buick LeSabre to its limit. She thought about the money. This one lick could have her set for life.

"You gotta do somethin' Layla." She told herself. "Improvise!"

Tank blazed through the other motorist like they were standing still. He was a man on a mission. Dickinson, Tx. was his goal.

Tank weaved through the three lanes of traffic treating the brake pedal like a bitch with A.I.D.S. He wasn't touching it for shit.

Flying down the middle lane Tank was watching the bumpers of all of the cars in front of him. If any of them made any sudden moves he needed to be on point.

Tank squinted his eyes. It looked like the two cars in the outside lanes were trying to merge into the car in the middle.

"What the hell?" He mumbled, shaking his head.

The cars returned to their starting positions.

Tank gripped the wheel and blinked a few times. His vision had begun to blur slightly. He licked his lips and tried to stay focused. Now was not the time for his mind to start playing tricks on him.

Much to his frustration, Tank stared straight ahead as the middle car split into three cars.

"Shit." Tank cursed as a throbbing pain

began pounding against the inside of his skull.

"Wha… what's happening to me?"

Tanks entire body started to feel like it was being robbed of its strength. Like he had taken a bottle of extra strength muscle relaxers.

Layla looked on as the Chrysler seemed to slow down some and swerve slightly. Tank was having trouble keeping the car straight. She knew what that meant.

The drug was kicking in.

As Layla's mind struggled to find a way to do what she had to do, a blessing came her way. Tanks blinker came on.

"Oh, thank God." Layla said. "He's going to pull over."

Layla gratefully prepared to follow Tank off of the crowded and dangerous highway. She wasn't sure if the Alpha and Omega condoned doing wrong if you were doing it to an evil person, but she gave credit to her higher power for Tank exiting the highway none-the-less.

Maybe the Man upstairs was just trying to spare some innocent child from being pinned under countless tons of steel?

Or maybe He… or She… was using Layla to punish Tank for his sins?

Or maybe…?

"Who am I kidding?" Layla asked out loud. "Even if there is a God, He's probably waaay too busy to get involved in all of this. Tank is pulling over because of self-preservation. He feels that shit creeping up on him and he don't wanna get fucked off in no crash."

Tank's reasoning may not have been clear in Layla's mind, but it was as clear as crystal in his own. The more his senses seemed to go off track, the more he struggled to compose himself. And by doing so, he noticed an all-white Buick LeSabre trailing him in his rearview mirror.

"Layla?" He had thought, straining to remain focused in the face of an ever-growing headache. "What is… what is she doing?"

The drug that the Doctor and Ashanti had slipped on him was clouding his thinking and bombarding his body with burst of soul numbing pain. He was lucky to be coherent enough to recognize the vehicle she was in. One of his workers that had been assigned to watch her movements in the days after Sticky's murder had given him a heads up about her change in cars.

As Tank maneuvered off the exit, he summoned up all of the energy he had left. He was fading fast. The drug had him no longer even comprehending his situation clearly.

Drool oozed from the corner of his mouth and his head dropped back onto the headset.

Layla followed as Tank's Chrysler slowly made the exit, cruised in a straight line towards the feeder roads curve, rocked as the two front wheels jumped the curb, and finally came to a stop half on the road and half in the grass.

She surveyed the area.

The highway was still packed but the feeder was virtually deserted.

"Good." Layla thought.

He didn't have a wreck and there were not a whole lot of witnesses. The only hard part would be picking up all of his dead weight and relocating it to her car.

She eased up behind the still running Chrysler and threw her Buick in park. Layla knew that she had to work fast.

Reaching over the passenger seat she unlocked the side door and hopped out on the driver's side. The sound of multiple vehicles whizzing by helped to calm her nerves.

It was obvious that no one was paying them any attention. They were too busy living their own lives.

Layla rushed over to Tanks car and yanked the door open. She found tank slumped over across the two front seats mumbling in a barely audible voice.

"La… LaMita." He muttered through a mouth full of spit.

He had lost all function in his limbs and his tongue was growing heavier by the second. Fear had begun to creep up into what little consciousness he had left. His heart felt funny. It felt like it was trying to stop beating.

Layla ignored Tank's ramblings and tugged at his lifeless body. She knew that he was a big dude, but she had no idea his frame could be so heavy. The man was barely moving, and she was using every ounce of power that she possessed.

In Tank's intoxicated mind, Layla must have known about the kidnapping and come to offer her assistance. His mind wasn't working good enough to wonder why the kidnappers would call her and he was the target. And his mind definitely wasn't functioning well enough for him to ask himself, "if she did know about the kidnapping, how did she just happen to find him on the highway speeding away from Dr. Abu-Kahr's Houston home?"!

No, his brain wasn't operating correctly at all. He remembered the kidnapping and he recognized Layla. To him, the only two things he could still focus on had to be related.

He needed to talk to Layla about the situation before it was too late.

"LaMi... ita." He strained to say as Layla continued to fail to move him. "LaMita... and... Aliii... ungh."

He took 3 quick breaths.

"Ali... J!" he said through the pain.

Layla stopped tugging on him.

Had she heard him wrong?

Did he just try to say Alize?

Layla grabbed Tanks head and made him face her.

"What did you say?" she asked wide eyed. "Did you say Alize?!"

Tank used his lead tongue to force a glob of the accumulated saliva out of his mouth. He didn't even feel it as it slid down his chin and was soaked up by his shirt. It was still hard for him to see but he heard Layla's voice clearly. He was getting through to her.

"LaMita." He groaned again. "And... and Alize. Kkkk... Kkkk... Kid... napped."

Tanks eyes closed, his head hung low, and his tongue dangled from his mouth. The drug had won. He was no longer aware of anything. This was as close to dead as a man could get and still be able to come back without a word from Jesus himself.

Although Tank's final words were garbled and broken, it didn't take a rocket scientist to decipher their meaning. Layla had gathered enough insight from Ashanti to piece together a basic understanding of what was going on.

She stared at Tank through horrified eyes. The Doctor had already told her that once he slipped into a state of unconsciousness the only thing that would be able to bring him back was time. And as Layla stood halfway inside of Tanks vehicle, she quickly analyzed the situation.

Ashanti had said that a situation with Tanks girlfriend, LaQuisha, had caused him to leave from the Doctors house prematurely. Layla now knew for sure that Tanks LaQuisha was indeed Alize's home girl LaQuisha. And it wasn't a fight that had Tank spooked, it was a kidnapping. A kidnapping that her daughter was caught up in.

Layla frantically looked up and down the feeder road. There was no way she was going to be able to drag tank from his car to hers. He was just too big. She could not just leave him there though. For one, she needed him in order to get to his money. And two, she needed him to find out exactly what was going on with her daughter.

"No! No! No!" she shouted, shoving Tanks shoulder in a futile attempt to wake him.

Tears of frustration began to build up in her eyes. Once again, a brick wall had risen out of nowhere like a dangerously steep mountain range forbidding any and all explorers from reaching their goal of standing atop its snow covered peak.

Layla felt herself losing control. It seemed like just when she had an actual opportunity of providing for her daughter the type of life, she herself never had, another problem popped up.

Layla pulled herself from the vehicle and wiped the moisture from her now red cheeks.

"Come on Layla." She encouraged herself speaking slowly. "You gotta get it together. Now's not the time to fold girl. Just relax."

She took a deep breath.

"Relaaax. Relax and think. For every problem there is a solution."

She glanced up and down the road again.

"You just gotta figure out what the fuck is going on."

Layla knew that time was a luxury she didn't have. She needed to make a move and she needed to make it fast. The only question was which move to make. She weighed her options.

Somebody has my daughter.

Tank knows who that somebody is.

But tank won't be able to talk for another two hours.

Shit!

O.K. Tank has the money I want.

I need tank to access the safe.

But Tank won't be able to talk for another two hours.

Fuck!

Layla glanced down. It seemed like Tank was the key to both of her problems. Tank was the solution, but Tank was too heavy to move.

Damn it!

Just when Layla was about to feel as if all hope was lost, a glare from the sun shined in her direction. That's when she saw it. The keys to the Chrysler were still dangling from the car's ignition. The sight caused her spirits to rise.

She had an idea. One that seemed airtight in her mind. Layla sprinted back to her LeSabre, grabbed a few key things and darted back to the Chrysler.

After a couple of strenuous lifts and pushes, Layla was back on the highway speeding towards Dickinson. Tank was cramped up headfirst into the floorboard with his legs twisted and carelessly tossed onto the passenger seat. The LeSabre was left for the tow trucks.

CHAPTER TWELVE

"… in Jesus name I pray. Amen!"

LaQuisha listened to Ming's heartfelt prayer for protection and she wanted to cry. How could a day that started out so perfect end up like this? One minute the Valley Park Girls were riding around in style, laughing and joking with one another, and the next thing they knew they were all tied up and held hostage inside of an empty apartment bedroom. They had also been gagged and blindfolded on the ride over, so they had no idea where they were at.

The kidnappers had removed the blindfolds and gags once they were inside the building, but they were still tied up and very much afraid.

LaQuisha struggled against the restraints that held her wrists together behind her back. She had been trying to loosen them up ever since they had been put on. The kidnappers had tied the rope so tight that it was beginning to cut off the blood circulation in her hands.

"Fuck." She mumbled, loud enough for her friends to hear her but low enough so that her abductors in the other room could not.

"Whichever one of them dudes tied me up must've been a boy scout when he was little." She continued. "He tied this shit up like a pro."

All of the girls' hands and feet were tied. The restraints weren't all of the girls concerns though.

Alize was still aware of what was going on, but the basketball player had left the entire right side of her face swollen, discolored, and bloody. It wasn't easy to make such a pretty girl look bad, but

Alize was on hull. For anyone out there who didn't really know, Steel beats skin any day.

As the shockwaves of pain danced across her bruised face, Alize sat awkwardly with her back against the far wall. There was nothing inside of the room except a maroon colored carpet and matching maroon walls. The solitary window inside of the makeshift prison was hidden behind a thick black blanket. Apparently, the kidnappers didn't want their hostages being able to see the outside world. Their drive time away from the scene of the kidnapping wasn't long enough to have taken them out of Dickinson, so Alize knew that if she could somehow manage to get a quick peek outside, she could figure out where they were at.

Alize peered through her one good eye at the line her home girls had formed on the wall to her left. Immediately next to her there was Krystal, then LaQuisha, then Ming, and finally Melissa.

Winking at the pain, Alize whispered to Ming, "Hey. Is she gonna be alright?"

Ming looked down at Melissa and quickly turned away. It hurt her to see her friend suffer. Melissa was tied up just like the rest of the girls, but she wasn't sitting with her back against the wall. She was curled up on the floor whimpering. The crotch of her pants was stained with blood and the smell of death was freely flowing from the material. No one in the room wanted to verbalize what had happened but they all knew exactly what went down.

Melissa had had a miscarriage.

Between the back to back cramps and the outpouring of tears, all Melissa could do was roll around slightly and do her best to endure. The emotional trauma of losing a child that she had already carried for so long was compounded by the kidnapping and being held hostage for ransom situation.

"It's alright Ming." LaQuisha said, trying to comfort her. "We're gonna get out of..."

"Alright?! Ming shouted with grief. "How are things alright?"

As the seconds ticked by, Ming was becoming more and more unstable. Anger, fear, frustration, and intoxication were not a good mix.

"Look at her." Ming said, motioning towards Melissa's writhing body with her head. "She's in pain. We need to get her to a hospital."

"I know." LaQuisha said calmly. "But..."

"Ain't no buts!" Ming interrupted. "Melissa has had a miscarriage. A MISCARRIAGE! That type of thing is dangerous to both the child 'and' mother."

Tears rolled freely down her cheeks.

"And look at Alize." Ming offered. "Look at what he did to her face!"

She closed her eyes and rocked back and forth.

"We... we gotta get out of here." Ming told them, opening her eyes back up. "We gotta do something."

LaQuisha could her desperation within her eyes. The kind of desperation that was dangerous. The kind of desperation that overrode good sense and logical thinking. She knew that she needed to calm her home girl down and she needed to do it fast.

In the living room of the small one-bedroom apartment, the three kidnappers were debating about what their next move should be.

"I say we call tank back right now."

Basketball player suggested.

Gucci shades checked the time on his wristwatch.

9:25am.

"It's still too early." He replied. "We'll call him back at about 10:00am. He ain't sweated enough yet."

Basketball player paced the room.

"Fuck makin him sweat." He growled. "This kidnapping shit ain't my type of gig no way."

He pointed his gun towards the door that led to the hostages.

"If it was up to me, we'd just smoke all of those little bitches and dump they bodies in the Bayou. Well, we'd smoke all of 'em except the one we really need."

The short man wearing the white tee hit the blunt he was holding.

"Just chill dog." He told him. "The boss already said we gone get to do 'em all. But right now, we need to keep 'em alive. It's the only way we gone get what we want."

Basketball player frowned up and continued to pace the room.

"I'm telling you niggas," he said. "Keeping them hoes alive gone backfire on us. If we kill one or two of 'em, at least that bitch will know we serious."

The short man shook his head. His partner was a damn fool and nothing anybody said was going to change his personality.

"Naw." Basketball player said. "I'm bein' for real. Like that Mexican chick for example. The bitch probably gone die anyway. I mean, ya'll been back there. The hoe done lost her baby and everything. We can't possibly take her to no hospital. So naturally her pussy probably infected by now."

He shrugged. "Why wait 'til later to kill her? She needs to be put down right now."

Gucci shades stared at his Basketball player weirdly.

"Do you even hear yoself bro?"

"What?"

"You say the girl need to be put down like she some kind of horse, or dog, or something."

She is a dog." He said smiling. "A female dog. Ha! Ha! Ha! Ha!"

The short man jumped up suddenly from his seat on the couch and snapped his head in the direction of the bedroom door.

"Did ya'll hear that?" he asked, moving with determination towards the door.

Gucci shades and Basketball player immediately stopped their bickering and got into gangsta mode. They quickly followed their comrade with their guns in hand.

LaQuisha whispered. "Ming stop it. You're gonna get us all killed."

Ming had done all the sitting around and waiting that she could do. She had reached her breaking point. All she could think about was getting the hell out of there.

It had proved impossible to untie the knots in the ropes that held them in bondage, so Ming decided to make her escape with the ropes still on. She carefully maneuvered her hands under her body and brought them around to the front of her. Then she crawled over to the only window in the room. Using the windowsill to rise to her feet, Ming pushed the blanket back and struggled to raise the window.

To her disgust and disappointment, the window wouldn't budge. The kidnappers had had enough foresight to nail it shut before they brought them there.

"Nooo." Ming whined, still tugging at the window and silently praying that it would somehow open.

Unfortunately, it never did.

The bedroom door flew open as the three, armed men, came rushing in. All of the Valley Park Girls, except for Ming and Melissa, gasped as Ming was caught in the act of trying to escape.

"What the hell is going on in here?" the short men asked, surveying the scene with his pistol aimed towards the girls.

Ming spun around so quick that she lost her balance and fell to the floor. None of the girls could respond. The three men had already made it painfully clear that they had no hang-ups about hurting them, and Ming had just allowed her fear to give them the perfect reason to abuse them all.

Basketball player rushed into the room last. He quickly studied the area. The Chinese girl had moved. She was now under the window. The blanket was pushed to the side. One word lit up inside of his head like a high-class neighborhood on Christmas Eve.

Escape!

"I told you!" he grumbled to his companions while moving towards Ming. "I told you all of these extra mothafucka's was gone be problems. Let's just kill 'em all except for the one we need."

His statement echoed in the minds of Krystal, Alize, Melissa, and Ming. They were all expendable. Expendable was a bad thing.

Basketball player walked up to Ming, who

was lying on her back, and pointed his weapon directly at her forehead. In one slow motion instant, Ming's entire life flashed before her eyes. She thought about all of the things that she had done over the years and she regretted all of the things that she had not done.

She had spent her entire life saving herself for a husband that she would never get to meet. All of the pleasures she had denied herself. All of the sacrifices she had made. The hard work. The no play. The short-term goals and long-term goals. All about to be snuffed out by a mad man's bullet. A mad man who didn't even know or need her.

Basketball player glared down at a trembling Ming with a stare so cold it chilled her to the core. His finger embraced the trigger of his weapon like it was a long-lost love finally found after years of searching. Ming and the others watched helplessly as the kidnapper prepared to squeeze.

"NO!" Gucci shades shouted, rushing up behind his partner in crime.

There was no way he could allow his out of control friend to murder one of their hostages.

Basketball player hesitated long enough for Gucci shades to reach him. Not wanting to get into a wrestling match with an armed man, Gucci shades simply stood on the side of him.

"The boss said not to kill 'em." He told him calmly. "At least not yet. He wants 'em alive."

Basketball player turned to face Gucci shades, but he kept his gun pointed at Ming.

"Alive?!" he repeated, with hatred for the order seething through with each syllable. "Why we gotta keep these hoes alive? I mean, I know what the boss said, but the boss ain't know how disrespectful these… these little fucking sluts were gonna be."

He kneeled down and pressed the barrel of his pistol to Ming's temple. She closed her eyes and prayed silently.

"And not only that." He continued. "This one just tried to escape. ESCAPE?!!"

Basketball player grabbed Ming by her shirt.

"If we can't punish their disobedience, how do you suggest we keep them from studdin' up?"

Gucci shades looked down at his homeboy and the frightened Asian girl. He had been in these types of situations with him before. Not the exact same situation but something similar to it. He knew from experience that once his friend had his heart set on fuckin' someone up, someone was going to get fucked up. There was no if, ands, or buts about it. Basketball player was sick. Sick with a dangerously short fuse.

Gucci shades knew that he had to keep a cool head though. They had specific instructions to keep all of the hostages alive long enough for them to be interrogated by the boss. If the boss showed up and they were all dead… let's just say that the boss was the kind of man you disobeyed.

"Aiight Clipso." Gucci shades said, slipping up and using Basketball player's street name. "You think we ought to punish them? Fuck it. Punish 'em"

"That's what I'm talking 'bout!" Clipso said excitedly.

"Wait a minute though." He told him, once again saving Ming from a bullet to the brain. "We still gone have to do this shit clean. The only way we can murk one and be able to explain it to the boss is if we murk the one that's already wounded."

Clipso glanced over at Melissa. Her eyes

were now wide with fear and everybody else's eyes were on her.

"And use the knife." Gucci shades added. "That pistol gone make too much noise."

A wicked grin slowly formed on Clipso's face. The bitch was already enduring the physical and emotional pain of having a miscarriage. Now, as if the gods of suffering and grief had smiled upon him, he was given the opportunity to torture her further before the reaper showed up to collect her shattered soul.

"You can't kill Melissa!" LaQuisha spoke up. "I'm... I'm the one you really want. Just let my friends go. Please?!?"

"Yeah." Ming added. "Melissa didn't do anything wrong. I'm the one who tried to escape. Don't kill her because of me."

Krystal sat and admired how brave her two home girls were. They were actually offering themselves in the place of Melissa. She had to admit, she cared a lot about her Hispanic friend, but she was not about to die in her place.

"A.K." Gucci shades said to the short man wearing the white tee. "Help me stuff these gags back into these hoes mouths so they'll stop all that damn yelling."

"Aiight Duke." A.K. replied.

All of the girls protested as they were once again silenced by the dirty rags used as make-shift gags. All of the girls except Alize. Her mind had no choice but to contemplate on their situation, but other things had entered her mind also. None of the other girls paid much attention to the kidnappers slip in saying their names. She did though.

Thinking to herself, she thought, "Clipso, A.K., and Duke? I know those names from somewhere. But from where…?"

She struggled to place the names, but she couldn't. None of them were wearing a mask so she knew for a fact that she didn't recognize them by face. She had heard their names before.

"Maybe A.B. mentioned them." She thought. "Or maybe my mama?"

As A.K. crammed the rag into her mouth, she cut her eyes at the still slightly pushed back blanket. Alize had a damn good idea where they were being held hostage at, but she couldn't figure out what those names had to do with LaQuisha's man or their location.

Deciding to ensure that they wouldn't have a repeat of Ming's attempted escape, Clipso, A.K., and Duke hogged tied the girls after gagging them. When Duke and A.K. left Clipso to finish off the Mexican chick, all five girls were lying face down with their hands tied to their feet behind their backs. It was no possible for them to get free. Their restraints had them at the mercy of the kidnappers.

With all of the girls incapacitated, and the room to himself, Clipso slowly pulled the blanket back in place in front of the window and sat his pistol down over near the far wall.

Oh, how he was going to enjoy this!

Gleefully looking from terrified face to terrified face, Clipso rubbed his hands together.

"Mmmm." He hummed sadistically, making the girls skin crawl. "I got a nigga bitch, a cracker bitch, a mixed breed bitch, a wetback bitch, and a chink bitch. That's every color of the rainbow ain't it?"

Clipso took a step closer to his prey. He couldn't help but to chuckle as they all flinched in unison.

"Don't worry." He told them. "Although I would love to murder four of you right now, I don't think the boss would approve."

Melissa tried to swallow but a lump got caught in her throat. It had already been decided that she was the most expendable. She thought about her dead baby, her baby daddy she was supposed to marry, and all of here family members.

"Will they ever find out the truth about what happened to me?" She thought. "Will this sick bastard have to pay for what he is about to do to?"

Clipso rubbed on his chin as he scanned his captives. They were all pretty in their own unique way. Especially the little Asians one.

Clipso stared at her slender legs and small butt. She wasn't as developed as the other four but the navy-blue shorts and matching button down shirt she was wearing made her look innocent. Clipso loved to defile the innocent.

He glanced over his shoulder at the closed door. A.K. and Duke were back in the living room. He was all alone with the hostages. His mind ignited with lustful thoughts and desires as he turned back to face Ming. Duke told him not to kill any of them other than the Mexican. He didn't say Clipso couldn't fuck one of them.

Clipso grabbed his dick through his red Dickies shorts. It was already beginning to grow before he even touched it.

"I ain't never fucked no chink pussy before." He mumbled under his breath.

Clipso weighed his options. The only way he could fuck her was to get her naked. The only way he could get her naked was to untie her. If he untied her, she might try something slick again.

He didn't want to risk all of that.

Clipso looked at Ming again and could easily visualize the exotic faces the young foreign girl would make when he shoved his 13-inch tool deep into her stomach.

The girls watched confused as Clipso made his way over to his gun and then picked it back up. Once again pointing it at Ming, he walked over to her and knelt down.

Pulling the gag out of her mouth, he asked, "Do you really want me to spare your friends life?"

Confusion spread across Ming's face.

"Wha... wha... what do you mean?" she asked back, not sure what he was getting at.

"Earlier," he answered, "earlier you said that she shouldn't die for your mistake. Did you mean that or was it just talk?"

Melissa cut her eyes in Ming's direction.

Ming returned the gesture.

Yeah, she had said that Melissa shouldn't die because of her, but she wasn't implying that she should die in her place. It was more like a suggestion to keep them all alive.

Ming struggled to find the right words.

"Yes." She mumbled. "But I don't want to die neither."

"Ooohhh." Clipso cooed, in a strangely calm tone of voice. "I don't plan on killing you. I was thinking more of a... a trade. You know? The Mexicans life in exchange for... something else."

Clipso ran his fingers through Ming's hair and she cringed.

"Dear God," she thought, suddenly becoming mortified. "Is he saying what I think he's saying?'"

Ming noticed an extremely large bulge twitching in the crotch of Clipso's shorts.

"But but but…" she stammered out.

Clipso gripped Ming's hair tightly and quickly switched his attitude back to aggressive.

"Ain't no mothafuckin' buts." He growled, shoving the barrel of his weapon directly between her eyes.

She could feel the cold steel on the bridge of her nose.

"Either you gone lay there and take this dick or I'm gone shoot you hoes one by one."

He motioned towards the door with his head.

"Before my soft ass homeboys make it back in here, all of ya'll 'll be dead."

Ming couldn't believe what was happening. The ugly one had been begging to kill them all along. She knew he wasn't bluffing.

"Now." Clipso said, releasing his hold on her hair and sliding his hand slowly across her shoulders. "The ball is in yo court. Whether you and you r friends make it out of this alive is on you."

His words hit Ming directly in her stomach. Had she really been saving herself all of these years only to be deflowered in a sick and twisted act of rape? Her mind raced to find a way out of it that wouldn't result in a bullet to her brain, but she just couldn't come up with one.

Her silence was like a green light to Clipso. He sat his gun back down and re-gagged her. Once he started fucking her like he planned on fucking her, the little teenager would be sure to howl like a banshee. The average grown woman with kids found it hard to take his tool so he knew that he would kill the young Asian.

After he had finished limiting the amount of noise Ming could make, he warned the rest of the girls.

"And just in case the rest of ya'll are thinking about trying something, the same rules apply for ya'll. If ya'll don't lay there quietly…"

He pulled out a pocketknife and popped out the blade. Then, he slowly ran it through the air in front of his throat.

They got the point. LaQuisha couldn't believe she couldn't help her home girl. Alize started to cry out of her lone good eye. Krystal didn't want to die for her friend, but she would've had sex for her. Anybody but Ming would've been a better choice to her. Melissa, on the other hand, was the only one happy about the turn of events. If Ming had to get her cherry popped in order for her to stay alive, so be it. Death is worse than sex any day

Clipso was eager to dive in the Asians flesh. He quickly untied her hands and feet and then ordered her to strip.

Ming slowly stood to her feet trembling like a leaf. Her shaky hands eased up to the top button on her shirt and she hesitated. She couldn't believe she was about to be raped. It made her feel so helpless and dirty. She let her head hang as she undid the top button. There was no way she was going to look her assailant in the eyes. If she did, his predator stare would probably be chained within the chambers of her memory for all eternity.

Clipso felt a surge of adrenaline shoot through his body. It tingled like pure power. The power to completely control another human being. He had done a little bit of everything in his lifetime. Robbery, burglary, assault, drug hustling, car theft, attempted murder, etc… But he had never actually taken the pussy. Of course, there were the times when he would press the issue until the female finally gave in, but he didn't count that as rape.

There was no weapon, no threat of injury, and definitely no tears. Oh, the tears. He watched them run down Ming's cheeks and eventually fall to the floor. The whole ordeal was lifting him into stages of pleasure he never even knew existed. Clipso slowly undressed as he stared hungrily at Ming.

The buttons on her shirt had all come undone. She dropped it to the floor and stood before him wearing her shorts and a plain white bra. Her size B breast might as well have been 44DD's to Clipso.

"Hurry up and take that shit off." He commanded her, while at the same time tossing his jersey to the side.

Ming closed her eyes and prepared to remove her shorts.

"What's takin' Clipso so long?" A,K, asked.

Duke shrugged. "You know that fool throwed off. He probably playing with that hoe before he kills her."

A.K. smacked his teeth.

"That nigga needs to go ahead and do her and get it over with."

Duke hit the blunt.

"As long as he occupied." He said, holding in the smoke. "I don't give a fuck what he does with that bitch."

He exhaled slowly and watched the smoke rise into the air.

"Ah say." Duke said, leaning forward on the couch. "Turn that shit up. This hoe right here be jamming like a mothafucka!"

A.K. looked back at the bedroom door and sighed. Then he picked up the remote off of the end table and increased the volume on the radio.

Atlanta rapper T.I.P. blasted over the

airways.

"… niggas hangin' out the window mouth full of gold teeth. When the guns start poppin' wonder when it's gone cease. Choppa hit you in the side and create a slow leak…"

"FOR REAL!!!" Duke shouted, jumping to his feet. "These faggot ass niggas don't know me!"

Clipso momentarily diverted his eyes towards the door.

"Damn," he thought. "That extra noise came right on time."

Ming was completely naked and already lying on her back. Clipso was standing over her in nothing but his boxers with his abnormally huge weapon sticking more than a full foot out in front of him. If Ming's eyes wouldn't have been closed, just the sight of his mutated manhood would have sent her into shock.

All of the other girls were looking at it though, and they all were thinking the same thing. "Clipso is about to literally bust Ming's virgin hole wide open." There was no way on God's green earth she was going to be able to handle him. Hell, none of them were sure that they could handle him. Not even Krystal. His dick was made for female horses, not humans.

Clipso licked the tips of his fingers and used them to lubricate the head of his penis. He wasn't about to jeopardize the feeling by using a condom. The Asian looked clean enough.

Ming laid perfectly still and braced herself for the pain she'd always been told would accompany her losing her virginity. Holding her breath, she felt Clipso's grimy hands part her legs.

Clipso laid down on top of her and smiled as he lined his dick up with her pussy. She was so afraid, embarrassed, and disgusted, she wasn't even wet.

After hesitating for a couple of seconds, Clipso thrust his hips and forced half of his massive meat inside of his victim.

Ming's body tensed up and her eyes shot open wide.

"Nnnnngggghhhh!!!" she screamed through the gag as her walls stretched wider than she ever imagined.

Out of instinct she tried to back away and remove the large intruder from inside her but Clipso wrapped one of his arms around her neck and held her in place.

"Don't run now." He whispered in her ear, jabbing her intestines by pushing all of his 13 inches inside of her.

Ming tried to holler but the gag muffled her cries. She tried to get away but Clipso was too strong. She wiggled, squirmed, and yelled through her gag as Clipso began long stroking her with more and more speed.

"Fuck." He groaned, as he plunged deeper and deeper. "You so tight."

He pumped harder.

"Like a… like a virgin."

Ming struggled to close her legs to prevent him from punishing her, but it was to no avail.

She dug her fingernails into his back but that only made him fuck her rougher. As if it turned him on.

Ming bit down hard on the rag that was in her mouth. She had no idea how her friends could subject themselves to this kind of abuse consensually. Absolutely nothing about sex felt good to her. It hurt like hell.

Clipso held poor Ming and drove his dick into her like he had never done another woman. They had never let him continually put all that he had in them. No female actually wanted to be ruined. The chink, however, didn't have a choice. He fucked her like he had always wanted to fuck a woman.

Fast! Hard! And Raw!

"GGGGGOD Damn!" Clipso moaned. "I ain't know that that overseas pussy was this good. Mmmm. Shit girl. You got that bomb."

As Clipso pounded away, he felt Ming go from dry to super sloppy wet.

"Yeeeah." He told her, getting pleasure out of the fuck faces of agony she was making. "You can't fool me. I feel how wet this pussy just got. You like this shit, don't you? Hell yeah you like it. You lil trash ass bitch."

Clipso got off to talking dirty.

"You and all yo home girls some little fast ass hoes. Ain't ya'll? Ya'll was probably on ya'll way to let some niggas fuck when we picked ya'll up. I know one thang though."

Clipso bit his bottom lip and started hitting Ming's hole as hard as he possibly could.

"Yo... boy... friend," he said with each thrust. "Gone... know... I... been... here. You hear me girl? Yo... boy... friend... gone... know... Clip... so... been... up... in... this... exotic... ass... pussy!"

"NNNNN!!!" Ming wailed, wondering when it would all be over.

As LaQuisha laid there helplessly and listened to her home girl being brutally raped, all she could think about was making Clipso and his two friends pay for what they were doing. Knowing

250

that Clipso was too preoccupied with his cruel act of sexual assault to really be paying her any attention, LaQuisha began trying here hardest to break free from the ropes. She wasn't sure exactly what she was going to do once she got loose, but she just had to trey something.

Clipso penetrated deep inside of Ming until he felt his nuts about to explode. That familiar feeling of orgasm tingled down below and caused goose bumps to pop up all over his body.

"Mmmm." He moaned. "Here it come baby. Here come that cum."

Clipso's strokes became uneven as his body jerked in anticipation of his coming release. He had nutted countless times before but something about forcing the Asian girl to have sex with him was making his eruption buildup 1000 times stronger.

Clipso's dick slid in completely as the cum rose quickly up his 13-inch shaft.

"Uuunngghh!" he groaned, as he contemplated depositing his load inside of her. He knew it would feel sooo good to shoot his sperm within her wetness and warmth. But at the last second, he changed his mind.

With only a fraction of a second to spare, Clipso pulled out of Ming's goodies and aimed his penis at her breast.

"Ahhh." He hollered, as his testicles pumped his baby making cream out of his tool and sent it spraying across Ming's body.

Cum landed on her stomach, breast, neck, and face. He gripped his thickness and masturbated on top of Ming's nude and trembling frame until he was completely empty.

"Fuck!" he exclaimed, as the final drops dripped into her pubic hairs.

Ming couldn't believe it. She felt like a slut. A tramp! He had gone the extra mile in degrading her. He had left her vagina split open and his sperm scattered all over her. All she could think to do was to roll up into the fetal position and cry. He had made her endure all of that just to save Melissa's life. But the way she was feeling after the ordeal made her think that death would've been far better than that.

Satisfied, Clipso rose to his feet to start getting back dressed. The blood stains on the carpet and on his dick didn't surprise him. He had made several women bleed before.

"Look how you got that hoe." He said to his piece as he slid back on his shorts. "You make daddy sooo proud. Ha! Ha! Ha! Ha!"

Clipso looked at the door. Once Duke and A.K. found out that he had raped one of the hostages they would no doubt talk shit. But fuck 'em. It's done now. Point seen, money gone. He didn't even see fit to try and hide what he had done. After he finished getting dressed, he tied Ming back up while she was still naked and covered with his cream.

LaQuisha watched angrily as Clipso stood over them all again with that same devilish ass grin on his face. Oh, how she wanted to just wipe that smirk right off of his face.

"You wanna hear something fucked up?" Clipso asked, reaching into his pocket and withdrawing his blade. "I never had any intentions on letting the wetback live."

His statement made all of the girls, including Ming, look up.

Clipso extended the blade of his pocketknife.

"It's true." He admitted, moving into position over Melissa. "I just said that so the chink bitch would take this dick and not fight back."

"Mmmm-ummm! Nnnnmmm!" all of the girls moaned, as he dropped down next to Melissa and pulled her head back by her hair.

Clipso chuckled as the realization set in that he had played them.

"Dumb ass hoes." He mocked.

Melissa cringed as she felt the extremely sharp metal slice into the left side of her neck and slide quickly all the way to the right. Blood squirted from the wound and rained down on the carpet. Clipso released her hair and her head fell to the floor.

With her last little bit of life, Melissa blinked four times and convulsed. She could hear her friends whimpering but their voices were swiftly fading. To her disgust, her murderer's voice was the last one she heard.

"Every time someone tries something funny," he warned, "one of you will die."

Then, out of pure disrespect, he kicked Melissa in the face and spit on her back.

CHAPTER THIRTEEN

Layla noticed the time on the radio display screen as she weaved from lane to lane doing about 85mph down I-45.

It was 9:30am.

Layla glanced over at her still unconscious passenger. Tank was stuffed upside down into the floorboard to her right. He looked uncomfortable as hell, but she knew that he didn't feel a thing. In all actuality, Tank was clinically dead. And by Layla's calculations he would be that way for another hour or so.

Mumbling in a soft but very frustrated voice, Layla cursed her predicament.

"Damn." She said, only minutes away from Dickinson. "I can't believe this is happening."

Once again, her master plan had hit an enormous snag. Her daughter, her flesh and blood, her everything, had been abducted by God knows who, taken God knows where, and forced to do God knows what. If it wasn't one thing it was another.

Layla did her best to come up with a possible explanation. What she knew for sure was that Alize had been snatched up along with one of her best friends LaQuisha. And since Tank was contacted by the kidnappers, and Tank was LaQuisha's boyfriend, common sense told her that the whole thing revolved around Tank somehow. Either he had so serious beef going on in the streets or her and Ashanti weren't the only ones trying to rob the hood rich street king pen.

As much as she hated it, she knew she was going to need A.B.'s help if she ever wanted to get her daughter back.

"A.B." she thought sadly. "I'm sorry I keep dragging you deeper and deeper in all of this. I really do love you though. It's just… just…"

Layla shook her head and refused to let herself get sentimental. Sometimes the things that were necessary were the hardest things to do. Like using the man you love for monetary gain and financial stability. She had just hoped she could just clean out Tanks stash and transform into nothing more than a distant memory from his yesteryear. Only to be seen in mental images of times long ago. And only to be heard when the winds blow gently and somehow disturb the order of past, present, and future.

It was defiantly going to be hard explaining why she went after Tank alone, but she knew that she had to come up with something. Without A.B., she would have no help in finding her daughter.

Layla sucked up her reservations as she neared the exit that would escort her back into her hometown. She slowed down once she got within city limits because there was no way she could stand getting pulled over with a clinically dead body in the passenger seat. A run in with the Dickinson Police Department would really fuck things up for her.

Luckily it was still early in the morning. Not many patrol cars would be on the streets. Their main hours for street patrol were afternoon to about 2:00 in the morning. Dickinson was known locally as Wicked City, so the police tried to keep crime to a minimum while there were kids out and about. During school hours they mostly kicked back and relaxed.

After seeing only one police car about 4

blocks ahead of her, Layla pulled safely into the driveway of her Valley Park home. It was 9:50am and A.B. was laid up in the bed smoking on a BossPlaya blunt. He was in deep thought about the News Broadcast, the possibility that his mother and Menace snitched him out, and the fact that his road dog Steel wasn't coming back no matter who he put that iron on. It was an awful lot for a 15-year-old boy to be dealing with.

BOOM!

A.B. heard the front door crash open and he instinctively reached for his .38 snub nose that was resting on the nightstand. He was moving fast but he was also thinking clearly enough to drop the lit blunt in the ashtray and not on anything flammable.

He rolled off the bed and got on his knees. The owner of the footsteps that were fast approaching would no doubt be aiming up high. He pointed his pistol at waist level and waited for the fool to show himself. There was no time to be afraid. He was in the middle of a street war.

"A.B." Layla called out, rushing to the bedroom door, "A.B. Where are you?"

Layla made it to the door and yanked it open. Her heart stopped when her eyes greeted the barrel of a pistol.

A.B. was just about to squeeze the trigger when his brain recognized the person at the door as Layla. She had become stiff as a board and her mouth was wide open like she wanted to scream but no sound was coming out.

A.B. lowered his weapon and rose to his feet.

"Layla?!?" he sighed relieved. "My bad baby. My bad. I ain't know it was you."

He sat the pistol back down and crossed the

room wearing nothing but a pair of black boxer briefs. When he reached her he hugged her. Layla was still in shock. She just knew that she was about to die. The scene kept playing over and over in her head.

"I'm sorry boo." A.B. apologized, realizing how shook up the situation had left her. "I didn't know it was you baby. I swear I didn't know it was you."

A.B. rubbed on Layla's back and held her close. Her body trembled slightly.

"I'm... I'm ok." Layla managed to stammer out. "We got bigger problems than this right now."

A.B. squeezed her one more time and the n released the embrace.

"What kind of problems?" He asked concerned.

Layla knew that the lies she had prepared would most likely be used shortly. She turned her head and broke eye contact with him. Then she walked around him slowly and over towards the bed.

"It's about Alize." She told him. "Somebody got her."

A.B. was confused.

"Got her?!" he repeated. "What do you mean, 'somebody got her'?"

"Just what it sounds like." She replied. "Somebody done kidnapped Alize. They got her friend LaQuisha too."

A.B. instantly thought about the plex they were involved in.

"But how? Alize is supposed to be at school. Did they run in the high school?"

A.B. thought about it.

"Wait a minute." He said, as if he was being

hit with a major revelation. "Ain't you supposed to be at work? How do you know they got Alize? How do you know they got LaQuisha? What is going on here?"

Layla took a deep breath.

"Just calm down baby." She said. "It probably would be best if I just showed you."

A.B. was really puzzled now.

"Show me what?"

Layla rose to her feet.

"It's in the car."

A.B. tried to question her further but Layla silently grabbed him by the hand and led him out the bedroom, through the living room, and out the front door.

"Whose car is that?" A.B. asked, when he noticed that the black Chrysler 300 was not the white Buick LeSabre he had expected to see.

After a few more steps in the direction of the vehicle, he gasped.

"Who the hell is that?"

A.B. had caught a glimpse of the upside-down man stuffed uncomfortably into the floorboard of the passenger seat.

Layla released A.B.'s hand and made her way to the side of the car that Tank was on.

"Look." She told A.B. "We need to get him inside the house before someone sees him. I'll explain everything once we get him inside. I promise."

She opened the door and used the palms of her hands to keep Tanks body from falling out.

"Come on Baby." She said. "Don't just stand there. We have to hurry up. Anybody could be watching."

A.B. was snapped out of his daze by Layla's

words. He nervously scanned the street and moved towards the body in the unfamiliar car. Layla had a lot of explaining to do. Unfortunately, though, he couldn't give it his undivided attention at the moment. On top of everything else, his girl had just pulled up with a dead body inside of what he assumed was a stolen car. Now she was asking him to help her get the body inside the house before she got found out.

A.B. eased to the side of the car and reached in to grab the man's torso. Layla stepped out the way.

"I'll grab his legs when you pull him out." She said, constantly looking around for witnesses.

A.B. didn't feel comfortable with what was going on, but he jerked the man out of the car with 3 hard tugs. His heart rate increased when the man's head rolled over revealing his face.

"I know him." A.B. thought. "That's Tank. One of the richest mothafucka's in Dickinson and the third person on my list of suspects in Steel's murder."

He cocked an eyebrow and peered at Layla.

"Why did she go after him without me?" he wondered.

Layla smiled awkwardly and placed each one of Tanks legs under her armpits. A.B. grabbed him around his chest and together they lifted him in the air.

"Shit." Layla groaned, wobbling. "We gotta move fast. This nigga heavy as hell."

The two of them carried Tank all the way inside and then laid his body down in the middle of the living room. Layla looked at the clock. It was 10:00am. Tank would be waking up in another 30 minutes. She had to move fast.

Layla left a puzzled A.B. alone with Tank and darted back outside to the car.

"Hey!" A.B. called after her. "Where're do you think you're going?"

Layla didn't respond. She just disappeared outside. A.B. looked down at Tank and scratched his head. Layla needed to fill him in on what was going on, and fast.

While he was waiting on Layla to come back inside, the sudden sound of 50 Cent made him jump.

"Many men. Many many many many men. Wish death on me LORD I don't cry no more. I don't look to the sky no more."

A.B. stared at Tank. The music was coming from his pocket. It must've been his cellphones ringtone. He knelt down to find the phone. Curiosity had him wondering who was calling.

"Have mercy on me. Have mercy on my soul. Somewhere my heart turned cold…"

A.B. found the phone and checked the caller I.D.

"LaQuisha?" he read out loud. "I thought Layla said that you and Alize got kidnapped?"

He looked towards the open door. Still no Layla. He shrugged and pressed 'Talk'.

Slowly raising the phone to his ear, he listened before he said anything. All he could make out was a radio playing in the background. It was too low for him to tell who the artist and song were.

After a brief hesitation, he spoke.

"Hello." He said into the receiver.

"It's been long enough." Duke growled into the phone. "Do you have the money and the weed, or do I have to kill your little girl friend and her home girls?"

A.B. tried to make out the voice, but he couldn't. It was no doubt the voice belonging to the kidnapper though. And from the sound of it, LaQuisha and Alize got snatched up as a tool to extort Tank with.

When Tank didn't respond, Duke got upset.

"Tank!" he shouted. "Don't play these games with me. Do you have what I asked for or what?"

A.B. didn't know what to say. If he said too much, the kidnapper would recognize that it wasn't Tank's voice. If he said nothing, the kidnapper would hang up and they might never find Alize.

Making a quick decision, A.B responded.

"I'm sorry." He apologized. "Yes. I have what you wanted. What do you want me to do now?"

Duke chuckled over the line.

"Good nigga. That's real good. I would've hated to have to fuck up someone as pretty and fine as yo lil tenderony here. But you a smart man. You realize that possessions can be replaced. A life on the other hand… well, once that's gone it's gone. Look, here's what I want you to do…"

Duke proceeded to give A.B. instructions for the drop off. Before he could finish, Layla came rushing back through the door with a whole lot of rope and duct tape.

"A.B." she said loudly, coming in with her heads down. "I know Tank looks dead, but he's not. He's just…"

She looked up for the first time only to see A.B. frantically motioning for her to be quiet. Fear was written all across his face. Layla saw him holding Tanks phone. Her stomach instantly knotted up.

A.B. wondered if the kidnapper had heard her.

"Ummm." A.B. mumbled into the phone.

"Who the fuck was that?" Duke demanded. "And who the fuck is this?"

"Damn." A.B. thought. He didn't get a chance to find out where Alize was being held at.

"This… this is Tank." A.B. lied, trying to salvage something.

"No it's not!" Duke replied. "I heard what that bitch in the background called you and it sure as hell wasn't Tank. What's going on here?"

A.B. was silent. The kidnapper knew he wasn't Tank. He stared at Layla and Layla stared at him. He was fresh out of ideas.

"Where's Tank?" Duke asked. "And who was that female I just heard?"

A.B. lowered the phone

"It's the kidnappers." He whispered to Layla. "And they heard you talking in the background."

Layla cursed under her breath. She was hoping that Tank would be back conscious by the time the kidnappers called back. Oh well. She would just have to improvise again.

"Here." She said, handing A.B. the rope and duct tape. "Tie him up good and give me the phone."

A.B. took the items and said, "But he's…"

"Just do it." Layla snapped.

The last thing she needed was Tank coming to and not be restrained somehow. Thinking fats, she raised the phone to her ear.

"Hello." She said.

"Listen here mothafucka." Duke instructed her. "I don't know what kind of games you and that

nigga over there playing, but ya'll done got ya'll
selves caught up in the middle of something that I
can promise you, you don't want no parts of. So,
either you tell me who the fuck you are and what
the fuck you doin' with Tanks phone, or so help me
God, I'll…"

"Oh really." Layla mocked, cutting him off.
She had had enough of this man's threats already.
"You think I don't know what's going on?"

Well let me tell 'YOU' something
mothafucka. We know exactly what's goin on. You
and you lil bitch ass homeboys got a couple of girls
held hostage. And you trying to do yo damnest to
make Tank drop out in exchange for their safe
return. But guess what? 'WE' got Tank. So, by
default, we got Tanks money. Now, if you wanna
get yo hands on any of it you gone have to deal with
me. So, check that attitude and call back when you
learn how to take some of that bass out of ya voice.
Bitch!"

CLICK!

The line went dead.

A.B. was listening to Layla check the
kidnapper while he tied up Tank.

"Are you crazy?" A.B. asked. "They got
Alize. How you gone hang up on the people that got
Alize?"

"Just relax." Layla told him. She was
nervous but she was hiding it well. 'I got everything
under control. He'll call back. Watch."

"Call back?!" What makes you think he'll
call back? You just talked bad to him and hung up
in his face. He probably killing Alize as we speak."

"Don't say that." Layla shot at him. "He
won't kill her."

She sat the phone down on the couch and

dropped to her knees. She wanted to help A.B. tie Tank up. He was a pretty big dude. If they didn't tie him up securely, he would no doubt break free.

"O.K." A.B. agreed. "Maybe he won't kill her. But we don't know anything about this dude. What makes you so sure he won't do her and LaQuisha both?"

"It's simple. The only reason they kidnapped them was to hold them hostage and use them to extort Tank. They may be killers, true enough, but they got money on they mind. If we got access to the money, we hold all of the cards. We make the rules of negotiation."

But Layla, they have your daughter."

"True. But they don't know that they have my daughter. They don't know who I am. As far as they know, we don't give a damn if their hostages live or die. That gives us the power. We have something they want, and they have nothing."

A.B. was beginning to understand. In order to gain control of the situation, Layla had to bluff them into believing they needed her, but she didn't need them. The woman was a genius. They had kidnapped the person the kidnappers were trying to extort.

"I see." A.B. said. "That's why you got Tank. You knew that the best way to get Alize back was to go and get the person Alize's kidnappers wanted."

Layla thought about what A.B. had said. It wasn't the lie that she was going to tell him, but a lie that you tell yourself is always more believable anyway. Hell, anything was better than the truth. How could she tell him that she had planned on robbing Tank herself and skipping town without him?

"Ummm. Yeah." Layla replied. "Tank is our bargaining chip."

A.B. smiled.

"You a fool wit it baby."

He laughed briefly and then stopped.

"But explain something to me. How did you know Alize got kidnapped with LaQuisha, and how did you manage to get Tank like this?"

He waved his hand at the hog-tied street boss.

Layla looked around nervously. She couldn't possibly tell A.B. the truth about how she knew about the kidnapping and how she got Tank hemmed up. It would call into question the story she had just agreed to.

"Well," Layla said, struggling to come up with something believable before A.B. got suspicious. "I just..."

"Many men. Many many many many men. Wish death on me..."

The two of them turned to face Tank's phone.

"Oh thank God." Layla thought. "Saved by 50 Cent."

She eagerly grabbed the cell phone and checked the caller I.D.

Seeing 'LaQuisha", she said, "It's them."

A.B. tensed up and Layla pressed 'TALK'.

"Is that attitude gone?" Layla asked calmly.

Duke gritted his teeth. He hated the position he was now in, but if the woman and man had Tank, he had to comply until he could get Tank from them.

"What will it take for me to get Tank?" he asked, getting straight to the point.

Layla gave A.B. the thumbs up.

"Now you're talking like a man with some home training." She said into the phone smiling. "And a man with home training is a man that I can make a deal with."

She began pacing the room.

"It seems to me," she continued, "that we are both after the same thing here. Tanks stash. But your M.O., the whole... kidnapping thing that you've done, lets me know that you don't even know where Tank's stash is located. Hell, you probably don't even know how to access it if you did know where it was at. So I'm left to analyze the situation I'm in. On the one hand, I got Tank, knowledge about his stash that you don't got, and an understanding of how to get to his stash. And the other hand... your hand, all you have is a couple of girls."

Layla placed her hand on her hip.

"If you wanna tell me why in the world I even need you, I'm all ears."

Duke stayed silent for a moment. The lady had a point. She didn't need them for anything. But she did make one mistake though. She falsely believed that he didn't know where Tank kept his money. He knew alright. He might not have known the actual combination to the safe, but he did know that it was located inside of the Willis, Winn, and Stone Law Firm building. Duke wasn't about to tell her that though. It might come in handy.

"You know what?" Duke asked. "You're right. You hold all of the keys right now, and I honestly don't see how we could be of assistance to you. Yet and still you continue the conversation. So obviously you believe that there is something that I can help you with. Instead of having me try to guess at what it is, why don't you just come out and tell me?"

Layla smirked. She had him right where she wanted him. Now, the only tricky part would be managing to keep her foot on his neck.

"You must be the brains of the bunch." She noted. "I like yo style. You get straight to the point. You're very perceptive too, because actually, I could use you and your crew for something. And in exchange for your cooperation, what do you say to a... ummm, I don't know. How about a 70-30 split? The 70 being my share of course."

Duke almost laughed out loud. There was no way in hell he was willing to accept a deal like that. True, he didn't have much to offer the alliance, but he wasn't about to get fucked over like that.

"How about a 50/50 split?" Duke offered. "I can't see involving my team in your little scheme for anything less."

Layla and Duke haggled back and forth for a while before Layla finally gave in.

"Alright Mr. Kidnapper," she said. "You win. We'll bust the pot right down the middle. 50-50. But only because you drive such a hard bargain."

"Then it's settled." Duke agreed. "Now tell me. What exactly do you want from me?"

"Oh, nothing major. Just a show of good faith and a little elbow grease."

"Show of good faith? Elbow grease? What are you talking about?"

"Pay close attention," Layla instructed him. "I'm only gonna say this once. First..."

CHAPTER FOURTEEN

Clipso and A.K. stood staring at Duke in anticipation of what he was about to say. He had just gotten off the phone with Tank's abductor and he did not look happy. The way his face was frowned up into an expression of rage, and the way his hand wrapped tighter and tighter around the cell phone, it was easy to figure out what the woman had said some things that he didn't necessarily like.

"So?" Clipso asked quizzically. "What'd she say?"

Duke slowly turned his head and gave Clipso one of those stares that would have ended his life if looks could kill.

"What'd she say?" Duke said in an extremely mocking tone of voice.

He sighed.

"She said we fucked up when we killed that Mexican bitch." Duke spat. "And 'YOU' fucked up when you raped that Asian bitch!"

Duke turned and began walking towards the other side of the living room. Just the sight of Clipso was burning him up. He knew better than to kill that girl. The boss specifically said to keep 'em alive. Now, their chances at getting at Tank and Tanks money had become very slim. All because he gave in to Clipso's whining.

"But…" Clipso sputtered, shrugging his shoulders. "How does she even know about any of that? And why does she care anyway? She doesn't even know them hoes."

Duke snapped his body around and spoke through gritted teeth.

"Of course, she doesn't know yet, you... you ignorant mothaf..."

He placed his free hand on his head.

"Look." Duke continued, closing his eyes and trying to remain calm. "Whoever the hell has Tank wants us to tell all of the girls go as a sign of good faith. To prove that we can be trusted. But how can we let them all go if one of them is dead? You get it?"

Clipso understood somewhat but he was still confused.

"O.K." he offered. "I get that part. But what I don't get is how us releasing will benefit her. Like I said, she doesn't even know them."

Duke looked back up at Clipso as if he couldn't be serious. Did his homeboy ever try to use his brain? Shaking his head, Duke turned his back on Clipso without answering the question.

"What?!" Clipso asked, becoming frustrated with Duke's attitude. "Why does she care about some hoes she don't know? That's crazy. It don't make sense."

"It's not about the girls." A.K. stepped in. "It's about leverage. Whoever this bitch is, she doesn't want us to just let the girls go so they can be free. She wants us to let them go so that she can hold them hostage. Under any other circumstances that would be crazy, but as things stand, she has Tank. So we gotta play ball however she sees fit."

"Ooohhh." Clipso said, as the realization of what was going on swept over him. "So if we only show up with four of the five girls, she gone think it's some type of game that we're playing."

"And," Duke added, "If we show up with four live girls and one dead one, she gone think we playin' some kind of game too."

He turned back around to face Clipso and A.K.

"They got Tank." He said seriously. "We cannot give them any reason to cut us out of this completely."

Clipso sat down on the couch. With Tank being held hostage, their situation was very sensitive. If they weren't careful, the woman and man would just rob Tank themselves, kill him once they were done, and then skip town and be gone forever.

A.K. passed the weed blunt to Clipso and then directed his attention

"So, what do you propose we do?" he asked.

Duke looked him directly in his eyes. He had been thinking the exact same thing ever since the woman told him to hand over the hostages. Duke was quick on his feet though, and it didn't take him long to realize that they were in bad shape. The entire mission had spiraled out of control in a matter of minutes. And the only thing that could get it back on track was a high-risk maneuver.

"We gotta let our nuts hang." Duke said in response to A.K.'s question. "We got one shot at getting back in control of this mission. One shot and one shot only."

Both Clipso and A.K. gave Duke looks that said, "Just tell us what to do and it's done!" Duke liked that. He wasn't the boss, but he was in charge of this particular caper. To have the loyalty of his fellow comrades meant a lot to him.

"Getting to Tanks stash is risky." Duke told them. "Even for someone who actually has Tank. The security that he has set-up is so elaborate, one slip and you'll have the entire Dickinson Police

Department on your ass in a matter of minutes."

Duke took a seat next to Clipso and accepted the blunt from him. After hitting the marijuana hard, he continued telling them the plan.

"The woman ain't no fool. She knows how hard it is to run up in the Willis, Winn, and Stone building with jackin' on ya mind. It's obvious she willing to try her luck, but now that we done came into the picture, she feels like she ain't gotta do the hard work no mo'."

He hit the blunt again.

"She wants us to do it for her."

Clipso and A.K. exchanged glances and then looked at Duke. He wasn't saying' what they thought he was saying'? Was he? The two of them considered the implications. The woman wanted them to break into the building and steal the money. She had tank though. Without Tank, it would be damn near impossible to gain access to Tanks money.

"So..." A.K. spoke up. "What 'exactly' are we going to do?"

Duke sighed. He had purposefully withheld a crucial bit of information from his team. Some information that he was now about to reveal to them. The woman had made one more request. It was sort of her insurance policy.

<u>....</u>

Meanwhile, over on the opposite side of town...

"Do you really think this is gonna work?" A.B. asked Layla as he hopped around the bedroom on one foot trying to hurry up and put his pants on.

"It has to." She responded. "It's our only hope for getting the girls 'and' the money."

In just a few minutes, Layla had come up

272

with a way to come out of this thing on top. She had accepted it was long shot, but she could see no other options. Someone had her daughter. There was no way in hell that she was going to leave town without Alize. Alize had been there for her through thick and thin. Ever since day one her daughter had been riding it out like a G. And she was only 13. That was the amazing part. The average 13-year-old couldn't hold down a position like she had been called on to play. But she not only held it down, she held it down like a pro. Layla was proud of her daughter.

A.B. got draped in his yellow and black unit. The same yellow and black Roca wear gear he had on the night Steel got killed. The outfit made him reminisce about his homeboy. It had been awhile since he just gave all of his attention to the memory of his road dog. A.B. stood in the middle of the room looking down at himself. He couldn't understand how something that began as seeking revenge for a fallen soldier could turn into... this. None of what he was doing lately seemed even remotely to be for Steel. It was like he had somehow gotten entangled into an endless web of fucked up situations. Fucked up situations that bred more fucked up situations. He no longer knew what he was doing any of this for. Was it for Steel? Was it for himself? Was it for Layla? Alize? Money?

"You gotta stay strong." Layla told him, as she finished getting dressed.

The two of them looked like twins with Layla dressed up in a matching black and yellow Roca wear unit. Hers was form fitting and made for females though. The material hugged her sexy curves.

"There are not too many people I trust with

my daughter. So just know that I trust you."

A.B. wasn't exactly feeling the plan, but he had no choice but to accept it.

"Are you sure you can get in and out by yourself?" he asked concerned. "You said it yourself. Security on that building is tight."

"Yeah. It's tight. But all you need to know is the layout of the building and the codes to the locks."

She stepped up to A.B. and grabbed him around the waist.

"I work there baby. And Tank got all of the codes."

She kissed him lightly on the lips.

"Don't worry about me. Just worry about Alize. By the time you get back here with those girls, I'll be back with the money."

She let him go and said, "Then we break camp, leave all the bullshit in Dickinson behind us, and live happily ever after.

Just that quick A.B. got mesmerized by the confident words, soft lips, and beautiful blue eyes of Layla. She had a hold on him that he didn't understand. Layla was a bad bitch and she was ride or die. That combination could win over a thug every time.

"Aiight." A.B. said, picking up the .38 and tucking it into his waistband. "Let's do this. I promise you boo. I'll bring Alize back in one piece."

"I know you will." She responded. "Now hurry up and get to the pick-up spot. You need to be there before the kidnapper gets there so you can peep out the scene. They want that money, so I doubt they'll try anything slick, but you need to be on point just in case."

A.B. nodded his head.

"Bet." He told her, turning around to head out of the bedroom.

Walking briskly through the living room with Layla close on his heels, A.B. called over his shoulder, "You sure you got a ride coming?"

Layla rolled her eyes behind his back. She was becoming frustrated with all of his questions. Her predicament was stressful enough without A.B. asking a thousand different questions. His many inquiries were threatening to rip to shreds the fabric of her elaborate lie.

"I tooold you." Layla whined, playfully nudging A.B. out of the front door. "My home girl that helped me get the best of Tank is on her way over here. Don't worry Daddy. You'll meet her. We just on a tight schedule right now."

She put her hands on her hips.

"If you don't leave soon, we might miss our chance to get Alize and LaQuisha back."

A.B. stepped out into the front yard and glanced back at Layla. His instincts were telling him that something was seriously wrong. Everything was happening so fast; he didn't have enough time to really get a handle on what was going on. He still didn't know why Layla wasn't at work. He didn't know how she knew about the kidnapping. He had absolutely no idea who Layla's secret "friend" was or what exactly they done to Tank to knock him out cold like that.

Suspiciously and wearily, A.B. returned Layla's smile with one of his own, and headed towards the Chrysler. His smile, just as he assumed hers was, was forced, fake, phony, and fraudulent.

A.B. made his way to Tanks car and climbed into the driver's seat. Starting the ignition, he thought to himself, "When all of this is over and done with, she gone have a hell of a lot of explaining to do!"

Layla watched, extremely relieved, as A.B. backed out of the driveway.

"Finally." She said sighing. "I thought he would never leave."

It was imperative that Layla got A.B. out of the house before her home girl Ashanti showed up and especially before Tank woke up. She had called Ashanti, as soon as she made the decision to steal Tanks car. With her daughter kidnapped, her car stranded on the side of the highway, and her boyfriend brought into the loop about her having Tank, she needed Ashanti by her side. And fast! Things had changed. Out of necessity she had changed the entire plan.

"Uuuggghhh." Tank moaned in a barely audible voice.

Layla's head snapped around at the sound. What she saw was literally right on time. Tank was twitching slightly and moaning. Drool slowly leaked from his mouth. It was time. He was coming too.

Layla looked down the road. A.B. was nowhere in sight. She liked that. Now she could do Tank how she really wanted to do him. All sorts of devilishly, evil, and wicked thoughts danced around in her head as she closed the front door and eased over to Tank. He was lying on the floor directly in front of the couch, so Layla just took a seat and watched him as he came back to life.

The Doctor said the process would take about 5 minutes for him to become coherent again. She couldn't wait to look him in his eyes and tell him just how she had played his ass. He thought he was sooo tough. Sooo in charge of everything. But look at him now. Hog tied and at the mercy of a woman he thought that he had total control over.

"You in charge?" Layla asked, putting her foot on the back of Tanks head. "By the end of the night, you'll have no choice but to accept who the badest bitch is. I don't need a nigga fa' shit!"

Layla threw her head back and laughed out loud. Her labors of the past few months were finally about to bring forth a harvest. A harvest she estimated to be worth at least 3.5 million dollars. And that was at the least.

.....

A.K. grumbled his frustrations as he drove the candy red Escalade to the designated place. His two homeboys, Clipso and Duke, sat patiently back at the apartment awaiting the call saying the handoff had been made. For now, it was just him, LaQuisha, Alize, Krystal, and a very distraught Ming.

Melissa's body was wrapped up in plastic in preparation for a late-night dip in the Dickinson Bayou. When some unlucky fisherman found her body, there would be no evidence on the body connecting Clipso to the crime. The only witnesses, her home girls, would all be dead by the nights end.

The S.U.V.'s rearview mirror allowed A.K. to constantly watch the movements of his still tied up, blindfolded, and gagged cargo. After seeing Clipso rape Ming and murder Melissa, they all ceased to resist. They were quiet and still. Just how he needed them to be.

As A.K. drove, he mulled over the woman's request in his mind. It was strange, and yet oddly meticulous. The woman had told Duke that she wanted all of the hostages turned over to her, she only wanted one of them to deliver the girls, and the one that delivered the girls had to also allow himself to be turned over.

A.K. was frustrated with her guidelines but he fully understood why she wanted one of them in her possession. After she had given up the codes to all of Tanks security, she needed to be sure that they wouldn't just hit the lick and bounce. A.K. was going to be her insurance policy.

She was smart. It would pose a real challenge for them to simply outwit her. The woman had seemed to cover all of her bases. She was systematically taking full control of the joint mission. All they could do was play her game and wait on an opportunity to present itself.

Duke had told them that they would just play it cool until the actual exchange. Money for A.K. Her whole strategy was so effective because she was managing to stay low key and out of sight. They had no idea who she was or where she was.

Her mistake though, was sending Duke and Clipso to pull off the heist. That meant she would have no choice but to come out of the shadows once they had the loot. And once they had the loot, they would have the one thing the woman wanted. If they had what the woman wanted, they would also have some power back. With the power, they could demand to meet face to face and exchange the money for A.K. When they met with the woman face to face… she would pay dearly for interfering in their business.

A.K. made it to the highway and merged in with the traffic. His gut was telling him that the woman was hiding out somewhere in Dickinson, and the only reason she had him traveling all the way to Houston to deliver the girls was to keep her true location a secret.

"You'll get yours by the end of the night."
He said to Layla but really to himself. Then he
leaned forward and turned up the radio a little. He
figured he might as well get comfortable. His
destination was about 1 hour 20 minutes away.

.....

Tanks head was spinning like a merry-go-
round and his body felt like it had been run over by
a Mack truck.

"Mmmm." He moaned, trying desperately to
compose himself.

He couldn't remember anything. The
thoughts in his head were all mixed up and
completely incoherent.

"What happened to me?" he wondered.

Tank strained to open his eyes, but his
eyelids seemed to weigh a ton. It was a battle just to
get them to crack.

Come on Tank. You gotta get a hold of
yourself. Just breathe baby. Breathe.

Tank sucked in some fresh air through his
nose, held it, and then released slowly. He repeated
that act about 2 more times.

Alright Tank. Now… open your eyes and
see where you're at.

"Nnnggg." He groaned, as his eyelids began
to split.

"Aaaahhh." He cried out.

The light from the room he was in attacked
his retina's and burned like hell.

"Ha! Ha! Ha! Ha! Ha!" he heard a woman's
voice laughing and echoing. The noise appeared to
be distant, but it was unusually crisp.

Tank tried to move.

What the fuck?

My hands? My feet?

Tank was slowly becoming able to sift through the jumble of words, pictures, and sounds that were floating around free inside of his cranium.

He opened his eyes up again, but only wide enough for him to peek. His vision was too blurry to make sense of what he was seeing though. As he struggled to bring things into focus, he heard the woman's voice again. This time she sounded closer.

"Taaaank." She cooed. "Are you alright alright alright alright? Ha! Ha! Ha! Ha! Ha!"

The voice still echoed.

Who is that female? Why isn't she helping me? Why is she here? Hell, where the fuck is here?

Tank thought back and tried to remember something. Anything! After a few moments of contemplating, his vision cleared up just enough for him to see who had been laughing at him. The colors and shapes finally blended together into something his brain could comprehend.

Tanks mouth opened wide as he gasped.

"What the hell is going on here? He thought.

Right there in front of him, sitting on a couch together like the best of friends, was two women Tank couldn't believe even knew each other. It was Layla and Ashanti! Seeing the two of them brought a tidal wave of memory rushing back. Their smiling faces assisted him in sorting through the madness.

That's right. I went to Dr. Abu-Kahr's house to pay him that $25,000. Ashanti was there. Ashanti was naked. She showed me to my seat, went and got Abu-Kahr, then gave me a cigar.

The cigar was exotic. It tasted weird. I liked it though. I puffed on it and spoke with the Doctor. We spoke about a plant. It had a strange name. Habi… Habi… fuck it. Some plant! Hmmm. What happened next?

Gasp! The phone call. The kidnapping.

"LaQuisha." He mumbled.

Layla leaned over and looked Tank in his eyes.

"Oh. I wouldn't worry about LaQuisha if I were you." She told him. "LaQuisha and Alize are alright. I'm going to get them back. Who you need to be worried about is yourself."

Tank looked from woman to woman. Their expressions were stone cold and square business.

"What is this all about?" he asked. "I thought we was in this thing together. Why aren't you helping me to get free?"

Both women laughed at the remark.

"Help you get free?!" Layla repeated. "Why would I help you get free and I'm the one who tied you up in the first place?"

Tank stared at her. He was right. She had double crossed him. The no good, dirty, dope fiend ass hoe had set him up. Now he was glad that he had made his first move. If he would've waited to go on the attack, he would be shit out of luck right now.

"That's right." Layla mocked. "I'm the one that did this to you."

She nodded her head towards Ashanti.

"Well, I couldn't have done it by myself. My home girl here played a major part in all of this."

Tank knew that he had an ace in the hole. Whatever game these women were playing… they would lose. All he had to do was chill and wait.

"Since when did the two of you become friends?" Tank inquired, trying to stall them long enough for him to figure out what was going on.

The women exchanged glances.

"We used to work together." Ashanti answered. "Well, technically we still do, but we used to work together legally too."

"That is," Layla added, "Until our boss fired us and everybody else that worked for the company."

"Yeah, that was fucked up." Ashanti said pouting. "We all got fired because of one person's mistake."

She shook her head.

"I heard Bunny paid for that mistake with her life. Tsk, tsk, tsk. Poor Bunny."

Tanks guard instantly went up when he heard the name Bunny. He knew that Layla knew who Bunny was, but she wasn't supposed to tell anyone. How did Ashanti know?

"Giiirl." Layla said. "Who knew that working for a Law Firm could be so action packed and drama filled?"

Tank was now extremely suspicious.

"Law Firm?" he asked.

"Oh, you ain't know?" Layla asked. "Me and Ashanti here both use to work for Willis, Winn, and Stone. And we both been knew that 'Stone' was just another alias name for the one and only Tank, A.K.A. Tony Quinten."

Tank was shocked. The expression on his face gave both of the women more pleasure then they thought it would. He couldn't believe it. If what they were saying was true, then there never really was a double cross move by Layla. In reality, she was never on his team to begin with. He now regretted not knowing any of his employees.

"Come on Tank." Layla said, reaching down to pat his head. "You should be a little smarted than that. Did you really believe that a heroin addict like Bunny could've infiltrated that building?"

"But… but… but…" Tank stuttered. "How… how did you know about me?"

"Ooo! Ooo! Ooo!" Ashanti said, raising her hand high in the air like schoolgirl trying to answer a question in class. "I know! I know! Let me answer this one."

"By all means." Layla replied. "Go right ahead."

"This is the funny part." Ashanti said happily. "You know those two dudes you took from pretty much nothing, and funded the opening of their own Law Firm?"

Tank thought about it.

"You mean Henry and Marshall?" he asked.

"Yeeeah." Ashanti answered. "Henry Willis and Marshall Winn. You would think that after you had showed them so much love, they would at least be loyal to you. Buuut unfortunately, like most men, Henry and Marshall were more loyal to their dicks than to you."

"Their dicks???" Tank wondered.

"You didn't know it," Ashanti continued, "But me and Layla here use to be receptionists at your little Law Firm. And your partners… we had them wrapped around our fingers."

She patted her goodies through the crotch of her black pants.

"Those fools were pussy whipped. Pussy whipped and paying to play. I mean, they had it so bad they would even have us inside of the office building after hours."

Ashanti looked at Tank and smirked.

"That's how we found out about you daddy."

Tanks eyes grew wide with the realization of what was being said to him. It was all so obvious. So plain. So... so... so right in his face that he felt like a fool for not seeing it before. He knew that all slippers could count. Even the slips that he himself didn't make. All he had to do was give someone else inside information about his business. And if they slipped and let the shit get out, he would suffer the consequences.

The two women continued to brag and boast about how they had so perfectly set Tank up for failure. They started at the beginning and weaved him a tale of non-stop deceptive and conniving actions. As they took him back to a night that had died several months ago, his anger was almost overshadowed by his awe of their persistence and intelligence. They were two bad bitches for real.

"You remember that night Tank here almost caught Henry and Marshall fucking us in the office?" Ashanti asked.

"How could I forget?" responded Layla. "That was the night that led to all of this."

With their words, the women took Tank back. All the way back to a night that happened about 5 months ago...

"Drink! Drink! Drink! Drink! Drink!" Layla and Ashanti chanted.

Both Henry and Marshall had bottles of Budweiser turned straight up in the air trying to see who could chug the most before the intense burning in their throats got to be too much. Neither one of the two guys were the kind you'd expect to see getting fucked up off of liquor and powder.

Henry was a 43-year-old white guy with hair only on the sides and the back of his head. The top had dropped long ago like a convertible Mustang.

His pudgy frame testified to the fact that he had never been big on physical fitness. While the other kids were playing sports, he was at home playing chess. With himself.

Marshall wasn't any different. The only thing that really distinguished the two apart was Marshalls glasses. They were huge with thick black frames. People often teased him saying that he had some T.D.C. glasses. That joke always went over his head because he had never been to prison. He didn't know that people in the penitentiary with bad vision got issued glasses similar to his own. The comparison between him and prison men ended there, though. He was flabby and balding just like Henry.

The two of them had bread though. A lot of motherfucking bread. They were lawyers. And one thing about them… they didn't mind using that bread to enjoy themselves. Even if it meant tricking with two of the sexiest females they had working for them.

Layla and Ashanti stood on the conference room table wearing nothing but their thongs and bras. Henry and Marshall were reclining back in two of the twelve chairs that lined the long cherry oak table. They were still clothed in their business suits. Well, sort of. Both men had their jackets off and white dress shirts completely unbuttoned. Their black slacks were pulled down around their ankles and they had their erect penises standing up through the hole in their boxers.

Five and ten-dollar bills were scattered across the table top. The women gave them an exotic and sexually stimulating strip tease while they stroked themselves to the idea of penetrating the two beautiful women. All of the various degrees, certificates, and plaques on the walls gave the whole scene the feel of an X-rated movie set.

Two almost naked women dancing on a conference room table. Two middle aged white guys lusting after them and using them as their very own personal sex toys. Bottles of Vodka and bottles of beer all over the place. And lines of coke the size of a man's thumb already prepped for inhalation into the nostrils of anyone who wanted to get higher.

"Ssssssss!" Henry hissed as the burning became more than he could handle.

He lowered his bottle and leaned over coughing.

Marshall, who was still chugging, cut his eyes at Henry. He knew he was going to win. Marshall detached the bottle from his lips and wiped his mouth off with the back of his sleeve.

"Ahhh." He sighed after swallowing his final mouth full. "Don't feel bad Henry. It takes a REAL man to handle his liquor like I do."

He winked at the girls.

"So?" he said, setting the bottle down in the cup holder on the leather chair and rubbing his hands together. "Tell me ladies. What prize did I win for coming out victorious in you little competition?"

The women looked at each other seductively, whispered back and forth in each other's ear, and then turned back to Marshall.

"You… win," Layla told him. "A… private… show. In which me and Ashanti both will work oh so hard at getting you off."

COUGH! COUGH!

Henry peered up through bloodshot eyes.

"What do you mean, private?" he

questioned.

"Private as in, you need to go somewhere else until we tell you to come back." replied Ashanti.

"Wait just one minute. I paid my money too. Ya'll can't just leave me out over some stupid challenge."

"Nooo baby. You got it all wrong. We fully intend on giving you your money's worth too. It's just that the only way to reward Marshall is by giving him some private ménage trio's time. Calm down boo. You'll get your turn."

Henry pouted. He didn't want to miss out on any of the action.

"Oh, come on Henry." Marshall said. "Like the kids say now-a-days, 'Don't Hate'."

Everybody but Henry burst out laughing. He was too busy mumbling and cursing under his breath.

"Ya'll just be sure to hurry up." He told them, reluctantly rising out of his seat.

Henry pulled up his pants and headed towards the door. He could hear them snickering behind him.

"That's cool." He thought. "But if they take too long, I want my $500 back."

Layla, Ashanti, and Marshall waited patiently while Henry left the room. He mumbled and grumbled the whole way out.

"What a sore loser." Ashanti said disappointedly.

"I bet if I had been the one to lose," Marshall added, "he would have probably dragged me out of here by my ears."

Marshall laughed at his own joke but the ladies did not. They had more important things on their minds that far outweighed some old white guys' idea of humor. Important things like the money they were being paid for tonight's entertainment.

Layla was experienced in the field of prostitution because of her drug addiction. Ashanti, on the other hand, didn't use drugs. Well, she smoked weed and sniffed cocaine, but she never touched crack a day in her life. The only reason she had gotten into the business of selling herself on occasion was because Layla was so damn good at convincing her that it would be the easiest money she ever made. Layla wasn't just looking out for her though. She knew that two beautiful women could bring in more feddy than just one.

This was only like their third time tricking with their bosses, but Ashanti had taken to the job like a pro. Her money-minded attitude made Layla start cutting for her for real. The two of them became friends as well as business partners.

"Fuck him." Layla said in an extremely sultry voice, referring to Henry. "We not gone let him ruin this for Marshall with his little attitude."

She turned to Ashanti and gazed deep into her eyes. Ashanti could feel the sexual energy surge from Layla, to her, and back again.

"Are we baby?" she asked.

Marshall watched like a hormone filled teenager as Layla closed the gap between her and the exotic looking Puerto Rican. From his seat he could look up like man viewing heaven. As the pearly gates swung wide, revealing the perfection of Adam's rib, Marshall silently gave thanks for the vision of paradise.

The full lips of Layla connected gently with the pouty lips of Ashanti. Four hands, sixteen fingers, and four thumbs all embarked on an exploration of sorts across the hill country. Layla and Ashanti touched each other on the tabletop. Their bodies collided at the breast, waist, and thighs. Their natural instincts were to squirm with delight.

Layla's mouth felt good. Lay's hands on Ashanti's ass felt great. Ashanti moaned as they kissed, falling deeper into the crevasses of pleasures unrivaled. She found that she enjoyed being with women almost as much as she enjoyed the rugged thrusts of a man. Especially when the woman was as skilled as Layla.

Layla's tongue danced with Ashanti's for a few more seconds then she pulled back. The two women were breathing heavy. Layla cut her eyes at Marshall. As expected, his mouth was hanging open and his hand was stroking his meat.

Layla smirked. Men were so predictable and easy to manipulate that if she actually had a conscience, she would feel bad about how she did them. But unfortunately for men, all she cared about was two things. Her personal satisfaction and her personal bank account. She knew that all men, or at least the straight ones, had a fantasy of seeing two sexy women make love to each other. And experience had taught her that the attraction was so strong they couldn't contain themselves when confronted with the fantasy.

Layla curled her lips and sucked in air through her teeth.

"Damn baby." She cooed aggressively. "You makin me sooo hot and sooo wet at the same time."

Ashanti ran her fingers through her hair like she could barely contain herself.

"Let's get naked." Layla suggested.

"Oh hell yeah." Ashanti replied.

The two women peeled off their undergarments in a frenzy. Layla kept checking on Marshall out the corner of her eye. As expected, he was working his tool more vigorously. At the rate he was going he would end up summing all over the place before Layla even touched him.

Ashanti and Layla squirmed and squealed until they were both fully exposed. They stood atop the table and fondled themselves. Layla's hands caressed Layla's body and Ashanti's fingers penetrated Ashanti's walls. She let out a sigh of ecstasy as her index finger located her spot.

"Mmmm." She sighed softly, squeezing her thighs together and smothering her hand.

Layla zoomed in on the two fingers that were sliding in and out of Ashanti's wet, shaved, sweet smelling love box. The streaks of Ashanti's juices reflected the fluorescent lights in the same way the drops of morning dew reflect the Sun.

Taking charge, Layla instructed Ashanti to lay down flat on her back on top of the scattered bills they had received for their seductive dancing. She had gotten hungry just watching her homegirls fingers slip and slide.

Ashanti complied without hesitation.

"Ooo... oo... oo... Yee... eah." Marshall's voice was choppy because he was bouncing up and down.

The way Layla had laid Ashanti's sexy frame down and then got on all fours in between her gapped legs really had him going.

"Eat that pussy Layla." He encouraged her. "Lick all on that pink ass pearl tongue."

Layla needed no direction. She cocked her

nice, round, soft ass up in the air and she lowered her lips to Ashanti's lips.

She kissed her vagina.

Ashanti moaned.

Layla's tongue extended past her lips and reached out to greet the special place of Ashanti.

"Well hello there." Her tongue said, with a series of flicks and licks. "Nice to meet you."

"Nice to meet you too." The special place responded, with a stream of clear slightly cloudy liquid.

Layla's tongue licked from Ashanti's hole all the way up to her clitoris. Ashanti's back arched and she rocked as the sensation of sexual satisfaction overloaded her brain.

Ashanti could fell Layla's tongue going in and out of her like a short but very effective penis. She grabbed two handfuls of Layla's pretty blonde hair and began grinding her hips into her face.

"Damn this bitch can eat some good ass pussy!" Ashanti thought.

Layla was making her feel better than the men she had been with could. She was slurping and sucking on Ashanti's goodies like oral sex was going out of style.

"That's right." Marshall said to himself. "Keep on licking. Daddy is about to cum."

He could feel his load preparing to explode at any minute. A few more pumps and it would be over with.

Ashanti's ample breasts rose and fell as she began to breathe heavily. Layla's neck swiveled and swerved, kicking it into overdrive as she sensed Ashanti's orgasm nearing. Marshall's entire body tensed up as he willed his testicles to induce the euphoric feeling that accompanied ejaculation.

"YES!" Ashanti hollered.

"Mm-hmm!" Layla moaned with a mouth full of pussy.

"SHIT!" Marshall cursed.

BAM!

The door to the conference room came bursting open.

"FUCK!" Henry shouted, as he rushed in with a panicked expression on his face.

"OOOOHHHH! YEEESSS! Ashanti wailed, as her orgasm hit her hard.

"Uuunngghh." Marshall groaned as his release shot straight up in the air and his body jerked.

Henry took in the scene quickly. The naked women were as threat for his eyes indeed, but they had a problem. A BIG problem.

Layla, Ashanti, and Marshall were all interrupted by Henry's intrusion, but they were all too far gone in the throes of passion to just stop what they were doing at the drop of a dime. So, Henry had no choice but to wait a few seconds while Marshall and Ashanti unloaded.

Squeals of pleasure echoed throughout the room. Beads of sweat sparkled on foreheads. Smiles and closed eyes covered faces. Moments like these are what make sex worthwhile. Feelings such as the ones being felt are the gasoline that fuel the raging fires of S.T.D.'s and unplanned pregnancies. Human beings will boldly and brazenly risk unimaginable consequences all for a nut. The promise of an orgasm quickly reduces the most dominant and intelligent species to the level of beast. Clear and conscious thought gets overshadowed by primal instincts.

Ashanti stretched out on her back and

rubbed her torso slowly. Layla had stopped eating her but it was like she could still feel her tongue on her clitoris.

Exhausted, Marshall reclined in the leather chair and allowed his softening member to fall to the right.

Layla simply tasted Ashanti's white reward and stared at her passionately. She didn't do women regularly, so it was a welcomed and unique treat to reduce a woman as lovely as Ashanti to the state of a quivering mass of sexually fulfilled flesh.

"I did that." Layla thought proudly.

Henry had seen enough. He knew that if they didn't clean that room up pronto, the shit was defiantly going to hit the fan.

"Get up Marshall!" he ordered his business partner as he made a beeline for the pile of cocaine. "Get up and get dressed!"

Everybody in the room could feel the strange vibe that Henry was giving off, but nobody knew what was going on.

Confused, Marshall asked, "Henry. What's gotten into you?"

Henry scooped all of the loose powder into the plastic baggy it had been dumped out of and blew the residue onto the floor.

"We gotta move fast." Henry told him, dropping the baggy in his pocket. "I just saw the boss pull up. If he catches us in here with... with them... like this, we out of there."

Marshall jumped up and started pulling up his clothes when he heard the bosses name get mentioned.

"What's Tony doing here?" he inquired, struggling to get himself presentable.

"I have no idea." Henry answered. "All I

know is that he's here. I just saw him pull up out back on the security camera."

The conversation had successfully spooked both Layla and Ashanti. They had sobered up real quick. Layla kept a level head though. She rose to her feet and began scooping up the loose bills. Ashanti didn't know what to do. Her first mind told her to get dressed.

"Who the hell is Tony?" Layla asked. "I thought ya'll were the bosses. What's going on here?"

"It's a long story." Henry answered, grabbing up beer bottles and tossing them into the trash. "We'll explain later. But for now, ya'll two have to hide."

The two women climbed off the table.

"Hide?!" Layla repeated. "You mean like some high school girls who snuck into their boyfriend's bedroom?"

She rolled her eyes.

"Boo please. I'm a grown ass woman. I don't do no hiding."

Henry sighed.

"Come on Layla. Just…"

She folded her arms across her still naked breast.

"What if we give you some more money? Would you hide then?"

Layla unfolded her arms. "How much money we talkin'?"

Henry dug around in his pockets and pulled out whatever loose bills he could find. Seeing a fifty-dollar bill on top, Layla snatched the whole stack and agreed to hide.

"Hurry up girl." She told Ashanti, grabbing her clothes off of the floor and table. "Let's get somewhere before Tony show up."

The two men did a rush clean up job on the room and the two women ducked off into the storage closet inside of the room. The space was cramped due to all of the extra office supplies, but they fit pretty comfortably. They had enough room to get dressed.

It was dark inside of the storage room, but the women were so close they could see each other. They stood there perfectly still, listening to what was going on outside. Layla estimated that they had been inside of the closet for about 7 minutes before the man Henry and Marshall called Boss could be heard. From the sound of it, he wasn't even mad at the two guys for being there after hours. They had shot him some bullshit story about working on one of their larger cases and the dude bought it.

"So, Tony." Layla heard Henry say after the small talk was made and the lies were set in place. "What brings you to the office this time of night? We don't usually see you around here. I know how you like to stay low key."

"Damn Henry." Tony responded playfully. "how many times do I have to tell you about that Tony shit? Call me Tank, man. Everybody else does."

Layla gasped, but only loud enough for Ashanti to hear her.

"What is it?" Ashanti whispered.

Layla swallowed hard. Could it be?

"I think I know who that is." She answered.

"For real?? Who is it?"

Layla pressed her ear harder to the door.

"Shhh." She shushed. "I can't hear. Let me see if I'm right first."

Ashanti was curious but she held her tongue.

She knew that her home girl would explain herself eventually.

"… didn't plan on coming up here tonight." Tank was saying, "but something came up. I fucked up around and hit an unexpected lick for a nice lil chunk of change and I need to put this cash up. You know how it go."

Layla's eyes popped open like saucers. If she had been a cartoon character, big ol' green dollar signs would've replaced her pupils. That last statement had pretty much confirmed what she initially thought. All she needed to do was sneak a peek at the man so that she could be 100% sure. Already though, at 95% surety, her brain had cranked up and was plotting a master plan. That was one thing about Layla. She never stopped thinking of ways to come up. Any opportunity she saw, she was going to do her best to capitalize off of it.

Knowing that whenever she cracked open the door to get a good look at the mystery man, she would be taking a major risk, Layla tried not to think about it.

"Just do it." She willed herself.

It took her a couple of minutes to build up the courage she needed, but eventually, her shaky hand clamped down on the doorknob and turned. Holding her breath, she pushed the door open just enough for one of her eyes to be able to see out. What she saw clenched it for her.

Standing alone in the room, with his back to her, was the unmistakable six-foot frame of a man she knew around the way as a street boss. With his solid red t-shirt, creased up black jeans, red and black ball cap, and all black Air Force Ones, it was obvious he was the type to hire lawyers to help him beat a case, not hire lawyers to work for him by beating other people's cases. The reason her two bosses called Tank boss was still a mystery, but she knew that she could get the information out of them easily. All she would have to do is suck one of their dicks. That always worked.

Tank quickly unloaded a duffel bag full of cash into his hidden wall safe. The safe was concealed behind a nice sized framed poster that blended in well with the certificates and degrees hanging all over the place. The poster was nothing more than a poem. A poem about hard work and never giving up.

Layla peered into the safe and her heart almost skipped a beat. All she could see was stacks of cash. The safe was deep and wide. And it was damn near filled up.

"Wait a minute." Layla squinted her eyes. "Is that what I think it is?"

Along with the money, Tank had pounds and pounds of marijuana stashed away inside of the safe.

"What do you see?" Ashanti whispered, tired of being left in the dark.

Layla eased the door shut. The grin one her face was from ear to ear.

"Ashanti," Layla whispered back through the darkness. "I see our meal ticket."

CHAPTER FIFTEEN

The streets were grimy.

The streets were heartless and cold.

The streets, and maybe 98% of the people in the streets, could not be trusted. Tank knew this. He had known this since he was young. And yet, his current situation seemed to have the power to drive that particular point home better than any other event in his life. He couldn't believe that a female smoker actually had the mind and the patience to pull off something so elaborate. Here he was, one of the most major figures in the Dickinson, Tx. underworld, hog tied and being ridiculed. The gangster inside of him was boiling hot and ready to kill. The man inside of him had his pride scarred and was ready to hide in shame. The plotting, scheming, planning strategist in him was intrigued and ready to figure out exactly how she had done it.

"So," Tank said, after finding out his two lawyers had helped to dress him up like a holiday ham. "Is that when you came up with the idea for all of this?"

Layla leaned back on the couch and crossed her legs. She was loving every minute of this. All of the nights she sat up wondering and worrying if everything was going to fall into place were now worth it. Only time now separated her from her prize. Licks like this came once in a lifetime. She saw her chance and she took it. Even when it seemed like a long shot, she continued to play her role. Now it was all about to pay off.

She interlocked her fingers behind her head.

"Although I would like to take credit for

masterminding all of this from the jump, I can't. Really, my plan done switched up on me so many times due to circumstances out of my control, the whole thing has sort of taken on a life of its own. In the beginning, I just planned on stealing yo shit. You know? A good ol' fashion burglary. But once I got inside the office building and reached the safe, I found out just how well protected your stash really was."

Layla whistled.

"I damn near went to jail fucking with that security system. I didn't leave empty handed though. I might not have gotten the money and the weed, but I did get some electronics up out that bitch."

Tank furrowed his brow.

"What?!?" he asked, clearly puzzled. "You broke into Willis, Winn, and Stone and stole electronic equipment?"

Layla smiled enthusiastically. She knew that that little revelation would shock him.

"Oh." Layla said in a sarcastic tone. "You didn't know that you made the right decision to fire everybody because it had the feel of an inside job?"

Ashanti smacked her teeth.

"Of course, he didn't know." She added, using the same level of sarcasm as Layla. "He also thought them niggas over there in the projects, Sticky, and Luck, had something to do with it. For some reason he thought they had sent Bunny up in there to clean him out."

"For some reason!?" Tank shot out. "Layla, you told me they the ones that sent Bunny in there!"

Layla twirled her hair around her finger like a dumb blonde.

"Oh yeah." She said, after a moment of

staring off into space. "I did tell you that. I was just lying though. I knew that my only hope of getting past that security you got set-up would be to get close to you. Sooo, I gave Bunny the shit that I stole, brought her to you with some bullshit story about Sticky and Luck, convinced you that Sticky and Luck were out to get you for moving in on their turf, and viola, I swear to help you pay them back, and with that, I'm in like Flin."

Layla knew that her underhanded tactic of getting in good with Tank had its fucked up parts, but she could see no other way. Yeah, manipulated Bunny into setting herself up to get killed, but she rationalized it in her mind. Bunny was strung out on heroine. She was out there bad. Layla figured it was only a matter of time before she checked out anyway. Why not make sure that her death was a blessing to someone else? It was easy too. A few hits of her drug of choice and Bunny was swearing on God, Allah, Jehovah, and whoever else that Sticky and Luck had paid her to rob Tank.

Tank thought about how Bunny looked when she realized that the liquid she had just injected into her veins was not what she had expected it to be. It was poison. Poison provided by the good Dr. Abu-Kahr.

Layla sighed and stood to her feet. She was now growing tired of the conversation. It was time she got on with the plan. After all, as long as she didn't have the actual money and drugs in her possession, she had to stay focused.

"Watch him." Layla instructed Ashanti. "I'll be right back."

Ashanti watched Layla walk off. She had a damn good idea what her home girl was going to go get but Tank didn't have a clue.

Layla sashayed into her daughters' room like she was on top of the world. Like she couldn't be touched. A couple of days ago she had given her daughter something very important to hold onto for her. Something that was vital to her overall mission.

Layla entered Alize's bedroom and went straight to the closet. She knew what she was looking for and she knew where it could be found. Waiting patiently on her, tucked away under a pile of dirty clothes, was a black trash bag. Layla dug the bag from beneath the pile and stared at it.

Just the sight of the bag changed her attitude. She went from happy to sad instantly. Deep down, she didn't want it to come to this. Enough people had been either hurt or deceived by her attempt to get rich. Even some people that she actually cared about. Like A.B. He had been to hell and back fucking with her. Layla knew that if A.B. was to ever find out the truth, his feelings for her would change instantly. That is why she couldn't take him with her.

Layla's body shivered as she thought about what must be done. Standing alone in the closet, she carefully untied the knot in the trash bag. Once it hung open in her hands, she took a deep breath and peeked inside. In her mind, she did a quick inventory.

Latex gloves. Check!
3 grams of crack. Check!
32 Xanax pills. Check!
Tape recorder. Check!

Layla knew that she had to be prepared for anything. She had plans A-Z already lined up. And even when Alize questioned the purpose of her stashing away such items, she knew that they might come in handy.

Layla gripped the bag and walked with purpose back into the living room. Tank and Ashanti were making small talk, but all of that ended when she dumped the strange items out onto the couch.

Ashanti knew what time it was.

Tank stared with a mixture of wonder and fear in his eyes as Layla silently began putting on the gloves.

"Wha… what are you about to do?" he stammered out.

Layla's silence and straight face told him that whatever she was about to do wasn't gonna end up good for him.

CHAPTER SIXTEEN

The Wal-Mart parking lot was just as packed as always. Mini-vans, sport cars, hoopties, and expense foreign vehicles were all packed between the yellow and white lines painted onto the pavement. Some people who had just pulled up were making their way towards the sliding glass doors while others were coming out with baskets full of merchandise. Cart-boys were collecting discarded shopping carts and returning them to their proper place inside of the store, the volunteer worker for the Salvation Army stood ringing his bell in front of the building seeking donations, and one of several security personnel was diligently circling the parking lot in his all gray uniform and electric golf cart.

A.K. was keeping his eyes on everyone. Even the Sheriff who was waiting to fill up his cruiser only 30 feet away. The Murphy gas station that shared parking lots with the Wal-Mart was always considered a welcomed convenience. But now that A.K. was forced to use the area to hand over his hostages as well as himself, it was proving to just be in the way.

He had been sitting in the last row in the very last parking space available for the past 10 minutes. He was keeping his eyes open for the person he had been sent there to meet, but so far, no one had even attempted to approach him.

"Maybe he's just waiting on that cop to leave?" A.K. thought.

If it wouldn't have been for the heat that the ever-rising Sun was creating, he wouldn't have been so eager to do what he had to do and get it over with.

"Mmm. Mmm."

One of the girls mumbled and A.K. turned around quickly to investigate. The last thing he needed was for one of them to start making a lot of noise and spark someone's curiosity.

"Mmmm." LaQuisha moaned.

She was tired of laying across the seat hog tied, blindfolded, and gagged. It was uncomfortable as hell how they were packed into the S.U.V. LaQuisha was tied up and tossed on the middle seat while Alize was tied up and tossed onto the floorboard in front of her.

Krystal was restrained and tossed onto the back seat and Ming, back fully clothed, was crammed onto the floorboard in front of her.

Even though they were told that they were about to be let go, none of them believed it. They felt as if they were all being taken somewhere to be executed and dumped.

LaQuisha had noticed that the vehicle had been stationary for a while now. The sounds that reached her ears let her know that she was in a public place. She could hear people, cars, and the opening and closing of car doors. The only thing she hadn't heard in a while was the voice of the kidnappers. She knew it was a long shot, but maybe, just maybe they had ditched the truck with the girls still inside and were putting some distance between themselves and the girls before they were discovered.

Of course, LaQuisha couldn't understand why they would just let them go like that.

"Maybe Tank paid the ransom?" she thought.

LaQuisha tried desperately to spit the gag from her mouth and to remove the rope from her wrist. A.K. watched her struggle for a few moments. He figured she was searching for a better position and would eventually stop of her own volition and free will.

It didn't take long for him to realize that she would not.

"HEY!" he growled, startling her into being still. "You betta calm yo ass down back there 'fo you end up like that Mexican chick."

A.K.'s voice made all of the girls straighten up. Especially by him mentioning Melissa. So much shit was going on that they still couldn't really come to grips with the reality that she was dead. It all seemed so surreal. Like a dream or a misty fog that rolled in and faded out in the middle of the night when there was no one awake to even notice.

Ming's entire body flinched as the throbbing pain in her lower parts sent shockwaves through her. To her, there was nothing dreamlike about it. Her intense pain was real. Her feeling of being violated and disrespected was real. Her mental thoughts of the dishonor she had brought on herself, her family, and her future husband was real.

Ming shuddered as A.K. threatened them again and again with death if they didn't shut-up and be still. For Ming, even the horror and fear were all too real.

All of the girls complied with A.K.'s demand to be quiet. None of them wanted to end up like Melissa. They could still visualize Clipso's blade slicing through her throat and they could still hear the gurgling sounds that she made before her heart thumped for the very last time. It was the kind of scene that stuck with a person for life.

A.K. turned back around in his seat and checked his mirrors. The last thing he needed was some 'concerned' citizen coming over to the Escalade to investigate. He already had enough on his plate. And threatening his hostages with the same fate as the Mexican had brought one of his biggest problems back to the fore front of his mind.

"How am I gonna explain what happened to her?" he wondered.

Duke had told him to just say that she tried to escape. The missing girl might pose a problem, but then again, it might not. But if it did cause a major problem, A.K. had orders to do whatever he had to do to keep the man that had Tank from getting away. Even if it meant gun play.

The Wal-Mart security guard turned his golf cart onto the row that A.K. was parked on. Scott, the security guard, was a 42-year-old, borderline obese, extremely racist, white man who loved the superficial power his job produced. He had his head shaved bald and his right arm was almost covered with tattoos of devils, demons, skulls, swastika's, and lightning bolts. Scott had never done any time in the pen, but he managed to look like he had.

Scott made his way down the row, and as was his job, he examined every single face and every single car he encountered. He had been working for Wal-Mart as a security guard for five years now and he had never encountered anything more serious than the occasional theft or a fist fight over a particular parking space. Yet and still, he always played the part of some bad ass street cop in his own mind. His golf cart was his squad car, his mace was his gun, the Wal-Mart parking lot was the neighborhood he was assigned to patrol, and the stores customers were the drug dealers, murderers, and robbers he was sworn to protect the citizens from.

Scott squinted his eyes at the bright red Cadillac Escalade that sat at the end of the row. A vehicle like that would stand out anywhere. He had noticed it when it first pulled up and parked, and his instincts had him watching it ever since. For one, the color of it and all the extra accessories on it just screamed drug dealer. And two, a young black male was driving it.

Something inside of him wanted to harass the driver immediately but he had done that before. The result... talks of racism, legal action, and a threat that he might lose his job. Scott longed for the good ol' days when the Constitutions description of black people as 3/5 of a person actually meant something. Nowadays affirmative rights made it hard for a white man to treat a black how Scott felt they should be treated.

"He's just been sitting there for fifteen minutes." Scott said to himself as he approached the DS.U.V. "Technically, I have an obligation to go to him and make sure that 'everything is alright'."

Scott smiled a mischievous smile and brought his electric golf cart to a stop behind the Escalade. Reaching down to his waist, he checked to make sure that his mace was still in place, then he struggled to climb his 5'7 315lbs. frame out of the cart.

"Shit!" A.K. cursed under his breath.

He was watching the security guard approach through his rearview mirror.

"Fuck! Fuck! Fuck!" he mumbled, as Scott wobbled his fat ass closer to the driver's side window. "I can't let that hoe see those girls."

A.K.'s mind raced to figure out a way out of

this. His eyes cut from side to side as if the answer would be found to his left or his right. He gripped and un-gripped the steering wheel nervously. He was drawing a blank. The fool had parked right behind him so he couldn't even drive off.

Quickly running out of time and options, A.K. pulled his black baby .380 out of his waistband and placed his left hand on the handle of the door. There was no way he was going to get jammed up by a bitch ass rent-a-cop. He'd blow that fools head off first.

Scott hiked up his ever-falling pants and strolled towards A.K. with a smug expression on his face. He could see him fumbling around in the driver's seat and he wanted to laugh out loud. It was always amusing to see one of those so-called 'thugs' get nervous in his presence.

A.K. sat his pistol down in his lap, placed his right hand on the door to assist his left, and braced himself. Just as he had hoped, the security guard stood right outside his door and tapped on the window. Scott could barely get out the words, 'Excuse me sir, but...'. Before A.K. pulled the handle back and threw his entire upper body into the door.

The door swung open with so much speed and force that Scott didn't even have time to protect himself. The glass window smashed into his face and the metal door collided with his body. Scott heard the cracking sound of his nose being broke but he couldn't even cry out in pain. The wind was knocked right out of his overweight belly.

Staggering backward, Scott's eyes instinctively closed and began to water. Fear took control of his emotions as he grasped at the air and tumbled down into the empty parking space beside the S.U.V.

A.K. had wished the unexpected blow would have left the due unconscious, but it was obvious by his squirms that he was not yet out for the count.

Running off of pure adrenaline, A.K. scooped up his pistol off of his lap and hopped out of the driver's seat in attack mode. A quick scan of the area revealed that no one had seen him yet, but there was no way to tell how long that would last. He didn't have a clue as to what he was doing, all he knew was that he had to move fast.

A.K. swiftly stepped around to the head of the security guard who was still rolling around in silent agony and prepared to compound the man's woes.

Taking careful aim, A.K. drew his right foot all the way back and kicked Scott as hard as he could in his temple.

"Auugghh!" he moaned, as his breath re-entered his lungs.

A.K. didn't want to make a lot of noise by shooting the man, but he desperately needed him incapacitated. So, with his .380 in hand, just in case, A.K. proceeded to kick Scott in his head over and over again.

"Go to sleep!" A.K. growled as he mercilessly stomped on the security guard's cranium. "Go yo bitch ass to sleep!"

Scott was extremely discombobulated, but he refused to black out. Something told him that if he blacked out, he might not ever wake back up. He was in a fight for his life. He had to do something fast.

Doing his best to guard his face from the onslaught with his left arm, Scott reached for his can of mace with his right hand.

A.K. saw his maneuver and analyzed things in an instant. If he let him get to his mace, he was as good as sprayed. If he gunned the man down, he would be committing a murder in broad daylight and in front of countless witnesses. The dilemma was a lose-lose situation.

Scott wrapped his hand around the can. He had to try something.

A.K. wrapped his finger around the trigger. He too had to try something.

BUCK! BUCK! BUCK! BUCK! BUCK!

Five bullets erupted from the barrel of the baby .380 and all five bullets tore into the fatty flesh of the security guard. A.K. was a good shooter. He sent the first two bullets directly into the brain of his victim. The other three he had delivered to his heart. Blood leaked from the wounds and oozed onto the asphalt.

A.K. stared down at the now motionless body. The security guard was stretched out like those images of Jesus on the cross. The only difference was Jesus had holes in his hands and feet. The security guard had holes in his head and chest.

A.K. shook his head. He now had four kidnapped teenagers and one murdered rent-a-cop. The handoff was compromised. There would be no exchange made today. He had to get the hell out of there before it was too late.

"Aaaahhh!" a white woman screamed a few rows over. "HE KILLED HIM! HE KILLED HIM!"

The entire parking lot full of Wal-Mart customers were positioning themselves so that they could see the area where the shots were fired but also where they were safe from being shot.

Out of frustration, A.K. pointed his pistol at

312

the heads that were peeking over and around the various vehicles. If he would've had enough shells left in his clip to air that bitch out, he would've been letting loose. Unfortunately, his aiming at the witnesses was nothing more than an idle threat. An idle threat that was wasting him valuable time.

The sound of the gunshots had all of the Valley Park Girls cringing. They had no way of knowing if one of their own was the target. They could overhear the struggle between A.K. and Scott but they had no way of knowing exactly what was going on.

A.K. stepped over the security guards' dead body and jogged around to the back of the S.U.V. where the golf cart was parked. If he was going to get away, he was going to have to move that first.

People were yelling and pointing but he was way passed the point of trying to move with stealth. He had been seen. There was no way around it. All he could hope for now was a successful escape.

Reaching the cart, A.K. hopped in and looked around for the ignition switch, or the go button, or whatever the hell started the contraption.

"Fuck." A.K. grumbled, hitting the steering wheel with his free hand.

He could see where a key could go but the key was missing. He looked over at Scott.

"He must have it." He thought.

A.K. swung one foot out of the cart and heard a sound that made his heart drop.

"FREEZE! PUT YOU GOD DAMN HANDS WHERE I CAN SEE "EM!"

Looking in the direction of the voice, A.K. was horrified to see the same Sheriff, who was waiting to fill up his cruiser, running in his direction with his weapon aimed directly at him.

He had forgot all about the cop.

"PUT DOWN YOU WEAPON!" the Sheriff yelled, stopping only a few feet away from the golf cart. "PUT IT DOWN! NOW!"

A.K. cut his eyes down at the .380. He had already wasted five bullets.

He cut his eyes at the Cadillac Escalade. Four hog tied hostages equaled four kidnapping charges.

He cut his eyes at the slain security guard. All he could see was life without parole.

A.K. took a deep breath and adjusted his grip on the gun.

The Sheriff saw something in his eyes.

"Don't do it man!" the cop warned, his heart about to jump out of his chest. "It ain't worth it. You don't wanna die today."

A.K. looked the cop directly in his eyes. He knew that the man wouldn't hesitate to pull the trigger. In the academy they're trained to kill. But, in the streets, A.K. was trained to kill too.

"You got it twisted." A.K. called out to the cop. "You got a family and kids. You the one that don't wanna die today."

With that, A.K. rose his weapon as quickly as he could but it still wasn't quick enough. The Sheriff let off seven shots in rapid succession. All aimed at the torso.

"Uuunngghh." A.K. groaned as the slugs caused his body to slam into the seat of the golf cart.

He pulled the trigger of his baby .380 one time before the pain made him drop it. The bullet flew up and to the right. It didn't even almost hit the cop.

A.K. frowned up as the hot lead ignited like

an inferno in his stomach and chest. He grabbed at his chest and slumped forward but nothing he tried eased the pain. He couldn't believe he was going out like this. At the hands of a pig!

"No!" he protested through gritted teeth.

"DON'T MOVE!" the cop yelled when he noticed that A.K. still hadn't given up.

"Fuck you!" A.K. thought.

He summoned up all of his energy to climb from the golf cart and woundedly hop towards the driver's seat of the Escalade. As he disappeared out of the cop's sight, he could hear the man's boots stomping and his keys jingling as he gave chase.

A.K. made it all the way to the door before the Sheriff reached him.

"Get on the ground or I'll shoot." The cop warned.

A.K. looked down at his blood-stained shirt as he struggled to climb into the truck.

"You already shot me." He mumbled.

The Sheriff aimed at his back.

"I said GET ON THE GROUND!"

A.K. pulled his body into the seat.

BANG!

Another shot rang out. The crowd that was watching the ordeal gasped.

A.K. flinched at the sound of the shot, but strangely, he didn't feel anything. Sitting down correctly in the seat, he looked back to see what had happened. What he saw was totally unexpected.

The Sheriff was sprawled out on the ground next to the security guard and a young nigga he knew from Dickinson was standing over him with a .38. The young nigga had put one in the cop's dome.

"A.B.?!?" A.K. asked confused.

A.B. didn't respond. He just rushed to the cop, took his weapon, and then shot him one more time to make sure he was dead. A.B. had been watching the whole drama unfold. His instincts told him not to get involved, but there was a lot of shit going on. The last thing he needed was to see A.K. get jammed up and then give the police all the info they needed to expose all of the dirt that had been going on in Dickinson.

Deep down he wanted to murk A.K. right then and there but just his presence brought on a lot more questions that needed to be answered.

With a mug on his face, A.B. pointed both guns at A.K. and ordered him into the passenger seat. A.K. was in no position to argue so he simply obeyed. A.B. hopped into the driver's seat, crunk up the S.U.V., and plowed over the golf cart that was behind him. Then, he threw the big body into drive and peeled out. The tires howled as he sped towards the highway. He knew that more law enforcement would be there shortly.

Checking the rearview mirror, he saw LaQuisha and Alize.

"Good." He thought. "I got the girls."

A.K. moaned and groaned as the loss of blood slowly threatened to become too much. The human body could only stand to lose so much before it shut down. And after it shut down, so did all of the organs that keep you alive. A.K. knew this so he fought the call of eternal sleep like a Viking.

A.B. didn't say another word until he had hit the highway and was flying towards Dickinson at 85mph.

"What the fuck is going on here?" A.B. asked finally.

Alize recognized A.B.'s voice and she

started making noises and thrashing about.

"It's aiight." A.B. assured her, looking at her through the rearview. "Yeah this me. A.B. You knew me and yo mama wasn't gone let nothing happen to you."

A.K. glanced at A.B.

"You and her mama?" he questioned. "How do you know her mama?"

A.B. turned his attention back to A.K.

Pointing his .38 at him, he said, "I'll ask the mothafuckin' questions 'round here. I know who you is. You work for Tank. So what the hell is you doin' kidnapping his girlfriend and holding her for ransom?"

A.K. grunted.

"How do you know about that?" he asked through the pain.

A.B. yoked the car hard to the left and swerved around a slow-moving vehicle. Everyone inside the Escalade jerked to the right.

"How do I know?" A.B. repeated. "I just got off the phone with you. Who do you think set this handoff up?"

A.K. thought about it. A.B. got Tank?

It can't be.

He stared at A.B.

But how else would he know I was at that Wal-Mart with the hostages?

Cough! Cough!

"Mmmph." He moaned.

The woman that had set this all up had to be Alize's mother, Layla. It was the only thing that made sense. But how? And why would A.B. still be working with her? Had he still not realized who Layla really was?

A.B. was watching the road as he drove but

he was also keeping a close eye on A.K. Something wasn't right. He knew A.K. as one of Tanks henchmen. When him and Layla had made the decision to bring the hustlers in the projects to their knees, he made it his business to learn as much about them as possible. He knew for a fact that A.K. wasn't an enemy of Tank. A.K. was a loyal solider. There was no way he would bite the hand that had been feeding him by holding Tanks girlfriend hostage. That scenario just didn't add up. Too many things were beginning to look funny to A.B. He needed some answers. Some answers that were believable.

His pointed his revolver at A.K.

"I'm gone ask you this again," he said. "What the hell did you kidnap Tanks girlfriend for if you work for him?"

A.K. looked at the barrel of the gun. He didn't know how much A.B. knew, but he had to assume that he knew enough to justify killing him in cold blood. He had to put the spotlight on someone else.

"Umph." A.K. moaned, adjusting in his seat. "We didn't kidnap Tanks girlfriend."

"WHAT?!" A.B. cried out in disbelief. "There she is right there."

He pointed towards the backseat with his head.

"O.k. O.k." A.K. said, moving his head out the direct aim of the gun. "Yeah, we kidnapped her, but she wasn't the target."

A.B. looked at him confused.

"But ya'll were holding her for ransom." Cough! Cough! Cough!

"That's just what we said." A.K. told him weakly. "But really, we had orders to get that one."

"Which one?"

"Layla's daughter." A.K. revealed. "Alize. She's the one the boss wanted. All the others were just extra."

A.B. was shocked. He glanced back at Alize and then gave his attention back to the road and A.K.

"Alize?" he wondered out loud.

All of the Valley Park Girls could overhear their conversation and they were just as surprised as A.B. Especially Alize. They all were wondering what was going on.

"Why Alize?" A.B. inquired.

A.K. struggled to stay conscious. The bullet wounds and the loss of blood had him light-headed and in agony. He kept talking though because the talking helped him stay awake.

"You... you really don't know." He said

"Know what?"

A.K. shook his head. He could now see that A.B. was a bigger pawn in Layla's little game than they were. And the sad part was that he still hadn't realized it.

"Alize's mother," A.K. began. "Layla. She isn't who you think she is. She's a manipulator. A backstabber. That woman cannot be trusted. She..."

A.B and the Valley Park Girls listened while A.K. painted a picture of Layla as being so cutthroat and underhanded, she might as well have been the devil in the flesh.

He told them how Layla was working for Tank. She had sworn to help him get rid of the competition in the projects. But she needed their help first. Her whole game plan was to trick someone else into committing the actual murders, but she needed help in convincing someone to do it.

That's were Tank and his boys came in. And subsequently, that's where A.B. came in also.

But somewhere along the way, Tank got the impression that Layla couldn't be trusted. He said that either Layla or her daughter was snitching. So he came up with the idea of kidnapping Alize just in case Layla was planning something stupid. Unfortunately, in the middle of the operation, someone who turned out to be none other than Layla, kidnapped Tank.

A.B. listened to A.K.'s story but he cut him off before he could finish. Something he had said was nagging at him.

"Wait a minute." A.B. cut in. "You said that ya'll helped Layla convince me to help her. I never spoke with you or Tank. How did ya'll help with that?"

A.K. sighed. He could feel himself slipping anyway so it didn't matter if he told him or not. All he was hoping for now was that with his deathbed confessions, he could destroy the unity between Layla and A.B., and maybe A.B. would do to her what needed to be done.

"Do you remember what brought ya'll together?" he asked.

A.B. thought about it. He really hadn't been close to Layla until…

His eyes got wide.

"Steel?!?" he said, picturing his friends body tossed behind the bushes in the projects the night that he had died.

"He wasn't supposed to die." A.K. told him. "We just beat him up real bad. You know? Give ya'll a reason to plex with everybody in the projects."

"What?" A.B. said, tears forming in his

eyes. "Yoo… yooo… you killed my homeboy?"

A.K.'s words were causing the painful memories to resurface.

"You murdered my potna?"

"No no no." A.K. answered. "We didn't kill him. We just beat him up. He was still alive when we planted him behind those bushes."

A.B. remembered hearing Steel's heartbeat. He recalled rushing him to the hospital. But once they got to the hospital…

"YA'LL WENT TOO FAR!" A.B. shouted. Anger mixed with his hurt. "YA'LL LEFT HIM BRAIN DEAD! YA'LL DID KILL HIM!"

"Steel wasn't brain dead." A.K. disputed. "That's just what Dr. Abu-Kahr had to tell you to make it sound believable."

"Abu-Kahr?" A.B. thought.

He pictured the doctor that said Steel was dead.

Gasp! It was an Iranian.

"How… how do you know that doctor?"

"I told you," A.K. said, realizing that A.B. was now starting to see that he was telling the truth. "Steel was alive. He wasn't supposed to die. But somewhere along the way, Layla decided 'by herself' that you would more readily go along with the… ugh… with the plan if Steel died. That's why she stayed at the hospital. She knew that Dr. Abu-Kahr was on Tanks payroll. Tank introduced her to the Doctor when he needed to get rid of this chick named Bunny. So Layla used that to convince the Doctor that Tank would pay him $25,000 if he… 'lost a patient'. That patient was yo homeboy. That Patient was Steel."

For the umpteenth time in just a few days, A.B. felt his entire world begin to collapse. He had been operating under a lie. He wasn't in a war to avenge his road dogs death. Hell, Layla was more responsible than them. His mind raced over everything that had happened since Steel got killed. Layla had been playing him for A fool the entire time. He was literally sleeping with the enemy. But little did she know, he knew now.

Anger seeped through his pores and fury boiled up in his blood. He had sworn to avenge Steel's death. And even though the truth had his mind in a spinner, he could clearly see that revenge must be had.

Revenge for Steel!

Revenge for the lies!

Revenge for the deception!

Revenge for the manipulation!

Revenge for… revenge for the sake of revenge!

A.B. rose his .38 and drove three shots into A.K.'s weary brain, No words, no warnings, no expression. Just blood and brain matter smeared across the window. He didn't care if any of the other motorists saw the dead man slumped over in his passenger seat. All he cared about was killing everyone involved in the killing of Steel. Especially Layla. That Bitch!

CHAPTER SEVENTEEN

"The handoff has been made." Layla said into the cell phone. "Ya'll go into the building and call me when you reach the safe. It's located on the fourth floor in the conference room. You won't be able to see it at first because it's hidden behind a poster. The poster is a poem. A poem about hard work and never giving up. Once you reach the safe and call me back at this number, I'll give you the combination. Is that understood?"

Duke gritted his teeth, but he held his tongue.

"Yeah." He forced himself to say.

"Yeah what?" Layla asked.

Duke rolled his eyes and sighed.

"Yeah. I understand."

"Good." Layla told him. "Now hurry up or yo homeboy here won't be breathing too much longer."

CLICK!

She hung up the phone.

As instructed, Duke and Clipso had been parked at the Jack-in-the-Box across the street from the Willis, Winn, and Stone Law Firm building. They were watching when all of the employees exited the building some 45 minutes ago. The woman who had Tank said that she was going to get him to call in and have the building evacuated.

She was true to her word.

"You ready to handle this business?" Duke asked Clipso.

Clipso rolled his neck around popping it.

"I stay ready." He answered. "Let's get this over with."

"Bet." Duke replied.

He turned the key in the Explorers ignition and brought the beast to life.

"She said that Tank told 'em not to engage the alarms." Duke informed Clipso as he pulled out of the parking space and prepared to cross the street. "So all we gotta do is walk in, find the safe, clean it out, and shake the spot."

Duke looked both ways then drove straight across four lanes of traffic and pulled into the Law Firm's parking lot.

"Simple." He said, parking in front of the glass doors and killing the ignition.

Clipso stared up at the office building that stood before them. In all his years of working for Tank he had never once been inside of there. The building was huge compared to all of the other structures that surrounded it. It was a four-story building made entirely of imported rocks and stones. The rocks and stones were from several different countries, but they were all from the same continent.

Africa!

There were black ones, white ones, green ones, brown ones, red ones, and blue ones. It made the building stand out. It looked exotic.

Both men made sure that they were not being watched, and then they dawned their robber's attire.

Black guns. Black gloves. Black clothes. Black duffel bags. Black masks. Even though the alarm wasn't set, the security cameras on the inside were always rolling. Tank had them installed after the first break-in. They had to be sure not to show anything incriminating on tape.

Pulling the ski-masks down over their faces, the duo exchanged head nods. That was their silent signal that it was time to move. They grabbed the two duffel bags and exited the vehicle.

Unbeknownst to them they were being watched. The Wash World Washeteria sat next door to the Willis, Winn, and Stone Law Firm building. Inside, pretending to be tending to a load of clothes, a very attractive Puerto Rican woman sat in a chair facing the window with her legs crossed. She was holding a copy of the Galveston County Daily News newspaper. She wasn't reading it though. It was just a front. A decoy. A smokescreen. It was something to keep her from looking obvious as she played her position as watch out.

When she noticed the two brothers infiltrating the building, she knew that her job was done. Very calmly, she folded her newspaper up, tucked it under her arm, rose to her feet, and politely headed towards the exit. The clothes she had in the dryer could now be considered a donation to the Asian family who owned Wash World. They could write a thank you note to Alize if they wanted to.

Nobody paid Ashanti any mind as she stepped out into the slowly warming afternoon air. She noticed that the two men had disappeared inside the building. She also noticed a woman wearing a black and yellow outfit come jogging out of the shadows behind Willis, Winn, and Stone with two large duffel bags over their shoulders.

Ashanti walked around to the driver's side of the fully loaded Maybach Benz that she had 'borrowed' from Dr. Abu-Kahr. The shady figure ran up to the passenger side. The two people climbed in simultaneously. The one in all black slammed the door on her side and pulled off the mask she was wearing.

Ashanti closed her door.

"They just went in." she informed her passenger.

Layla smiled from ear to ear and tossed the two bags into the back seat.

"This shit is just too easy." Layla declared.

Ashanti crunk up the luxury vehicle and peered at the bags through the rearview mirror. She knew what was inside of them. One of them contained all of Tanks cash and the other one contained some of his extra pounds of weed. The two women were officially rich. All they had to do now was get rid of anybody who could give them up to the police.

Still breathing slightly hard, Layla pulled out Tanks cell phone and dialed a number she knew she would have to use eventually. Ashanti merged with the traffic on the street and Layla listened to the phone ring.

After only two rings, someone picked up.

"Dickinson Police Department. Please state your emergency."

"Hello." Layla said in a panicked voice. "Oh my God! They got guns. GUNS! I don't... Willis, Winn... all black... oh my God! Oh my God!"

"Ma'am." The female dispatcher said calmly. "Calm down ma'am. Who has guns? Where are you?"

"I'm sorry." Layla apologized. "I'm at the Willis, Winn, and Stone Law Firm building off of FM 517. Across the street from Jack-in-the-Box. Two armed men, dressed in all black, just entered the building and took everybody hostage. I work there. Me and a few others barely made it out in time. They're demanding money. Oh my God! You gotta hurry. They look crazy. I think they're going to kill someone."

"O.k. ma'am. Just relax. I just notified all units in the surrounding area. They will be there shortly. In the meantime, I need you to stay on the phone with me until…"

CLICK!

"Hello?" the dispatcher called. "Ma'am, are you still there? Hello?"

Layla rolled down her window and tossed the cell phone out. Two cars behind her, a blue F150 truck rolled right over the phone, crushing it.

"Let's hurry up and get back to Valley Park." Layla said. "A.B. should be on his way back with Alize by now. We need to get my daughter and get the hell out of Dickinson."

"Right." Ashanti said, giving the Benz a little more gas and slightly increasing their speed.

Clipso pointed at the wooden door marked 'Stairwell'.

"There it is." He said triumphantly.

The pair had been searching the first floor of the building looking for the stairs ever since they entered. The woman had told them not to use the elevators, but she failed to tell them that the entrance to the stairs was tucked away at the back of the building.

Duke and Clipso had fumbled around the lobby and empty offices that littered the first floor in search of the stairs. It took a minute, but they weren't really pressed for time.

"Come on." Duke said, leading the way down the small hallway that led to the stairs. "She said we gotta go to the fourth floor and find the conference room."

"What's a conference room?" Clipso asked, following close behind.

"Shiiit. I imagine they'll have it labeled like everything else in this bitch. Don't worry. We'll know it when we see it."

Duke made it to the stairwell door and wasted no time opening it up. A stale smelling air escaped from the confinement of the stairwell and brushed against the noses of both men. It gave them the impression that nobody had opened that door in a long time. And why would they? The elevators were more easily accessed.

The two men stepped into the dimly lit room and found themselves facing their pathway to getting their boss back safe and sound. The stairwell was small. It was only about six feet wide. Directly in front of them was a section of stairs, with about seven steps on it, going up. It was only three feet wide. Duke and Clipso climbed those seven steps, reached a platform that connected to another set of seven steps over to their right, and kept climbing.

Duke gazed up as he climbed the black steps. The staircase followed that pattern all the way up. Every two sections, or every fourteen steps, was another floor. He tallied it up in his head. They had to climb forty-two steps in all.

In a semi-rush to reach the top, Duke started climbing two steps at a time. In his head he counted off the floors as they neared their destination.

"Second floor… Third floor… Fourth floor."

"Bingo." Duke said in a low voice, standing in front of a blue door labeled 'Fourth Floor'.

He had watched a lot of people exit the building, and the interior was quiet as hell, but still he wasn't 100% sure that they were the only two people inside. Duke was a firm believer in the 'better safe than sorry' concept.

Turning his upper body towards Clipso, he placed his index finger up to his mask.

"Shhh." He shushed. "Somebody might've stayed behind. Just stay ready."

Clipso nodded his head to let Duke know that he understood what he was saying. Then, he eased his hand into his waistband and pulled out the black 44 he was packing. A simple thumb movement was all it took to release the safety.

Duke quickly followed suit. Now they both had a black duffel bag in one hand and a black 44 in the other.

As quietly as he could, Duke grabbed the doorknob with the hand the bag was in and turned it. First, he turned it just enough to peek through the crack. Seeing no one, he swung the door open wide and pointed his weapon down the dark hallway.

The fourth-floor hallway was plush. The floor was covered with a bright red carpet that reminded Duke of a Hollywood premiere. The walls were an off-white color and covered with oil-based paintings of Africanized artwork. Knowing his bosses' taste in things, he guesses that all of the paintings were expensive. Very expensive. $5,000 and up expensive.

There were doors on both sides of the hallway, so Duke decided to just check them all until he found one labeled Conference Room. As he walked, he came across paintings of Black Pharaohs, Black Queens, tribal outfits, African Warriors, beautiful African landscapes, and a painting of what Duke could only call Black Jesus.

About four doors down, Duke found what he was looking for. A door with a gold-plated label on it marked 'Conference Room'. He stopped at the door and looked back at Clipso. The two of them stared at one another for a minute. They couldn't believe they were actually robbing their own boss for a woman who had their boss held hostage somewhere. They had to do whatever it took to get tank back alive though. Even if it meant playing some woman's twisted game of cat and mouse until she slipped.

"Remember," Duke said, gripping the knob. "Look for a poster with a poem on it about hard work and never giving up."

"Got 'cha."

Duke slowly opened the door to the conference room and stepped in. Directly in the middle of the room was a large cherry oak table with about twelve chairs positioned around it. The duo immediately began scanning over the various degrees and certificates that hung from each of the four walls. It didn't take long for one of them to catch Clipso's eye.

"Look." He said, pointing with his gun to a large white poster over on the wall to the right side of the room.

Duke turned to see what his homeboy had found. He followed the aim of the pistol and his eyes came to rest on what Clipso had seen.

"Hmmm." Duke mumbled.

He approached the poster so that he could see it better. As soon as he got up on it he read the first few lines in his head.

When the going gets tough, the
tough don't notice
When the road gets rough, the
rough keep rollin',
When the odds stacked against a

real man, he smile
When the opposition comes he
gone stand his ground
When everybody else fold, I'm
sho' to stay stiff
When the tale gets told...

"That's it." Clipso said, breaking Duke's train of though. "That's the kind of shit Tank would use to mark his stash. It's like his X marks the spot."

"I think you right." Duke agreed.

Duke laid his duffel bag and pistol down on a metal file cabinet that sat against the wall about 3 feet to the left of the poster. Then, he reached out in front of him and grabbed the sides of the poster.

Taking a deep breath and moving gently, Duke lifted the poster off of its support hook. He half-assed expected to hear some alarm go off, but he was relieved when nothing happened.

Releasing the breath, he had been holding, Duke sat the poster down on his right and leaned it up against the wall. The two men examined the huge steel safe. It looked big enough to fit a person inside of it. They knew their boss had loot, but they never expected he had enough cash put away to fill up a safe that size.

"Where does the combination go?" Clipso asked.

Duke scanned the smooth surface of the safe's door.

"That's a good question." He said, clearly stumped.

The only thing that looked like you could probably punch a combination into it was a small

3x3 inch black box that was attached to the wall on the left side of the safe. The box looked like a blank computer screen but there was no keypad in sight.

"Hold on." Duke said, fishing his cell phone out of his pocket. "Let me call that bitch back."

Duke punched in Tank's number and waited. He was shocked when it didn't even ring. It went straight to voicemail like the phone was cut off or something.

"Hey there." Layla's voice said, in place of Tanks regular recorded message. "I'm assuming you made it to the safe by now seeing as how I told you not to call me back until you reached it. Well, a jackass like you might go against my instructions anyway. But what should I expect from a fuck up other than a fuck up? Ha! Ha! Ha! Get it? Fuck up? Ha! Ha! Ha!"

Duke couldn't wait to kill that woman. Watching the arrogant little whore take her last breath would be like bustin' a nut.

"But for real though." Layla continued. "Let's get down to business. The combination is sort of like a key. You just have to put the key up to that small computer screen beside the safe. And how ironic is this? The key is taped to the back of that white poster that hid the safe. So look, you two get the money and I'll call ya'll back when this voice message reaches Tanks phone. Buh-bye!"

Duke stood there seething hot as he waited for the phone to beep so he could leave a short message.

BEEEEP!

Yeah, this me. Get at me."

He hung up the phone.

"Aaauuuggghhh!!!" he hollered. "I wanna kill that bitch so bad! She too fuckin' smart for her own good. Talkin' to a nigga like she can't be touched. Like she invincible."

Duke glared at his phone and squeezed it with all of his might. He could visualize the phone as being the woman's throat.

"Hey." Clipso said, trying to bring his homeboy back. "You gotta stay calm Bro. We on a mission right now. Somebody got the boss. We gotta get the boss back. Of course, whoever that hoe is she gone get it, but we can't focus on that right now. We gotta focus on getting this money first. If we don't get the money, we can't force ol' girl to come out of hiding. You feel me?"

Duke continued to choke the phone but Clipso's words had calmed him drastically. His potna was right. First things first. The bitch would die no doubt about it. But without the loot, they couldn't get to the bitch.

Duke took a deep breath and exhaled slowly.

"Aiight then." Clipso said, seeing his boy return to normal. "What we gotta do to open this safe up?"

Duke looked down at the poster to his right.

"She says the key is taped to the back of that poster."

"What?" Clipso asked puzzled.

Duke shrugged. "That's what the hoe said Bro."

Neither one of them could understand why the key would be so close to the safe, but Duke reached out for the poster anyway

Grabbing the top of it, he simply pulled it away from the wall and peered down at the back of it.

"What the... fuck?" Duke mumbled, seeing something strange taped to the back of it.

He reached down with his left hand and grabbed it. A slight yank was all it took to peel it away from the poster. Duke lifted the object up to his face and gagged. His instincts made him drop the key and the poster.

"Hell naw." He said, shaking the head he touched the key with as if it were covered in invisible dirt. "Tell me that ain't what I think it is."

Clipso sat his bag down then bent over to pick up the key. He was a little less squeamish than Duke, so he didn't gag. The key was a wretched sight though. The thing that the woman had described as a key was nothing more than a blood-stained ink pen with a human eye attached to the ball point.

Clipso stared into the pupil of the lifeless eye and it dawned on him what he was looking at.

Swallowing hard, he said, "You... you don't think the eye belongs to..."

Duke shook his head no.

"Hell no." he said, really trying to convince himself. "It can't be. Not Tank. Maybe... maybe somebody else. Yeah, yeah. Somebody else. One of them fools we had to do in back in the day. The boss probably kept they eye and made it useful."

Clipso looked at Duke with a raised eyebrow. He didn't believe that the eye belonged to someone else and he was willing to bet that Duke didn't believe that shit either. There was only one way to know for sure though.

With Duke watching, Clipso turned from the eye to the little black box. Then he shrugged his shoulders and raised the eye up to it. As soon as the pupil of the dismembered eyeball lined up just right with the black screen, the screen lit up a neon green color.

"Whirrrrr. Click, click, click."

The sound of some type of mainframe coming to life startled the pair but Clipso managed to hold the eye in place. After a few seconds, a red light shot from the neon green screen and moved back and forth rapidly across the eye. The two dudes didn't realize it, but the red laser light was actually charting the retina of the eye in an attempt to identify it.

The red light scanned the eye until a positive I.D. was made. Once the I.D. was made, the light shut off and the green screen turned sky blue.

"Beep. Beep. Beep."

Clipso and Duke stared at the screen as words began to appear on it.

"Identification Verified."

"Access Granted."

"Hello, Tony Quinten."

The two men looked at each other. It 'was' Tanks eye.

"Whirrrrr. Pssssss."

The sound of pressurized air being released came from the safe. Then, the door to it unlocked itself and slowly swung open. Both men took a step back to avoid getting hit by it.

Duke looked inside the safe bewildered.

"What the fuck is goin' on here?" he asked softly.

The safe was empty. There was nothing in it but a note. Duke was sort of afraid to read it but he reached in and grabbed it anyway.

The note was short and to the point. Only six words. Duke read it out loud and Clipso read it silently looking over his shoulder.

"Come out with your hands." It read.

Duke and Clipso exchanged glances. They

had no idea what the note meant. Just as Duke was about to say something…

"D.P.D. DON'T MOVE! DON'T MOVE!"

A whole swarm of fully suited Dickinson Police officers came rushing into the Conference Room with their weapons drawn.

Out of shock, Clipso dropped the pen and eye combo and turned to face the cops.

"HE'S GOT A GUN!!!" one cop yelled.

Clipso raised his hands to guard himself. The cops thought he raised his hands to shoot.

"BUCK! BUCK! BUCK! POW! POW! POW! BLATTT! BLATTT! BLATTT! CHIC-CHIC BOOM! CHIC-CHIC BOOM! BAM!... BAM!... BAM!"

There were about eight cops already in the room when the shooting starting. All of them had a different weapon of war and all of them began unloading in the direction of Clipso and Duke.

As the bullets, slugs, and pellets cut through the air and penetrated deep into the flesh of the men in all black, Clipso and Duke both did the same dance. With their heads tilted back, and arms fully extended to their sides, the two of them rocked from side to side as the hot lead reduced their once solid frames to the human equivalent of Swiss Cheese.

The crowd that had gathered around the police barricaded outside the building hollered and ducked as the one-sided gun fight blasted like the climax of a symphony. The police officer's arsenal was the bass, treble, horns, and wind instruments. The movements of Clipso and Duke were the conductor, encouraging the band to play with their refusal to fall down. The tragedy of the whole ordeal was the stringed instruments. The violins playing a solo titled, 'Ode to a Life Lost'.

Over the deafening sound of death, Police Chief Ortega was yelling.

"CEASE FIRE! CEASE FIRE!" he screamed.

It took a few seconds but eventually the room was silent.

"CEASE FIRE!" the Chief creamed one more time, waving his arm in the air.

All of the cops stood perfectly still. They stopped shooting but they kept their fingers on the triggers. Clipso and Duke blinked. Their bodies oozed blood.

"Finally." They both thought. "They stopped long enough to let me die."

Their bodies had passed the point of pain with the seventh or eighth shot. Now, with the number somewhere in the twenties or thirties, all they could feel was the numbingly cold chill of eternity.

The police watched as the duo practiced for the synchronized dying team. Together, they dropped down to their knees, hesitated exactly 3.5 seconds, then fell forward and landed flat on their faces. The only problem with a performance like that was you only got to do it once.

All of the officers lowered their weapons. Not even Superman could've survived and attack like that. They knew the dudes were dead. So simply following procedure, the Chief lifted his radio up to his mouth.

"We need an emergency medical team in the Conference Room on the fourth floor. We have two suspects down. Expect multiple gunshot wounds."

The Chief lowered the radio. They had been told that there were hostages inside. Where were they? And if they weren't in the building, where were all of the employees? And where was the person who called in the hostage situation? And why was the safe empty? Where was the money?

The Chief looked to his men.

"Find me the person that called in to report this." He told them. "Trace the call if you have to."

He turned back towards the two dead bodies. He wasn't sure why, but his gut was telling him that there was more to this thing than meets the eye. And he intended to find out what it was.

CHAPTER EIGHTEEN

After flying down I-45 in a complete and total rage, A.B. finally made it back into Dickinson city limits. His first and only stop was going to be the Valley Park sub-division. All four girls were still tied up, blindfolded, and gagged in the back of the S.U.V. and A.K.'s bloody corpse was still slumped over against the passenger side window. A.B. didn't care though. He had finally snapped. All of the bullshit he had been forced to endure over the past few days had stolen what little sanity the streets had allowed him to keep.

His brain bounced names, situations, and circumstances around as he went over each fucked up occurrence.

My closes road dog got killed. My bitch was the one who orchestrated his death. My mom's let some no-good ass nigga convince her to call the cops on me. My baby sister has to grow up just like me. I done killed two dudes and one cop. The cop's murder was in front of witnesses. I'll never see the light of day again.

A.B. sat his .38 down in his lap and rubbed the bridge of his nose. He knew that he was going to kill Layla on sight, but after that, then what? Where was he gonna run to? How did he plan on getting there?

He damn sho' couldn't stay in Dickinson. And once his plot hit the airwaves in connection with that shooting at the Wal-Mart in Houston, an all-out manhunt would begin. The media was going to make it seem like he was on a city to city killing spree. Well, in all honesty, he was.

A.B. thought about how much money he could get his hands on real fast. Waiting on the lick they had planned with tank wasn't gonna work. Layla didn't know it, but the cops were on their way. The 'hood was about to be on fire.

"The money we took from Sticky!" he remembered.

Yeah. That was like sixteen G's.

O.K.

I'll let Layla have it, find the money we stole from Sticky, and then I'll bounce. Fuck it. Sixteen G's can get me out of Texas. Once I get out of Texas, I'll post up in a hotel room and plot my next move.

Movement in the back made A.B. glance at the rearview mirror. The girls were wiggling and trying to talk.

"Damn." He thought. "What about them? They didn't do anything wrong."

A.B. felt sorry for the girls. They were really just caught up in the middle of something that had nothing to do with them. He especially felt sorry for Alize. She was so laid back and relaxed. Plus, she was pretty and intelligent. But it was her mother that stood at the center of all the drama. And it was her mother that A.B. was about to kill.

It took him awhile to make up his mind about what to do with the girls. He knew that they could all be called upon to testify against him in court one day if he left them alive, but so what? There were so many witnesses to his crimes and evidence against him that whether the Valley Park girls snitched on him or not, he was still going to get the lethal injection if he allowed the authorities to apprehend him. That was a given. So A.B. decided to let them live. After all, they had done him no wrong.

After entering the city of Dickinson, A.B. was turning into the Valley Park sub-division in no time. Instinctively he slowed down as he approached Layla's house. When he was about five houses away, he noticed a Maybach Benz parked in the driveway.

"That must be her 'friends' car." He told himself.

How her friend could afford such an expensive vehicle, he had no clue. But he figured he would have to kill the friend too. The projected body count continued to escalate.

A.B. eased the Cadillac Escalade into the driveway behind the Benz and killed the ignition. Butterflies had entered his stomach and he was beginning to feel a little nervous. It was easy plotting the murder in his head, but actually doing it seemed more complicated. He had real feelings for Layla, but he had learned that her feelings for him were all artificial. She only pretended to care so that he would blindly follow her lead.

A.B. stared at the front door of the house. Still staring, he opened the car door and inhaled deeply. He had two guns. A .38 and a .45 that he had stolen from the slain cop. He wasn't sure how many bullets he had left in both guns, but it should've been enough to do what he needed to do.

A.B. tucked the cop's gun into his waistband and gripped the .38 tightly. He stepped out of the vehicle and left the four girls mumbling and struggling to get free.

"It'll all be over with soon." He whispered so low they couldn't possibly have heard him.

The wind blew across A.B.'s face as he strode towards Steel's true killer. He had the element of surprise. If he wanted things to go off smoothly, he had to capitalize off of it. Sneak up on his target swiftly, and then fire without speaking. Even though he loved her, her treachery had earned her death.

Inside of the house, Layla and Ashanti were more prepared than A.B. thought. They were the real ones with the element of surprise. Not him.

They had already discussed what they were going to do several times. So as soon as they saw A.B. pull up in Tank's Escalade, they sprang into action. Ashanti played her part and Layla played hers.

A.B. turned the doorknob to the front door and pushed it open. He immediately pointed his pistol inside and was ready to shoot anybody he saw alive. He didn't see what he expected to see though. He saw something totally different.

Tank was still tied up in the middle of the floor, but his face was badly disfigured. It looked as if someone had cut out the man's entire right eye socket. There was a hole where his eye once was, and a large puddle of blood beneath his head. The stench of his death had attracted the flies.

A.B. gagged and covered his nose. Tank wasn't supposed to be dead yet. What the hell happened here?

"Hey!" he heard a female's voice call out behind him.

A.B. snapped his head and found himself looking into the eyes of a light skinned woman wearing black and yellow. He didn't look at her long though. The woman stood just outside the open doorway long enough to see A.B.'s gun then she took off running to A.B.'s right.

"Layla's friend!" he thought, as he rushed

towards the door to give chase.

A.B. sprinted out the door and made a sharp turn to the right. He didn't make it two full steps before he felt two sharp pains pinch at his back. Then, within a fraction of a second of feeling the two pinches, A.B. hollered in agony as 950 volts of pure electricity entered into his body and wreaked havoc on his pain receptors.

"Aaauuuggghhh!!!" he screamed.

His gun fell from his hands and the electricity brought him to his hands and knees. Layla released the tasers trigger.

"I'm sorry." She apologized, with a strange hint of authenticity in her voice. "I'm so so sorry."

A.B., still on his hands and knees, looked back at Layla. As the pain subsided, he remembered the gun in his waistband.

He went for it.

"AAAAHHHH!!!" he shouted, as Layla pulled back on the trigger, breaking him down further.

A.B. laid face down in the front yard breathing heavy.

"Wha… Why?" he managed to ask. "Why are you doing this?

Genuine tears welled up in Layla's eyes. She didn't want to do A.B. like she was doing him, but she saw no other way.

Layla covered her mouth with her free hand. Ashanti leaned down over the weakened A.B. and patted him down for weapons. He tried to resist but the electricity had knocked the fight out of him. Once Ashanti had possession of the .38 and the .45, she stepped away from A.B.'s writhing body.

"O.K." she said to Layla. "Go ahead. Give it to him."

Layla pulled the tasers trigger once more.

"Oh my God." She wailed, looking away but not releasing the trigger. "I'm so sorry." She said to the hollering A.B. "It's the only way Baby. It's the only way."

Layla shocked A.B. to the point where all he could do was slobber at the mouth and barely breathe.

"Drag him inside." She told Ashanti, after she was sure that A.B. was incapacitated. "I'll get the girls."

"Right." Ashanti said, setting the two guns down and grabbing A.B. under his arms.

It was a good thing he wasn't a big man because she wasn't a strong woman. He was just light enough for her to drag him. While she dragged, Layla jogged over to the Cadillac Escalade. She hesitated for a moment when she noticed the dead guy in the passenger seat but she figured that was the third kidnapper. Fuck him! He had held her daughter hostage.

Layla rushed to open the side door of the S.U.V. She gasped when she seen the condition of the four girls.

"BABY!" she cried out, reaching to Alize. "Look at you face!!!"

"Mmm. Mmm." Alize moaned, hearing her mother's voice.

Layla tore the blindfold off of her daughter and yanked the gag out of her mouth. Alize looked up into her mother's face and broke down.

"Oooooo!" she wailed. "Mama! Thank God it's you! I thought I was gone die."

"Shhh." Layla said, pulling her from the truck and sitting her down on the grass. "I'm not gone let NOTHIN' happen to you. You hear me?"

Layla pulled her daughters head to her chest and both of them cried like newborn babies. They were both overjoyed that Alize was safe.

Ssnniff.

"Look at me." Layla said, wiping the tears from her face. "Let me get these damn ropes off of you."

She went to work on the knots.

"And once I get you free," she added, "we'll get your lil home girls free."

Alize thought about all of the things that A.K. had revealed before A.B. shot him in the head. He had implemented her mother in a lot of shit. That gave them the power to compromise the whole operation. Alize could not allow that.

"NO!" she said, as the ropes finally loosened on her bruised wrists and swollen ankles.

Layla looked at her daughter strangely.

"No?" she repeated.

"We can't let them go, Mama." Alize told her. "They know too much."

LaQuisha, Krystal, and Ming listened in horror as their home girl, their ace, and their ridah, explained in detail why they had to die. Really, Alize didn't want to do it, but they had too much at stake to leave any loose ends behind. If her home girls survived, they would no doubt give up her mother. If they gave up her mother, the cops wouldn't rest until they had her in police custody. If they arrested Layla, they would lose all of the money they worked so hard to get. Alize wasn't a heartless killer. She was just a young girl looking for her ticket out of the madness. And now that she had found it, she didn't want to give it up.

Layla listened to her daughters reasoning and she could feel where she was coming from.

They had already made so many sacrifices in the name of financial stability that it would be foolish to ease up off the gas so close to the finish line. The only real choice they had was to play this thing out to the end. It was all or nothing.

Alize and Layla rose to their feet and stared at the three helpless girls. Life for cash. An exchange that many condemned, but when faced with the opportunity, many would embrace. Alize shed a few tears for her home girls as Layla shut the door on what would later become their final resting place.

"Mmmm! Mmmm! Mmmm! Mmmm!" were the last sounds the mother and daughter heard as they headed back inside the house.

Ashanti was already working diligently to set the scene up so that it would somewhat match the lie they had come up with. A.B. was still conscious and Ashanti was keeping him in line with the taser that was still lodged in his back.

When he saw Layla and Alize walk in, he couldn't help but to confront them.

"You... you killed... you killed Steel." A.B. accused.

Layla's heart instantly started to melt when she gazed upon A.B. in pain again. She knelt down in front of him but not close enough for him to touch her.

"Nooo baby." She said with grief. "I know that that is the lie you were told, but it's just that... a LIE. I love you baby. I wouldn't kill your friend."

Her words were sickening to hear.

"Baby?! Love?! How can you call me baby and you have been lying to me the entire time? How can you say you love me, and you keep shocking the shit out of me? Why wouldn't you kill my

346

friend?" he challenged. "You're about to kill me! Why not Steel too?"

"Baby…"

"STOP CALLING ME BABY! You don't care about me."

Layla rose to her feet.

"I don't care?!?" she repeated. "If it wasn't for me, you'd probably be dead instead of Steel. It was Tanks idea to use one of you, but it was my idea to take you to safety while they jumped on Steel. I didn't know they were gonna kill him though. How could I have possibly known that?"

"Oh you knew alright. You the one that told that shady ass doctor to kill him. I know all about the $25,000 he was paid to kill Steel."

"Is that right? Well, since you know so much, tell me this. Who paid the doctor? Me or Tank? And if Tank paid, why would he pay for my rouge idea? Think about what you're saying A.B. Think about who you are listening to. I was the one who consoled you when Steel died. I was the one who took you in when you fell off. I was the one who was right there when you killed Sticky. I'm just as guilty as you. ME! Not Tank and his henchmen. But they are the ones you believe?"

"Well what about this?" A.B. questioned, referring to the prongs in his back. "You done turned on me."

"You don't understand, A.B." Layla replied. "I didn't want it to come to this. Look at my face! Listen to my voice! Can't you see that I am just as fucked up about this as you? I never wanted to hurt you. I wanted to share that three million plus I just hit Tank for with you. I love you boo. What I am doing now must be done. There's no other way."

"But why? If you really love me, and if you

are really telling the truth, why is any of this necessary? Why can't we just take the money and go?"

Layla wiped a tear from her delicate cheek.

"Things got out of hand." She told him. "Too many people ended up dying. Now, if we don't feed the police the person responsible, they won't rest until we're found. There will be no peace unless justice is served."

"So I'm... so I'm the scapegoat?"

"Just trust me baby. If I could do this another way, I would. But I can't. I... I just can't."

Ashanti walked over to Layla with one hand still on the trigger of the taser.

"Here." She said, handing her the 32 Xanax pills, the 3 grams of crack, the tape recorder, and a folded-up piece of paper. "WE gotta get this over with, Layla. The clock is ticking."

Layla accepted the items and sighed.

"I really do love you, A.B." she confessed sincerely. "I pray you can see that."

Layla crotched down in front of A.B. and laid the pills and the dope down in front of him.

"I need you to swallow that." She said solemnly.

"What?!" A.B. replied. "You gotta be out of yo rabbit ass miiilIIAAAAAUUUGGGHHH!!!"

Ashanti pulled the trigger and held it for a few seconds before releasing it.

"A.B." Layla said, when Ashanti eased up. "Listen to me. I need you to swallow that. Somebody has to go down."

"Ugh." A.B. groaned. "Fff... Fuck you! AAAAGGGGHH!!!"

Ashanti fed his body a constant stream of 950 volts. When she released the trigger, A.B.

twitched uncontrollably. He knew that if he swallowed those narcotics, his heart was liable to explode. But that taser was like cruel and unusual punishment. He couldn't take much more.

"Swallow." Layla instructed him. "It's the only way."

"Ooofff." A.B. grunted. He was feeling hurt, afraid, and deceived.

He didn't want to be shocked again, so he struggled to reach the pills and the dope. Staring at Layla with hatred in his eyes, he started the process of ingesting the poison. It took him awhile to swallow it all, but he eventually got it down.

"That's good." Layla said, unfolding the paper. "Now, I need you to read this. And make sure you speak into the mic."

She slid the paper up to his face and held the tape recorder close to his mouth. A.B. looked down at the paper and cut his eyes at Ashanti. She wiggled her finger on the trigger. He knew what that meant. Read the paper or get shocked. A.B. sighed, feeling defeated.

"You wanna know what I hate?" he read out loud and directly into the tape recorders mouthpiece. "I hate people that try to make it seem like the ghettos, projects, and poverty-stricken neighborhoods across America is all that. They want you to believe that if you weren't raised in the slums then you missed out on some hell of an experience. I hate when people brag about how hard they had it…"

A.B. read down the page, realizing what he was being forced into as he read. This note was like a confession. His confession to all of the murders that had taken place. It was indeed a fucked up way to go.

"But at least," he thought, "I'm about to be reunited with my road dog."

"Well," A.B. said, still reading from the prepared note. "I guess I better fill ya'll in on how I got to this point before my heart bust. Like I said, don't nobody wanna tell a story like mine, so fuck 'em. I'll tell my story myself. Just consider this lil narrative as my suicide note. Hey, I like how that sounds. Say, whoever finds this tape recorder after I'm gone, do me a favor. If they do make a movie or write a book about my life, make sure that they use that as the title. Suicide Note! See, I grew up in the streets. I been dealing with the madness my entire life. But shit really hit the fan for me the night my comrade got killed. Damn! Steel! Man, I miss my nigga for real…"

CHAPTER NINETEEN

Channel 9 News reporter, Antoinette Hall stood poised in front of several cameras at the station and prepared to go on the air live. She looked extremely professional in her light blue business suit with the skirt that hung just below her kneecaps. Her hair was freshly braided, and her make-up was flawless. She cleared her throat and smoothed out her jacket.

"This one story is making me a household name." she said to herself, thinking about all of the ratings she had been getting in the past two days.

"O.k. Antoinette." The cameraman called. "We're going live in 5... 4... 3... 2..."

He pointed at her to indicate the number one. Antoinette put on her serious face right on cue.

"Thank you, Susan." She said. "Two full days after the most bizarre conclusion to what is hands down the most ruthless crime spree ever to rock the small town of Dickinson, Tx., the Dickinson Police Department has finally decided to go on record with their official story about exactly what took place. The Departments very own Police Chief Ortega released a statement to the News Station personally. In it, he provided us with the results of their investigation. In a tape-recorded confession, this young man, Anthony Tyrone Boon, sorrowfully admitted to all of the slayings that stretched form Dickinson all the way to Houston."

Antoinette motioned toward an enlarged version of A.B.'s high school yearbook picture that had just appeared on the screen beside her.

"Anthony, or A.B. as he was known in the streets, went on his murderous rampage when his best friend Steven Woolard was found beaten to death outside of the Highland Projects. A.B. admitted to going on a killing spree as a way of lashing out on a society that glorified the type of existence that led to his friend being murdered young."

"Primarily with the recorded confession, police were able to tie A.B. to a whole string of crimes. In his disillusioned state, Boon first broke into the house of the man he suspected to be responsible for his friends' death and cut his throat. That man was Orlando Green."

"Then, as far as we can tell, he went underground and plotted his next murder. For reasons still unknown, Boon next traveled all the way to Houston, Tx. to the home of a highly respected Doctor named Dr. Abu-Kahr. Somehow, the out of control teen managed to bypass all of the Doctors security measures and gain entrance to his home. The Doctor was found with his throat slashed and his Maybach Benz vehicle stolen. The car was never recovered, so police figure A.B. might have sold it to a local chop shop trying to make a quick buck."

"According to the time of death analysis, A.B. had to have killed Abu-Kahr, sold his car on the black market, and rushed over to the Super Wal-Mart in Houston, Tx. all in about an hour. The police know this because about an hour after Dr. Abu-Kahr was murdered in cold blood, Boon was seen killing a Sheriff in the Wal-Mart parking lot as the Sheriff attempted to stop a man who had just killed a security guard. Authorities believe that the other man involved was one of A.B.'s accomplices. And it just goes to show you that there is no honor among thieves because A.B. delivered the kill shot to his suspected accomplice shortly after they fled the scene in a Candy red Cadillac Escalade."

"Police say that A.B. knew that the walls would soon come down around him, now that he had killed a cop, and that's when he got desperate. Police don't have all the answers, but they do know this. A.B. had at least two more accomplices other than the one he killed in Houston. And the three of them somehow kidnapped the owner of the Cadillac Escalade in an attempt to rob him. The robbery is still an ongoing investigation, so police are not saying any more about it, but this station received a tip that the planned robbery was somehow connected to the police shooting that left two men dead at the Willis, Winn, and Stone Law Firm building across the street from Jack-in-the-Box."

"What police 'are' saying is that A.B. held the owner of the Escalade hostage inside of a home in the sub-division known as Valley Park. On the tape, police say that A.B. admitted to killing the mother and daughter that lived there, chopping their bodies up into little pieces, and consuming their flesh in a satanic ritual that was meant to give him extra souls that he could use to trade with the devil in exchange for money, power, and a long earthly life. The spell, or ritual, or whatever it was must have not worked because A.B. ended up taking his own life by ingesting so many prescription pills and so much crack cocaine that his heart had no choice but to shut down."

"Before he killed himself though, he took a few more lives with him. For reasons that the police figured were just the satisfaction he got from killing, A.B. hog tied, blindfolded, and gagged three teenage girls, loaded them up in the Cadillac Escalade with his murdered accomplice, covered them and the S.U.V. with gasoline, and then set them on fire."

"The coroner confirmed the grisly truth that all three girls were burned alive. The names of teenaged girls are not being released per their parent's request. But we can say that all of the girls went to the same school as A.B., and perhaps he wanted them dead because they rejected him or made fun of him. Who really knows the mind of a psychopath? And who can understand exactly why they do what they do? All we can do is try to move on, pray, and do everything…"

Layla turned down the volume on the T.V. screen in the back of the all black stretch limo. Her plan had gone off without a hitch. Herself, Alize, and Ashanti had a grand total of $3,662,530 and 30 pounds of weed to split amongst themselves. All of the people that could give them up and tell the real story had been conveniently taken out by a man who committed suicide.

The media got a monster to display before the public.

The police got the culprit, so now the streets were safe.

The three women got rich.

Everybody was happy.

"Look at them." Layla said with a mug on her face. "They don't care about my baby. They only here for show."

Ashanti and Alize sat in the back of the limo with Layla and gazed out of the tinted window. The people that Layla was referring to were Samantha and Sandra. Today was the last day that anybody could see A.B.'s corpse, as it laid in its open casket hanging over the six feet deep hole, they quietly got back in the car with Menace and drove off.

"They couldn't even pay for the burial." Layla said angrily. "I had to donate the money anonymously."

Ashanti looked around nervously.

"Why did we even have to come here?" Ashanti asked. "I know the police think A.B. done it all, but still. We don't need to be in Dickinson. We need to be out of the country or something."

Alize reached out and rubbed her mother's leg.

"Ashanti is right, mom." She said softly. "Don't feel bad. We all lost people that we cared about trying to pull this off. You did what you had to do mom. There was no other way."

Layla could hear her friend and her daughter, but her eyes were glued to A.B.'s casket. Tears rolled down her cheeks.

"But… but I really do love him." She told them. "I didn't want things to end up like this. I didn't want to portray him as a monster."

"We know." Alize assured her. "We know you cared about him. I did too. But if you wouldn't have done what you did, there's no way we would've gotten away with all of this."

Ssnniff.

Layla wiped her nose on a handkerchief.

"Do you think he understands?" she asked. "Do you think he knows that I love him?"

Alize stared into her mother's eyes and she could actually feel the pain deep down in the woman's soul. She hated to see her mother cry. She felt her though. A.B. was a good dude. He didn't deserve what happened to him. He was one of the good ones.

Alize sighed and grabbed her purse. After digging around in it for a few seconds, she pulled out a piece of paper and a pen.

"Look." She said, handing the items over to her mother. "You and I are supposed to be dead, so we can't risk being seen. So go ahead and write A.B. a farewell note. Let him know how you feel. And before we leave, Ashanti will place it in the casket with him."

"But how will he read it?" she asked.

"It's symbolic mom. You can bury a picture of yourself and a piece of your heart with him. That way, the two of you will be connected. I believe that he will be able to sense your love. Plus, it will give you some much needed closure."

Layla looked at the paper for a moment, and then decided to do what her daughter had suggested. She began to write.

"My dearest, dearest A.B...."

CHAPTER TWENTY

A.B. had been floating around in a sea of pure white light for what seemed like an eternity. He didn't feel any pain, any sorrow, any grief, any hurt. He didn't feel anything negative whatsoever. All he could feel was joy, peace, love, and happiness. His best friend Steel had been floating around in the bright light with him. They both wore white robes and no shoes.

"Is this... is this heaven?" he asked his friend, still not use to the way his voice seemed to vibrate in this place.

Steel smiled the most beautiful smile.

"I guess you can call it that." He answered.

A.B. thought back to all of the havoc he had caused before he was forced to commit suicide. He had killed people.

"I don't mean to question... Gods... judgment," he said, choosing his words carefully. "But how did I get here? I mean, why didn't my actions get me sent to hell?"

Still smiling, Steel began doing the backstroke through the light.

"The people on earth have it mixed up." He told him. "They read the Word but they do not understand the Word. This is why the Book says that the people perish because of lack of knowledge. Their misconceptions about the meaning to the Book is what causes their state of struggle. You see, all humans were created in the image of the Creator. This means that we have the power to create. And with this creative power we can either create a heaven or a hell. In your case, you died, or went to sleep as the Book calls it, striving to make things right by me. In your heart, at the time of your death, you were engaged in a righteous act. So now that you have entered the realm of eternal sleep, your eternal dream, or afterlife, is one of pure bliss with the homeboy you strove for. This is what you desired, so this is what you created. But for those who go to sleep greedily hording away money and oppressing the poor, their eternal dream is one of all the turmoil that comes with trying to lie, cheat, and steal. They have created an afterlife where they must constantly defend their possessions against the people who wish to take them. That is that person's hell."

A.B. stared at Steel. He didn't sound like his homeboy from back in the day. He sounded… what's the word… he sounded Enlightened.

"So what about you?" A.B. asked. "If you are here with me because I wanted to be with you, am I here with you because you wanted to be with me?"

"Not exactly." Steel said. "See, the me that is here with you is not the me from the earth. Rather, I am a version of the real me that you created as part of your eternal dream. Every person that has ever lived has created their own personal eternal dream. No two people share a dream."

A.B. scratched his head.

"So where is the real Steel?"

"The real Steel is existing in his own eternal dream. And unfortunately, his eternal dream is one of hell."

A.B. gasped.

"What are you talking about?"

"The real Steel went to sleep with fear, hatred, and vengeance inside of his mind and his heart. Dwelling eternally with him is a version of Tank, a version of Duke, a version of A.K., a version of Clipso, and a version of the doctor that revived him just long enough to tell him that Tank wanted him dead. The real Steel will clash with theses personages for all eternity. Or until the ultimate Creator intervenes."

"No!" A.B. shouted. "It can't be! Not Steel!"

A.B. began thrashing about in the midst of the white light.

"How… how can I find him and help him?" he asked frantically. "Where is he at?"

Steel watched A.B. struggle in a futile attempt to reach another man's dream.

"You cannot find him." Steel said calmly to the panicked A.B. "No man may exit the reality in which he created and enter into someone else's. If that were possible, the people who created hell for themselves could escape into someone's heaven and bring to naught that persons bliss. That would violate the rules."

"Rules?!" A.B. spat. "Violate the rules? How about this for a violation of rules? If my created heaven is one of blissful peace with my homeboy Steel, how is it possible for you to destroy that by telling me you aren't really Steel, and the real Steel is enduring eternal torment?"

A.B. swung at the light.

"How is this heaven?" he challenged. "How is it heaven for me to face that reality for all eternity?"

Steel suddenly became silent, and the smile he had been wearing faded away.

"Maybe," he said, with a less cheerful tone. "Your eternal dream is one in which you must constantly face the reality that all of your efforts to help Steel were in vain. Regardless of how hard you tried to save him; he was already gone. You were powerless to reach him. Powerless to help him defend himself against Tank and his goons. Powerless to bring him back!"

Steel's face suddenly began to look evil. His features began to shift and morph. The bright white light slowly began to be consumed by darkness.

"And when you did have one shot at saving your friends pathetic little life, what did you do?" Steel asked in a wicked sounding voice.

A.B.'s eyes grew wide as Steel's face transformed into the face of Dr. Abu-Kahr.

"What did you do?" he re-iterated in the voice of the Iranian Doctor. "You entrusted his recovery to a man who was on his attacker's payroll. Ah-ha! Ha! Ha! Ha! Ha! You handed him over to the enemy like the fool you are! Ahh-ha! Ha! Ha!"

Fear suddenly entered into the heart of A.B. He tried to back away, but he could not. It felt as if the light had turned solid on his back and sides and he couldn't move. As the darkness closed in, so did the Doctor.

The Doctor laughed a wicked laugh as his face too began to change and morph like Steels did. He laughed and transformed until his face, surrounded by only darkness now, sat perfectly still in front of A.B.'s face.

A.B.'s body rocked as pain began shooting through him. He closed his eyes and cried out in agony.

"Aaauuuggghhh!" he hollered.

"Your eternal dream is HELL!" he heard a strange mixture of several voices say. "Ahh-ha! Ha!

Ha! Ha! WELCOME, A.B.! To the pits of HELL! Ha! Ha! Ha!"

A.B. opened his eyes.

"No!" he cried, when he saw the latest face of his tormentor.

"Yes!" a smiling Layla said back to him. "I love you baby! I love you baby! I LOVE YOU BABY! I LOVE YOU BABY! Ahhh-ha! Ha! Ha! Ha! Ha!"

Layla leaned in and kissed A.B. on the lips. Her kiss sent a jolt of electricity through his torso.

"AAAAUUUUGGGGHHH!!!" he screamed. "AAAUUUGGGHHH!!!"

A.B. rocked and wailed as his eternal suffering began. Every time his eyes opened, he saw Layla's face. She was telling him that she loved him. Excruciating pain bombarded him. Tears formed in his eyes. A.B. had never believed in God sincerely until that very moment. And at that moment, he summoned up all of his faith and strength to call upon HIM.

"GOD! He hollered, as the pressure got too be too much. "GOD! HELP ME! HELP ME PLEASE!!!"

And just like that, the pain stopped.

The mocking laughter stopped.

The mean and hateful words stopped.

A.B. sat with his eyes closed, afraid to look up again. He sat like that and waited for the torment to begin again. He waited and waited. Then he waited some more. His heart raced and his breathing was heavy.

Nothing happened.

Taking a deep breath, he decided to open his eyes. Cautiously, A.B. stole a peek. He blinked a few times.

Darkness.

Only this darkness wasn't like the other darkness. This darkness came with smells.

Ssnniff!

"Hmmm." He thought. "Is that… is that…"

Ssnniff!

"Is that wood?"

A.B. tried to stretch out his arms but they would only go so far. He felt around. He was in some sort of box.

"What's going on?" he wondered. "Am I still in hell? Did God save me? Is this all another way to torture me?"

A.B. tried to roll over and he felt a small slender object poke him in his left shoulder.

"Ooowww." He said, reaching within the cramped space to investigate.

Finding the object that poked him, he used his fingers and hands to try and guess at what it was.

"Hmmm." He hummed. "Feels like… feels like a… a pen?!"

A.B. pressed down on the ass end of the pen and a skinny beam of light shone forth from the tip of it.

Curious as to what was going on, A.B. used the light to examine his surroundings.

O.k. There go my feet.

Hmmm.

I'm wearing dress shoes.

And black slacks?

A.B. swallowed. He could see the thing that he was in.

A wooden box!

Me lying on my back!

GASP!

I'm in a casket!

O.k. A.B. Don't panic. It's o.k. It's not what it looks like. Just chill. They're just trying to scare you. Or… are they?

A.B. regulated his breathing. Inhale. Exhale. Inhale. Exhale. After calming himself down, A.B. pointed the light at the roof of his casket. He almost dropped it when he encountered Layla's smiling face. But this Layla wasn't the demon Layla. This Layla was just a photograph. Someone had taped a photograph of Layla to the inside of his casket.

But who?

And why?

And how did he survive that overdose of drugs?

And if he survived, what the hell was he doing in a casket?

As these questions and many more swirled around in A.B.'s head, he continued to search with his pen light.

He slowly directed the light below the picture. At first, he thought he was seeing things, but then he realized he wasn't. It was a letter. Someone had attached a letter to the inside of his casket along with the picture.

His heart began to race. He swallowed hard and prepared to read it. Maybe it would provide him with the answers he sought.

The letter read:

My dearest, dearest A.B.

By now you have realized that I did not

actually kill you. After I had you swallow those drugs and recite that confession, I injected you with something that would make you appear to be dead for a couple of days. It was all just a trick to fool the police and provide the two of us with a fresh start. My share of the lick we hit was somewhere around 1.2 million dollars. I will gladly share that with you if you will still have me. I told you to just trust me Baby. I love you. Everything I did was necessary. Please forgive me. Right now, I am working to dig you out of there. Just hold tight, and breathe shallow. Layla's coming Daddy. Layla's coming!

Yours Forever, Layla

A.B. read the letter two more times. Suddenly, everything that had brought him up to this point had begun to make sense. Maybe Layla did do some shady things along the way, but if she really was out to get him, why wouldn't she have just let him die?

A.B. considered his options. If Layla was really working to dig him out of his grave, he could switch up on her and kill her for putting him through all of this. But then again, he could forgive her for not telling him the entire plan and go somewhere and live happily ever after.

Searching his heart, A.B. admitted that he did still love Layla. And he no longer believed that she made the decision to kill Steel.

A.B. stared up at Layla's picture. Just being honest with himself, he knew that he would take her back. He had fallen in love with her. Love was arguably the strongest emotion on the planet. Stronger than hate, envy, and greed.

A.B. gazed up and smiled.

"Hurry up Baby." He said to Layla. "Hurry up!"

If A.B. had x-ray vision, he would've been able to see through the top of the coffin, through the dirt, through the worms, through the roots, through the twigs, and also through the grass. And on top of all of that, he would've been able to see three women, dressed in all black and covered with dirt, using the blanket of darkness to conceal what they were doing.

"I appreciate ya'll sticking around to help me." Layla said, shoveling dirt and sweating like a slave.

"Hey." Ashanti and Alize said. "We're in this together, right?"

"Yeah," Layla answered. "We're in this together."

The three women smiled at each other and then went back to work. They were vigorously digging like someone's life depended on it.

And it did too!

THE END

By:
MATTHEW DANIELS
A.K.A.
The Real Bookworm

Just a little something extra for the in-depth reader.

If you were REALLY paying attention, which I KNOW you were, (Ha-ha) you would have noticed that back in chapter 2, on page 28, I quoted two scriptures found in the Bible but I never mentioned exactly where they were located in the Bible. To be honest with you, the thought to include this information in this section of the book originated with my extremely supportive "Big Sis".

Yeah, gotta give credit where credit is due. I love you Sis. Mrs. Director of Marketing and Sales. Without you I might have never figured out how to act as my own publisher, print up my own book, distribute it myself, and always keep my business professional, legit, and 100. Appreciate it Sis. From the heart!

So, for all who may be interested...

Proverbs 6:25, 26
Lust not after her beauty in thine heart; neither let
Her take thee with her eyelids. For by means of a whorish
woman a man is brought to a piece of bread:

Proverbs 7:25, 27
Let not thine heart decline to her ways, go not astray
in her paths. Her house is the way to

hell, going down to the
Chambers of death.

If you have a Bible somewhere close by, feel free to take a minute to look those verses up. I'll wait. By no means should you ever just take someone's word for something. Not even mine. Especially when you can easily verify the information. Plus, I guarantee it won't hurt to crack open your Bible. Go 'head.

O.k., you back? Good. Say, do you remember the quote I used at the beginning of the book? The one about creating an enemy for the people to hate. Back when I first came up with that quote, it had absolutely nothing to do with this book. But one day someone pointed out to me that a lot of other books that are being sold in the stores have quotes at the beginning of their books. So, I looked through my list of quotes and tried to find the one best suited to the book. If you can't tell, I chose that particular quote because to me it symbolizes Layla. Ya dig? And even though I wrote the quote before I wrote the book, to me it just sorts of embodies her whole style of manipulation.

I enjoy doing that though. You know, using my own creativity to enhance my creative works. Like the poem found in chapter 17, on page 294. It's one of mine. Now don't get me wrong, I didn't write the poem before I wrote the book like I did with the quote. Instead, I wrote the poem as a result of the book. I basically just came to a point in the book where I needed a poem, so I wrote a poem.

Well, I wrote about 98% of a poem. If you remember, I didn't quite finish the last line. It wasn't until my Big Sis asked me how the poem ended that I realized I needed to finish it. As sad as it might sound, I was content with leaving it how it is in the book. But, when I found out that my sister was interested in how it ended, I thought to myself that other readers might be curious about it too.

So, for all who may be interested...

When the going gets tough, the tough don't notice
When the road gets rough, the rough keep rollin',
When the odds stacked against a real man, he smile
When the opposition comes he gone stand his ground
When everybody else fold, I'm sho' to stay stiff
When the tale gets told, Money, Power, Respect, and No Fear

You know what they say. All good things must come to an end. And alas, it's time for me to end this book. Expect more books from me in the future. Everything from poem books, children books, spiritual books, activity books, and even more novels.

Hope you enjoyed it!

Special Thanks to:
My wife Raquel Daniels, my daughter Samiah Jayde Daniels, my son Heru Aamir Amen-Ra Daniels, my son Gabriel Cantu III, my father

Rev. James Edward Daniels, and my mother Mrs. Judy Ann Colvin.

I also would like to offer a special thanks to all of my brothers and sisters. My Sister Hope Daniels, my Bro. Jason Robinson, my Bro. Joshua Daniels, my Bro. Joe Daniels, my Bro. Damon Robinson, my Bro. Eddie Daniels, my Bro. Bobby Robinson, and my Sis. LaShelle Long.

There are so many friends that I can't possibly name them all by name, so I'll just say that you know who you are. Keep ya' head up and never get fed up. One Love!

Other Books By Matthew Daniels
Thicker Than Water.

Matthew James Daniels
Facebook Group: The Real Bookworm
Email: MatthewDaniels720@yahoo.com
Facebook Page: Everything Matthew Daniels
Facebook Name: Matthew Daniels
YouTube: TheChosenPhew
Website: www.TheRealBookWorm.com

www.ingramcontent.com/pod-product-compliance
Lightning Source LLC
Chambersburg PA
CBHW032227010726
47494CB00002B/382